Ella Garcia
20 Harbor Cir
Freehold, NJ 07728

WHERE REBELS ROAM
A Civil War Novel

BY

KEN ROBERTS

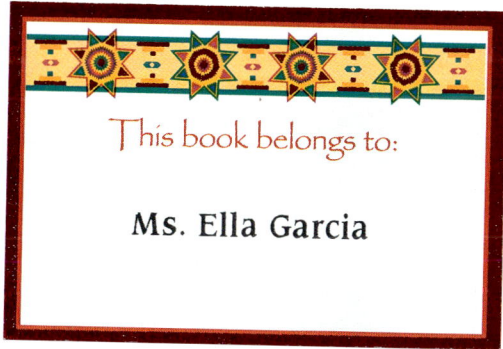

This book belongs to:

Ms. Ella Garcia

SAILAWAY BOOKS
Lakeville, Connecticut, USA

Copyright © 2013 by Ken Roberts

All rights reserved. No parts of this book may be reproduced or distributed in any printed or electronic form without the author's permission. Please do not participate in or encourage piracy of copyrighted materials in violation of the author's rights.

This is a work of fiction. Names, characters, places, and incidents are the product of the author's imagination or are used fictitiously. Any resemblance to actual events, locales, or persons living or dead is entirely coincidental.

Where Rebels Roam

First print edition

ISBN-13: 978-0615923512
ISBN-10: 0615923518

BISAC: Fiction / Historical

Cover art and design by Dorothy Trojanowski, *www.freshlysquozen.com*.

Cover background photo:
Brandy Station Battlefield, Culpeper County, Virginia.
Brandy Station photo courtesy Civil War Trust, *www.civilwar.org*

Sailaway Books | Published by arrangement with the author
P.O. Box 312, Lakeville CT 06039 USA
www.sailawaybooks.com

Dedication

To Robert J., my dad and childhood hero, loving father, husband, grandfather, friend, and Korean War combat veteran. You are with me always.

To William Smith, USMC, of North Carolina. Our dream was to become pilots and fly. For a short time we were the modern-day cavalry, and you lived your dream to your very end. Bill, I miss flying with you. Semper Fi, brother.

To Todd B. Our friendship and brotherhood were way too short. But those last few days were heavenly.

Acknowledgements

A special thank you to my first victim, reader, editor, translator, and supporter, Katie.

A big thank you to Ginger for reading and supporting me through this experience.

Thanks to the Civil War Trust for the use of the Brandy Station Battlefield photos that appear on the background of the book cover. To learn about the preservation of Civil War battlefields, please visit the Trust's website, *www.civilwar.org*.

Thank you to my family and friends who have supported me throughout this project.

Thank you to my new friends for sharing that amazing day with me and introducing me to a new world of racing.

Thank you to Lauren for posing for the cover photo.

Preface

My wonderful journey began by revealing some nasty twists and turns in the spring of 2006. It sent me down a strange yet challenging rabbit hole where several remarkable events began to influence my life. Finally in the spring of 2012 I ascended into a new world full of amazement, the vibrant new land called Oz.

In the spring of 2006 I signed over $205,000 worth of horse transportation equipment, not realizing I had been conned. For several years I was hemorrhaging money. The first big step was to separate myself from a situation I had put myself in and rethink how I would now manage my horses. Then I began the slow process of repairing the financial damage.

That's when my horse trainer recommended a young couple in Pennsylvania. This change would lead me toward a new way of looking at my life.

No matter how things go, remember it is part of the journey. Faith will teach you there will always be a reason to enjoy the ride, no matter how tough it gets. We can't really appreciate spring until we go through winter.
— K.R., August 2013

On June 20, 2012, I began to write a story…

Table of Contents

Introduction 7

PART ONE: Raid, Rain, and Redemption 8
Battles Can Be a Pleasure 35
Minutes, Moments, and Memories 65
Silent Stalker Sanctifies 71
Dominate or Be Dominated 81

PART TWO: Here I Am 104
Fighting to Die 107
Fervor Flows and Surges 123
Perilous Deeds Lead to Promotion 126

PART THREE: The Beginning of the End 134
Love Is a Battlefield 159
A Night to Remember 168
Social Season to Soar 205

PART FOUR: Letters, Lies, and Love 211
The Fragrance of Flowers and Fire 219
The End Is Near 221
Captains, Damsels, and Destiny 234
Conscience and Consequences 255

Epilogue 261

The Inspiration and Real Story cclxiv

Where They Are Today cclxxiv

About the Author cclxxv

Introduction

The Civil War was the deadliest war in American history, with estimates of the cost in military lives approximating 650,000. Both the North and South reaped what many described as a "harvest of death." Above all it devastated a generation of young men in their 20s and 30s, both North and South. Add to this the estimated civilian deaths of 50,000 to 250,000, including women, children, and slaves, bringing the staggering death toll to over 850,000 people. These deaths would forever impact families and communities. An equivalent proportion of today's population would be about nine million.

Our Civil War has been called the last of the ancient wars, and the first of the modern wars. With the development of new weapons, the killing would escalate and begin a massive new level of lethality reserved for the combination of technological proficiency and inhumanity characteristic of a later time.

In the East there was a great obstacle to both armies that was at the center of significant battles. Toward its western source rests ground that has been described as the most fought-over and occupied in our nation's history. Control of this ground and that great barrier changed hands many times during the course of the war. It was an especially difficult barrier for the Union troops to overcome, as it stood in the way of their attempts to thrust into southern Virginia. This splendid creation where men spilled their blood and fought to the death is the Rappahannock River, an Indian name meaning "where the tide ebbs and flows." That meaning would be most fitting as the battles raged around it.

PART ONE
Raid, Rain, and Redemption

April 22, 1863.

Late that evening as she slowly rocked her well-worn but comfortable rocker it creaked softly, telegraphing its age. Draped over her shoulders was a wool shawl that barely kept the damp night air from chilling her bones. She watched the moon struggle to light up the night as it tried to show its self through the thick fog and heavy rain clouds that rolled in and out over the last several days in this part of Virginia.

Concerned, she rocked slowly as her mind kept repeating the same question over and over. *Who are you?* Having moved outside, the thought seemed tamer, more like curiosity ... gentler, less urgent. For the first time all day she began to relax and to feel how tired and drained she really was. But she knew that going inside and seeing him would bring back that feeling again, like he was trying to get to her, like he needed her to know who he was.

Then the heavens opened up again and the rain began to soak her small front porch. She watched the mud and water move past her toward a small gully where it would drain into the river, turning it into a raging torrent. The wind howled as the trees swayed and banged into each other, and together with the raging current of the river it made that all-too-familiar roar that once scared her as a child over twenty years ago. But this night, even though she felt safe, she also sensed there was a change blowing in with this storm. The rain and her desire to sleep grew stronger than her need to stay away, so she went back inside her small, two-room home.

Sitting on the large chair next to his newly made bed she stared at him for what seemed like hours. It was almost completely dark as the last small candle struggled to light the main room.

Her mind raced through the events of the day, then again she whispered softly, "Who are you?"

He was not the first, and she was sure he would not be the last, but she sensed he was different. The war had brought many wounded to her little farm. Some needed care and attention to go on their way, but others were the unknown, mortally wounded and permanent residents to the landscape, stones marking the last proof of their human existence, barely noticeable to even those who knew where they rested for eternity, never able to go home.

The light flickered as the candle slowly burned out, leaving the room to the dark, sleep, and dreams.

* * *

Early the next morning his moaning awakened her. She rubbed her face and realized that her husband was staring at her as he stood over them.

"Did you get any sleep?" he asked.

"A little. I had a strange dream." She paused to stretch and yawn. "It was like I was watching him, like I was a witness or observer."

"Watching over who?"

"Him, the sergeant." She pointed and stared at the sleeping man. "Not watching *over,* just watching. I think I was dreaming of what happened to him, after he got wounded, before we found him."

"You are right, that is strange, Kate. You don't even believe things like that are possible."

"I know … that's why it seems so strange, but so real."

"Maybe you took care of him before."

"No. I remember all of them, and I have never taken care of him."

"You have seen many soldiers come this way, and many were hurt badly. Maybe you were just trying to feel you can do more—you know, make some sense out of this war."

"If he makes it, I'm going to ask him about it."

"If your dream took place after he got wounded, he might not remember."

He walked toward the front door and turned back to her.

"I was right, Kate."

"What were you right about, Alex?'

"Your new horse is gone."

"Are you sure?" she asked, jumping up from the chair. "Were you able to go all the way to the back of the field?"

"No, but I called and brought him some oats, and he didn't

come. Go check for yourself."

"I will. Maybe the storm scared him and he went through the fence."

"Damn it, I knew I should not have left that troublesome colt out in the west field last night," she said to herself as she angrily walked back to the house. "That's the second horse one of those stupid armies has taken from me this year. I wish they would both just kill each other off and leave us alone. You think that all the horses they took these past two years would be enough. Now we only have the mule to ride and pull our wagon."

* * *

For the second time during the war he arrived to rejoin his troop, the First New Jersey Cavalry Regiment. It was late on the evening of April 12, and the Union Cavalry was camped north of Falmouth, Virginia, on the north bank of the Rappahannock River, when Private Lewis Michael saw him first and yelled out.

"Nice try! You can't sneak up on us."

"You are all lucky you were not Rebels and were warned I was on my way, or you'd all be dead now," he joked.

"You feel better, Sergeant O'Shea?"

"Why—did you miss me?"

"No, we just missed your weapons," said Private Mott.

"You all healed up?" Private Smalls asked.

"Yup."

"Where you able to bring him?"

"Yup, Private Gregory, nice to see you're still with us. He's with the other horses."

The sergeant greeted many of the other members of his troop, noticing that a few were missing.

"O'Keeffe, where's Robert and Tom?"

"Both gone last month. Robert from sickness, and Tom we believe was taken prisoner."

"Hmm." He was silent for a moment, then looked toward the men. "Meet the new guys I brought you to play with."

"Hey, you new guys, don't worry about the fear of dying by the hands of Jonny Reb… this winter we had more go down by sickness, so fear your friends," said Private Smalls.

"Yup, and most of the rest were taken prisoners. Our KIA's so far have been low," added Corporal O'Keeffe.

"I would rather be a KIA then die by disease—there is no honor in a death like that," said Private Michael to the new men.

"Watch out, here comes 1st Sergeant James."

"Men, it's getting late," said 1st Sergeant James. "Square yourself away and get some sleep. We are moving out at 08:00. Sergeant O'Shea, it's time to get back into this war."

"Yes, 1st Sergeant."

"You're responsible for getting the new guys ready for tomorrow morning."

"Yes, 1st Sergeant."

"Where to, 1st Sergeant?" one of the new men asked.

"Back to *hell,* where else?" He turned and walked back to his tent.

"That's not where we're going—he's just trying to scare you new guys," said Corporal O'Keeffe.

"So where are we going, Sergeant?"

"Most likely down South, across the Rappahannock."

"Not down to hell, just down south—and that's as close as a man can get to hell on earth. Private Michael, tell them who owns hell."

"That's the land of the Southern cavalry devil himself. That's JEB Stuart country."

* * *

April 13, 1863.

Early the next morning the Chancellorsville campaign began, when the Union Cavalry, under Major General George Stoneman, was ordered west to cross the Rappahannock and embark on a long-distance, ambitious, and daring raid.

General Hooker, commander of the Army of the Potomac plan, was to dispatch his 10,000 cavalrymen far upstream around the left flank of the Army of Virginia, commanded by General Robert E. Lee. Once deep in the Confederate rear areas they were to destroy facilities and crucial supply lines and depots along the railroad from the Confederate capital in Richmond to Fredericksburg, which would cut Lee's lines of communication and supply.

8 A.M.

General Buford's Cavalry Brigade included the 2nd Division, led by General Gregg. Under his command was the First New Jersey Cavalry Regiment. They broke camp at Falmouth, Virginia, and the next day they engaged the enemy at Kelly's Ford, Virginia. The rebels fired at the brigade with cannons, and the Union light cavalry four-gun cannon battery replied and drove the rebel guns away.

Buford's report noted:

> *At 11 A.M. on the 15th of April, the ford was swimming. After the brigade arrived we were ordered to await further instructions. The country at that hour was like a sea. The regiment reached Morrisville on the 16th, having had Marsh Run to swim, then started for Kelly's Ford; was prevented from reaching Kelly's Ford by bad roads and fog.*
>
> *From the time that the brigade struck the river at Rappahannock Bridge on the 15th, up to the crossing of the river on the 29th, it seemed as though the elements were combined against our advance; such rains and roads I had never seen. During the whole expedition the roads were in a worse condition than I could have supposed to be possible, and the command was called upon to endure much severe discomfiture.*

* * *

On the morning of April 19 the sun struggled to shine between heavy rainclouds.

"Sergeant O'Shea, pick five men from the company, and go reconnoiter to Kelly's Ford. Cross it if you can without getting anyone killed, and that includes yourself," ordered 1st Sergeant James.

Before midday the six men were able to find a safe place to cross the river near Kelly's Ford. Later that afternoon the rain returned. That evening they were fired upon by Rebel pickets, scattering some of the men.

Riding erratically to avoid the shots from sharpshooters and pickets, Sergeant O'Shea smashed his head just above his right eye on a low unseen branch. He managed to stay on his horse, though dazed and barely able to see from the blood running down his face.

Then the heavy rain came again, separating him from his men.

After many quiet minutes and light rain, another shot rang out. This bullet passed between his thigh and holster and opened up a three-inch slice in his right leg. It whizzed past his mount's right cheek, causing the animal to break into a canter to his left and through some heavy briars.

O'Shea walked the rest of the day in circles searching for the river, both bloody and lost, needing medical assistance, food, and rest—but not water, it was everywhere. His lifelong companion had dozens of small, deep irritating cuts all over his exposed chest and legs.

They continued to wander most of the night and through the next day and night as the sergeant slipped in and out of consciousness, until finally early on the third day the exhausted animal stumbled in the mud and lost his rider, and both collapsed on the wet, dense forest ground while the rain continued to fall.

"The rain, when is it going to stop? It feels like it's been raining for days." He looked at the horse. "Don't you want it to stop?"

His companion just looked at him with his head down and his nose very close to the right side of his head, funneling more water onto the brim of the sergeant's hat.

"You know, you're making me wetter, if that's even possible. Move your big, hairy head and find your own tree to sit under."

Lifting his left hand he reached up and across his body to push the big head away, but the horse gently swung it right back into place.

"I can't take this killing anymore. Why can't these Rebels just learn to shoot straight, and save me all this misery? I can't stop my leg from bleeding, and my head and eye are killing me." As he tightened the rag that was tied around his leg wound he continued rambling. "Rascal, you need to go before I pass out again."

He pushed the big head away again, but this time he also raised his right hand, which was clutching his revolver, and he pushed the barrel into his own right temple.

Rascal wouldn't leave his lifelong companion. The sergeant's hand shook as he glanced at his weapon, his mind wandering in and out, filled with delusions caused by his condition.

"You know, besides you—because you are not a person—there were only two other people who really understand me," the sergeant rambled. "One is dead, 'cause I killed her, and the other is so old she may be pretending to be alive. If she finds out I shot myself and I splattered blood all over the jacket she made me, she would kill me. That old lady knew that was one thing she could not protect me from. Myself. What do you think? What will you do when I'm finally dead?"

The horse reached down and put his mouth around the revolver, pulled it out of the sergeant's hand, and walked away.

"I know what you should do when I'm gone, find someone to teach you to count, because that's not going to help—I have another pistol here somewhere."

He struggled to pull his other pistol from its holster and again began to mumble and rant.

"I just hope my ammunition is still dry enough to do its job. It would be really bad if I blew my head off and didn't die. I should put clean, dry rounds in it just in case—that's if I can find any."

His senses were becoming overloaded from delirium. His right eye was swollen shut, and his left could hardly focus as his mind kept wandering.

"Hey, you over there—when I count to three, let's draw and see who's the last man standing. If you don't want to, I'll make you a deal—if it stops raining before I can get this pistol ready, I will try and mount you, and we can look for help. What do you think about that?"

It was a long struggle to reload and ready his weapon, then suddenly he stopped and glanced around.

"Listen. Do you hear that?"

Silence.

"Neither do I."

It wasn't what he heard, but what he didn't hear. It was quiet; the noise of heavy rain had gone silent, and the only sounds were of drops landing in puddles or onto large leaves.

"Do you hear it? No rain. Look—is that the sun trying to break through the clouds? Yup, and it's creating a faint rainbow."

He drew a deep breath, smelling the cool forest dew and the musty leaves from days of rain. The effort brought his attention to his empty stomach, causing it to start grumbling and reminding him that he hadn't eaten in some time. Water was plenty, but not edible food, and the rain would not stop for long.

"OK, you win. Let's go. I guess someone wants me to do my job. Come here and help me up so we can kill more Rebs."

Using Rascal to pull himself up he struggled first to his feet, then into the saddle.

"Maybe we should find help first. I don't feel too good." These were his last words before slumping forward onto his companion's neck.

* * *

Born in November 1835, his parents named him Robert Gabriel O'Shea, but his grandmother who was raised and educated in Europe made sure he was called Gabriel, Latin for "an angel of the Lord." Gabriel's father, Joseph, was her second son, and his mother, Adeline, were as opposite as two parents could be. The benefit of that union allowed Gabriel to grow up in a very diverse world, enjoying and learning from different lifestyles and perspectives, each teaching him to adapt quickly to different situations, which was critical if he was to have a future. He was tough and bright, charming, well mannered, and loved his family, and he had a keen sense of humor. His piercing eyes were unnerving to some and alluring to others. He grew up loving life and the world God created, with all the surprises and pleasures it would bring.

He adored his grandmother. When he wasn't in New York City with his parents or at school, he loved to spend as much time as he could at her Bay View Stable in Middletown, New Jersey. The estate overlooked the lower New York City bay and the great city beyond. Thanks to her he received some informal military education, which she insisted on. As a transplanted matriarch of old Europe, where war occurred almost as often as the change of seasons, she was wise to changes in fortune.

She had been grooming him his whole life for his biggest adventure. As a child she allowed him to have free range of her magnificent estate, provided he would take full advantage of a longtime companion's knowledge as a retired French Cavalry officer. He loved to play and joke around, but his training helped him to develop a no-nonsense attitude he would need in war.

Gabriel never imagined he would one day be putting the knowledge of military tactics he received every summer to use in an actual war, much less one being waged against his own countrymen.

Private Robert Gabriel O'Shea finally got back to the First New Jersey Cavalry Regiment, now attached to Bayard's Cavalry Brigade, Department of the Rappahannock, in early May, 1862, just over a year after the war started. His return had been delayed for more than six months. During those months he had been a horse solider without a horse, at least without the right horse.

His childhood training prepared him to quickly prove he was a strong leader, with little patience for babysitting other soldiers—especially officers. He was made to be a cavalry soldier, athletic and agile, and an excellent rider with the ability to think quickly, which is very important in war; as he soon learned, battle situations change very quickly. His sophistication and determination helped him become one of the Union's better young cavalry soldiers.

What his grandmother could not help him with was what worried her the most: the grief he carried. He was becoming daring and reckless, a perilous combination to bring to war, especially when you are fighting two of them. In his personal war, he was facing issues for which no training could ever prepare him. But he kept it buried underneath, releasing the internal conflict with a determination to kill the enemy every chance he gets. Since joining the cavalry, he had walked the line between sorrow, pending death, and an unknown future. Though his wartime actions hadn't always been honorable, over time the bonds fused in war would change his view of life and himself.

However, good intentions don't always amount to good deeds. Slowly he would come to realize he still had an extraordinary life worth keeping and fighting for. When forces conspired to make him nothing more than a killer, he and his companion did the only thing left to do: they ran—advantageously, right into a falling tree-branch. Given time to contemplate what the future holds, he could now have a reason to live. The question was whether he would survive.

* * *

April 22, 1863, just after sunrise

Kate ran into their cozy little home. Her husband, Alex, blurted out, "Look what I found! Union rags." He held up a torn blue Union jacket.

Kate tried to catch her breath. "I got you beat ... I found what goes into ... that Union rag." She pointed to the east field. "Go hitch the wagon, I'll get some blankets and bandages. He's a mess, but alive."

After throwing some things into the wagon, Alex drove them out to the field.

"Over there, by the far tree-line toward the river." Kate pointed. "There—there he is."

She did a quick check of the man's wounds, and they rolled him onto a blanket and lifted him into the wagon.

"He's not that heavy," Kate said.

"Cavalry soldiers are not usually big men," Alex explained. "That makes it easier for both horse and rider. I'll drive. Jump in the back with him, Kate."

"I would have been perfect for the cavalry," said Kate. "I'm only five foot three. Too bad they don't allow women."

At first Kate sat at the edge of the wagon dangling her legs and feet, but as she turned to look at their cargo she slid closer to him. "So this is what a Union cavalry soldier looks like. Haven't had one of these yet. Now, where is his horse?"

"Maybe dead, maybe ran off. If he's alive, someone's cavalry will get him," Alex replied.

"Let's hope the rain holds off a bit more."

"There, over there, Kate—to your right."

A bloody, wild-eyed bay horse with white socks on diagonal legs came running out of the trees and up to the wagon, rearing and striking at them.

"Whoa," Kate said to the animal in a soft, slow voice. "Easy boy, easy."

She turned toward Alex. "Stay slow, go very, very slow ... I want him to calm down and follow us."

Kate again slid to the edge of the wagon and held out what looked like a piece of old, rolled-up green rope, her legs dangling off the wagon. As the horse moved closer, she broke up the object into small pieces and dropped a few.

"Come on, I know you can smell it. Easy, boy." The bay animal picked up the pieces, chewed them up, and trotted closer to the wagon, then he reached out to her and took a piece from her hand.

"He's calming down—he should follow us to the house. When we get home, can you carry in the soldier? I want to catch his horse."

Alex carried the wounded rider in and put him on a large chair next to the fireplace, then took off his holster and boots. After returning from their small bedroom where he'd gone for supplies he scanned the room, but there was no sight of Kate. He then assembled a small bed, a task they have repeated many times before, and settled the man in it.

When she finally walked in, Alex blurted out, "What have you been doing with that stupid horse for so long?"

"I had to hide his saddle and things just in case we had visitors. If this soldier is around, there could be Rebels. I also wanted to check on the horse's wounds, and I cleaned a few. He's resting in a stall now." She looked at their human patient. "How is he doing?"

"I started to clean his head wound, but his eye looks to be swollen shut. I don't think it was a gunshot; it looks like he was struck by something." He reached down and tipped back the man's forehead slightly. "See, he is bruised all around it, and no markings from a rifle butt."

"Yes, I agree—but it is a big area, and badly swollen. He must have a concussion. What about his leg?"

"As soon as I removed the leg wrap he had on it, and before I could cut open his pants, it started bleeding, so I quickly rewrapped it. You need to handle it."

"How long ago, and did it smell?" she asked.

"Maybe ten minutes. And yes, it does."

Kate frowned. "Damn. OK, please get some more clean linen, and I'll mix up some of my meds."

"Are you going to use your horse meds on him?"

"What else do we have around? Everything else is used up." She waited for Alex to respond, but he said nothing. So she pushed him again. "Well, do we have anything else left—like laudanum?"

Alex was silent.

After a pause, Kate blurted out, "Alex, I have no time for this—go get your bottle, and don't act like you don't know what I was talking about. 'Cause I do. We don't have time for this now. Please, go get it."

He avoided her gaze and then spoke. "OK. I'll go to the barn and get it." In less than five minutes he came back with a bottle of clear liquid.

"Is that Bobby Brown's stuff?" she asked.

"No, it's from Doc Wilson—it's the good stuff. How did you know?"

"I'm your wife, I'm supposed to know. What I don't know and hoped you'd tell me is how bad the pain is." Together they unwrapped the leg wound.

"My lower back and my gut have been hurting since Easter, and my leg's OK."

Kate sighed. "OK. We'll talk about it later. Please pour a bit here." She gestured toward the edge of the five-inch-long, one-and-a-half-inch-deep wound that was now open to the air.

"Good—put pressure here, and here." She pointed to the upper left and right sides of the leg just above the injury. The torn flesh was oozing blood, a dark, putrid liquid, and a smell that the dead know well. They alternated between pouring liquor on it and cutting out the infected flesh.

The strong smell made Kate catch her breath. "Thank God he is out cold, 'cause this would hurt so much he might think we were trying to cut off his leg."

"Or worse, maybe kill him," her husband mumbled.

"Alex, it looks really bad. It could be four days old."

He nodded. "All this rain didn't help it, probably made it worse."

Kate thought aloud. "The horse looks like they went though some thick briars, but he has no deep wounds. He's mainly just exhausted and hungry. We know the Union cavalry has been all over the area. It seems like they're trying to move through and get through the rain, but so far from what I've been told, there have been no battles around, just some skirmishes."

Alex nodded. "I think he may be part of that movement that started at the same time as the heavy rains. When I went to town to fill up my bottle, the doc said that the Union cavalry was trying to move in mass, maybe a raid heading to Richmond."

"Well, this one never made it. He could have been wandering around for longer than four days. I guess we'll find out when he wakes up."

"You mean if he wakes up."

The man on the bed suddenly stirred and started to mumble. "*Aaaahh … aaaah …*"

Kate quickly leaned forward and whispered, "*Shh, shhhh,* it's all right. Go back to sleep."

The man mumbled again, this time more clearly. "G'ma, whisper in my ear, whisper to me … goodnight, my majestic warrior."

Kate and Alex looked at each other and watched the soldier fall back to sleep.

* * *

For two days he slept while the young couple sweated his fever, spooned chicken broth and the clear liquid down his throat, and monitored his wounds. Finally very early on the third day, sometime after two in the morning, he was coherent enough to open both his eyes, even if one was only partly open, and tried talking.

Still delirious, he started with a mumble. "Rascal, Rascal … where are you, boy?"

A moment later he yelled out with fear and concern for his companion. "Rascal!"

Then louder, as loud as he could: "Rascal! RASCAL!"

Kate and Alex quickly emerged from their bedroom. Looking around with the help of the bit of moonlight coming in a window, they watched the front door swell and shake in rhythm with an eerie squeaking and groaning.

"Hurry, light a candle!" Kate told Alex.

"I'm trying."

BOOM.

The door suddenly blew in, letting in enough moon-glow to illuminate the room—and the stunned expression on their faces as they watched Rascal enter the room and turn as he nickered to his injured companion.

The soldier raised himself up as much as he could. "Easy boy, I'm OK, just checking on you. Go back outside and close the door behind you."

After watching the horse turn and walk back outside, Kate and Alex stood there and stared at each other for a few seconds.

Then the trooper asked, "Where is my wife? If I am a prisoner of war or I'm dead, please tell her."

"OK ... but you are neither," Kate said.

"Neither what?"

"Don't bother to explain—he can't focus," Alex said.

Kate was determined to set the trooper straight. "This is our home. I'm Kate, and this is my husband, Alex. We found you in our field three days ago."

"I'm not dead?"

"No—not yet," Alex said.

"What does it take to die in this war? No one else seems to be able to avoid it."

Kate and Alex just stared in puzzlement.

The soldier changed his focus. "Are you bloodletting me?"

"No. The Confederate army medical staff sent us a warning to avoid it. Besides, I think you lost enough on your own."

"Not enough; you just said I'm still alive. Where am I?"

"She just told you—in our home," Alex said.

"No, I mean, am I still in Virginia?"

"Yes. Where do you think you would be?"

"It's just, you sound like you're from the North, not from the South."

Alex explained. "We're both from Pennsylvania, and that's why you're not a prisoner, and are still alive."

The trooper looked at Kate wistfully. "I'm not in Virginia, I'm in heaven. What is today's date?"

"It is early morning, the 24th," Alex replied.

"Yes, it's very early," said Kate. "How do you feel?"

He seemed to think about her question for a few seconds. "I have a bad taste in my mouth, my head hurts, my eye feels like it's being squeezed out of my head, and my right leg feels numb. Thanks—I think?"

"You think so?" she replied.

"Yeah. If I were dead I wouldn't feel this bad."

"We can arrange that," she mumbled.

"It's OK. Rascal would miss me. I am Lieutenant Gabriel O'Shea, First New Jersey Cavalry Regiment. Thank you for saving him and me."

While Kate was explaining his and Rascal's injuries to him, he passed out. This time he looked comfortable and relaxed and fell into a deep sleep as if not to have a care in the world.

"He looks like he's happy and sleeping at home with his wife."

"Did you hear what he said?" asked Alex.

"Which part?"

"He introduced himself as Lieutenant O'Shea, but his uniform jacket is that of a sergeant."

"So which is he, Alex—can you tell?"

"I don't know. I guess we will find out when he wakes up again."

"I will bet you he won't remember any of this when he wakes up again." Kate picked up a lantern and lit it.

"Yup, you're probably right, Kate, so I won't be betting you. I'm going back to bed. Where are you going?"

"I'm going to check to make sure Rascal went back to the barn and is not wandering around outside."

* * *

Until the war wounded him, Alex was a strong, outgoing man. Now in his early thirties, at five-foot-eleven he was thin, tall, physically limited, and reserved. He came from an average, hardworking family in a small Pennsylvania town. Growing up, his good looks, strong body, and polite manners got him a lot of attention from the ladies in town. But his size did not compare to his heart, which in comparison was much bigger. He helped everyone in town; it was always "Alex, please help carry this," "Alex, cut this for me," "Alex, can you do this?"—he never turned anyone down. Now, however, only a shell of who he once was, he struggled to keep his vivacious and ambitious wife happy. His emotions bounced daily from depression to inadequacy to anger and finally love. Focusing on their little farm and getting from day to day just so he could lie by her side were what kept him going.

The smell of food stirred the trooper's empty stomach to grumble, speeding up his groggy awakening. Straining to open his eyes, he looked around to see a man cooking.

"I'm so hungry, and that smells good—what is it?"

"It's eggs with a little venison mixed in."

"I have some other questions. Who are you, and where am I?"

Yup, we were right, he doesn't remember last night, Alex told himself. "Last night when you woke up, my wife told you that you were not a prisoner of war."

"Your wife. Where is she?"

"Kate is not here. My name is Alexander, but please call me Alex. Kate and I are both Northerners."

"That's why you don't sound like a Southerner. Besides being my unwanted saviors, how did the two of you end up in Virginia, in the middle of this war?"

"We met in Pennsylvania eight years before the war started. I was working for a guy who was hired by Kate's family to build a new barn, and we were married five months before the war started. Kate's uncle owned this farm for years. He always loved her and knew how much she loved it too, so in his will he left it to her. We needed money to get and keep it, so after we moved in I volunteered with a Pennsylvania Infantry Regiment. By the time I got wounded we had just made enough money to keep the farm, and after I got out of the hospital I made my way here. What about you? How did you end up at our little farm?"

Pausing to think about an answer, he decided to tell Alex what many would say. "To save the Union."

His hesitation in answering was to conceal the real reason he joined. He did not fear death; he feared living, haunted by his guilt, until he died old and alone. This was what he was not ready to reveal.

Alex had been listening closely and had some suspicious about Gabe. "Last night you woke up and asked us, 'What does it take to die in this war ... no one else seems to be able to avoid it'—and just now you called us 'unwanted saviors.' What's going on?"

"Nothing ... I'm just tired of the killing."

"From one Union soldier to another, why do you want to die?"

"You know, Alex—you served, fought, and were wounded."

"Yes. So what is going on with you?"

Lowering his head, he stared as he rubbed his hands together. "Before the war I lost someone close to me, and I feel I could have done more." He paused. "I should have been prepared. Many times I feel overwhelming guilt. So every time I go into battle, I do so with a cavalier desire to remove my misery. I kill in hopes of being killed. I know that if I die, I will die gloriously, doing so with Rascal and my fellow horsemen. Then I can be—" He stopped quickly.

"Can be what?" Alex asked.

"Once I have died, I will then be with—" The soldier broke off his sentence, changing the subject. "Your wife, what's her name? Where is she?"

"Katherine, but she likes to be called Kate, or Kat. She went to town to get us some supplies."

"When will she be back?"

"Why?"

"I hear someone outside. It could be Rebels."

Alex looked out the window. "Don't worry, it's not Rebels."

"How do you know?"

"They are all gone, most likely chasing after your cavalry."

He sat up to position himself to look outside. "I stink. How can you stand it?"

"We were out of soap. Kate will bring some, and we'll help you with a bath. Try to take off your blouse and your undershirt, then put these clean clothes on. She will wash everything."

"Where are my trousers?"

"We took them off so we could work on your leg wound."

While seated he struggled to take off his blouse and then his undershirt. When he was finally able to stand, the clean blouse fell to the floor. Suddenly the morning breeze helped the broken door open quickly, and a young woman stood in the doorway and looked in. She was stunned at what she saw, but she stared anyway at the scars of war on the back of a nearly naked man.

Gabe turned quickly, hoping not to see any Johnny Rebs, but the blinding morning sun created a glowing silhouette, revealing a woman's dress that flowed up and around her. The light lit up his face so clearly she could see his fresh head wound and several other scars on his unshaved face. But what she fixated on was his wide-open, bright blue eyes. They drew her in, but what her essence felt surprised her more: *Oh, God, this young man needs healing, and not just for his external wounds.*

Gabe fell back onto his bed, unable to put any more weight on this injured leg. She moved quickly to the bed and tried to hold him steady.

"You smell like flowers," he said softly.

"You stink like a swine."

"I know. I need help dressing and bathing. Can you help me?"

Alex turned to her. "He is still delirious; I told him Kate was going to wash his clothes and to take them off. He just needs help putting on the trousers I loaned him."

"That explains his rude and forward behavior."

"No, I think that is just him."

"Sorry—you are not Kate?" Gabe asked.

"No, I'm not."

"She is right about that," explained Alex. "Elizabeth Lynn Jefferson is a Southern lady. She is Kate's childhood friend and our best neighbor. Call her Ellie. Ellie, this is Lieutenant Gabriel O'Shea."

"Lieutenant? Who said I was a Lieutenant?"

"You did, last night."

"I must have not been thinking. I am a sergeant. Is Rascal OK? He is OK, right? I think I do remember talking to him last night. He did tell me he was, didn't he?"

"Yes, he came in at two in the morning to let you know he was OK," Alex said.

Gabe could not take his eyes off of Ellie, who looked puzzled. After staring for several seconds, he softly said, "Your hair is as dark as a moonless night sky, and stars twinkle in your eyes with approval."

"Yankee, you are delirious—and smelly! Lay down so I can help you put these trousers on."

"I thought Kate would be back by now," said Ellie as she worked to pull them up.

"We got a late start because he had us up last night," said Alex.

"Is that how the door got broken?" she asked.

"Yup, he called for his horse, and the damn thing pushed his way in."

"What kind of flowers?" Gabe asked.

"What are you talking about?" asked Ellie.

"I said you smell like flowers—what kind?"

"You smell my lavender perfume."

"It smells wonderful." Gabe closed his eyes.

"Maybe you should put some on him," Alex said.

"I don't have enough to mask his smell."

"I don't smell anything anymore, except the food and you," Gabe said.

"Let's eat—it's ready," Alex announced.

"Gabe, put this blouse on. You're not sitting at the table

without it."

While eating, Ellie and Alex glanced at each other and turned to stare at Gabriel, who was shoveling it in as fast as he could. "This is great," he said between huge mouthfuls. "It even tastes better than it smells. Can I have more?"

"You also eat like a pig. How long has it been since you ate something?" Ellie asked.

"What is today's date?" he asked, with a full mouth.

"The 24th."

"The 21st," he mumbled.

"I said the 24th, not the 21st," Ellie corrected.

"No—the 21st was the last time I had something to eat. You wanted to know when I last ate." Looking up into her eyes with a grin on his face, he continued. "I don't usually eat like a pig, but you try not eating for nearly four days, and let's see if you eat like a lady."

"Actually, Kate and I were able to get some chicken soup in you a few times," added Alex.

"Thanks so much. Can I have a bit more now?"

Ellie got up and filled his bowl again. As she put his bowl down she looked at Gabe. "I believe you had more manners when you were sleeping."

This time he took a deep breath, paused, and whispered, "Thanks for the food." He ate slower, held the fork correctly, and did not speak with food in his mouth, and this time he wiped his mouth with the small hand-towel by his bowl and not his sleeve.

Ellie just stared. *I wonder what he has been through these last few days. He has manners and poise, and he showed a bit of charm, but I sense something more.*

As he ate he kept glancing up at her. *She is so wonderful to look at … I want to remember her face in case I don't ever see her again. I want to remember her. She has a small scar on her left eyebrow, and her lips are pink and full. The yellow flowers on her dress make her eyes even brighter, and with those very short sleeves I can see that each time I look at her, her arms get little bumps, and the tiny hairs stand up. I wonder what she is thinking.*

After eating she helped him back to his bed, and he fell fast asleep again. Within the hour Kate returned, to find Ellie cleaning the dishes.

"Where is Alex?" she asked.

"In the barn feeding the horse, I think."

"How is he doing?"

"I'm not sure about his wounds, but his mind is full of life, he even ate at the table."

"Ellie, I'm sorry but while you are here … I can use the help to wash him. Alex can only help so much."

"Is his pain back?"

"Yes, and he has been hiding it and drinking again. I'm going to wake this one up. Can you get Alex?"

"Gabe, wake up." Kate nudged him.

Opening his eyes, he looked directly at her.

"How did you do that?"

"Do what?"

"Change the color of your eyes?"

"What are you talking about?"

"They were blue before."

"No, they weren't."

"Your eyes were blue, and your hair was darker." He paused. "Who are you? I'm Sergeant Gabriel O'Shea."

She realized that as far as he knew, he was just meeting her for the first time. He clearly did not remember last night.

"Hi. I'm Kate Sheppard. I thought you were a Lieutenant? That's what I heard you tell us last night."

"Nope, just a sergeant."

Alex and Ellie walked in.

"Ellie is going to stay and help bathe you. You are making my house stink," Kate said.

"You two ladies are going to bathe me?"

"Can I shoot this Yankee instead?" Ellie asked.

"Alex, please help Ellie get him outside. I will start getting water for the tub. Gabe, don't say a word, and get your little ass outside before I shoot you," Kate said.

"Strong words from a lady. Alex, your wife—she is a lady, right?"

Alex pulled off his blouse, and Ellie now had a clear view of the dressing on the leg wound. "Kate, this looks like it needs to be checked," he said.

Kate looked at it quickly and then spoke to him. "Gabriel, Ellie stops by several times a week to help me out, so if you behave you may see her more often."

"OK. I will make my family proud."

"Don't get that wound wet," Kate firmly told both of them.

Ellie looked at Gabe. "Sometimes I may stop in several times a day. Also, from time to time one of my two brothers Mark or Tommy John—we call him T.J.—might stop in, or both of my younger sisters, Ann or Teresa. So don't shoot any of them, and watch your manners."

"If you need anything, we can ask T.J. to get it," Kate told him.

"Even information on where my army is?"

"Yes," Ellie replied with a grin.

"Ellie, is that it, or are there more of you?"

"Just one more: Robert the eldest is in Richmond."

"There is another one, Gabe, named JJ, but he hasn't been around since '61," Kate said, with a serious look at Ellie.

"JJ?" Gabe asked.

"Yes—he ran off, and we haven't heard from him since."

Still wearing what was left of his drawers, Gabe was helped outside and into the tub and sat on an upside-down bucket that was placed in the bottom.

"Sit still," Kate told him.

"It's cold."

"Here, Ellie—use this to wash him." She gave Ellie a small cloth.

"Where is Rascal?" Gabe asked.

"Over there, in that field." Kate gestured out to the east field. "He is doing great, eating very well, and his cuts are mostly closed and clean."

Ellie was clearly uncomfortable to be touching a nearly naked man. "Kate, I have never …" she said. "Kate, I can't …"

"If it makes you feel better, just keep your eyes closed," Kate told her.

Ellie tried to keep her eyes closed as she washed his back, but she could feel large scars, several on his left shoulder and one across his upper back. She motioned to Kate, and they both stared for a few seconds, trying not to have him notice.

Ellie had never felt anything like this, partly because she had never touched the naked back of a man nor seen such battle scars. She could not help herself; she tried to be discreet, making sure to feel each scar with just her fingertips, moving them end to end, but finally her curiosity got the best of her.

"Do these still hurt?" she asked.

"Not the one on my back—it was not deep—but sometimes the short ones on my left shoulder do."

"What are they from?" she asked. "They don't look like saber wounds."

"Where are my things?" he blurted.

"I hid your things in the barn. We found a jacket that may be yours; it was tore up some."

"Can I see it, please?"

"I'll get it after you are clean. Your things must stay hidden," Kate told him.

"Ellie, the long one on my back is from a saber, and the others from a cougar."

"No," Kate blurted out. She looked more closely at the scars on his shoulder then placed her left hand on top of them, lining up her three middle fingers as best she could with the marks and moving her hand from left to right, gently following the path as it moved from his shoulder to his back. "How?"

"We were scouting in the mountains around the Staunton and Strasburg Road, in June of '62. My mind was not focused, but Rascal was. As the cougar leaped off a large overhead rock toward us, Rascal quickly turned to our left, and the animal went flying by—but not before it reached out and caught me. It fell to the ground, and I drew and pointed my revolver ready to shoot. But as it turned over to get up, I noticed her teats, and I realized she must have young ones nearby. I could not kill her. She glanced at us and ran off. At that time I was a new private with my regiment, and my troop joked about it for weeks—my first war wound was from a female. They also joked that so far as they knew, I'm the only one in the Cavalry to be nearly killed by a female cougar. They had many laughs about that."

With a pained pitch to her voice, Ellie blurted out, "In nine months you went from a private to a sergeant—how many Southern boys did you have to kill to move up so fast?"

After a slow, deep breath, Gabe turned to look straight at them. First he glanced at Kate, and then he looked into Ellie's eyes. He said softly, "You mean how many of my friends had to suffer for me to move up? At least eight, maybe more—some killed in battle, others mortally wounded and died later, one died by disease, one missing, maybe dead or taken prisoner, mostly fallen by JEB

Stuart's cavalry. He is beating us in every battle; sometimes I wonder when it is going to be my turn. Don't worry, as well as your Southern cavalry is doing, we don't stand a chance. All this is for nothing, and I'll be dead by summer."

At that moment Kate dumped fresh water on his head, mostly to get his head cleaned but partially to change the direction of the conversation. Then she began to wash around his head and eye wounds. *His eye is healing nicely,* she thought. "Are you two done fighting the Civil War? We have work to do. Gabe, look at me. Can you see out of this eye?"

"It's still blurry."

As they continued to clean him up, Gabe softly said, "I'm done. Are we done?"

Ellie threw the washrag at him. "You're not done until your feet are washed. If you're in a hurry, maybe you should wash your own feet."

"While you do that, I will get the jacket to see if it is yours," Kate said. "Alex, don't dump the water, I want to wash his clothes. Can you bring the rest of his clothes out and kill a chicken so I can prepare it for dinner, please? Ellie, come with me to the barn."

After they entered the barn, Kate asked Ellie to move two barrels several feet across the barn floor. Moving the straw from that section of the floor, she opened a small door that had been uncovered. She hesitated for a moment, then climbed down a ladder that went into the hole and threw up two rolls of Union blue cotton. She unrolled one to reveal a long, flowing, dark blue cape lined with silk the color of red wine, and the other his jacket.

"Look, both of these are monogrammed 'RG O'Shea,' and look at his jacket—I already washed it and sewed the sleeves. They were ripped up, but inside it has leather sewn in the back and neck. Have you ever seen this in the cavalry, North or South?"

"No, never. 'RG O'Shea' … didn't he say his name was Gabriel O'Shea?"

"Yup, look at this." She went back down and brought up one of his saddlebags. "Look here." She pulled out wads of rolled-up money.

"It looks like he has eighty to a hundred U.S. dollars in here," Ellie said.

"He has less now; I took some to pay for supplies, including those for his wounds."

"Where would he get so much money—his pay?"

"Could be, if he hadn't been paid for a while. Alex sometimes didn't get paid for months."

"But on sergeant's pay he couldn't have that much, could he, Kate?" Ellie's brow furrowed.

"A Yankee sergeant's base pay is about seventeen a month, and cavalry soldiers get extra to keep their horses," said Kate.

"Like you said, there is almost a hundred dollars in here."

"He did say something about being a lieutenant, and they make a lot more money, fifty to a hundred dollars a month," said Kate.

"That's if he is a lieutenant."

Kate's eyes narrowed. "He could be stealing it."

"From who?" Ellie asked.

"Don't know."

"He seems nice, but we shouldn't trust him," said Ellie.

"Ellie, you don't trust any Yankee."

"Do you think he is looting?" Ellie asked.

"Maybe ... I don't know. Maybe it's his money."

"No matter how he got all this money, why would he be carrying it around?" Ellie examined one of the rolls. "Fascinating!"

Kate gathered them back up. "Don't worry. As soon as he gets better and leaves, we won't see him anymore. Like he said, he'll probably be dead by summer's end."

Kate brought out another item from the saddlebag. "Look—he even has two of the new Colt 1860 pistols."

"Our boys would love these," Ellie said.

Kate put the pistol back in the bag. "Strange man. It would be interesting to find out more about him." She furrowed her brow for a moment. "Let's go."

Returning to the tub just outside the house, Kate handed Gabe the jacket.

"What's been done to it?" he asked. He looked over the outside cotton; the rips had been carefully sewn. He discreetly reached in and found that the inner linings were still hiding the leather.

Kate reached over and took hold of the jacket. "Discreetly yours?" she whispered.

"Yes, discreetly mine," he whispered back.

"I could be dead from that saber strike on my back if I wasn't wearing it," he told them quietly.

Ellie picked up the soap and started to wash his lower back. "Gabe, we saw the leather. Why is it there?"

"Can I trust you not to tell anyone?"

"Yes, but we think we know now," said Kate.

Gabe looked at Ellie. "You? I know you are a Southern lady, and you have family fighting for the South."

"OK, I will not tell anyone."

"My grandma told me that in Europe, some cavalry soldiers put leather in their collars to protect their neck from sabers cutting their heads off. She sent me two items to help protect me in this war—this jacket, which has linings sewn inside to hold leather. But you saw that already."

"Go on. And the other item?" Kate asked.

"She sent me an angel."

"An angel?" Ellie repeated.

"I don't believe in angels," said Kate.

"Yes, an angel. She sent Rascal. *Shhhhh,* he is a very special creation—and don't ever call him an animal."

"He's an animal, not an angel," Kate said. "A horse is a horse—some smart, and others better-looking than most, but still an animal."

"You'll see. Be careful, he's not an animal," said Gabe.

"I think your head might be damaged," Ellie told him.

Kate gathered up the wash supplies. "Let's go inside so I can check your bandage and change it if it needs it, since you got it wet."

"Last night, did I ask you why you don't sound like you're from the South?" he asked her.

"Yup, and Alex and I told you we are both from Pennsylvania, and that is why you are not a prisoner and you are still alive."

"Did I call out for Rascal?"

"Yes, you did."

"Did he respond?"

"Yes, he did."

"You ain't seen nothing yet. So I guess I'm still in Virginia?"

"Yes, same as last night."

"Sorry, I don't remember waking up last night. In fact I feel like I'm dreaming now. I may even be starting to like Virginia. I can't remember ever being taken care of by two beautiful women."

"One more time, and I will ask Kate to turn you over to the

local militia as a POW."

"OK. I'm sorry. Now I know I'm awake and not dreaming."

Ellie looked at Kate. "Kate, I'll help you bring him in and help with his wound, then if you don't need me anymore I'm going home. I need to get up early tomorrow—T.J. and I are going to Culpeper to get supplies."

"Alex, please help Gabe back inside, and Ellie, come with me to get his new leg wrappings ready. I want to show you what needs to be done."

Kate cut the bloody bandages away to find a piece of his thigh muscle pushing up and out of the opening; it was also stuck to the bandage. She was relieved to see that most of his injury was clean and red, and the rotten smell was going away.

"Here, take some of this." She handed him the clear liquor. They all knew what was coming next.

"Alex, hand him a piece of wood. Ready?" she asked them.

Gabe then put the small piece of wood into his mouth. He shook his head, indicating that he was ready. Alex held his shoulders down, and Kate began to cut away the rotten, infected flesh she had missed, and as gently as she could she pushed in the protruding muscle. She tried not to look at him, not wanting to see the anguish in his face. But as hard as he tried to stay calm, she could feel the torment in his somber agony as his body began to shake.

When she was finished she rinsed the wound with cool water and added some of her Indian remedies and rewrapped it.

Turning to look at him she could see tears on his checks, and even more tears running down Ellie's face.

"Do you want more liquor?" Ellie asked Gabe.

"No, I will be OK. I want to stay clear." Looking up at her he noticed that her eyes had swelled up with tears, one beginning to run slowly down her cheek. He reached up and let it continue to run down his finger. "Thank you. I will be OK now, because of all of you."

"Everything will be OK," Kate said.

Those were words he once said some time ago that were lies. He looked away and closed his eyes.

As Kate rewrapped the wound she drifted off in thought, wondering how much pain he had already endured in this war. On his first conscious day she had learned a little more about him, and she wanted to know more.

As they cleaned up Kate glanced over at him and saw he had fallen asleep.

She looked at Ellie. "Bye, Ellie, talk to you later."

Ellie nodded, then looked down at the patient. "Bye, Gabriel. It was interesting to finally meet you," she whispered, knowing he did not hear her.

While hugging Kate, Ellie whispered, "All clear for a while. The word is, nothing going on around here."

Kate gave a sigh of relief. That was the message she had been hoping for.

Battles Can Be a Pleasure

Kate was dynamic, powerful, and independent, with a flair for fun and the ability to show strength and confidence without appearing dominant. In her little world she was the boss, but she was young and naïve enough to think she could deny a Civil War from getting in the way of her dreams. Those who she let into her world were close; she treated them well and considered them family. They believed in her, looked up to her, and followed her. At times she was mature for her age; she was patient, responsible, and a hard worker. At other times, however, she revealed her inner child; warm, encouraging, playful, rebellious, and with the ability to appear innocent, she brought out the child in others, making those she touched feel young again. That child wanted someone to challenge, appreciate, and provide her with what was important to her. But it was hidden behind a mask built to lock out the controlling world, and ironically was responsible for her self-preservation. The shine in her eyes and the delicate, subtle smile were signals that she would prefer not to be alone but that she will be in control. To live her dreams and control her destiny, she would dig deep inside—determined, creative, and strong. She was a fair person, but she could also be cruel if her control or loyalty were threatened.

Each time the war came knocking, it got brutal, but it also presented opportunities to put her desires first, the belief that she could make life fun and challenging again, and in return she would get her rewards. But her desire and choices could destroy everything.

Kate had gotten the message she'd been hoping for. Now all she needed was a horse.

Thinking back, Gabe's words hung in her mind: *She sent me an angel, she sent Rascal. He is a very special creation. Don't ever call him an animal.*

Yeah, right, she thought. *I know horses. We will see what his animal is made of, first thing tomorrow.*

After going through her house chores quickly and quietly while Gabriel slept, she planned to be gone before he woke up.

She realized she'd need to get quicker at her morning chores so she'd have enough time for training. Once finished she went to the small field next to the barn and brought Rascal into the barn, where she quickly brushed him, checked his legs, and tacked him up.

"OK, good boy, let's see how smart you really are. That was a nice trick opening the door and coming into my house. You know what would impress me? If you can fix it." She pulled his girth tight.

"Ready. Let's go for a ride."

She peeked outside and looked around, making sure nobody was watching. Off they went down the tree-line, through a field scattered with large, white stones, toward the east field and the river.

"OK so far. I think you like me."

An hour later, on her way home, his words now stuck in her heart. *She sent me an angel. She sent Rascal.*

I can't tell him I'm going to take his horse, she thought. *He will kill me. I won't tell him until the last moment. Alex won't be any happier, but he understands why I need to do this.*

After a week of sneaking out and working with Rascal, she decided to tell her husband. That night in bed she whispered her plans to him.

"I'm going to take Rascal to the race."

Alex turned his face toward her. "I know. I saw you leave on him today. How was he?"

"Amazing. He is extremely smart and brave."

"Why do you say that? What happened?"

"He spotted some Confederate pickets near the river long before I did. I was wondering why he was not focusing on me and began to walk differently. He walked slowly and very quietly, and each time he was careful where he put his feet. He also was using the large trees for cover, as he kept his head turned to the pickets and the trees between us and the soldiers. That's when I saw them. What surprised me the most was that he did it without me telling him to."

"I had heard stories of troopers falling asleep or being wounded, and their horses would carry them back."

"Then later he spotted some Union scouts, and he turned to look at me as if to ask, 'What do you want me to do?' I said *shhhhh*, and we walked quietly away, and each time he was careful where he put his feet. He did everything I asked. We were jumping three feet and higher, and I know he enjoyed it as much as I did. But he does this strange thing that concerned me: He jumps beautifully, but a lot of the time he is not watching what he is doing, like he is not paying attention."

"You need to find a way to tell Gabe you will be taking him. Feel him out. Try to soften the blow and tell him. I don't want him asking me to see Rascal once he is gone. Maybe he knows why Rascal doesn't pay attention."

Kate spoke with resolve. "OK. While he rests tomorrow I will tell him."

Late the next day, after she'd stalled long enough, Alex said, "Now, go do it. I have never seen you apprehensive about asking a man to do anything."

"This is different. I'm trying to feel him out, and I don't really know him. What if he gets mad and takes him and leaves?"

Alex was firm. "Lady, that's a chance you will need to take."

Kate looked down. "I know. I'll do it."

Gabe had been sitting in a rocker under a big shady tree that was between the house and the barn.

Kate swallowed hard and wondered how to begin. She took a deep breath and walked over to Gabe. He seemed relaxed and comfortable.

She began. "Gabe, I want to tell you a true story that happened to a sad little girl and how it changed her life. I don't share this with many people."

"Is it about you?"

"Yes."

"Then I want to hear it."

"Ellie's grandpa and his family started going to The Fauquier White Sulphur Springs resort on the banks of the Rappahannock River in Warrenton, Virginia, when it first opened in the early 1800s. My family started going there too, when my mom was a young girl. It was a year-round spot for friendly and competitive events. My grandpa and Ellie's met there and became friends. They would tell us stories of the famous people who would go there. It was only a one-day stagecoach ride from Washington, and we could take the railroad from Harrisburg, which was also a day's ride. We made a little adventure in getting there. So, many Southern plantation owners would spend a month or two each summer with their families, and Ellie and I tried to meet all of them. It was so beautiful and exciting." Kate seemed momentarily lulled by the old memories.

She looked up at Gabe all of a sudden. "Do you want to hear more, or am I boring you?"

"Please, go on," he said. *It's not like I can do anything else,* he thought. *Besides, she looks so happy, like a child who just got the best news ever. This is the happiest she has been since I first saw her. She is barely stopping to take a breath ... I guess she doesn't know.*

"It has a grand hotel, known as the Pavilion, four stories high with tall columns, and a large dining room that would seat 400 guests, and a huge, beautiful ballroom. The ladies wore so many beautiful gowns, and the musicians would play the finest music in the country. They had medieval-style jousting tournaments, bowling, billiards, cards, fox hunting, horse racing, and fancy dress balls. My and Ellie's favorite thing to do was watch the races and the balls and listen to the music. Many celebrities would also come. I remember even seeing a president once, I just don't remember which one.

"Ellie and I would dream and talk about the same two things, but we had different priorities. I wanted to one day be able to be in a race first, then marry a Southern gentleman who also was a bit arrogant—you know, to add some excitement, someone I had to keep in his place. Also, his family had to own a big plantation. Ellie wanted to marry a handsome and sophisticated Southern gentleman who would treat her as an equal and whose family also owned a plantation, it didn't matter how big. A bit boring. I told her to train one to treat her as the queen, but she likes to play it safe.

"Ellie and I first met when I was seven. It was the first time my family took us to The Springs. Then one day in a store she watched me start an argument with a store manager over candy. I wanted more, and he said I needed more money, but I told him I didn't have any more and I was not going to give up. She came over and handed the store owner the difference, and I got my candy. I asked her why she had paid, and she said she needed the store owner to help her with what she needed to buy, and she got tired of me wasting her time. We have been friends ever since. Sometimes we would visit each other, and at other times we would write. That's why when I got the chance to get this farm I had to have it.

"Each summer we would make sure our family's came to The Springs at the same time, and we would talk and play together with the other children. Ellie and I—well, mostly Ellie, because she would read the stories to us—one summer she read stories to us about the great American racehorses. We would dream about owning a few. Guess what we wanted to be?"

"Riders, breeders, or both?" Gabe seemed amused by Kate's detailed reminiscence.

"Yup—riders first, then breeders! We were only in our early teens. We loved to watch the horse races, and my dream was to one day ride in one. Before the war I was working hard on my reputation as a very good rider and trainer in a man-dominated culture. Several lady friends who were also riders and wives of influential men finally convinced the racing group to let us have a race just for ladies to compete. I finally got a horse I felt I could compete with, but the Confederate Army made sure it became theirs. Then one day Ellie sent me this newspaper story. Can I read it to you?"

"You saved it?"

"Yes, to remind me, and to motivate me, because one day I want to rebuild it."

> The Fauquier White Sulphur Springs resort, on the banks of the Rappahannock River in Warrenton, Virginia, was also located directly in the center of the greatest concentration of fighting so far in the War Between the States and was destroyed.
> Taking advantage of Union General McClellan's pause in his offensive advance to Richmond, General Robert E. Lee turned his attention to John Pope's Union Army of Virginia. Lee divided his troops, immobilizing McClellan while sending Major General Longstreet to reinforce Jackson's Confederate forces along the Rappahannock River near Fauquier Springs. Lee

arrived at Gordonsville on August 15, hoping to defeat Pope by cutting bridges along the river and then attacking before McClellan's army could arrive to reinforce it. Lee needed to be able to cross the river even though he was cutting bridges to foil Pope. To that end, the Confederates built several bridges themselves, including a key crossing at Fauquier Springs. Unfortunately, this bridge created a strategic target, and there was a series of skirmishes.

On the afternoon of August 25, 1862, while the Springs was occupied by Confederate troops, a shell struck the main hotel at the Springs, known as The Pavilion, which burst into flames and burned to the ground. The Fauquier White Sulphur Springs now lay in ruins.

"I dream of one day returning to The Springs after the war to help rebuild it and restore it to prominence as the grand resort I remember."

"Why are you telling me this story?"

"Well ... because even though The Springs is gone, we still meet once a year to race." She paused.

"And?"

"And this year would have been the first time I would have been able to compete, but both armies took my horses ..."

Turning his head to look straight at her, he spoke in a soft but firm tone. "You want my horse."

"No, I don't want him—I just want to borrow him."

"You are crazier than I thought. I know you're ... insistent, and—"

While he was at a loss for words, she cut in.

"I'm independent and strong willed. When I set my mind on something I do what it takes to get it done. I'm one of the best young riders in the state, and I'm better than most men, and this is my chance to prove it. I ride to win."

"Fauquier Springs is Yankee territory. What if you run into Yankees?"

"I have a plan."

"OK. Report your battle plan to me. I want to review it—

strategy, route, and objective."

He could feel how serious she was about her journey, and her sparkle and drive were starting to stir him up. As she began to outline the plan he regained his focus.

Kate explained each step. "Ellie had created the plan, and we improved on it ever since the war started. In two weeks we head north to Remington to meet some friends, hopefully ten in all. Then it will be about seven miles north to the race grounds, near Lees Mill Road. The race area will be about two miles south of Sulphur Springs, west of Warrenton—about twelve and a half miles in all. We plan to leave Remington in groups of two or three, fifteen minutes apart, in case we run into Yankees or Confederates. We should be there in three hours. We will leave at five o'clock in the morning, and would return by midday on May 14th."

"Objective?"

"Win a three-mile race, against six to ten other women. Some jumps, maybe two water crossings."

"Size of gathering?"

She paused and took a breath.

"As many as one hundred, but fewer have been coming each year since the war started."

"You don't think one hundred Southerners' gathering in a field for three days won't attract attention?"

"No Southern soldiers will be there, and if any Union soldiers show up they will only see the local families with children playing, wagons, and a few tents and horses. You know many of your officers know the history of that place, also."

"What about rain?"

"We'll see what the weather is like before we leave."

"How is Rascal feeling?"

"Great—bored, and ready to ride with me."

"What about his bad hoof? His cuts look better, but he may need more rest."

"No, he doesn't."

"He doesn't what?"

"His bad hoof will be ready, and he will get all the rest and good food he wants. He will be ready."

"He doesn't like many people, and he never lets anybody ride him ... how do you expect to get him ready for a race in two weeks?"

"Like you said, he is smart. He told me he was ready, so I started to ride him, and we have been training."

He wanted to push her; he felt the need to push her. *I'm enjoying our little debate*, he thought. *She's putting up a good fight. She came prepared, and I can see the determination in her eyes. She's not going to give up. I realize she is going to take Rascal no matter what I say. This is her way of telling me where she and Rascal were going to be for those three days. Unless I take him and leave first ...*

"Did you take better care of him than me so you could steal him?"

"I never lower my standards of care, not even for a Yankee. You both got the best of my attention and time. Why don't you feel like I deserved this?"

She deliberately raised her level of emotion. *Now I have him where I want; I sense his uncertainty. He is going to give in and say yes, or a least he now knows I am going to take him anyway, and he isn't going to stop me.*

"Do you know why he doesn't pay attention when he is jumping?"

Damn it ... think. "No, not yet, but I'm working on it."

"What day is the race?"

"May 13th."

"You have to do better than that. You have about two weeks to be ready. What's the reason?"

Now I have her off balance, he thought. *Let's see what she comes up with. I'm enjoying this.*

"He is not focused," she said.

"Why?"

She did not know, so she looked up at him, and with her playful, flashy smile and with a hint of dubiousness she said, "I don't know. I need your help with that, Gabriel, please."

Not bad. She can be nice and polite, if only to get what she wants. That must have been hard for her, but she did put it back on me.

Gabe explained. "He's not focused because he is not being challenged. Go out early tomorrow and challenge him. Every once in a while I need to shake him up. He gets bored like the rest of us."

"How?

"I make him jump really high, or take him through a loose

fence. You should set up a high jump, and don't lead him if he's not paying attention—have him crash into it. But be careful. I've done that before, and at the last second he catches on and jumps, and sometimes he loses me, and sometimes he doesn't. OK, you have my blessings. But I want to see both of you before you leave that morning."

"You do realize I will be racing Rascal against Ellie and one of her horses?"

"Yes, I figured that."

"Thank you so much. You don't know how much this means to me. You know I'm very lucky, right?" She sat on his bed and hugged and kissed him on the check.

"I don't believe in luck," he told her.

* * *

April 30

It was the first time in nearly two weeks he had gotten up and dressed without help. At first he started by walking around the inside of the house, and later in the day he included the outside area to and from the barn. He was sitting on the porch resting when Alex rode in on the wagon with supplies from town and pulled up next to Gabe.

"Gabe, the Union cavalry crossed Kelly's Ford in force yesterday, heading south toward Richmond," Alex said.

The rain caused a two-week delay, he thought to himself.

"Thanks for that information, Alex. Can I help you unload?"

"Sure, if you feel up to it."

"Yes, I do, if I plan on getting back into this war."

"OK, let's do it. Jump in, and I'll take you to the barn."

By the third day of moving around, he tried to help Alex around the farm more and more, at first with light loads and loading and unloading the wagon. *As each day passes I feel stronger and stronger, and I can see Rascal is doing well. He is focusing on his training. Maybe in a few days after they return, I may be able to ride him again. Tomorrow I will include some bending and carry heavier loads to strengthen my leg.*

* * *

May 11

"Alex, could you please bring in some more wood for the night?" Kate asked her husband.

As soon as Alex left, Gabe spoke to her. "What about Alex? You know he is not doing well."

She shook her head. "He is fine. He's felt like this before, and besides, he has always wanted to see me race. Don't worry I trust you with my husband." She slapped his back with her hand.

"I thought about this very carefully," Gabe insisted. "I don't want to be responsible for you getting hurt. I don't think you should go …"

"How would you feel if someone could help you live a dream, and they tried to stop you? Who are you going to be in this dream? You would be dead if I—" She stopped herself and took a breath.

Gabe spoke up. "I needed to know how much this means to you. I will not hold you back. Have fun, but don't let either army take him."

"I won't, I promise. And I never make promises."

"Get up, say goodbye now. You won't be up tomorrow when we leave."

"Yes, I will, and I already said goodbye to Rascal, and I told him he better take care of you."

5:00 A.M.

She was quiet, trying not to wake both men, but as she headed to the door she heard, "Aren't you going to say thank you, or at least goodbye? You know I would love to be there and see you both cross the finish line first."

She walked over and sat on the edge of Gabe's bed and whispered, "I didn't want to wake you; you still need your rest. Besides, I expect you to be ready to ride when I return, so you can ride your winner."

"I once needed someone to help me with a dream."

"How did that go?" she asked.

"She gave me Rascal. Now I'm going to let you take him to live yours. Take—"

She cut him off. She leaned over and kissed him on the check, then whispered, "Thank you for trusting me. See you in three days."

Like two children going to live an adventure, she and Rascal slipped off into the early morning fog.

* * *

Ellie was waiting for her on the road to Remington, along with her brothers T.J. and Mark and their friend Brandy.

"You're late."

"I know. Gabe woke up, and we had a nice goodbye chat. He's not so bad for a Yankee."

"That sounds like something I should be saying," Ellie said softly.

"I see you're going to race Rebel. He's your best, but he still won't beat Rascal."

"We'll see, Kate. We'll see."

Mark, Ellie's younger brother, was not allowed to enter the war until he turned 16. Then he would be assigned to support his oldest brother Robert in Richmond, who was attached to the headquarters of the Army of Virginia. Brandy was one of four children, whose family lived on a modest-sized farm north of Kate. Brandy and Mark were planning to get engaged after Mark turned sixteen.

Mark would ride in the race for older boys, those 14 to 16 years old.

In Remington they met up with a few more friends and fellow riders, code-named The Breeders.

"Are we all here?" Kate asked.

"Yes. Caroline and James can't make it … they have no horse to run."

"Taken by the Yankees?"

"Yup."

"What about young Seth and Mary?"

"They're coming, but they'll be taking a different route." Ellie looked around. "OK, let's get going. We should try to stay on schedule."

"So, The Breeders will be the ten of us this year," said Kate.

"Thirteen, Miss Kate. George and John Stuart will also be there."

"Good, thirteen. Thank you, Thomas."

"Let's go," Ellie said. "I heard that twelve were entered for the ladies' race. Kate, four years ago when you thought up this plan for a ladies' race, I thought you were nuts." She paused to look around at the group. "We all thought this was never going to be possible, especially when The Pavilion was destroyed by the war."

"Peter, tell her what Mrs. Sara Johnson told you," said Jill.

"She said that a few of her friends are thinking about a day when women race against the men," Peter announced.

"That would be a miracle," said Brandy.

"Hallelujah!"

"Thomas, it's a miracle of God that he made a few women able to soften the cold, narrow minds of ancient men," said Jill.

Brandy turned to Kate. "When you first started The Breeders, it was to protect good horses from being destroyed in the war and breed them. Hiding them from the Union and Confederate armies was easy compared to us getting to race—and in a few days we will be racing."

"Don't forget, we need to split up into smaller groups and separate," said Kate. "Keep your eyes and ears open. We don't want anybody asking questions about our horses. Does everyone understand?"

"T.J., you are with Brandy. Stay behind me and Kate."

"Peter, you are with your sister, and take the lead. Mary Ann, you stay with him."

"Aww … I was…" Peter moaned.

"Forget it, Peter. We promised Jill's folks to keep an eye on you," Kate said.

"Thomas, you and Jill are with Mark, and you trail the group."

"When we make camp today, the gentlemen will take one tent, and the ladies will be in the other," said Ellie.

After walking for a while, Ellie turned to look for Brandy and T.J., who as usual were moping behind.

"Brandy, T.J., move closer. Can you hear me?"

"Yes, Miss Kate," they responded together.

After rotating to the rear, Ellie and Kate fell a bit behind the rest. Ellie thought about asking Kate about Mac.

Ellie's thoughts started to wander as she remembered the first time she saw William Randle McMurphy. "Mac" was a handsome, strong sixteen-year-old cadet from the nearby military academy. He was also the second son of a graduate of the U.S. Military

Academy at West Point, New York, and a wealthy landowner in the Tidewater area of Virginia. He was expected to follow in his father's and older brothers' footsteps by attending West Point.

My father was hoping I would marry him but I couldn't ... he was not right for me. Boy, did that make him mad for a few weeks. I knew his family would not approve of Kate, but she tried anyway. For most people that would have been the end of it, and impossible to pursue, but she is not like most.

"Do you still dream of seeing Mac at The Springs?" asked Ellie.

Kate paused to think about her response. "Yes, you know I do. Why?"

"What I still don't understand is what happened between to two of you—I mean before you got married. You stopped writing me, and then I did not hear from you again until you showed up at my door nearly three years ago with Alex."

"I don't want to talk about it." Kate looked away.

"We have a long trip and nothing else to do but talk. Besides, I think you owe me an explanation. Remember, I introduced the two of you."

Kate sighed. "OK, only because you will nag me about it the whole way. That last summer you saw me, he was not acting the same way he had every other summer. Something had changed."

"I'll say. He was a man."

"Besides that ... he waited until midsummer, then told me his family wanted him to marry a woman they had picked out for him. He could not spend time with me anymore. She was arriving the next day so they could get to know each other. I tried not to see them together, but there were times when I could not avoid them."

"No wonder you were so hard to talk to and so mad at everything. I didn't know."

"I was so angry. You finally found someone you liked, and you were having a great summer. I didn't want to bother you."

Ellie looked distressed. "I'm your sister; you should have shared that with me."

"Let me finish. I found out in a Richmond newspaper article that their wedding plans were put on hold because of the war, and they have not married."

"Why?"

Kate shrugged. "I don't know. All I could find out was that he became an officer—1st Lieutenant with the 7th Virginia Cavalry, also known as Ashby's Cavalry."

"Let me see if I have this straight: You live in Virginia, married to a discharged wounded Yankee. You will be riding in a race on a Yankee horse whose wounded Yankee owner is lying in your home, with your husband taking care of him. You still think about a childhood memory of a Confederate cavalry officer who would kill the other two without a second thought. Lady, you like living dangerously." Ellie smirked.

"I am a woman of the times. There are other women going through extraordinary circumstances during this war. Besides, I think it's exciting. Aren't you having fun?"

"Compared to the life you live, this race is going to be the easiest thing you do all year."

"I hope so. If you think three men are one too many, I can spare Gabriel. He is really good looking when he's cleaned up."

"He's married," Ellie said.

"He is? Who told you that? He doesn't act like it."

"Alex told me. Anyway, you're married, and sometimes you don't act like it."

"Good point." Kate smiled.

Ellie looked distracted for a moment. "Before I forget, I want to show you something." In a deep but soft voice she called out, "Thomas did you bring the *Weekly?*"

"Yes. Here it is, already folded to the page."

"OK, good. Have everyone ride in closer so they can hear too."

"This is from the April 1 issue of *Harper's Weekly*."

She read loud enough for all to hear:

"Saratoga Race Course, a Thoroughbred horse-racing track, will open in Saratoga Springs, New York, on August 3, 1863. It will open for four days of racing from late July through early September. John Hunter and William R. Travers are building Saratoga Race Course across Union Avenue. The dirt track will be known as Horse Haven, and Steeplechase races are also to be run on the turf."

"There is a drawing by Winslow Homer included, if anybody wants to see it," she added.

"Let me see that," Kate blurted.

Peter looked indignant. "The Yankees burn down Sulphur Springs in '61, then they go build a place in Saratoga Springs, New

York? Let me see."

T.J. chimed in. "Kate, maybe you should move to New York."

She smirked. "Funny, T.J.—but not unless they allow women riders."

Everyone laughed.

Kate's smile faded. "Thanks. Thomas, who made you our resident race historian?"

"Ellie did. I have something else."

"Let's hear it," Ellie told him.

"OK. Almost forty years ago to the day, May 27, 1823, American Eclipse, the North's fastest horse, raced against Henry, the fastest horse in the South, from North Carolina. American Eclipse won two of the three races that day, but Henry did beat him in the first race—the only time American Eclipse was ever beaten."

"So, what's the point? That was a long time ago." Kate said.

"Tomorrow, you from the North will be riding a horse from New Jersey against Ellie and Rebel, from the South. Sounds like a modern rematch with women."

"Kate, do you think they only let us ladies race because of the shortage of men and horses?" Brandy asked.

"I hope not, cause if that is true, then when the war ends we won't be racing."

"Kate, I don't understand why tomorrow's race is so important," said Thomas. "You've beaten some of the best young men and women riders in the area before."

"Those races were not official. We raced in places and times when no one would see us. Besides, the boys I beat would never admit it. If you and the rest of this group hadn't been there to watch our race, nobody would know."

"I have another old race story for you, Kate."

"OK, Thomas, tell us."

"On May 2, 1778, another legendary race took place at Tucker's Path, a quarter-mile course located along North Carolina's border with Virginia. This race pitted Willie Jones, a planter from Halifax County, and his horse, Trick-em, against Mud Colt, an impressive Virginia thoroughbred that North Carolina planter Atherton had rented. Trick-em won handily, ridden by Austin Curtis, a slave whom many experts at the time called North America's finest rider and trainer. Slaves and free blacks filled many winner's circles at both Southern and Northern racetracks in the mid-1700s."

Kate cut in. "OK, everyone, the history lesson is over, we now need to keep quiet—eyes and ears open, and only hand signals. Spread out in groups. Thomas and T.J., take the lead for now."

"You know, you should have been in the cavalry," Ellie whispered to her.

"Yup. And my side would have won already."

* * *

After they rode silently for some time, Kate spoke to the group. "As soon as we cross over the next ridge, we'll be there."

Ellie's eyes widened as they came to the top of a rise. "Wow, it's beautiful—look over by the trees over there, look how many tents are up already."

"I love how it is nestled between all these rolling hills."

"Look to the west—the clouds are beginning to clear," said Jill.

"If we have time before we leave, I'd like to take a ride over to The Spring and look around," Kate told the group.

"We should check first."

"Why?"

"I heard in Culpeper that the Union army has some troops there."

Shortly after they arrived at the gathering they unpacked and set up their small tents.

"What time is it?"

"Four-fifteen," Mark yelled out to Kate.

"I'm going to take Rascal out to get used to the area. You want to come, Ellie?"

"Yes, definitely. Let's get tacked up."

The two women walked out toward the horses together and tacked up.

"I was hoping we would be able to ride in trousers instead of dresses."

"Me too. Kate—"

"What?"

"Peggy is coming up on your left. Hurry, mount and go to your right."

"Peggy Jones?"

"Yes, go—I'll try and catch up, but don't wait."

"OK. If I don't see you, have a good ride."

Kate was quick, and up and off she galloped.

"Hi, Peggy. How are you doing this fine spring morning—out for a walk?" As she spoke she positioned her horse to block Peggy's path.

"OK," she replied.

Peggy was the second-youngest child from a large family that lived southwest of Culpeper, closer to the mountains. Several of her brothers were fighting for the South. Peggy and her younger brother were spoiled and selfish, trying to take what wasn't theirs. She tolerated Ellie but despised Kate.

"Did you come by to wish me luck?"

"No, I came to talk to Kate."

Ellie spoke cheerfully. "Ah, you just missed her! See, there she goes. Better luck next time."

"I'll get her next time," Peggy mumbled as she walked off.

When they returned from their rides an hour later, Kate went up to Ellie. "How was your ride, Ellie?" she asked.

"Good. How was yours?"

"Fine. What did she want?"

"She wanted to talk to you."

"Why?" Kate narrowed her eyes.

"Didn't say—but do you know she lied?"

"I know," Kate replied.

"She is getting too close; she is never this interested in us. She is up to something, Kate."

"I think she wanted to get a good look at Rascal."

Ellie nodded. "You expected that. I think it is more than that, though ... you know she has always hated you."

Kate smiled. "I know. But I don't know if I had more fun beating her up, or taking her suitors."

Ellie laughed. "I'd bet on taking her suitors—especially after you dumped them! You were one mean little girl when you were sixteen."

"I was, wasn't I? I was so mad at so many things back then." Kate looked thoughtful.

"You should be careful with her," warned Ellie. "She is definitely up to something."

"I know—but what?"

"The only thing I can think of is that she may try something with Rascal." Ellie scowled.

"To win the race, or to hurt me?"

"Both, maybe? But don't let her bait you into a fight, either. That wouldn't be good. The consequences for this race and future ones could be bad."

"I won't. I'll stay far away from her." Kate smiled. "With the team's help, of course."

May 13, 8:00 A.M. Race day.

"Kate, look to the west! It looks like rain clouds are rolling in again." Ellie told her friend.

Kate looked at the sky and frowned. "They sure are. Let's hope the rain holds off for the rest of the day."

9:30 A.M.

As the group prepared for the event, Ellie came over to Kate. "Kate, our race organizer Mr. Pitts is looking for you."

"Here he comes now," Brandy cut in.

Even though Mr. Pitts was tall and thin, he was always eating something. You could see it in his beard; he always had food in it. He acted like he was running and coordinating the races, but everyone knew his wife ran the events.

"Miss Kate, please come over here. What is that wardrobe you have on?"

"You like it?"

"Miss Kate, this dress is not appropriate."

"I have pantalets under my dress."

"What happened to your dress?"

"I cut it."

"Why?"

"It ripped when I rode yesterday."

"Your dress and petticoat can't be ripped like that." His face was stern.

"It got in my way and nearly caused me to fall."

"Are you trying to tell me a ripped dress is safer?"

"Yes! It is not just me. Many of the ladies think it is safer. I know you don't want me or anyone to fall and get hurt, do you, Mr. Pitts?"

He looked around to the ladies, each shaking their heads or commenting that they agreed. Some showed him that they had also cut their dresses, but not nearly as high as Kate's, and none had cut their petticoats.

"Fine, but don't any of you cut any more."

"We won't."

As they watched him walk off, Jill was the first to speak up. "Thank you, Kate. I didn't think you were going to pull it off."

"Great job!" said Brandy. "Now I feel I can ride like a man."

"Me too," said Mary Ann.

Kate looked pleased.

"Kate, you could ride sidesaddle with your dress wrapped around both your legs."

"We know that, but he doesn't. I feel more comfortable with less dress rolled up in front of me."

"You sure you are not trying to make a point?"

"Me? Never!" she exclaimed, with a smug expression on her face. "Brandy, get our girls together and head back to our tent."

As the group walked back together, Ellie asked, "What's wrong Kate?"

"I ripped my dress late yesterday after I rode off to avoid Peggy, remember?"

"Yes."

"I cut my petticoat this morning."

"Yes. So?"

"So, how did Mr. Pitts find out so fast? Peggy?"

Three ladies replied in unison: "Peggy."

"I will not be outdone by her," Katie whispered to Ellie.

Ellie frowned for a moment, then moved on. "What's the plan for the race?" she asked.

Kate answered with a smile. "Easy. I win, you're in second, Brandy third, and Peggy goes down."

Ellie feigned annoyance. "Hmm! How about I win, you're second, Brandy third, and Peggy goes down."

Kate showed off her predictable glare and smiled. "Whatever, as long as that witch loses."

"Hey! What about the rest of us?" asked Mary Ann.

"All of you are good riders, but you need more experience and better horses. Maybe next year you'll be able to keep up!" Kate told her.

1:00 P.M.

Mrs. Pitts smoothed her wide dress and cleared her throat before announcing the rules. "Ladies, listen. The rules are twelve riders race for four miles. Seventeen jumps, three over water. The course is marked by color banners—red stay to right, and lavender stay to left. There will be judges along the course watching you. Stay on course, and no fighting or deliberate bumping of horses. Do you all understand?

"Yes, Mrs. Pitts," the group responded.

"You have thirty minutes to get to the starting line. We run at two o-clock."

* * *

2:00 P.M.

"Line up, ladies," shouted Mr. Pitts.

The twelve riders carefully circled, each trying to get the best starting position. Ellie watched Peggy circle around Kate, trying to position her horse to block Kate's start. Just then Brandy steered her horse to cut in between Katie and Peggy.

"Get over, you senseless witch, before we push you over!" Brandy yelled out.

Brandy was riding Beth, the biggest and oldest horse in the race. That mare could get mean as hell if Brandy let her.

"Ladies, move away from each other," Mr. Pitts yelled out.

At the starting line the horses shuffled and moved into each other in preparation of the start.

"GO! Go … go."

Off they ran, down a gradual slope to the first turn and over the first jump. All went over in good form and moved to circle a large field in the distance. The spectators watched as they all cleared the next jump, then as a group they disappeared into the woods.

Brandy was in front—she was using Beth, her big mare, to block and intimidate some of the riders. Behind her was the rest of the field, except for three who were further back. They rode three across—Ellie, Kate, and Peggy.

Each rider was trying to get the best angle to the next jump.

"Move over, you Yankee wench!" Peggy yelled to Kate, as she moved her horse into Rascal.

"Witch! Stay away, or you will end up on your ass."

Several ladies giggled.

One of the judges yelled out as they approach the next jump. "Ladies, ladies, move apart."

Kate looked over to Ellie and softly asked, "Did you see where that judge was?"

"Yes, but not until she yelled to us. They could be spread out across three jumps."

"Yup, seems like it. Keep checking. When it's time, follow my lead."

A mile into the race and past several jumps, Peggy tried to pull out ahead and move in front of Katie and Ellie.

"You two have no idea who you are dealing with," Peggy yelled. "That colt you had in the west field three weeks ago, Kate—I took it and sold it to our cavalry."

With that comment, Kate let Peggy move up, then dropped in behind her. Ellie moved in close to Peggy's right side as Kate then moved up her left side.

"Ladies, what are you doing?" Peggy asked.

"No ladies here," Ellie said. "Not today we aren't. We're Rebel cavalry, and we're goin' to squeeze the witch out of you."

"No, stop. No!" Peggy tried to reach for Ellie's horse's reins, but Ellie quickly slapped her hand away.

Ellie and Kate moved their horses in tight, then moved away a bit. With each squeeze they placed their legs in front of Peggy's, then again moved in tight. They repeated the squeeze, each time squeezing Peggy longer and longer, until Peggy checked her horse and pulled him back.

"Go, Ellie!" Kate yelled.

Ellie and Kate began driving their mounts side by side, faster and faster, each stride bringing them closer to the leaders. They glanced behind them, watching Peggy trying to stay with them. Over the next half-mile they passed the remaining riders. Then Ellie and Kate were side by side in the lead, with Peggy trying to get past Brandy's big mare.

Ellie finally broke the silence. "We still have about a mile and a half to go."

"I know," said Kate.

"Let's ease back a bit."

"OK. You first."

"OK." Ellie eased Rebel back, then Kate eased Rascal. Together they went over the third water jump.

After running about a mile and clearing several more jumps, Ellie said to Kate, "We don't have far to go, and no sign of Peggy. I guess it will be the two of us."

Kate let out her reins to encourage Rascal to move out, and Ellie did the same to Rebel. But both horses just looked at each other, and neither picked up speed. Then a quarter-mile from the finish, both beasts began to move out, extending their strides.

Ellie and Kate began driving their mounts side by side, faster and faster, each horse taking the lead as they alternated head-bobs—Rebel's head in front, then Rascal's. With each stride their head-bobs begin to synchronize, until they were a nose apart.

The crowd lined up along the straightaway to the finish line, their cheers growing louder and louder as the horses raced toward them. *Whoosh*—the horses and riders flew by in a blur, and it was unknown to the spectators or judges who won, the finish was so fast and so close.

As the ladies pulled up their horses, they glanced over at each other.

"Wow! That was great," said Ellie.

"It sure was," Kate replied. "Congratulations on winning."

"I thought you won."

"I guess we'll need to wait for the judges to decide."

As they began to walk around to cool their horses, they saw Brandy coming in to finish in third, followed by the rest of the riders.

Brandy circled around them and yelled out, "Who won?"

"We don't know yet! Too close."

After several minutes' accounting for all the riders, the head judge yelled out though a megaphone.

"The winners are Ellie on Rebel, and Kate on Rascal—too close for us to call."

"Brandy, where is Peggy?" asked Ellie.

"Um, maybe in the water at the last water jump."

"'Maybe'?"

"OK. In the water," Brandy confirmed.

"What did you do?"

"When she tried to get past me she kept hitting Beth, so I let

Beth do what she does best."

"She slammed into her?" Kate asked.

Brandy smirked. "Yup, right off her horse and onto her smug wet ass."

"Brandy! Watch your mouth. You are still a lady," Ellie scolded, with a grin.

"Yes, Miss Ellie," Brandy said, smiling.

"Just like you wanted, Kate," said Mary.

"Thanks, ladies. Let's hope no judges saw you—I don't want anybody disqualified. Let's go and take care of our horses."

"Kate," said Ellie.

"Yes?"

"You can have my winnings."

"Thanks, Ellie. You know, I expected that."

"I know."

Kate moved closer to Ellie. "Don't you wish you could find a man who responds like our mounts do? These boys were so smooth, so easy to balance. I felt as if we were one creation, with one mind and one purpose."

"Yup, woman and horse become one," Ellie agreed.

"Ellie you mean rider and horse become one."

"That's what I said."

Kate smiled at her.

Peggy was angry about how the race turned out and that Kate had gotten another horse, so she went to pick a fight. Kate and Ellie were still together, and the three had a brief, loud discussion until Mrs. Johnson came over and broke up the argument. Mrs. Johnson was not related to Ellie, but she knew all the large farm owners in northern Virginia. Her family had settled in the tidewater area of Virginia in the early 1700s and then expanded westward some sixty years ago, just before she was born. Her family had been intimately involved in many areas of our revolution. She was influential and benevolent.

"Stop it, all of you," she told the women.

"Yes, Mrs. Johnson. We are all very sorry. Right, ladies?" Ellie apologized.

"I'm sorry," said Peggy.

The three looked at Kate.

"OK," Kate finally said. "Me too."

"Do you want to ruin this for all of us?"

"No."

"That was a fine race and a good start, ladies, but we have a long way to go. Now, stay away from each other."

"Yes, Mrs. Johnson."

"Miss Kate, Miss Ellie, will you join my family for dinner tonight?" Mrs. Johnson asked.

"I don't think we can. We need to keep an eye on our group," said Kate.

"I'm sorry—of course, all of you are invited."

"Thank you, Mrs. Johnson. What time?" Ellie asked.

"About six o-clock, an hour after the older boys' race. We're behind the Morgan family's tent. We're the big gray tent over there. Will that give you ladies the time you need to clean up and put on new dresses?"

"Yes, Mrs. Johnson. Right, Kate?"

"Yes, ma'am."

Ellie turned to Mark. "Mark, run ahead, and tell everyone to meet at our tent at five-thirty."

Shortly after all had arrived for dinner, one of the older guests spoke. "Nice job, ladies. We are proud of you."

"Thank you, Mrs. Johnson."

"Mark, congratulations on winning your race."

"Thank you, Mrs. Johnson."

"Please call me Martha, and this is William, my husband—and you already know Mr. Pitts and his wife, and Mr. and Mrs. Morgan."

"Yes. Well done to all of you." Mr. Johnson shook Ellie's hand, then Kate's.

"Mark, Brandy, make sure everyone eats, then you can leave this tent area, but make sure you are all back at our tents by eight-thirty. I want the both of you there before it gets dark."

"OK. See you later."

Mr. Johnson gestured to Kate and Ellie. "Come sit here, please. Tell us, it was better than racing only friends, right?"

"Yes, it was."

"Why?"

"It was more competitive, because not all of us riders like each other," Ellie said.

"I wanted everyone to know that I'm the best lady rider in this part of Virginia."

"Well, not all the riders were able to compete—you know, with some losing their horses and all," said Martha.

"We know, so next year it will be better… maybe we won't have to wear dresses."

Kate got a lot of stares for that comment.

"I mean, we can wear trousers instead!"

"Miss Kate, you are a young woman ahead of your time. Maybe one day," said Mrs. Pitts.

"Kate, where did you get your horse? He did very well," Mrs. Morgan asked, with a curious smile.

"Um … he showed up one day and wouldn't leave, so I put him to good use."

"I think he is a classy little rascal," Martha cut in, glancing at Kate and smiling. "Let's eat."

After dinner and a few quick chats, Kate wanted to leave.

Back at their tent, Kate called over to Ellie. "Can you please light the fire, Ellie?"

"Got it. That food was great."

"Yes, it was. I was so hungry after the race, I could have eaten anything!"

"Me too."

"Let's celebrate."

"How?" asked Ellie.

"The way we deserve. Sit." Kate motioned toward the blankets laid out on the ground. She pulled out some rolled-up brown paper from her saddlebag and unrolled it onto Ellie's lap.

"Tobacco cigars!" marveled Ellie. "Where did you get these?"

"A friend. Here, light up." She handed Ellie the stick she had pulled from the fire to light her cigar.

"Good thing we are behind the big smoking tent the men are in, so nobody will notice our smoke," said Ellie.

"You mean, good thing I put us here," said Kate with a smile.

Ellie looked over her cigar. "It smells and feels fresh."

"Do you really need to examine it? It's not like you have a choice. Just light it."

They puffed away, and after several relaxing minutes of staring up at the early evening sky, Kate reached back into her saddlebag and pulled out a small flask.

"Try this." Kate took a swig, then handed it to Ellie.

"Wow, that's sweet," Ellie said. "Bourbon?"

"Yup, the real good stuff, like your pa used to get. Ellie, good thing you stopped me today, cause I was gonna pop Peggy right in her smug nose."

"I know, and as usual you started to get loud, and a lot of people started gathering around."

"Did you hear Jeffrey Jackson?" Kate smiled. "He kept yelling, 'Hit her!'"

"He does that every time he sees you get mad," Ellie said. "He likes to see you hit someone."

Kate tipped her head back and looked up at the sky. "Maybe next time I should hit him, I would like to see what he does. Maybe tomorrow I will." There was a gleam in her eye.

"No, not here, girl," warned Ellie. "You really don't think about consequences, do you?"

"Nope, I don't even recognize it as a word. I do what I do, then sometimes things happen, and we go on."

"Limited conscience also, then?" asked Ellie.

"Yup." They both smoked in silence for a few minutes, then Kate spoke again. "So, you kiss anybody or see someone you want to court since we last spoke about it?"

"You know I haven't," said Ellie, sighing. "All the good men who are the right age are off fighting."

"Tomorrow, go over to that wounded soldier—you know, the one who lost his left hand. Dismount and act like you're passing out from exhaustion, and fall into his good right arm. Then thank him with a kiss."

"Why?" Ellie asked.

"'Cause you need to practice how to talk to a real man and get him to look at you."

"You know I can't do that, Kate. The old men may use it as an excuse not to let us race next year."

"Too bad. Anyway, you know the men liked watching the ladies race."

"I know, and so did their wives and lady friends."

"Next time the Confederate Army comes around, just walk up to a good-looking second lieutenant—you know, the baby of the officer class. Press your lips to his, and tell him thank you for fighting for the cause. And he will remember that until the day he dies, which may be sooner than later."

"And if he lives?" asked Ellie.

"Even better: Marry him. Any man who can make it though this war unharmed is my kind of man."

"I can't," said Ellie. "I'm not like you. I want my man to kiss me, not the other way around. Besides, you act like I've never been kissed before."

"I know you kissed Tom Henry, Paul Anderson, and ... what's his name? You know, Peggy's brother?"

"You know his name is George Jones."

"Tom and Paul are both dead. Killed at Antietam," said Kate.

"I know." Ellie looked away.

"I remember how mad your father got each time you ended your courtships after a month," said Kate.

"I just couldn't pick one just to make my father happy. I know deep down he wants me to be happy."

"What about George?" asked Kate.

"I don't like him; there is something about him that's not right. I just can't put my finger on it," said Ellie.

"As a person, or a suitor?" Kate asked.

"Both. I don't like the way he treats the workers on his farm, almost cruel. He has a real mean side to him."

"That's what you saw," said Kate. "Imagine what he does when nobody's looking. I don't think he's right in the head. Ellie, do you remember when he was fourteen?"

"Of course I do. You beat him up—twice!"

"Do you think that's why he hasn't joined the army yet?" asked Kate. "Somebody won't let him ... either his family, or the army."

"I don't know, but I really need to like a guy before I can let one get close," said Ellie. "And I just haven't met anybody."

"Listen, girl, you're not getting any younger. You're nearly twenty-four. At the snail's pace you're going, and at the pace this war is killing them off, there won't be anybody left but widows and children."

"Yuck—and Kate, I'm nearly twenty-*five*."

"Come on, kiss someone before we leave tomorrow! What about that guy who came in second in the third race, the one you said was good looking?"

"He's too young. But I'll talk to some of the wounded soldiers, maybe the cute one who lost his left hand," said Ellie.

"You wouldn't want me to have to use the money I won to pay someone to kiss you."

"If you didn't need the money, you might—but I know you need every dollar."

"How do you know? Maybe I took more of Gabe's money." Kate gave a wry grin.

"Maybe," said Ellie. "But you still won't use your money when you can get it done for free or with someone else's money."

They both puffed on the cigars and took turns sipping the bourbon for a while as they lay on their backs looking up at the night sky.

After some moments, Kate blurted out, "What about Gabriel?"

"No, no," Ellie said. "He's so … Yankee."

"We know he's not an officer, and we don't think he comes from money. But he is good looking and a fighter, and he has this way about him," said Kate.

"Did you forget that he's married?" asked Ellie.

"He flirts real good, though," said Kate. "He could die tomorrow, and he has experience. You should try flirting with him. What if he grabs you, holds you in his arms, and kisses you—would you kiss him?"

"He is married."

"It would be a good kiss," insisted Kate.

"Then you kiss him!"

"I wish I could, but I'm married."

"Yes, you are, and so is he—besides, you told me he has a death wish."

"So, that's perfect! He won't be around to talk about the kiss." Kate took a sip of bourbon and smiled.

"Kiss! I'm looking to get married." Ellie took the flask from her.

"One step at a time for you, lady, I'll teach you."

"That's what I'm afraid of." Ellie paused. "You and Alex don't make love like you used to."

"What makes you think that?" asked Kate.

"You don't talk much about him or it, like you usually do. Is it his wounds?"

"Yes, I think so," said Kate. "But he won't talk to me about it."

"Is that why you seem crazier lately?"

"I don't know … maybe." Kate was silent for several minutes after answering. Finally she said, "You know, you made me and Rascal work today."

"Would it have been better if I made it easy for you?"

Kate smiled at her. "No. I wanted a challenge. You know I crave it."

"You almost beat us by a nose," said Ellie.

"I know, but you and Rebel have been together a long time. I just got started with Rascal two weeks ago."

"I'm still a better rider," said Ellie.

"What makes you think that?"

"Next time I'll ride Rascal."

Kate turned to look at her. "Over my dead body."

They both laughed, then Kate asked, "Do you ever wonder, what if Gabriel was not married and was cleaned up?"

"Yes, I have," Ellie said.

Kate turned to look at her again and smiled. "That's my girl."

At first light the next day Kate was already dressed and prodded Ellie, who still drowsily lay curled in her bedding.

"I need to get back, I can't stay," she told Ellie.

Ellie sat up abruptly and rubbed her face. "OK, I'll go with you—it looks like rain anyway. Why so frantic? That's not like you."

"I had a dream last night," Kate said, a worried look on her face.

"A dream, or a nightmare?"

"I don't know, but in it Alex died."

"Let's get going," said Ellie. "The men may need us."

She quickly dressed then came out of the tent and called out to the others in their group. "Mark, Brandy, T.J.—pack up and tack up fast, we need to go now."

On the way home a heavy rain fell for most of the trip. Ellie gave all the blankets to the kids, hoping they would help them stay dry. Kate had pulled out Gabriel's long, flowing cape and draped it over the both of them.

"Did you take his uniform, too?" Ellie asked.

"I would have, but he was in most of it."

"Why would that stop you?"

Kate just looked at her and smiled.

Ellie looked serious. "Have you had dreams of Alex dying before?"

"No, but since …" Kate's face clouded over.

"What? You had other dreams?"

"The night that we found Gabe, I think I dreamt that I was watching him, and he was already wounded. It must have been just before he showed up at my farm. I have had two more since."

"When did these bizarre dreams start?" Ellie asked.

"The night Gabe showed up." Kate paused. "Something bad is going to happen."

"Have a little faith," Ellie said.

"Faith? I lost what little I had many years ago. Now I rely on me."

"Faith … is what makes a good life meaningful," said Ellie.

"I wished that in my next life my husband would be like my dead dog Rocky —tough and loyal. He tried to follow me everywhere, and he would protect me even if it killed him. Too bad it did. I have to get another dog like him."

"That's crazy, believing in next lives," said Ellie. "Why wait? Just fix the one you have now."

Minutes, Moments, and Memories

May 13
Something is bothering Alex. Over the past two weeks I'm noticing he is getting quieter than when we first met, and less engaging. What could be bothering him? Could it be me? Three times I reached out to him since the ladies left to distract him and get him to open up, but nothing.

Gabe watched Alex as he stared out the window, watching the rain.

"Hey, you over there! You may be bigger than me, but you're still the younger brother I never had, and you better behave or I might have to get up and whip you into shape."

Nothing. He looked up with a blank stare, then looked back down at whatever he was doing, like he was a shell of the man he once was. Well, that did not work. I'm going to tell him something I've never told anyone before. Something is telling me he needs to hear it.

"Alex, why don't you have children?" asked Gabe.

"Before I was wounded, she wanted to wait. Then after ..."

"That's OK. I understand." *I have seen this before—the untold of the walking wounded; whether it was in their heads or somewhere in their body, the pain made it difficult for some to be with a woman again.*

"She only wanted children, if only to pass on her dream of her plantation. Now that won't happen."

Gabe was silent for a few seconds, then spoke. "Alex, do you believe in God?"

"Yes."

"But do you know for sure God exists?"

Alex just looked at Gabe. "What are you talking about?"

"If you lived my life, you would know God exists, even if sometimes you hate him."

Nothing. He continues to just stare at me.

"Kate does not believe in God, does she?" asked Gabe.

"No, she ..." Alex stopped and stared out the widow with a wide-eyed gaze.

Gabe paused and then began to speak.

"I need to tell you a true story that happened to me on August 8, 1862, on Slaughter's Mountain. I fell off Rascal, and I jumped up on a loose gray Confederate horse that was circling around me. After mounting him I noticed he had the right half of his face hanging from his head—I saw into his upper jaw. Then the frantic ghost of a monster rushed up a steep incline. Higher and higher we went, and near the top he reared up and started to fall over backwards. I was looking into the sky and saw a cloud where only seconds ago there were none in the sky at all. As the animal's head went higher into the sky, I knew I was going to die—not thought it, I knew it. Then everything slowed down, like we were hanging in the air. I couldn't tell if we were moving. I felt as though I was floating, and the world was still—no gunfire, no wind, no sounds ... nothing. At that instant I felt a rush of energy penetrate my stomach. It raced up inside my chest to my head, and my mind told me, *This is the energy of my life.* I felt wonderfully happy and proud; *I had a good life,* that's what I felt. *I can go, I am ready to go.*

"I'm not sure how much time had passed, but the next thing I remembered I was oblivious of my pain. I sat up and realized the horse had flipped over on top of my chest and face and driven me into the earth as it rolled over me. As I tried to sit up, sand was coming out of my ears. My face hurt, and I felt blood running down my face, I looked back to see the gray horse at the bottom of the hill, on his side.

"The battle had moved away, leaving me to ponder why I'm not dead. I walked over to the still beast, his war now over. Just then Rascal walked up to me and let out a soft groan that told me he could not understand why I got on a horse that lost its mind and half its face.

"My vision was blurry for five days, and my chest felt like I had been run into by a train. Deep breaths were a struggle to take in. The regimental surgeon told me I also had a concussion. As the horse rolled over me, his head smacked me across my face, and his withers most likely had landed on my chest, driving me into the ground. I should have been crushed to death, but I wasn't. Why?"

Alex did not respond, so Gabe continued. "Knowing that feeling, that message, but losing it is like missing something that was not really there, but it should be. You crave that feeling again but you don't know how to bring it back or explain it. I can't wait to taste a glimmer of it. I long to feel that way again."

Gabe waited again to see if Alex would respond.

Alex started, slowly at first.

"I was with ... the 4th Pennsylvania Reserve Regiment, attached to Hooker's I Corps. We arrived at Antietam on the afternoon of September 16, '62. We formed north of a cornfield on the morning of the 17th, advanced about 600 yards south, and became engaged with Hood's Confederate Division for the fight in the cornfield. I was wounded that morning. I was hit by small pieces from a cannonball—one caught my right hip, and two others went into my lower back. At the time I did not realize how bad my wounds were. I initially thought they were just deep cuts. But the next day I could barely walk, and it stayed that way until the piece in my hip was removed. But the two small pieces in my back could not be removed for fear of killing me. I learned later that five had been killed and forty-three were wounded that day from my regiment. Do you remember what the date September 16, '62 represents?"

Gabe answered quietly. "Of course. So far it's the bloodiest single day of the war, and it ended in a draw."

Alex looked at him, his brow furrowed. "I don't understand you—why do you want to die? You have a wife waiting for you back home."

Gabe paused and looked down at the floor. "Why do you think that?"

"You said so one night in your sleep."

"No, I don't," Gabe said. "What I have is as beautiful as a spring sunset and as adventurous as a lioness. Her name is Jacqueline."

"You must really love your wife."

"Sherry." Gabe looked down and took a breath. "Sherry was her name. Yes, I loved her more than life. She was killed less than a year after giving birth to Jackie, who will be four next month."

"Sorry, I didn't know," said Alex. "And you have a daughter. Do you mind if I ask how long you were married?"

"Just three years, but I knew her for nearly twenty. It felt like it was my whole life."

"Where is your daughter now?"

"With my grandmother. She has a big farm in New Jersey that overlooks the bay and New York City. She is the reason I have Rascal. I don't want to bore you with stories of home. I just felt that you need someone to talk to."

"Yes, please, I want to hear more. Besides, we still have some time before Kate gets back."

Gabe continued. "Several times a year my father would take us to the farm so he could help his older brother with the horses. One year while I was still a young teenager they got an older Thoroughbred mare that I began to ride, and I loved her. She was tough, bright, a quick learner, and very loyal.

"One spring day they were breeding some of their best mares to a Thoroughbred stallion they had, and I saw the old mare watching over the fence waiting for her turn. But I found out that she had never been bred, and she would never be, because my uncle said that as long as he was alive his stallion would never be bred to that old mare. I always thought he was a mean man, but his words proved to me he was also stupid. He did produce good stock, but nothing extraordinary. He could not see the opportunity in front of him. He ignored the mare completely. Someone who owed him money was trying to give the mare to him to pay off his debt, but he did not want her. My grandmother liked the old mare—I think they had some strange, old-lady connection. She also respected her previous owner; he was a hardworking man and took good care of his stock. The old lady told my uncle to take her. She was the one who ran the farm—you know, the brains—and her sons did the work.

"The next spring, I watched the old mare as she was watching several mares get bred, and when everyone went into the house I knocked a part of her fence down, and without hesitating she cantered by, glanced at me, then jumped over the remaining fence, and jumped over the next fence into the stallion's paddock. She knew what to do; she had seen it done many times before. When they were done she jumped out and back into her field. I fixed the fence and could not wait for the next spring.

"As time passed and we came back in the fall for weaning and other farm work, my grandmother kept looking at me with an eye that said, *What have you done?"*

"Was the mare getting fat?" Alex asked.

"A little, but you do not know that woman … she knows everything. One evening the following spring my grandmother told me to go sit outside and keep an eye on the mare. She said she thought the mare was getting sick. In her little field the mare stood next to me, glanced, and laid down. She let me watch her foal a colt. The next morning, my uncle was furious. He wanted to shoot them both, but my grandmother told him that if he did she would shoot him."

"She would like Kate," said Alex.

"Yes, she would," Gabe agreed.

He went on. "My uncle always called me a rascal because when I got bored I would get into trouble. When I was five, the men went out hunting, and they would not take me along. They said I was too young and I had no experience. 'Wait until next year,' they told me. So after they left, I got one of my uncle's guns and went out to practice. I shot four chickens before the ladies made me stop. I got more birds in thirty minutes then they did in four hours. When my uncle told me that the little colt acted like me, I decided to name him Rascal. I always knew he was special, and as a yearling he showed many people at the farm—even our visitors. One day I was throwing an old leather ball to two of the young dogs that were also born the same spring as Rascal, When it rolled into Rascal's field he stood over it, waiting to see what the dogs would do. One dog crawled closer, and Rascal waited until he stopped, scared to get closer. So Rascal slowly backed up until the dog got brave enough to run in and pick up the ball and ran away with it. Rascal would then chase him until he dropped it, then Rascal would pick it up and run with it and the dog would chase him. You could sense that he enjoyed the people watching him, and he enjoyed entertaining them."

"How did you get him into the cavalry?" asked Alex.

"After the first two horses that the army gave me nearly got me killed, I asked my grandmother to use her influence to get the army to let me have Rascal, and they did. He was cantankerous as a foal, and if he doesn't like you—and there were few he likes—watch out. During battles he is brave and alert, always anticipating what the other horses were going to do. He even puts himself between me and danger. I knew if I fell in battle, no one would ever be able to ride him."

They heard a rider trot toward the barn. Alex looked out and saw Kate going into the barn.

"She's back, and it looks like the rain has stopped," he said.

Silent Stalker Sanctifies

May 14

Kate arrived home just before dark set in. She went straight to the barn to take care of her race partner. Walking into the house, she shook Gabe's cape, trying to remove some of the rain. By the bright candlelight she could see Alex and Gabe talking at the table.

After a few seconds of silence, Gabe blurted out, "Welcome back. Did you show them your skills?"

"Yes, but I'm hungry. Let me eat first, and I will tell you all about it." She paused and looked at the men. "Thank you both."

"You're welcome—but for what?" Gabe asked. "Loaning you my horse, or my cape?"

"You fixed the door." She ignored him as she addressed Alex. Gabe waited, but Alex said nothing. "Not me. Alex did."

Alex got up and served Kate the dinner he had saved her.

"Thank you," she said to him. "How are you feeling?"

"Me?" Alex replied.

"Yes, you."

"Good, I'm doing well."

She looked over to Gabe and just smiled.

Gabe looked back at her. "In case you were wondering, I'm feeling great. I got up and out yesterday and did some walking, took some deep breaths out in the sunshine. What a beautiful spring day it was—"

"I did not ask." She cut him off with that little smirk in her smile that told him *not now*.

"The race was a tie between Ellie and me. Here is the money I made." She handed Alex her winnings and asked, "Do we need supplies?"

"Yes," said Alex.

"I want to go to Culpeper early tomorrow with you. Are you up for it?"

"Yes," replied Alex.

"I'm ready to take care of myself," said Gabe. "You two go have some fun together."

"We are only going for the day, and Ellie will be stopping by to check on you. Don't make her mad, do you hear me?" Kate frowned at him.

"Yup," he answered. "I will be nice. I will tell her how pretty she looks, how good she smells, and …"

Kate's voice was insistent. "Gabe, be a gentleman, or she may shoot you."

"OK. I'm just getting so bored, I want someone to play with."

"Go play with the chickens or the piglets, they at least tolerate you."

As Alex and Kate went over the list of things they need to pick up, Gabe lay down on his bed and quickly fell asleep.

Kate spoke quietly to Alex. "I see his first full days out with the boys wore him out."

Alex glanced over at the sleeping form. "Yup. He tried to help me, but he had to move slowly."

"I'm tired too, from the trip home. Do you mind if we go to bed early?"

"No."

"Alex, I wish you could have been there to see me ride."

He looked into her eyes and held her in his arms, but said nothing.

"Give me a few minutes to clean up, then let's go to bed," she mumbled.

Early the next day they slipped out without waking him. On the trip she could not stop talking about the race and how much fun they had.

Stopping the wagon in front of the general store, she asked Alex, "Can you handle getting the order together? I want to walk over to the post office and see the doc. We need more medical supplies."

Outside Doc Wilson's place she passed by three disabled local veterans. The good news was there were still only three.

"Good morning, Mrs. Kate," said the man on the near end of the bench.

"Good morning, boys. How are we feeling today?"

"Great, now that we see your smiling face," said the man on the far end. "Yup it's going to be a great day now. This morning we heard about your race at The Springs. You and Miss Ellie."

"Ellie and I had a wonderful time, but I'm glad I'm home to see all of you." She smiled at them.

"Ah, that's sweet, Mrs. Kate."

She looked at the man named Henry, on the step, but did not address him. "John, I see you have a new leg. How is it working out?"

"The Doc and Joe the blacksmith did a wonderful job with it, I can move real well."

"Edwin, how's the arm?" she asked the man on the far end.

"Ok had it drained again yesterday."

She called out to the young man sitting on the step. "Henry, can you hear me?" She knelt down next to him and whispered to him words that only he could hear. She looked for any response in his face, but as usual there was nothing. Henry was young, strong, and confident when he went into battle at the age of eighteen; he came home with one eye and with part of his brain scrambled.

She looked at the other two men. "You boys taking care of Henry for me?"

"Yes, Mrs. Kate."

"You will let me know if he needs anything, right?"

"Yes, Mrs. Kate."

The local people had known Kate's uncle, Arthur Sheppard, all his life, and he was well liked. Most of the people remembered her as a child running around town and spending time on his little farm, and once he had passed they were happy to hear she was going to move in.

"Morning, Doc."

"Good morning, Kate."

"I'm getting a bit concerned. He seems to be withdrawing more and more each day. Has he said anything to you, Doc? I think he is drinking more. Is this part of his normal recovery? It has been two years."

"Easy, Kate. He had me send over more liquor—he told me it was for that wounded soldier you're helping. How is he walking? How is his back? Have you tried to have a baby?"

"Baby? No way! Not now, I have enough work." She saw his smile. "Oh ... um ... no, he hasn't touched me in a few months. He has been walking less, and his back hurts him sometimes real bad."

"Any blood?"

"Not from the entry wounds, but if he is bleeding from the inside he is hiding it from me."

"I know how busy you are, but you need to try to pay attention. I need to know if he is bleeding again from inside. If either or both those two pieces of metal start to move again, it could be real trouble. He could be getting sepsis caused by the remaining projectiles."

"OK. I'll keep a closer eye on him." She looked at the doctor with a grave expression on her face. "Is he dying, Doc?" she asked softly.

"If it is sepsis caused by the remaining projectile, yes. Sometimes it can take years for the sepsis state to become potentially deadly. Look for a whole-body inflammatory state … it can be triggered by an infection. His body may develop this inflammatory response, also known as blood poisoning. Look for organ dysfunction."

"Like blood in his urine?"

"Yes."

"OK, Doc. We're going to have lunch and spend the day together in town before we head home. If I notice anything, I will let you know.

When Kate and Alex arrived back at their farm early that evening, Gabe peeked out to see if it was safe to go outside. He limped over to the door and went out to greet them.

"Good evening, Mom and Pa. Did you bring me a toy?"

Kate smiled and bent over to touch the ground. "Did you clean the house like I asked you?"

"I tried, but Rascal wanted to play."

"Then here is your new toy." She flipped a rock at him fairly aggressively, hitting him on his chest as he tried to catch it. "'Mom,' my ass … I'm glad you're not my kid. Besides, you're older than me."

The three of them help unload the wagon, and they sat down to a quiet dinner.

"Please pass me some more water," Gabe asked, nodding at Kate as she complied. "Thanks. So I heard Rascal took very good care of you, on the trip and in the race."

"Yes, he did. He is a wonderful horse. Did Ellie stop by?"

"No. T.J. popped in to see how I was doing, and I told him you both went to town. Then he left."

"Maybe tomorrow she will come by. She must be very busy."

Gabe smiled to himself, then looked at Kate. "So you now know Rascal's not just an animal, he is my brother. While you were gone I told Alex that I added him to my short list of men I would treat as brothers—especially since I did not grow up with a brother."

Kate looked over at Alex, but he said nothing and continued to eat.

"Kate, if something happens to me, do you want to keep Rascal?" asked Gabe.

"Nothing is going to happen to you," she insisted.

"But if something does. You know, soon I will be going back to the killing."

"Don't say that," said Kate. "Nothing is going to happen ... not with all the work ... I put into that leg." Her voice started strong then grew weaker, almost uncertain.

"Do you want him?" asked Gabe.

"Yes, I want him," she answered hastily. "Now, stop talking like that. Besides, if you die in battle, how is he going to get to me?"

"Don't worry about that. I own him not the army, and I will tell my troop. But most importantly all I have to do is tell him tomorrow. He will take care of the rest."

Alex and Kate just turned and looked at each other, puzzled.

"Gabriel, are you sure your head doesn't hurt anymore?" asked Kate. "Because sometimes the things you say tell me different."

"Nope. I feel better than before I hit it."

"You must have knocked something loose in there. Do you feel like there is more room up there?" she asked.

"Yup, something like that."

After cleaning up, Kate took her husband's hand. "Alex, please sit outside with me on the porch," she asked him.

Gabe watched them go outside together. *I wonder what's bothering her,* he thought.

* * *

Feeling the first morning light splashing on his face, Gabe rubbed his eyes and sat up. Looking around, he saw the sunrise coming in through the open door. "Who left the door open?" he called out. "Alex? Kate?" No one responded. It was an unusually quiet morning.

He dressed and limped over to the door to close it, then he paused to observe Rascal on a hill, grazing. Off to the right he saw someone near the wagon.

"Is that Kate?" he asked himself out loud. "What is she doing?"

Limping his way outdoors, he started toward her. With each hobble he felt a twinge of pain, a pain he had felt many times in this war. He grabbed his stomach and staggered forward. Each step brought pain to his leg and his gut. But the pain in his leg grew numb; it was the pain in his gut that grew stronger as he became more focused on his objective. Extending each stride, he was more and more determined to get to her. As the vision became clearer, the pain in his gut increased.

He finally reached the hill, and the objects that were not visible at first became clearer with every step, so much so that understanding what he was seeing soon became unavoidable. He could not deny what the objects were any longer.

The first one he focused on was that of Arthur B. Sheppard, Kate's uncle. Neatly carved into the stone was BORN 1802 DIED 1860.

Looking up, Gabe now had to accept what she was doing. Walking as if he were healed, he reached Kate, sat down on the ground, and slid into the thigh-deep hole she had managed to dig.

She was oblivious to his arrival. He had to take the shovel from her filthy hands; he could see that at some point she had been digging with her hands and fingers. The soil was encrusted on her fingertips and under her nails.

She lowered her arms and looked up at him. He would never forget her face. The tears had made it so wet that with each rub to remove them her face had grown dark—dark with dirt, but mostly dark with sorrow. Smudges of dirt covered her once pink, glowing cheeks, and her shiny hair was matted with clumps of grass and dirt. The left side of her nose was partially unsoiled. Her bottom lip remained clean and full, but only because she had been biting it. A little blood had dried in one corner.

He took over the digging, and she leaned back on the wall and struggled to show a smile. At that moment, her secret became visible; her smile, eyes, and white teeth revealed the child in her face, a little girl who had been playing in the dirt with her friends all day, running home with tears in her eyes because she had gotten hurt by the big boys. She closed her eyes and leaned on his shoulder, and he could feel her weight, which confirmed her exhaustion.

Gabe wrapped his arms around her to keep her from falling. She was cold and drained. *How long has she been out here?* He glanced over to the form that was rolled up in a blanket only a few feet away. He had so many questions to ask her, but he kept silent. He had not heard a thing last night. *Why didn't she wake me? When did he die? Why?*

Looking around, he could see this was not the first grave she had dug on this hillside, but it would be the most heartbreaking. *There must be thirty or more soldiers buried here,* he realized.

At that moment he had to stop, and as he looked around he felt a bit of sorrowful energy take hold of him, similar to when the horse fell on him. He now felt the toll of this war, he felt her sadness, and he began to feel the consequence of his killing, what so many mothers, wives, and children had to deal with. He was just one of many who have to live with the burden of killing and death. He held her away from his body, looked into her eyes, and hoped she'd not had to dig them all.

They worked together in silence. After they finished his grave, she knelt down by the body.

"Please come here. I need you to do something for me."

"Anything," he replied.

She moved aside part of the blanket to uncover the face beneath.

"Look, is this Alex? Can you identify him?" she asked.

"Yes."

"Thank you."

Slowly she began to rewrap him, and then she whispered "Goodbye" and kissed him on his cold lips. Together they laid him in the hole. Gabe could now hear the birds around them, and as he looked up at the morning sky, in tribute to a fallen American soldier a bald eagle flew along the tree-line that hid a small creek that flowed into the Rappahannock River. That's when Kate placed two objects in the hole beside her husband: a pair of worn boots and a half-drunk bottle of whiskey. Together they began to fill the hole.

Turning to leave, he realized the graveyard had been divided up into three sections: Union, Confederate, and the family. "Did you dig all of these?" he asked, pointing to the graves of the soldiers.

"No. Alex and I buried a third of them, and the armies dug the rest."

"Why did you bury him with the Union soldiers, and not with the family?" asked Gabe.

"He told me to. He said to make sure the doctor documents his death as being the result of wounds received as a Union soldier in battle, so he could at least leave me with my authorized volunteer benefits. I hope I still can receive the pensions of eight dollars a month for him being disabled."

"You drive the wagon back, I'll get on Rascal. Now that Alex is gone I don't want to leave Rascal this far from the house anymore," she told him.

"No, you—you're always telling me to be the gentleman. You take the wagon."

"I would, but your leg is bleeding."

Looking down, he saw that his trouser thigh was oozing blood. In his mission to reach and help her, he had opened his wound. But he did not care.

"Look what you did. Let's hope it's not opening again, or I'm going to have to put one of us out of our misery." At that moment Rascal turned his head and nickered to her.

"Not you, boy," she told him. "You're the only good thing to come out of this war."

She turned toward Gabe. "When we get to the house, I want you to lay down while I get cleaned up, then I'll check your leg."

The short, peaceful trip back to the house used up what remained of the morning. Entering the house, Kate looked around at the work she needed to do, took a deep breath, gathered her strength, and returned to the world of the living.

"While I clean up, try to get your trousers off," she said to Gabe.

Unable to remove his boots, he rolled down his trousers.

"Lay down," she told him. "Let me look at your leg."

After several minutes of quiet as she applied a clean bandage to his wound, she had a strange thought: *Why Alex, and not Gabe? He wants to die ... but why?*'

"Why did you bury him so fast? Didn't he have a family?" asked Gabe.

"No. His parents are gone, and his older brother died at twelve years old, when Alex was only ten."

"What? And there I was telling Alex he was my younger brother. He didn't say anything about a brother."

"I know."

"Just before you came back yesterday, I was telling Alex about a feeling I got in battle, when I thought I was going to die."

"Was it when you got up on a white horse?"

"Yes—how did you know that?"

"Last night after dinner, we went outside to the porch and sat on our rockers, and we had a really nice talk. Something we hadn't done in some time. He told me he really liked your sense of humor."

"I didn't know he had a brother who died."

"I know, and he never said anything to you when you joked about you being his older brother. Why did you say you were two years older than him?"

Gabe shook his head. "I don't know, that's what came to me. If I had known, I wouldn't have joked about that."

"We both knew that. He talked about your ability to feel things and then say what you feel, and the way you know things are going to happen before they do. He also told me about you and your life before the war … he tried to tell me about your ghost horse, but I wouldn't listen. He started to open up, and I shut him down." Her eyes start to swell with tears. "I lost my husband, my best friend, and my business partner. What am I going to do now?"

"You have a lot of people around here who will help you."

"I know."

"Do you want to hear about the gray horse?"

"Yes, I do."

"OK. One day, but not today."

Gabe sat up and wrapped his arms around her. She needed to let it out and mourn.

He then whispered in her ear. "I have a question. Were you with him, or did he die alone?"

She moved back. "I was next to him, in my rocker. He got very quiet, and when I looked over, he was shaking. I put him on the ground and asked what was wrong, and a few seconds later he stopped shaking, looked into my eyes, and took his last breath." More tears raced down her face. "I felt so helpless. I could not help him."

He wanted to tell her, *My wife had been in my arms, and I too felt helpless and could not help her.* He wanted to, he tried to tell her, but his guilt and shame would not let him share what he felt from his loss. He was not ready ... this was not the time.

They stared in silence. *She is too proud to ask for help,* he thought. *She will suffer her hurt and sorrow alone, and no one will ever know how she feels about her loss.*

Kate was deep in her thoughts as well. *He is holding back. What is it that he won't or can't share with me? Is it about his wife being killed?*

They shared their loss and pain in silence.

The war had intruded into her world once more, and this was going to be as much as she was going to let it, at least for now.

Dominate or Be Dominated

The next day he was up with the sun, and he began to stretch and put more weight on his leg. *I need to get strength in this leg*, he thought. *I must go. I can't be a burden to her anymore.*

He worked hard for more than a week helping Kate around the farm, maybe too hard.

Kate stopped to talk to him while going about her chores. "Gabe, your leg looks good, but it bothers me that you still can't ride well on it. When you get back to your army, you should get it checked by a military surgeon."

He nodded. "I will, and I'm going to leave in a few days. I want to help you with some chores around here before I go."

As the days passed, his leg was slowly getting stronger. Ellie stopped by one afternoon and was shocked to learn of Alex's death.

"I should have walked her home," she said to Gabe, her voice full of emotion. "I didn't even get a chance to say goodbye."

"How could you have known?" he reassured her.

Ellie looked at Kate. "You knew he was going to die."

Gabe seemed startled. "Kate, how did you know?"

Ellie turned to him. "She had a dream our last night at the spring, that he was going to die."

Gabe gave Kate an intense look. "You have dreams of people dying?" he asked.

"No, just Alex, but she had one of you—"

Kate cut her off, a hint of anger in her voice. "That's enough, Ellie. No more of that talk, do you understand me?" She paused for a moment to collect herself. "Can you please stay with Gabe while I go into town to notify the doctor about Alex's death?"

"Yes, I will."

After Kate left, Ellie sat next to Gabe for a few moments and then finally spoke.

"Gabe, do you know what happened to Alex?"

He spoke softly. "The day after she returned from the race, Kate said they were outside talking when he died. When I woke up she was already trying to bury him."

"She knew something was wrong," said Ellie.

Gabe nodded. "I've only known him a few weeks, and I could see something was not right."

Ellie turned toward him. "How are you doing?"

He frowned. "OK, but getting frustrated that my leg still feels weak and painful, and I'm still having trouble putting more weight on it. It should be a lot better by now."

"Did you tell Kate?"

He shook his head. "No. I did not want to bother her, she has a lot on her mind. But she has some idea."

"When was the last time she checked it?" she asked.

"Two days ago. It is fine."

"Take your trousers down, please."

He laughed. "Why, Miss Ellie, you are being forward—and polite about it!"

"Ha, ha! Take them down, or I will cut them off."

"OK, OK, but it is fine," he repeated. "I will need help with taking off this boot."

I knew he would say that, and I'm sure he's enjoying this, thought Ellie. For him to remove his riding boot, Gabe was implying he would need her to hold it while facing away from him, and he would put his left foot on her buttocks and push.

"Forget it. Hold still," she told him. "Pick up your leg and set it here."

She began adding pressure around the wound but not over it. Each time she moved closer and added a bit less pressure, until he winced.

"Uh." He flinched and tried to pull away.

"She needs to take a closer look. I don't like that you still have pain."

He tried to change the subject. "Why do you hate me?"

She looked surprised. "I don't hate you."

"So, you tolerate me?"

"Tolerate is the wrong word. I accept you. Besides, God tells us to love our neighbor."

"Why do you hate your Northern neighbors?"

She sighed. "I hate this war, the destruction; it and you Yankees nearly took my older brother, and you are destroying this beautiful region."

"He is a Confederate soldier?"

She nodded. "Yes. As soon as the war started, he was gone. He is Major Robert Jefferson, Army of Virginia, but he was wounded last year at Antietam, near the place where Alex was wounded."

"Where is he now? He doesn't know I'm here, does he?" He was trying to get her to smile, but there was nothing, not even a smirk.

"After he recovered with one less arm, he was assigned to Army Headquarters in Richmond—no, he doesn't."

She is so serious and proper, he thought. *How can I get in?*

He looked down at his leg as she continued to work her hands over his thigh. "How is this?"

"OK."

"It feels swollen around the lower part of the wound."

"Over here, toward the side of my thigh?"

"Yes. Hold still. When she comes back, you tell her—and if you don't, I will."

"OK. But can you take me for a short ride?"

"To where?" she asked.

"The river."

"Why?"

He looked toward the window. "I haven't been out in nearly a month. I need to see it. I hear it at night, but I can't see it."

"OK. We'll take my horse. Give me a minute to get him ready."

In a few minutes they were both outside. Gabe moved to the edge of the porch. "Ellie, move him closer to the rail so I can mount up."

"Gabe, let me mount first, then you can mount up behind me." She swung easily into the saddle. "OK, I'm ready."

Gabe climbed on behind her, putting his arms around her waist.

She glanced back at him. "Let go! You don't have to hold on to me. We won't be going faster than a walk."

"OK, I was just..."

"You were just going to keep your hands to yourself, like a gentleman, right?"

Gabe smiled. "Right."

"Thank you."

This slow walk is boring, he thought. *I wish she would learn to enjoy and try playing along. She's used to playing word games with Kate—but with a man, especially a Yankee, never.*

He asked, "Do you know how to have fun? You know, laugh?"

Ellie paused a moment before answering. *Kate told me he enjoys trying to get me to relax and have fun just like she does. Maybe I'll play along and see where he takes this.*

"Yes, I know how to laugh."

"Are you sure? Can you make others laugh?"

"Yes, of course. I just don't find you funny."

"I'm not trying for funny."

"Then what are you trying for?"

"I'm trying for curiosity covered in intrigue wrapped in playfulness."

She smiled. "Oh, my, that sounds like a lot of work."

Gabe wouldn't give up. "Let's try this again. How about you close your eyes and let my voice take you somewhere."

"Where?"

"Close your eyes and you'll find out."

"No, not while we are riding."

"OK. I'll wait until we get to the river."

She was not sure what he was trying to do, but she trusted him not to do anything inappropriate. Arriving at the riverbank they dismounted.

Ellie turned to him, eyes closed. "I'm ready."

He had just straddled a freshly downed tree and looked up at her. "Yes, you are."

She couldn't see the big smile on his face, but she knew he wouldn't be ready for her. He reached out to hold her hand.

"First come over here and sit with me," he said.

She immediately complied and faced him.

He started, quietly. "Close your eyes again. You are eleven years old, playing by the river. Can you hear the water rippling by?"

"Yes."

"Can you hear Kate laughing as she runs by you?"

"Yes."

"She tells your big brother Robert, 'OK, stop! I'm wet enough.' Why is she wet, Ellie?"

With her eyes still closed she paused for a few seconds, then responded. "He was trying to teach us how to swim, and I was twelve and Kate was ten. She was giving him a hard time about going in the water."

"Why?"

"She said she did not want to get wet."

"Is that it, Ellie?"

"She doesn't like someone telling her what to do."

"Why?"

"She wants to do what she wants, when she wants to, not what others tell her."

"Maybe she doesn't like being told what to do—you know, being ordered around."

"Kate doesn't like being ordered to do anything."

"She likes challenges. Why?"

"She likes to be convinced?"

"Why, Ellie?"

"She likes to be motivated?"

"Why?"

"I don't know, Gabe."

"When she first meets someone, she immediately tries to figure them out. She looks for their strengths and weaknesses."

"I know," said Ellie. "But why?"

"So she can get them to do what she wants, instead of the other way around."

"OK, but why, Gabe? Is it because she needs to be in control?"

"Sometimes, but what she really enjoys is someone who challenges her mentally, not someone who tries to force her. She likes the process and challenge—sometimes from people she just met, and sometimes from people she trusts. She likes it when each one of them tries to get into each other's head. I told her that I call it verbal stimulation."

"Oh, my word—why would she like that?" Ellie furrowed her brow.

The more into it she got, the harder it was becoming for him to concentrate on where he was trying to go with his example. He kept focusing on her facial reactions and expressions. They were showing him how innocent, pure, smart, and naive she was—or pretended to be. He could feel his body getting warmer.

"Because she enjoys it when someone can get deep inside her and touch her senses, so she can see other possibilities and not be pushed into submission."

"You mean she wants to convince or be convinced?" asked

Ellie.

"Yes, and she wants to be part of the process. She enjoys it when someone takes her deeper into herself. When your brother told you to go in the water, what did you do?"

"I went in and tried to swim."

"Without questioning him?"

"I did not question him."

"Was the experience fun?"

"Yes. I learned how to swim."

"No, not the outcome—the experience of being persuaded to try to learn how to swim."

"Hmm. I guess not … I did not feel persuaded."

"Exactly. So when Kate finally went in, how did that go?"

"He grabbed her dress and pulled her over to the water and told her to go in."

"She refused, right?"

"Yes."

"Then what?"

"He reached into the water and splashed her, and she tried to get away but couldn't. He asked her, 'Do you want to go in now?' She laughed at him and said, 'No—do you?' Then she tried to push him in, but he was too big for her, so she kept splashing him. They both laughed and splashed each other until they were both so wet it looked like they had gone swimming, then he let her go. She could hardly move with all the water soaked into her dress. She could not get away. He said, 'I'm going to give you one more try: walk into the water and swim.' She said no, so he threw her over his shoulder and carried her deeper into the water. He was wet up to his upper thighs, then he threw her in. She couldn't swim, but she sure splashed a lot. He stayed next to her until she could get herself up. That's when he told me to get in, and I did. Later, on the way home Kate said to him, 'So, how did you like your swim?' With a big smile on his face, he said, 'It was refreshing.' He was almost as wet as we were, and she really liked that. They each had a smile on their face the whole way home."

Gabe picked up a small stick and tossed it into the river. Sweat dripped down the sides of his face. "That's why she does it, for the challenge. She knew she was not going to win and he was not going to hurt her, so why not? She made him pay, and they both got something out of it—they had fun."

"She did have a lot of fun as a child."

"So what happened to you? You did play with her back then."

"I guess I thought she was being difficult. My dad said she could be a cantankerous little girl."

"Not difficult, she just wanted to have fun. Let me guess: She was always laughing?"

"Yes ... some did say she was always having fun."

He smiled. "OK, so I'm going to ask you again. Do you know how to have fun?"

She smirked. "With you? No."

"Good. Now we are getting somewhere."

"Gabe, I'm just beginning to realize how similar you and Kate really are," she said.

He looked at the river. "Ellie, do you want to go into the water with me?"

"Even if I did, you can't, not with that leg like that. Let's go back ... there may be soldiers around here."

"Yours, or mine?"

"Both." She turned to look at him with a devilish grin.

As he stood and put weight on both his legs, his right leg gave out, and he fell back onto the log.

He winced. "Ellie, my leg feels weaker and painful ... I think it is starting to swell."

She placed her hand on his head and the back of his neck. "You're sweating. You're burning up —hurry, we need to get you back to the house."

"I thought it was because of you." Looking up at her with a blank gaze in his eyes, he managed to get out "Miss Ellie, I'm getting to feeling real bad."

"Yes, you are, and you sound like it. Let's go now."

Later that day his fever started to climb dangerously high, and he began mumbling. Ellie listened quietly as he rambled on about his home and his wife. It was confusing to her, because he would call his wife one name and then another. As he rambled on about many things, she sat quietly and listened.

"When I die, I will be with the one I have loved my whole life." He paused. "I know she is waiting for me. Where are you?" he called out. "Boy, why did you make me kill you? Why, boy? Why did you make me kill so many?"

He would sleep for a few minutes and then start mumbling again.

"Where is the division? Our poor leadership is getting all our boys killed!"

"My troop. How are they?"

For a moment he seemed more aware of his surroundings. "Who's there?" he blurted out.

She leaned forward. "It's me, Ellie."

"Talk to me. Please tell me anything to keep my mind from crazy thoughts."

"It's the fever," she told him.

She said a prayer aloud: "Lord, please help me to ease his pain, if it is your will for him to heal, help me to help him. Amen."

I want to ask him about his childhood, she thought, *but I know he won't be able to focus.*

She tried to think of a topic that would keep his attention. "Kate ran a good race," she said.

"Ellie, you mean all of you did."

"True."

"I'll bet you wonder what would have happened if you rode Rascal."

"I do, and I would have won."

"It would have been wonderful to have seen the both of you competing like that."

She smiled. "It would also have been better if the race was run before the war. It was a heavenly place for all, especially for children. There was so much to do, and so many children from several states. Am I boring you?"

"No."

"Then why are your eyes closed?"

"Because I can see it. I was there."

"Where?"

"Fauquier Springs."

"Before the war?"

"No, after it was destroyed. My regiment was at The Springs in August of '62. I was resting under a tree. Looking around, I wondered what it must have been like before the war. When I listen to your and Kate's descriptions, I can feel the life it once had and how you felt about it."

"So you want me to continue?"

"Yes, please share more with me."

I'm glad he can't see how his words touch me, how they make my emotions swell up inside. As long as his eyes are closed, he can't see the goose-bumps growing on my arms. It's exciting that he wants me to share my childhood stories with him.

"That's where Kate and I met," she said.
"So, it was memorable for both of you."
"Yes, it was, for many people." She paused. "She told you about this already?"
"Yes. She said she asked you why you paid for her, said told her you needed the store owner to help you and you were tired of her wasting your time."
"That's right. Did she tell you the rest?"
"No."
"When I left the store she was outside waiting for me. She handed me back the money I had given her to buy her candy. I asked her why, and she said she had the money but was trying to see what it would take to get the man to sell it to her at her price, and not his. Needless to say, I was both shocked and intrigued by her actions."
"She started feeling people out early."
"We became good friends. Then one summer at The Spring I was walking around and saw her with six boys, ages eleven to sixteen. They were close enough to hear the band, and she told them to get in line if they wanted to dance with a teenager. She told them it was her thirteenth birthday. They struggled to form a line, mostly the oldest and toughest first. Another eleven-year-old came up to her and gave her the drink she sent him for. The older boys told him to get in line, and he went to the end. She followed him to the end of the line and asked him if he wanted to dance with her, and he said yes. She asked why, and he thought about it and said, 'Because you're pretty, and all these boys want to, so you must be worth it.' She said, 'You win,' then danced with him. After a few minutes, her dream boyfriend, William McMurphy, tapped the boy on the shoulder and asked to cut in. He did, and that was Kate's first up-close meeting with Mac. Later that day she told me she had turned twelve, not thirteen."
"That sounds like her."

"Gabe, what about you? What was your childhood like?"

"It was fun. I did lot of riding, fishing and hunting. I didn't care for school much. That did not please my father. What about you?"

"I did like school, because I liked to read a lot about business, and especially about adventures in far-off places. Then I would dream about what it would be like to live like that."

"I liked making up my own adventures," she said. "I can be creative like that."

"Ellie, I'm getting sleepy. Will you lie down next to me?"

"There is no room." She reached out to feel his neck and head. *He doesn't feel as warm as he did earlier,* she told herself.

He whispered a few last words before he drifted into sleep. "OK, but if you wanted to you would find some room."

She pulled up a chair next to his bed and watched him sleep. As the day started to come to its end she walked over to the door and opened it to watch the sunset. The view was breathtaking, with the few silver clouds that spread across the western sky silhouetted in purple, deep red, and orange. She turned to see a colorful glow on Gabe's face. She looked back at the sky, and the colors began to slowly get darker as the sun slowly descended.

Just before the sun touched the horizon it broke through the clouds, and its light touched her face. She felt him in the instant the sun touched her. She turned and stared at him as he slept, then quickly turned back to the sun.

"That's twice you did that to me … Why him?" she whispered, as she slowly closed the door in sync with the setting sun.

She turned and grabbed the extra blanket that was folded at the foot of the bed and lay down next to him, nudging him over a bit.

"We fit nicely," she said softly. *I want to ease his stress,* she thought. *The first chance I get, I'm sending T.J. to town to find out where the Union army or cavalry is.*

Ellie's thoughts drifted to how Tommy John, or T.J., her youngest brother, looked and acted younger than his age, and how it tended to make people underestimate him if they didn't know him. But in fact he was very cunning, and that's why her parents put him in charge of information gathering—mostly to find out where the armies were and where they were going. Yes, to help win the war, but above all to protect their home.

Ellie and Gabe slept together until Kate returned early the next morning. Immediately Ellie got up to speak to her about him. "What happened? I was beginning to worry."

"I'll tell you later," said Kate. "How is he?"

"For heaven's sake, Kate, you may have to consider him being a POW, or send him back to the Union army to save his life."

"No, Ellie, he's not going to be a POW, and those Union docs are just butchers. He stays here."

"Suit yourself. What are you going to do?"

"I don't know. I need to figure this out. I'm going to open up his wound and see if I can figure out what the problem is. Can you stay and help?"

"Yes, I'll stay, but I will need to get back when we are done. After that I'll stop over when I can—is that OK?"

"I like that fine."

By late morning his fever had broken.

Ellie was unable to stop over for almost two weeks. When she did, Kate hurried outside to meet her.

"Ellie, he is sleeping. I need you stay with him for a few hours."

"What is the matter? You look worried."

"Brandy stopped by this morning, and she heard that our cavalry is back in Culpeper, and the army is also on its way. I told her when you got here I would meet her at Brandy Station to find out what's going on. She was with T.J. and Mark."

"OK, go."

Gabe stirred awake. "What's going on?"

Kate walked back inside. "This should be it. The fever seems to have passed." She paused and looked at him. "How do you feel?"

"Better, but groggy. I need to get up. I want to sit outside"

"OK. Ellie will help you out so you can sit in a rocker. I have to go to town, but I'll be back real soon."

She was off to the barn, and in a few short minutes he watched her ride off in the wagon. He then closed his eyes.

As he rested Ellie distracted him with some news.

"I know you feel bad that you have been gone so long from your regiment."

He opened his eyes. "How do you know that?"

"You were taking while you were delirious with fever."

"How delirious?"

"Not enough to talk about any secrets, if that's what you want to know."

"No, I'm just wondering if I asked you to marry me."

She was caught off guard and smiled. "No, you didn't."

"If I did ask you, what would your answer be?"

"No."

"Why?"

"You're married."

"But what if I wasn't?"

"Well, if you weren't, I would say you did not ask me, so 'no' does not mean I would not marry you—it means I can't give you my answer."

"Good response."

She changed the subject. "I used my sources to get word that the Union Army is still in Falmouth, Virginia, but we're not sure where the cavalry is."

"You need to get stronger and get riding."

He looked at her. "I know. Before this last fever, Kate and I had been working on that. I hope we can continue now."

Ellie noticed that even when he was vulnerable he still projected an attitude of strength and confidence.

Later that day, while resting in the rocker on the porch, he found it impossible to sleep. It was partially because he enjoyed feeling the sun on his face, but what he enjoyed most was the sight of Ellie working in the garden, especially digging up vegetables.

Suddenly they both heard a wagon quickly headed toward the house. Both of them froze.

It was Kate. She quickly jumped off the wagon and motioned to Ellie.

"Can you talk?" she asked.

Ellie looked over to the porch to check on Gabe. "Sure," she whispered. "He's sleeping. What is it?"

With his eyes closed and head back as if asleep, he tried to listen to them.

"Captain Mac is on his way. The army is moving this way."

"Your Mac's a Captain now? He was a Lieutenant last time he was at Culpeper. How much time do we have?" Ellie asked.

"Three or four hours, no more—before sundown. The cavalry is also on the move."

"Do you think he knows about Alex?"

"I don't know, but the whole town knows by now. It's just a

matter of time until the cavalry knows; they have been in and around Culpeper for a few weeks."

"OK. I'll help you get Gabe out of here."

"Brandy and Mark were with me in town when we got the news, they are going to help us get him across the river."

Ellie nodded. "Good. From there I'll need to get back to my family."

"OK. Tack his horse and the mule for me, and I'll get him dressed."

Kate went over to Gabe and shook him gently. "Gabe, wake up. When do you think you will be feeling well enough to travel?"

"What?" He rubbed his eyes.

"Can you ride now?"

"Maybe. How is Rascal doing?"

"He is fine—better than you."

He looked around, his eyes focused on the wagon. "Anything going on I need to worry about?"

Kate's voice was urgent. "Ellie is getting the horses ready to ride. Soldiers are coming this way."

"How can you be so sure?" He pushed her for more.

She sounded impatient. "Because one of the officers is a friend of ours, and he is on his way to see us. I think someone from town must have told him about Alex's death."

"OK, I'll go in and start getting dressed. Can you bring me my pistols and holster?"

He got up and slowly walked in to the house. Kate followed him and glanced at his bare feet, then went into her bedroom. In the bedroom doorway, she paused to watch him pull his socks up.

"Here are your boots, let me help you with them," she said.

"They look great. Thanks for cleaning and polishing them."

"Thank Ellie, she did that. I cleaned your holster and weapons ... they were getting rusty."

He smiled. "Rusty like me?"

"Think of it as a nice, long rest. Besides, we talked about it, and we couldn't send you back looking the way you did when you showed up. That wouldn't be fitting."

He buckled his belt and put on his hat. "OK, I'm ready. How far to my cavalry?"

"The last word we got is at least a week old."

"How far?"

"Falmouth, about twenty-three miles east, is where your army is."

"The cavalry?"

"Some units could be there, some could be south of Warrenton Junction—but I do not know where they were going."

"If I can do four miles per hour in my condition, it's going to take me—"

"Six hours. About the same time it will be getting dark—so focus, and don't go any slower."

"I know. I don't want to run into any scouts and pickets in the dark."

He looked at her. "Can you tell me where I am now?"

"At my farm," she said.

"You know what I mean."

"Why do you need to know that?"

"What if I want to come back and say good day?" he asked.

She shook her head. "Don't."

"What if I want to thank you?"

She shook it again. "You just did."

"What if I want to thank Ellie?"

"Do it now, before you go."

"You are not going to tell me, are you?"

"Nope. Here she comes now."

He turned to Ellie. "Goodbye, and thank you for helping to save my life." He moved in closer. "I'll never forget you. Miss Ellie, would it be OK if I hugged you?"

As she leaned toward him, he moved in close and slowly reached around her. At first his arms were loose, then he tightened them to a snug embrace. She also tightened her hold. He whispered, "Thank you, I hope to see you again someday." Then quickly, before she pulled away, he kissed her gently on her cheek.

She blushed. "I didn't say you could kiss me."

Kate impatiently waved his gloves that she held in her hand. "Will you two lovebirds finish? We need to ride and move now. Here, take your gloves."

"We need to get along before you get caught. Rascal is ready." Ellie handed him Rascal's reins.

He gave her a tender look. "Maybe one day, if I survive the war, I'll come back, and—"

Kate interrupted him. "Gabe, I know you got soft these past few weeks, but we need to ride quickly and quietly. Mount up, move out. Do you remember how to be a solider?"

As they rode away from her home, the reality of his situation returned, and his journey back to the war started.
When the raid started over a month ago, he thought, *the Union army was also in Falmouth. But where would the cavalry be now?* At that moment all he could think about was mounting his riding companion and getting back in to the war. *I feel my regiment needs me.*

He looked at Kate. "I want to head to the last known Union army camp, at Falmouth, just north of the Rappahannock River. Which way do I need to go?"

"You don't need to worry about that. We will take you across the river," she said.

"How can I ever repay the both of you?" he asked.

Kate smiled. "You already repaid me. I took a lot of your money, and I borrowed your horse ... that should be enough for now. But if you ever feel generous and find this place as you ride by, please stop in and leave some more money, and then move on." She added her menacing but teasing grin.

"What about you?" he asked, turning to Ellie.

Her eyes were somber. "You don't owe me anything. I just want you to be safe and make it through this war."

"Faster, Ellie. Hurry, get going."

They were only three hundred yards out when Mark and T.J. came galloping toward them. *Even though T.J. is eleven,* thought Gabe, *he thinks he is the best horseman in the army. Even if he learned to ride from the ladies.*

T.J. gasped for air as he tried to speak. "Can't take him to Kelly's Ford—" His older brother Mark cut him off.

Mark was big and strong for a young man of fifteen. Most boys of his age would already be fighting, but since his older brother had already lost an arm and was working on General Lee's staff, his parents were keeping him home until he turned sixteen.

"Ellie, we need to move to our second option," said Mark.

"OK, I understand," said Ellie.

They knew that Confederate soldiers were around Kelly's Ford, but they did not want Gabriel to know. They were well trained on how to behave and travel when troops were around.

"To the quarry," Ellie quietly ordered.

"What's the quarry?" Gabe asked.

"That's where we bury all the Union soldiers we catch," Mark said, trying to act tough.

T.J. chuckled out loud.

"Gabriel, um ... Mark is going to put a hood on you," Kate said.

Gabe looked momentarily alarmed. "What?"

"Don't worry my man of war, I will protect you," Kate whispered to Gabe as she glanced and smiled at him.

T.J. chuckled again.

Looking straight into her eyes, he whispered back. "OK, only because I know if something goes wrong, the last thing I will have seen is your devilish smile."

Swoosh, on went the hood. Gabe was sure Mark enjoyed doing that.

He stayed very quiet so he could hear and feel as much as he could soak in. He wanted to remember where this crossing was. He could tell they were still going east. He could feel the warmth of the sun on the front of the hood as it warmed his face.

After walking for what felt like less than a mile, Gabe heard Mark talk to the others. "He's trying to figure out where we are going. Talk to him, keep him distracted."

Ellie leaned over to Gabe and whispered, "If you find out where we cross and you give its location away, these boys would love nothing better than to kill you, and Kate and I will let them ... this time."

"The quarry?" he asked.

"Gabe, this is for your protection," she explained. "We can cross almost anywhere, as long as there is no rain. But there are Rebel troops around, and if they approach us, we need to make them think we are treating you as a POW and moving you south."

"We're almost home," T.J. blurted out.

Everyone but Gabe turned to look at T.J. "Shut up!" said Mark, taking a swing at him and missing.

They rode for a few more minutes, then stopped.

Everyone is very quiet, thought Gabe. *All I can hear is the flow of water moving across rocks and my own breathing. Now I hear someone slowly and very quietly wading across something that sounds like a babbling brook. Now no sound but a few birds in the trees, buzzing bees behind me, and the river flowing in front of me. Everyone is still being very quiet and careful.*

Ellie broke the silence, whispering to him. "Stay very quiet... we sent someone to scout the far side." Then he recognized a voice. It was T.J. talking softly to the group from up high above them, to Gabe's left.

"Gabe, grab the rope I'm handing you." Kate put a rope into his right hand. "Pull the rope hand over hand—it will guide you across. Go slow; there are a lot of rocks. Don't make any other moves. Mark will be on the other side waiting for you. Any last words?"

He paused for a moment. "I guess it's goodbye."

Kate reached over and placed her hand over his. With a slight squeeze she whispered, "Off you go—back to your side of the river, the North, where your army and your brothers in blue will be happy to see you. If we ever meet again, please don't be bleeding."

Ellie whispered, "I hope you find what you need to quiet your ghosts and make it through this war. I mean this from the bottom of my heart. I trust I won't see you again."

The world of peace and care they had shared was over and behind them. Baptized first by water, then by fire, then one last time by water, with each pull of the rope, Rascal took him another step forward—but also back, back to their world, the world of the living dead, of kill or be killed, of slaughter, suffering, and destruction.

It only took a few seconds until he could feel Mark's arm. "The hood will stay on for now, do you understand?"

"Yes."

"Stay quiet."

Mark grabbed Rascal's reins from Gabe's hands as they walked off.

"We'll ride for a bit, then I'll hand you off to a few friends who'll take you the rest of the way past any Rebel pickets or scouts on this side. Then you are on your own."

After fifteen minutes of slow walking, they stopped. He could hear several horses moving from in front of him and to the left.

"Don't move; our friends are coming for you," said Mark.

Gabe's mind started to race. *What if Mark is passing me off to Rebel pickets or scouts? Can he be trusted? Kate and Ellie trust him, but this could be Mark's way of secretly turning over Union soldiers as prisoners of war?* After a pause, he realized that was unlikely. *He would have just turned me over when I was found—'cause I was the biggest pain in the ass they probably have had to deal with in this war.*

Suddenly a female voice was near. "*Shhhh*—I'm Brandy Morris. I'm one of Kate and Ellie's friends. Hold still while I take this hood off. Here, Mark, take this stupid thing with you."

Brandy introduced the petite woman near her. "This is Mary Ann."

"Good day, ladies!" Gabe looked at the two women. "What a beautiful way to end this wonderful day."

They giggled. "Ellie is so right about him," Mary Ann whispered to Brandy.

"I have sense also. I can see and hear, Mary Ann," Brandy replied, then she turned to Gabriel. "Let's walk. Rascal is an amazing horse. We were with Kate and Ellie at the races. He made winning look fun, and he took real good care of Kate for us."

"Thanks," said Gabe. "The place where we crossed the river … how did you find it?"

"We learned about the river from our grandparents, who learned from their parents, who learned about it from the local Indians—how else? We play different games on different parts of it. At some places we cross on swings, others we slide down the cliffs in the mud then into the water, and at others we swing and jump in and swim. The part you crossed is shallow and rocky. You just need to be careful with things below the surface, especially after heavy rains." She suspected that he was trying to find out how to find the crossing, so she gave him only information he already knew then changed the subject.

"You got anybody special waiting for you up North?" she asked.

"Nope, just the Army. I hope they don't shoot me by mistake." *It's a miracle we are still in this war,* he thought to himself. "Do you live close by?"

"I live just north of Kelly's Ford Road, about one-third of a mile from Kelly's crossing—closer to Wheatly's Ford. Mary Ann lives over by Norman's Ford, on this side of the river."

"*Shhh,*" said Mary Ann, "we must be silent for a bit."

"OK."

They walked in silence for nearly a mile, then Brandy spoke. "This is as far as we go. Keep going down this road, and I hope you find what you are looking for."

He smiled and thanked the two young women, and then he and Rascal walked off.

What am I in for now?

* * *

After a few hundred yards he heard voices.

"Stop, or we'll shoot!"

"Don't shoot—I'm Sergeant O'Shea, 2nd Division, First New Jersey Cavalry."

"Move forward slowly," a voice ordered.

He walked up to find Union scouts from Buford's Calvary.

"What are you guys doing here?" he asked. "Where is the 2nd Division?" The lead cavalry scouts took him to General Buford's headquarters, where he checked in and explained where he had been for more than a month and a half.

"Sir, the Confederate Cavalry is not in Culpeper any more," he said. "They moved to Brandy Station."

He kept his report as brief as possible and told them what they needed to know. This way they wouldn't ask too many questions. *Thank God it looked like they'd just finished having their pictures taken and were too busy packing up to care,* he thought.

"Hey, boy, we got the latest information—we know the Reb cavalry is still in Culpeper," roared a major. *This could be why we're losing most battles,* he thought. *They don't listen or ask the right questions, and they take too many pictures.*

"It's OK, son. Over there—see those men? They're loading a wagon with supplies. They are from Gregg's 2nd division. Go with them to find your regiment." He turned to see a large sergeant major with red hair and beard.

He trotted over to the wagon. "Corporal—are you riding back to the 2nd?"

"Yes, sergeant. We're leaving now."

While riding back the men told him about how poor the raid went, and about the major Union defeat at Chancellorsville during the raid. That news did not surprise him.

After riding north for about two miles and passing several pickets, one of the troopers pointed left and yelled out to him go that way.

As usual he could hear Lewis Michael's loud mouth and raucous laugh.

"Why two first names?" he yelled out. All heads turned.

Private Michael blurted back, "So all you slow Yankees don't ever forget me."

"Where have you been? It was reported you were taken prisoner," asked Corporal O'Keeffe.

"No," Gabe said. "I was wounded."

"Well, look who finally decided to join us again. We thought you'd turned chicken and changed your mind about fighting," Private Smalls added.

Gabe smiled. "I did, but then I realized, who was going to keep you non-riding city slickers alive?"

"So what happened to you?" Corporal O'Keeffe asked.

"I was riding with Private Mott when someone started shooting at us in the heavy rain. When we rode away I hit my head on what I think was a low branch, and it almost knocked me from my horse. Then after wandering around for a while in the rain, I got shot. Then I died, and out of nowhere two of the most beautiful Southern belles took me to heaven, where they gave me a choice." He paused.

"What was the choice?" several asked.

"They said we can let you die, or you let us take care of you and then you go back to war."

"I asked them how long would they take care of me, and they said a month. I thought about it for a long time, and then they asked what my answer was. I told them, I'm yours for the next month ... do what you wish."

"I can't wait to see some Southern belles."

"Ding, dong, ding, dong ... do you hear them, Private Michael?" Corporal O'Keeffe joked.

"I hear you," said Private Michael. "Why?"

"It's your prayer bells. Start praying, cause the only bells you are going to see or hear are ones ringing in the church when they bury you."

"Do you still have him?" asked Private Mott.

"Yup." Each soldier in his company came over to greet him.

"Philip, Richard, and James—nice to see all of you still alive."

"Good to see you, Sergeant. We need you," said Private Philip Gregory.

"Yup, we's gonna need you," added Private Smalls. "Since the raid, all we do is drill and clean our stuff."

"O'Keeffe, how did the regiment do in the raid? I heard the army got their butts kicked at Chancellorsville."

"The raid was a waste of good horses. We rode about 180 miles in nine days. The predicament of our horses was appalling—dead and crippled animals marked the route of our ride. At times we remained on the move for so long that dozens of men fell asleep in the saddles of their emaciated, sore-backed horses. Your wounds probably saved Rascal's life."

Life has a way of interfering with our plans. The raid had done more for Sergeant O'Shea than it did for the Union Army's war effort. It may have given him a chance for a future and altered his reason for being in the war.

In General Buford's report of the raid, he praised the performances of his staff. The raid lasted nine days. It was unimpressive in central and southern Virginia but caused a lot of destruction in the rear of the Army of Northern Virginia. It accomplished little strategically and failed to attack any of the objectives Hooker established, and they withdrew into Union lines east of Richmond to the peninsula north of the York River, across from Yorktown, on May 7, ending the campaign. Major General Alfred Pleasanton replaced General Stoneman in command of the Cavalry Corps. General Buford was soon elevated to the command of a cavalry division.

"Fill me in," Gabe said. "What is going on now? When do we move?"

"Don't know when we move, but we hear that General JEB Stuart is still kicking our ass since the war started."

Just then 1st Sergeant James walked up. "I see you decided to come back."

"And I thought you didn't care, 1st Sergeant," said Gabe.

"Good news travels fast," said Private Michael.

"Get some sleep. Tomorrow we move out," yelled out 1st Sergeant James to the group. Then he spoke directly to Gabe. "Welcome back, Sergeant O'Shea. Walk with me. How's the leg?"

"What do you mean, 1st Sergeant?"

"Don't try to bullshit me—I saw you ride in. I know a lame horse when I see one. It's your right leg, up high," he told him.

"Yes, but it's fine. I just lost some fitness, and I'm a bit sore from riding all day."

"How long have you been out of the saddle?"

Gabriel looked around, knowing the 1st Sergeant would not like his next words. "Just a few weeks."

The 1st Sergeant frowned. "Try again: Do you want me to send you to medical?"

"No. OK, about seven weeks. But just give me a few days in the saddle, drilling, and I'll be ready."

"I wish I could."

"Don't send me to medical. I just need a few days, and you need me."

"You have two days to prove it to me, only because we do need you. Hell, you made it back just in time to try to get yourself killed again.

If they had only known, he thought.

After taps was called that night, he looked up to the stars and wished he were sleeping in the bed Alex and Kate made for him instead of on the hard ground. *Boy, I miss that straw-stuffed bed, warm cover, and the pillow filled with goose-down. She did have nice things in that little house.*

The sequence of events around Alex's death had him wondering about his ghosts and his life. *For some unknown reason, Rascal and I were supposed to be there for those people at that time—but why?* Finally he let himself consider the possibility that he was also supposed to be there for his own healing, and not just for his leg.

Then a bright star caught his eye, and his perspective grew wider. *Those young people always knew where both armies were and how to avoid them or help them. It was like a game to them. They knew their land like the back of their hand, even young T.J. They knew the roads, trails, who to talk to, and where the telegrams would go and come from. Most of all, they knew the river. This river was always hard for an army to cross in force. Neither commander wanted to get part of his army trapped on one side, with reinforcements and supplies unable to help, because they could not get across fast enough. I estimate Kate's farm is about half a mile southwest of Kelly's Ford.*

His thoughts grew fuzzy as he was overcome by weariness. *This was the busiest day I've had in well over a month.* He was asleep in seconds.

PART TWO
Here I Am

On the 8th of June, 1st Sergeant James informed the regiment, "Tomorrow the U.S. Cavalry heads back across the Rappahannock, to attack the Confederate cavalry at Brandy Station."

During the start of the Gettysburg campaign, General Lee's stealthy troop movements away from the Fredericksburg area caused Union concern, and General Pleasonton was ordered to find out where they were heading. Launching a surprise attack on Major General J.E.B. Stuart's cavalry at Brandy Station resulted in the largest predominantly cavalry engagement of the war—and in the western hemisphere. The initial assault crossed the Rappahannock River at Beverly Ford, under command of Brigadier General John Buford.

While Buford's cavalry attacked, General Gregg led the 2nd and 3rd Divisions across Kelly's Ford to attack the flank and rear of the Confederates on Fleetwood Hill, where General Stuart's headquarters was located and captured in the attack by Gregg's troopers.

The fighting was fierce, saber-wielding, and hand-to-hand, and it completely surprised the Confederate cavalry.

Initial report June 1863 to His Excellency Joel Parker, Governor, state of New Jersey:

> *Governor,*
> *I have the honor to report that the Regiment has been engaged in another very severe cavalry fight. On the 8th inst. the Division broke camp at Warrenton Junction and marched to Kelly's Ford, where we bivouacked for the night. The next day (the 9th inst.) at 3 A.M. we crossed the river and moved on Brandy Station.*
> *As is normal in times of danger we were in the*

advance. Meanwhile Genl Buford was fighting hard opposite Rappahannock Station. The object of our movement was to turn the right flank of the Rebels. Col. Wyndham was in command of the 2d Brigade, composed of the 1st N. Jersey 1st Md. and the 1st Pa Cavalry, and the command of our Regt. devolved upon Lt. Col. Brodrick. Capt. Yorke of Co. I had the advance guard composed of Cos. C & I—he moved his men so carefully that he captured every vidette in the road, so that the first intimation that the enemy had of our being in their rear was by seeing the head of our column debouch from the woods.

Col Wyndham moved his troops with such celerity that we were upon them almost before they were aware of our vicinity. The fight lasted four hours and was a continual inception of the most brilliant charges ever made. Every officer behaved with the utmost bravery and coolness, and it is impossible for men to behave better than did ours—they proved themselves well worthy of the State from which they come. More cannot be said in their praise.

Lt. Col. Brodrick and Major Shelmire were both wounded and taken while leading one of the numerous charges–accounts of the nature of their capture are so conflicting that I defer sending any statement regarding it till I learn something definite but that they both behaved with the greatest daring and gallantry there can be no question.

Capt. Sawyer Co. K and Lt. Crocker Co. H are also prisoners but not thought to be wounded. Capt. Lucas Co. F Capt. Maulsbury and Adjt Kitchen while in the thickest of the fray had their horses shot out under them—that of Adjt Kitchen fell dead carrying him along with it–his escape seems almost miraculous. When the order was given to retire our Regt covered the rear. I am told that Genl Gregg expressed the greatest satisfaction at the conduct of the Regt. Towards the close of the engagement Col. Wyndham recd a bullet wound in the calf of the leg

> but we are thankful to know that it will not prove dangerous—he kept the field for sometime after being hit but was finally obliged to give up—he goes to Washington today. We hope he will soon return as he can ill be spared from his command. He also paid the Regt the highest compliments for its steady and dashing charges.
>
> The fight was hand-to-hand throughout. We had in the engagement four Field officers, 14 line officers, and 281 enlisted men. Our loss in killed wounded and missing is at present 3 Field officers, 2 line officers, and 52 enlisted. This of itself speaks volumes for the bravery of the Regt. The morale of the Regt has been greatly benefitted by yesterday's work and I am confident that the men will fight better now than ever. Major Beaumont will probably soon return from his present command to assume that of the Regt and will be able to collect further accounts of the capture and wounds of the missing officers than I am now able to do.
>
> I have the honor to be Governor
> Very respectfully
> Your obdt servt
> Hugh H. Janeway
> Major Commanding 1st New Jersey Cavalry

The Confederates managed to repel both Buford and Gregg. The battle was a draw, although it surprised and humiliated Stuart, and orders left behind in his headquarters on Fleetwood Hill provided valuable intelligence about Lee's intentions to invade the North.

After the Battle of Brandy Station, General Stuart wanted to again establish his headquarters on southern Fleetwood Hill—where they were situated prior to the battle. Stuart's staff persuaded him otherwise, as Fleetwood Hill and its slopes were covered with dead bodies.

"When we reached the place," a staff engineer wrote, "it was covered so thick with the dead horses and men, and the bluebottle flies were swarming so thick over the bloodstains over the ground, that there was not room enough to pitch the tents among them."

Fighting to Die

June 9

After the day's battle, that evening Gabe's four-man squad helped cover the retreat near the approach to Kelly's Ford. As they approached the river, Gabe thought he recognized the spot where Mark and Brandy had escorted him across just a few days ago.

"Men, I'm going to scout this side of the river and look for stragglers. I want the three of you to cross the river here, then stay and wait on the other bank, for no more than one hour. If I don't return by then, report back to the regiment. Try to hold off any small units of Confederates, but if a large troop tries to cross, report back to the division." He was worried the ladies might live dangerously close to where the day's battle had taken place.

It was hard to find her house, as there weren't many roads in the area. But he had a good idea where to go.

He arrived to find Kate gone and Ellie there, who blurted out, "What are you doing here, now?"

"Looking for Rebel cavalry or Union stragglers—have you seen any?"

"Like you? You know that even if I did I wouldn't tell you."

"And you know I had to ask. Where is Kate?"

"I don't know," she said. "Do you have the time?"

He pulled out his pocket watch, the last gift his wife gave him. "It's five-thirty."

She looked at the golden object in his hand. "Nice watch. Who is that in the picture?"

"Nobody," he sternly responded, starting to walk off.

"She wasn't here when I arrived nearly thirty minutes ago."

"I hope she is OK," she mumbled, then noticed his new injury. "You're bleeding."

"It's just a flesh wound. It will be all right."

"What about your left leg?" she asked.

He looked down as the blood soaked through his trousers. "It's also nothing. I'll get it looked at when I get back to my side of the river."

"Rascal looks a bit cut up too," she said.

"What happened? Why do you look worried?" he asked.

"It's Brandy and—"

Just then Kate rode in on the wagon.

"What are you doing here?" She looked startled to see him.

"Where were you?" Ellie asked her, worry in her voice.

"I heard the battle and tried to go to town to see if anybody needed help. I tried to wait it out but the fighting was too close, so I came back home to get some things."

"I'll get my medical things," said Kate. "We may find some wounded souls in need of help. Ellie, can you and Gabe get some sheets and blankets?"

"Yes, but we need to find Brandy and T.J. first."

Gabe hesitated, and for some unknown reason he quickly tied Rascal to the deck.

"Why? What happened to them?" Kate asked.

"We don't know."

They all went inside to quickly gather supplies.

"I think we have enough. Let's go," Gabe said after a few minutes.

Kate was out first, but just before Ellie could clear the doorway, four Confederate cavalry soldiers came riding up, surprising them.

"Sir, that looks like a Yankee horse," a corporal shouted out.

"It sure is," shouted another.

"I smell a Yankee," added a lieutenant. Then two of the men drew their weapons.

"Easy, boys," a captain ordered.

They tipped their hats to Ellie and Kate. "Good evening, ladies. Have you seen the man who owns that horse?" Captain Mac asked, pointing to Rascal. Rascal was trying to untie his reins with his teeth—he knew they were coming, and he would have walked away and tried to hide, but Gabe had tied him too tight, and he never ties him.

"That's my horse, and you can't have him, Mac," Kate said.

"Your horse, Kate? It has Union all over it—and since when do you tie your horses?"

"Yes, he is mine, and I tie them since the war started. For some reason they keep wandering off." As she untied him she said quietly, "Now watch, Rascal, go in the barn now." She swung her right arm toward the barn and pointed.

Rascal looked at her, then toward the house, then after

hesitating he walked over to the barn.

"Nice try," said the lieutenant. "He may know you, but he's smarter than you think. Hey, Yankee, your horse gave you away. Come out of the house."

Just then Gabe stepped out of the house, a pistol in each hand.

"She is right, it is her horse. I promised this lady my horse if I should die in this war, and this looks like today is that day."

"Hold on boys, there has been enough killing today—right, Corporal Wilson?" Ellie yelled.

"Yes, Miss Ellie, nice to see you again."

"Sergeant, it is six against one, and your words tell me you know you don't stand a chance, so why don't you surrender, and join your fellow prisoners we took today?"

Gabe smiled. "Nope, I am a rotten soldier, and I know I will make a real rotten prisoner. Why don't you just surrender to me and make me look better?"

"We can't do that. Right, boys?"

"No, sir, we can't—and we won't," Corporal Wilson blurted out. Then the riders started slowly moving their horses away from each other.

"Captain, not only am I a rotten solider, but many of my officers think I may be fighting with you Rebels."

"Nice try."

"Captain, we both know your army needs you more than my army needs me. I will kill you first, and at least one more, maybe wound a third man before one of you gets a good shot at me. Besides, Captain, you need to learn how to count. I see only four of you."

Just then two more riders came from the other side of the house behind Gabe.

"OK, six to one—now that's better, God."

"Stop it—that's enough, Gabe. Mac listen to me," Ellie yelled out, then she slowly walked over to Mac's horse. "Mac, last night there was a party at our house to announce Mark and Brandy's wedding. They wanted to wed before Mark went off to the war—he is sixteen now. Brandy left early this morning to go home, only Mark could not get up, so T.J. went with her. We can't find either of them. So we need all of you to stop the war and help us find them now. Please … we have known each other and our families most of our lives. You know Brandy. Remember when you were going to join the Cavalry, and she gave you flowers and kissed you on your cheek? She was just twelve years old then."

"I remember," said Mac. Turning to Gabe, he said, "Sergeant, a gentleman's truce? These ladies need our help."

Gabe nodded. "Yes, truce. Captain, I also want to help them look for the kids, if that is OK with you and your men, sir?"

"Yes, it will be, Sergeant. Men, it is an order: None of you will engage the sergeant as long as we are looking for the kids."

"Yes, sir," they all replied.

"Miss Ellie, we will find your brother and Miss Brandy."

"Brandy lives just north of Kelly's Ford Road, about a third of a mile from Kelly's crossing, north of Wheatly's Ford," Kate added.

"I just checked from my house to here, so we need to head north," Ellie said.

"This morning after we crossed at Kelly's Ford there was an engagement of our infantry against a cavalry-sized Rebel brigade on Kelly's Ford Road. I wonder if they got mixed up in that," added Gabe.

"Our cavalry regiment pulled back and headed north at about five o'clock," Mac said.

"Let's split up, sergeant—you go with Ellie up the east side of the road, and Kate will go with me and my men up the west side." He looked at Gabe. "Sergeant, until the next time we meet."

Gabe tipped his head slightly. "Yes, sir. Let's hope it's after the war."

"By us splitting up, maybe we'll get lucky," Kate added.

"I will pray for all of us," Ellie said as she looked at Kate.

Leaving Kate's farm, Gabe tried to keep Ellie's mind off of Brandy and T.J. "Ellie, how big is your farm?" he asked.

"My farm? It's not a farm. Kate has a farm; my family lives on Blue Larkspur Plantation. We have about one hundred workers who raise livestock. We still have horses, both for racing and for work, and we have dairy cows, mules, some cattle, sheep, chickens, and hogs, but not as many as we had before the war. We grow corn, both for people to eat and as feed for our animals. My grandpa grew a lot of tobacco, but we don't do too much of that anymore. We harvest hay, wheat, and barley grains. Most of the wealthy planters, including my father, believe in fertilizing their fields with dung and lime and rotating their crops to keep the soil fertile. We also have expanded our production of flaxseed and corn, since flax is in high demand in the Irish linen industry, and a demand for corn exists in the West Indies."

His mind wandered a bit while she spoke. *Good thing I'm not real tired, and I hope we find them soon, because she may go on like this for hours.*

"Why 'Blue Larkspur'?" he asked.

"That was one of grandmother's favorite flowers. She taught my mother all about flowers, and she passed that love onto me, especially in the spring. Don't you love their aromas?"

"Yes. Do you have slaves on the plantation?"

"No, not anymore. Early on they figured out we live so far north they kept running away. Then we found out a long time ago that people work much better when they're fairly compensated for their efforts. On a few acres my father brought in some merchants who have been employing newly arrived immigrants who were textile workers in Ireland and Germany. They work in their homes spinning the materials into yarn and cloth. Large farmers and merchants have become wealthy, while small farmers like Kate's only make enough for subsistence. That is why we help her. But by now you realize she wants to succeed on her own."

She continued. "The war made it hard for everyone, but it will be much harder for her now that Alex is gone. I know she loves breeding, raising foals, and training and racing horses."

"Since the war started, we have lost nearly 60 percent of our stock. If we make it, after the war I will make sure she gets some mules and a few horses and help her get back in business. We also have been blessed that our plantation is not in the areas the army and cavalry have been moving in."

"Mules?" asked Gabe. "I thought they were just pack animals. That's how we use them in the Cavalry."

"We made the mule our preferred draft animal—they can withstand the heat of summer better, and their smaller size and hooves are well suited for crops like cotton, tobacco, and sugar. Today we do most of our mule breeding for the army."

Gabe looked at her thoughtfully. "Because your family has lived here a long time, you seem to have learned how the culture of farming this region has evolved—what trends to move toward, and which to avoid."

"Sorry if I'm boring you, but I love this business."

"No, you're not boring me—please go on. You know more about this business that most men I know." *I can't believe I said that*, he thought. *She is getting a bit boring with all the details, but she seems so excited to share her knowledge, and so businesslike. Her talking will help me to stay focused on the search for the kids— and keep her mind off of it.*

She smiled. "'Bread colonies'—that's what they used to call the tidewater area of Maryland and Virginia. The wheat culture spread after George Washington diversified away from tobacco, and tobacco moved west."

"Your father must be proud that you know so much."

"Not really," she said. "He'd prefer that I was married to a plantation owner and had children by now."

"I have wondered why you're not married."

"You have? I don't want to just be a pretty woman on a man's arm who looks for ways to spend his money. I want to help run the plantation. I have yet to meet a man who will treat me more like an equal and at least listen to my ideas. I want the marriage and the running of a plantation to be something we do together, like a team."

"You're very different from what I thought you were like when I first met you. I like that you understand the business of what it takes to run a plantation. Personally, I prefer the breeding, training, and riding of the horses."

She quickly looked over at him. "What did you think I was like?"

Hearing a horse approach from the left, they froze. In a moment they saw Kate riding up in the wagon.

"Perfect timing, lady. Where is your Southern escort?" Gabe asked.

"Yes, where is your captain?" Ellie asked.

"Her captain?" Gabe asked, looking at Kate.

"After half a mile Confederate scouts arrived, and they told him that they are pulling out. He needed to return."

Ellie turned to Gabe. "We need to keep looking. Can you stay with us until it starts getting dark?"

"I'll stay for a while, but I must head back before it gets dark."

"Over there." Ellie pointed to a trail on the right. "This is the shortcut we use to get to Brandy's farm."

"Kate, leave the wagon. We should walk the horses from here,"

Gabe said.

Just off the road they walked into a clearing. Kate stopped abruptly. "Look, there's a dead horse."

"There is another one over there—and there," added Gabe.

There were a few weapons here and there, and a lot of military rubbish all over the place. Walking around they all started to notice the damaged trees. They could tell many rounds of ammunition had been fired, but there were no bodies.

"Was this the battle?" Ellie asked Gabe.

"Just a small part ... most of the big battle was at Brandy Station, at St. James Church and Fleetwood Hill. This is where a Southern brigade-size cavalry troop fought Union infantry, which also covered our retreat back across the river."

"Where were you?" Kate asked him, quickly adding, "Did you see the 7th Virginia Cavalry?"

"My regiment fought on Fleetwood Hill. And I don't think we engaged the 7th—is that the troop your captain is in?"

"He is not 'my captain,'" Kate said.

"Over here, down there—look!" yelled Ellie.

Kate and Gabe ran over to the edge of a small ridge and looked down. Ellie was already kneeling next to a body of a woman, whose dress spread out on the ground.

"It's Brandy!" Ellie yelled to them. "She's still alive, but she's bleeding and unconscious."

Gabe rushed to her side, then yelled over to Kate. "Kate, hurry! Try to get the wagon in here. This looks real bad."

"My God, what happened to her?" Ellie asked.

"Looks like a gut shot at close range."

"Oh, no—that's always bad."

"*Shhh,* I hear something ... stay quiet and with her," said Gabe.

He searched the nearby woods and soon called out, "I found T.J. He is also alive."

"Thank God," said Ellie. "How bad?"

"His head and lower right leg are bleeding; he looks like he was hit by a rifle butt. I'm going to carry him over. Stay with Brandy."

Just as he reached Ellie and Brandy, Kate arrived with the wagon.

"Wait, let me set the blanket," said Kate. "OK, put him down. Get Brandy. I'll tie Rascal and Rebel to the wagon."

She looked at Gabe. "Gabe, you drive, and Ellie and I'll work on them. Go slow. We'll guide you to Brandy's."

As they approached the house, Kate looked at Ellie and started to whisper, "He can't—"

Ellie cut her off. "Gabe, get out here and take Rascal. Wait for one of us. Do not go near anybody else or near the house. Do you understand?"

"Yes, ma'am." He knew she was serious.

Hearing them arrive, several people from inside the house ran out to help them get Brandy and T.J. inside.

Brandy's uncle Thomas was a doctor. Since he was near seventy years old, he'd been assigned to the Confederate headquarters medical staff, in Richmond. He performed many surgeries on soldiers throughout the war. He had stayed over after the evening's festivities. He often tried to teach Ellie and Kate the latest medical research techniques when he had time. Brandy's father was holding a woman back as she kept yelling over and over again, "How is she? Is she alive? Will she live?"

As Doc Thomas washed his hands, Ellie opened his bag.

Kate quickly gave him their assessment of the wounds. "Brandy has a gut shot, T.J. a leg and head wound. She has been unconscious since we found them. We could not find an exit wound, so we focused on trying to stop the bleeding. T.J. was moaning when we found him, and he's been unconscious since."

The doctor cleared a treatment area. "Kate, I want you with Brandy, and Ellie, you with your brother. Clean his leg wound and tell me what you see. I need quiet, so only Mrs. Jones and Mrs. Anderson please stay and help. The rest wait outside. Mrs. Anderson, please clean T.J.'s head and tell me what you see."

He walked over to a woman who was bigger than her peers; her flowered dress could cover most large dining room tables. The kids all called her Mandy. Her skin was usually pale, with a hint of rose on her cheeks, but that day she was as white as sun-bleached bones, with the only red in her eyes. Ordinarily she ran the house, but today she was silent. She said nothing, just listened.

"John, Amanda, please give me some time. Can you both wait in the next room?"

They left the room together, but John walked out the back to escape to his world, the running of their farm. Amanda paced in the main entrance hall.

The doctor turned his complete attention to Brandy and T.J. "Kate, check her pulse." He listened to Brandy's heart and glanced at her skin and lip color. He cut open her dress, which was soaked with blood. As he wiped blood away from her white, soft midsection, searching for the entry wound, he quietly said to Kate, "She's lost a lot of blood. Help me turn her on her side—we need to look for an exit wound. Cut her dress open."

Kate found a spot of torn flesh. "Over here." She wiped blood dangerously close to Brandy's spine.

The doctor examined the area. "It went clean through. Let's hope it didn't hit too many organs."

He handed Kate a small bottle. "Here, give her this morphine. Pour a few drops into her mouth."

"Even if I can stop this bleeding now, she may have already lost too much." He desperately tried to stop the bleeding by packing the wounds, as Kate listened to Brandy's heart.

Within seconds the bleeding stopped, along with her heart.

"Kate, check her breathing."

She leaned in close to Brandy's face to check her breath. She turned her head to look at Ellie, who was now aware of the eerie silence and stared back at Kate. They saw the tears filling each others' eyes, tears shed for their lost little sister.

Mrs. Jones burst into tears and had to be taken away, prostrate with grief.

Kate walked over to Ellie.

Ellie unbuttoned the neck on her dress and went back to work on T.J. Kate reached out to Ellie to pull her close, but she pulled away.

"Ellie, she lost too much blood. I will take care of T.J. now. Go get some air."

"No, I'm OK. I want to stay and help Doc Thomas."

"OK. I'll get some air and tell Gabe to leave."

"Please thank him for me."

"I will."

As Kate walked away from the house she began to wipe the tears and blood from her face. Looking down at her hands, she realized they were covered in Brandy's blood. She reached down under her dress to rip off a piece of her petticoat and walked over to the water pump. Slowly she pumped it several times until the water burst out and splashed her boots and the lower part of her skirt, creating a red puddle as the blood-tinged water washed onto the ground.

Pausing to wipe her hands and face, she looked up at the sky. "Now how do I look? Is this better for you? I hate you; this is another reason why I don't believe in you." She held the blood-soaked linen up to the sky. "How many more are you going to kill? Why so many innocent women and children? How many more are you going to take from me?"

She gently fell back onto the stones that surrounded the pump.

"Are you OK? Who are you talking to?"

Turning her head, Kate saw Gabriel standing over her.

"Yes, I just needed a moment. I was coming to tell you … What are you doing here? You can't let them see you."

"Who?"

"Brandy's family. They don't like Yankees, they will kill you. Why are you here? You are too close to the house. You should go before someone sees you." Her face was drained and weary.

"Not until you tell me how they are."

Just then, with no warning, Mark came flying up in full gallop, jumped off his horse, and ran up to Kate. "Did you find her?"

"Yes, she is inside."

"Thank God. I was so scared that something happened to her."

"Mark, she has been shot."

"What? No, no, no—is she going to make it?"

"Sit," Kate said.

Mark's face grew suddenly pale. "No. You tell me now."

"She never woke up. She died a few minutes ago."

With fire in his eyes, Mark turned toward Gabe. "It's your fault."

"What are you talking about? What is his fault?" Kate asked.

Gabe had seen this look on the battlefield. *It's the mind looking to get satisfaction, to create an escape. It's the beginning of the internal journey for revenge.* He knew the best thing to do for now was stay quiet. He had to let Mark say what he needed to.

Mark continued. "Your army came here. It brought the war and the killing."

Kate spoke up. "Mark, no. He had nothing to do with Brandy. He found her and T.J."

Mark pulled a pistol out from under his shirt.

Just then Ellie ran out of the house. "No!" she cried. "Mark, please don't! Hasn't there been enough killing?"

His hand shook as he held the gun. "Not yet. I'm going to kill all those that hurt her."

"Vengeance, is that what you want?" Gabe's voice was steady.

"Gabe, don't," Kate cut in.

"Have you ever killed someone, boy?" asked Gabe.

"Gabe, no," Ellie added.

Mark's voice was raw. "No. You will be the first of many."

Realizing he had felt like Mark and said similar words not so long ago, Gabe was not going to let Mark go down the same road. He stepped toward him. "OK, Mark, look at me. Look into my eyes. Squeeze your trigger and shoot me."

"Gabriel, stop," Kate pleaded. "Mark, don't do it. Gabe's a trained killer. He will kill you."

Mark reached up with his left hand to help steady the pistol. "No, I will kill him first."

"No, Mark you are not a killer, you are my brother," said Ellie.

"Shoot—I won't draw on you," said Gabe. "If you want to be a cold-blooded killer, let me be your first. Unlike you, I want to die, I'm ready." Gabe could see the puzzled look on their faces.

"Mark, killing him won't bring Brandy back. Look into your heart," begged Ellie. "You know she would not want this. She met Gabe, remember?"

"No, it won't, and it won't make that guilty feeling you have go away either," Gabe told him.

"I am not guilty, I did not kill her," said Mark.

"You're not guilty of killing her, you're guilty of neglecting her," said Gabe.

"What are you talking about?"

"If you were a killer, I'd be dead already," said Gabe. The minutes and seconds before battles had taught him to notice what drives a man. Above all, he feels their guilt and fears, the guilt of past wrongs and the fear of not being able to make the past right or whole if they should fall. Then after the battle the relief that they have more time, but he sees they rarely make things right. "You know you should have been with her," he continued.

"I–I couldn't," said Mark.

"Your little brother did your job."

"Gabe, stop it, stop pushing him, please," Ellie begged, reaching over to hold his hand in hers.

Gabe did not let up. "Look at him, he wants to be a man, but he is still a boy."

"Mark, if you had been with her, both of you would be dead now," Kate said.

Kate and Ellie looked at each other; Ellie knew what Kate was thinking as they slowly moved closer.

"Mark, I know how you feel." Gabe tells him.

"No, you don't, you can't."

"You feel grief and rage at the same time."

Mark lowered the gun slightly. "I guess I do. So?"

"My wife and I met as young children. After eighteen years of friendship we were allowed to marry in '58. One day we went into New York City, and we were attacked by four men. I was unprepared, and in the struggle we both died that day. I will never forgive myself for not being able to protect her, to save her. I'm not fighting to protect the Union. I did not join the Northern Army, I joined a war. I could be a Yankee or Rebel—whose side I die for means nothing to me."

"Then what are you fighting for?" Mark asked.

"What am I fighting for? I am fighting for the right to die, fighting to rid myself of my guilt. I joined the war to die. I want to fight someone who is able to kill me. That is what I want, so I could be killed like she was—she died fighting for another's life. She died a good death."

"Yours?" Ellie asked.

Gabe yelled, "No. Shoot."

BOOM.

The pistol went off at Gabe, filling the air with gray smoke.

"Oh, my God, I didn't mean to—"

Gabe flinched to his right, toward Ellie, as cloth from his right inside trouser leg flew into the air.

"Gabe!" Ellie yelled.

"I'm sorry," Mark yelled.

Gabe was still standing, and he was a bit surprised to be, considering he was less than fifteen feet away from the pistol.

"Your leg! Let me look," said Kate.

Gabe did a quick assessment. "No, I'm fine. It's just a nick—see? No blood." He looked up at the sky. "Hey, you up there? Can't you create anybody who can shoot straight?"

"Thank the Lord I did not realize my arm was slowly dropping," Mark said.

A few people came out of the house. Several stood on the front porch and stared. Amanda slumped down onto a large padded rocker. Someone yelled out, "What happened?"

"It's OK, go back inside," Kate yelled back to them as she reached for the pistol, but Mark moved away from her.

"No, Kate."

"I came out here to tell you that T.J. is speaking. He told us what happened to them, and the doc is trying to get more information." Ellie tried to shift the focus of the situation.

Mark started to move toward the house, then turned to Ellie, his face grief-stricken. "Who hurt her? Did he say?" he asked.

"Three Union men, the leader with a scar across his right eye," she said.

"Another was a big guy, and the third was a small, slow fellow," said Gabe.

"Yes—how did you know that?" Mark asked as he stepped back, raising the pistol again. "They're your men, aren't they? You know them," he shouted to Gabe.

Gabe quickly shook his head. "No—but I have seen them before. I think they rob the dead, they're most likely deserters."

"Can you find them?" Kate asked.

"I don't know, but I will do everything I can."

"How?" Ellie asked.

"I can start by checking to see if they were temporarily attached to the regiment that covered our retreat route. How is T.J.?"

"Doc Thomas says he has a severe concussion of the brain without fracture, most likely from a rifle butt," said Ellie. "He has a mine ball in his lower leg that he is taking out. Mark, please go inside and help wrap him in hot blankets, and apply bottles of hot water to his extremities. I'll be there in a minute. Go, now."

Gabe looked at Mark. "Mark, when I was growing up, I thought my life was going to make a difference, but now I have no life. Don't go on like me. Make a difference—a good difference—to as many people as you can. Do you understand?"

Mark paused and thought about Gabe's words. "Yes, I do."

The ladies just stared in puzzlement.

"Gabe how does it feel to kill in battle?" Mark asked.

"If you really want to know, ask your brother."

"I want to hear it from you."

"Why me? Why do you want to know?"

"I understand that killing those men won't bring Brandy back, and I know I will be safe serving with my brother away from battle. But you, now, can help me to begin to understand why a man fights and kills, or kills a child or a young woman … what they might have felt, and the cost of their soul. I want to learn it from someone like you who has lost their soul. From someone who has no interest in which side thinks they are in the right or on the same side as God."

"Are you sure? Remember, killing does not make you a man; choosing not to kill does."

"I don't want to hear this," Ellie said as she walked over to the water pump, needing to wash the blood of killing off her hands.

Kate stayed by the men and listened, her heart beating faster with every word.

"As a young man I was taught the realities of war and what to expect in battle. A soldier puts up with much hardship—long hours, stressful conditions, danger to personal safety, separation from loved ones, the loss and mutilation of friends, and more. The initial response of excitement ends as we are more and more submerged in the blood, terror, and carnage of the battlefield. As a battle starts, it's as if your body is taken over and you lose control of yourself. First you're full of emotions, then none at all as your training and experience kick in. You become intensely focused at doing your job so as not to let your fellow troopers down. It's so intense you can go at the enemy all day, until dark or death. A pistol, rifle, or cannon can kill. But you won't really know what it feels like until you look in their eyes in the instant both of you feel it—whether it's a point-blank shot or the thrust of your saber penetrating his body or slashing his throat, causing his blood to gush out in a black-red stream into the air. You're so close it splashes on your face, sometimes you taste it, the eyes still fixed as they stare at you or through you until the body falls over, dead." He paused. "Should I continue?"

"Yes," both replied together as they stared. Ellie sat by the water pump and listened from a distance.

"After your first few battles some drop to their knees,

exhausted. Your hands and body begin to shake, and you start to feel sick. Then a few troopers approach you and stare as if they expected you to fall over dead from the loss of so much of your blood—only to find out very little of it, if any, was yours.

"The first time is the most intense. With each kill you begin to harden or feel indifference. It becomes an act much like breathing … you do it without thinking much about it. That's when some begin to get reckless, careless, some overly cautious, and others fear they lost their soul."

He paused and took a slow, deep breath. "Killing is not what matters; you kill to keep from dying. The most important thing is the bond that soldiers share while killing and being killed. That bond is formed because we know we are all in it together, and we will help one another get through it. This mutual self-sacrifice, teamwork, and covering each other's backs contribute to individual bonding, a unit's cohesion, that fighting spirit. It is a very old pattern, the relationship of unity among troopers, a spirit of familiarity and trust existing between friends. It is the understanding of a soldier's behavior.

"We are taught that a soldier's courage must never fail. We must be manly and independent. Some retreat into silence and do not allow themselves to contemplate their physical or psychological wounds, in part because of a sense of disillusionment by the 'real' nature of warfare in contrast to the civilian vision of a war. Disturbing memories are to be kept to oneself. Yet we group together because we all understand the silent language of the warrior."

"How do you survive a brutal war that kills indiscriminately?" Kate asked.

"You justify your actions by creating rules that you can live with in case you survive."

Ellie walked back over and looked at Gabe. "You should go now. Some soldiers may have heard that shot."

"I know. I'm going." He turned toward her. "Ellie, I will find them and make them pay."

She hugged him and whispered, "I know you will. But at what cost?"

He addressed Mark one more time. "Until I met these ladies,

the only thing I lived for was to die by someone else's hand. It's too late for me, but not for you, Mark. That's my world. Welcome to my hell."

"I will pray for your soul." Ellie gave him a strong hug and a weak, touching smile, hopefully showing him she would rather he not find them if it would cost him his life.

He looked at her. "Save it. Don't waste your prayers on me. You're too late to help me ... use your prayers for the people in that house."

He gave Kate a hug and whispered, "I hope that helped you understand what Alex went through." He ran to Rascal and mounted. Gabe shifted position, his body weight forward, and touched Rascal's right knee with his hat, whispering, "Bow."

Rascal extended his right leg, slowly rocked back on his hindquarters, and lowered his head to his leg, giving them the dramatic exit they sought.

"Goodbye, my ladies." They rode off.

Ellie turned to Kate. "Didn't you say we won't see him anymore?"

"Yes, I did, Ellie."

"So why did he come back?"

"To see you, of course"

"You mean to see you, Kate. Did you learn anything more about him?"

Kate sighed. "He showed us he really does want to die. His pain goes deep. Ellie, are you sure he didn't come to see you?"

"Kate, he knows how to find you."

"Yes, he does—and since he did come back, I'll have my family in Philadelphia see what they can find out about him."

"They can start by checking the roster of the 1st New Jersey."

"If he comes back again, maybe we will know more about him and his money."

"Kate, now who sounds like a thief?"

Fervor Flows and Surges

After letting out a long yawn, Ellie looked around the room. Only Brandy's body was there, wrapped in a bed sheet. On the table next to Ellie were a nearly empty glass and a note from Kate:

Ellie,
 I had to go home. I did not want to wake you, the bourbon knocked you out. Stop in on your way home.
  Love you,
  Kate

The large wall clock said it was 10:30 P.M. After Gabe left, Ellie and Kate had helped take care of Brandy's body and tended to T.J. and the family, then they washed the blood from their bodies and changed their clothes.

Ellie was exhausted and had slept for over an hour in the chair. *I can't stay here any longer. I need fresh air.* She picked up the glass and lifted it in the familiar gesture of a toast. "Thanks, Kate, I needed this." She finished what was left of the drink.

Going out the front door, she went over to the large rocker Amanda had sat in until her husband took her up to bed.

Rocking gently, she sat and looked across the fields, then up to the clear night sky. This was the first time all day that she was able to hear the river, the soothing sound she had first learned and loved as a child. *The water should be warm by now,* she thought. During the hot summer nights the sound would help rock the children to sleep. Each day the river was capable of playing a different tune. Dry days were quieter ones. During and after a storm, it would be roaring like a lion. Each object in the current brought with it new notes, and she rarely sang the same song twice. The notes would tell the kids how deep and what was where in the river. They just needed to listen, and they all learned how to listen to her.

"Lord, hear my prayers ..." Ellie stopped. "I can't find the words, but you know what is in my heart. How many more need to die before we learn the real price of this war, the slaughter of our children? Please end this war soon, and take care of the young."

Minutes felt like hours, but only a few moments had passed. From behind she heard the sound of boots walking across the deck toward her.

His walk was familiar to her. Without turning around she asked, "Why have you come back?"

He stopped very close behind her but did not touch her.

His scent flooded her senses. "Why now?" She asked.

"*Shhh …*" he whispered into her ear and then kissed it softly. "Listen to the river. Feel it flow across your body. What is it telling you?"

His lips moved down and below her ear, kissing her exposed neck. The fragrance of her perfume filled him.

"Oh, no, I forgot to button my—"

"*Shhh …*" Gently he soothed her alarm and moved down, each kiss releasing a bit more pain that had surged in during this miserable day.

"That feels so good," she whispered.

He threw his hat onto the rocker.

Reaching around her, he firmly took her hands and placed them below the base of her neck, just where her nightdress was still buttoned.

"Close your eyes and breathe," he whispered.

She did, and then she opened her hand to free one more button, releasing more anxiety, letting it slip away with the current.

"Breathe slower and deeper."

I should be allowed to loosen up, she told herself, unlocking another.

I deserve this. She loosened one more.

His hand opened then slowly went up to her left shoulder, grabbing it firmly. He turned her to face him, her eyes still closed.

Pulling her body up against his, she could feel his chest taking in deep, slow breaths.

His lips touched her lower lip, holding it firmly, then he moved to her top lip. His hands now grasped both her shoulders, and she wrapped her arms around him. He moved his fingers firmly and slowly down her back. The sheer cotton nightdress could not hide her slender frame, and she leaned back as his fingers slowly moved further down, pausing at her lower back. His hands continued, stopping at her curved hips.

She pulled her lips from his, leaned back to unbutton one more. Nearly all her tension now washed away by her river, her nightdress was opened below her navel.

His next kiss went for her neckline, and then he kissed lower to its base. Each kiss one after another, like the river flowing across her body, sent a melody to her lonely soul, like the hum of passion echoing her freedom. Then the flow rushed over her heart, like a sharp, sandy bend in the river, pausing just long enough to feel how fast it was pounding. Slowly and meticulously it first flowed left, then right around soft, white, fresh mounds of firmness. Then returning to its anticipated course, moving downstream to the inevitable, but not before circling her navel, as if caught in a splendid whirlpool of warmth. She reached down and ran her fingers though his hair. He looked up at her moonlit face as it illuminated her smile, revealing her pleasure. He returned to his tender flow of kisses and again picked up her scent of lavender. Her blood flow was pulsating through her body as she started to tremble.

Out of nowhere a mild gust of wind blew, chilling her body and causing her to open her eyes. She was alone in the rocker, her nightdress closed, and looking around she saw no one.

I must have had a dream ... a real nice one, she thought. Then she was motionless as she remembered the blue Union hat thrown onto the rocker. "Oh, no! Lord, not him, I'm so sorry. Why him?"

Perilous Deeds Lead to Promotion

He returned late in the evening to the regimental camp and reported back that he was not able to find any stragglers or wounded men. He spotted several Rebel patrols and overheard that they had taken many prisoners. He also reported that the rebel Cavalry was moving out, and that he thought they were heading north. Again, none of the officers listened.

"You were right the last time you reported. The Reb Cavalry was at Brandy Station, and not at Culpeper. I will let the General know about your report." Standing off to his left was the large, bearded Sergeant Major whom he'd met when he returned to the war a few days ago. Someone was paying attention. "You're Sergeant Major Canse?"

"If that was a question, then yes I am."

"Thank you."

"Don't thank me, we're both doing our job. Now, get back to your company, and get some rest."

In camp, during their morning meal the men again started talking about yesterday's battle and their lost troopers.

"Gabe, what do you think about how we did?" Corporal O'Keeffe asked.

Carefully thinking about his next words, Gabe looked around at the men.

Before he could respond, Private Lewis jumped in. "I know what you're thinking, Sergeant. So far it was the largest cavalry fight we have ever been in."

"Yes, I agree," Gabe said.

"Yes, by far. What do you think, Sergeant?" Corporal O'Keeffe asked again.

"Yes, it was, but we did not win the battle, and our division lost too many good men." Gabe was trying to send the deliberate message that a victory that costs too many lives is no victory. "But this time we were able to face them as equals."

He saw a change in the faces of the men; they were pleased and proud of their efforts in the clash.

"You men should be proud. Since June '62, when we were covering the Staunton and Strasburg Road, our cavalry has been fighting better against the Southern cavalry."

"Yup, that ninety-mile stretch south to north through Harrisonburg in the Shenandoah forced us to work together."

"Sergeant, what's bothering you?"

"The Army of the Potomac fights three vicious, losing battles against General Lee, with three different generals. It doesn't matter that our army outnumbers them, outguns them, and is better supplied ... we still lose. We need what they have: great leadership. General Lee is a man I have come to admire."

"Do you wish that he was on our side, or that you were on his?"

"Hell, I would have settled for the Black Knight."

"Yup, Colonel Turner Ashby gave us hell in the valley," Private Smalls added.

"His cavalry did a great job screening our cavalry from the rear of Jackson's army."

"Then we finally gave him hell on the 6th of June '62 at Good's Farm, before we were forced to retreat. Good thing the 13th Pennsylvania infantry joined the fighting and killed Colonel Ashby."

"Since then we have been fighting better, and yesterday proves it—right, Gabe?"

He nodded. "Men, you did fight well."

Private Smith ran up, and while trying to catch his breath he leaned in and whispered. "Sergeant, when I walked back from the latrine, I passed the officers' tents, and I heard one say that a complaint from another regiment was made about you."

Gabe looked up at the private, then looked back down and continued to clean his carbine rifle. "I think it is time we get the Army to issue us the new Henry rifle," he said.

Just then 1st Sergeant James walked up. "O'Shea, come with me. The Major wants to see you."

"Can I finish cleaning my weapon?"

"Are you nuts? Get moving."

"Private Lewis, please assemble my weapon. I'll clean it later."

"Don't worry, sergeant, we will take care of it for you," Corporal O'Keeffe responded.

"Yup. It will be all cleaned up by the time you get back,"

Private Smalls added.

"Are they going to make me a General?" Gabe asked the 1st sergeant.

"Don't think so. Maybe a private again. Just watch your mouth."

Arriving outside the tent of Major Hugh Janeway, temporary commander of the regiment since yesterday's battle, he could hear him talking to Captain James H. Hart, the Company A commander since the fall of '62, when Janeway was promoted to Major.

"Sergeant O'Shea, reporting as ordered, sir."

"Come in, Sergeant O'Shea," ordered 1st Lieutenant John Hobensack, also from Company A. He was with Gabe's company since the summer of '62 and was promoted in the fall that same year. Gabe felt he was a good young officer.

"Yes, sir."

Gabe made a mental assessment of the room. He quickly looked around then stood at attention in the middle of the tent. It smelled of sweat, leather, and stale cigar smoke. *Major Janeway is seated in a corner at my far right, sipping what appears to be a cup of tea. Captain Hart is standing next to him, and they both appear to be waiting for Lieutenant Hobensack to address me.*

1st Lieutenant John Hobensack cleared his throat. "At ease, Sergeant O'Shea."

"Yes, sir."

"It was reported to me that you have been hustling some troopers from one of the Michigan Regiments. Do you have anything to say about this?"

"I would not call it hustling, sir."

"What would you call it?"

"Training." Gabe could see both the major and the captain turn their heads slightly so as not to reveal their smiles.

"Training? Please explain what training," he said as he walked around Gabe.

"I was training them on basic military strategy and to take better care of the generous amount of pay the army issues them."

"What basic military strategy?"

"Never underestimate your opponent, and always be prepared for each confrontation or have to deal with the consequence, sir."

"Explain how you did this."

"I would pick a trooper bigger than myself, entice him to arm-wrestle for a cash-in-hand wager, and explain the rules and purpose of the match."

The lieutenant interrupted him. "Did you plan to use the money as your own private account?"

"No, sir. The winner would pick which dead trooper's family with children the money would go to. If they agreed, we'd begin. After I won I would tell those around us to never underestimate your opponent and always be prepared, sir."

"They of course expected to win and keep the money. But from what we understand, you always won. How?"

"Before the war I was taught how to arm-wrestle, which muscles to keep strong. The lessons I received taught me how to take advantage of large men with small hands and even smaller brains. Mostly it's the same arm muscles that we use wielding our sabers. The techniques I learned are what make the difference."

The major then nodded to the captain, who said, "OK, we've heard enough, Lieutenant."

"Sergeant, at attention," Lieutenant Hobensack ordered.

"Yes, sir."

"Remove his stripes." Captain Hart ordered the 1st sergeant to cut the stitching that attached the sergeant insignia to his uniform; first his right arm, then the left, each fell to the ground.

Major Janeway approached and looked Gabe over. "I received an order form the War Department about you. After receiving it, I started to check into your background. Do you know what I found?" he asked with a slight smile.

"No, sir."

"It so happens that in the winter of '61 your family was working with our Governor Charles Smith Olden for your appointment as a 2nd lieutenant, but somehow his order was lost in Washington. I wonder how that happened." He paused to observe Gabe. "You fought well yesterday, even if you were reckless with your own safety. I know the regiment is fond of you, and you are close to your troop, but you will now need to make a change. Are you ready to take on the responsibility that has been granted to you when this regiment was formed?"

"Yes, sir."

"You will stop arm wrestling, and if you choose to send money to widows, do it from your own pocket, which apparently are deep. Do you understand?"

"Yes, sir."

"As you may well know, at Brandy Station we lost our brigade and regimental commander, Colonel Percy Wyndham. He was wounded in the leg and will be gone for some time. We also lost Lieutenant Colonel Virgil Brodrick and Major John Shelmire, who were both mortally wounded in the melee and we now believe may have both died on the field. Captain Henry Sawyer was badly wounded and was captured. So the 1st New Jersey Cavalry lost its colonel, lieutenant colonel, senior major, and a squadron commander all in one day. Needless to say, our regimental command structure was devastated. So, by the order of the Department of War, you are now a 2nd lieutenant in Company A. After yesterday and what we have seen of you since joining the 1st, we would have recommended you for promotion anyway. Even though these orders are more than a year and a half old, don't expect any back pay. With what you have shown us, I would now be promoting you to captain."

He turned and started pacing back and forth, picking his next words very carefully. "I have a feeling that achieving rank is not what drives you. Whatever it is, you need to control it for the sake of your men, do you understand?" He handed Gabe his gold 2nd Lieutenant bars.

"Yes, sir, major."

"You're dismissed. Lieutenant Hobensack, make sure you brief him about tonight."

"Yes, sir."

Newly promoted 2nd Lieutenant Gabriel O'Shea and 1st Lieutenant John Hobensack left the tent together.

Back in the tent, Captain Hart asked, "Major, do you know who was responsible for his orders getting lost?"

"O'Shea, of course, if your family and the governor commissioned you an officer, wouldn't you know?"

"Yes, sir."

"Then why hasn't he asked about it?"

"I don't know, but I think he will make a fine officer."

"Due to his informal military training and lack of discipline, he unfortunately may never go beyond Lieutenant."

"Sir, if I may, I don't think he cares about promotion."

"He doesn't. Did you read his record? He has proven to be a gifted military leader. He once defied a direct order and charged into a large enemy force to rescue two trapped cavalry troopers. That act cost him a promotion. He presents a tough exterior and hides his perceptive ability. Have you noticed that he distrusts authority and always goes with his gut, letting his strong, commonsense morality lead his actions?"

"I'm aware that he dislikes incompetent officers. Do you think he will survive this war?"

"No. I don't think he is trying to do that either, Captain."

"I agree with that, sir. Not without God's help in dealing with what's driving him."

Outside after leaving the major's tent, Lieutenant Hobensack asked, "Sergeant—sorry, Lieutenant—O'Shea, do you have the time?"

"Yes." Gabe pulled out his pocket watch. "It's three thirty-five."

"With my help, you should be able to move in to my tent, clean yourself and your uniform up, get your bars sewn on, and be ready by six-thirty. Then dinner at the major's tent and your first officers' briefing."

"Clean up? I thought I was clean."

"Not clean enough for a lieutenant. But I think you know that. You have passion, Gabe, and your military skills are growing. But to survive as an officer and a leader in battle, you must possess something that many take a lifetime to understand and appreciate."

"And what is that, sir?"

"Patience."

"I know, and I can't wait to get some."

Lieutenant Hobensack shook his head. "At dinner I'm thinking about asking the major whether the army will be issuing us the new Henry repeating rifle."

"Don't."

"Why not?"

"It was discussed; the Army is not planning on replacing the carbines any time soon. You know the government is more concerned about the dollars rather than saving lives."

"Firing 28 rounds per minute with a 16-round magazine can save many of our boys' lives," said Gabe.

"I heard a few of the Michigan regiments got them," one of the men said.

"They got Spencer repeating rifles, not the Henry. Either the state bought them, or the men bought them. I don't know."

"Is there talk about asking the governor to issue them to the regiment, or at least help us pay for them?"

"Yes, but don't expect anything to happen before the fall."

"I was thinking of getting a few for my squad."

"But now you need to think about the whole company."

"I know the men would put up the $35, plus $15 for the bullets of their own money, for a weapon that would improve their chances of surviving this war."

"Company A, armed with new sixteen-shooters sounds good. We can talk to the captain about getting a few for the men."

"Let's try to restart the discussion again after dinner tonight."

During dinner Major Janeway announced the promotions and began briefing the regiment's officers.

"Earlier today I received Brigadier General David Gregg's battle report. A summary follows:

"This command suffered severe casualties. Two regimental commanders were wounded or missing, our brigade commander Percy Wyndham was confirmed as wounded in the leg in the melee, a third field-grade officer wounded, two line officers were killed and 15 wounded, 18 enlisted men were killed, 65 wounded, and 272 missing are presumed prisoners of war. Our men captured eight commissioned officers and two colors. ... The field on which we fought bore evidence of the severe loss of the enemy.

"Gregg singled out our commander Wyndham and Kilpatrick for particular praise, as well as Captain Martin for the fight put up by his artillery battery. He placed blame for his failure to carry Fleetwood Hill on Colonel Duffié, both for delaying his crossing and for his tardiness in arriving on the battlefield.

"It was reported to Gregg that some Pennsylvanians heard a familiar cry: 'Put up your sabers, draw your pistols, and fight like gentlemen!'

"As you know, the First New Jersey has sustained major losses. Especially from our regimental command structure, which was devastated in the fighting for Fleetwood Hill. We have and will continue to promote new leaders from those who proved they are our best. Some officers feel the battle may have been a draw, even if Stuart may claim victory, as he held the field at the end of the day. But for nearly fourteen bitter hours, our troopers battled an enemy that outnumbered our cavalry. Our regiment was the first in battle, and when the order was given to retire, surrounded, we cut our way out and covered the rear.

"Get your men ready—our new orders say that General Lee is on the move. Lee's troop movements away from the Fredericksburg area again have caused Union general Pleasanton to order us to find out where they are going.

"You know what to do. Any questions?"

All were quiet.

"Well done, then. Dismissed."

At the onset of the battle, General Gregg's objective was to take Fleetwood Hill, where the Confederate cavalry had their headquarters. The 1st New Jersey Regiment led the charge and held the Heights for a time but could not keep it. The fighting involved charge and counter-charge and fierce hand-to-hand combat. When more Confederate cavalry arrived, General Gregg and General Buford withdrew to the north bank of the river. Information was received by Gregg that indicated the movement of the Confederate infantry. The invasion of the North was discovered through Confederate dispatches captured on Fleetwood Hill. Confederate casualties were listed as 523, while the Union troops had 936, of which General Gregg's division had 376.

From that time on, the Federal cavalry were to be rated as "worthy antagonists" by their Southern opponents.

PART THREE
The Beginning of the End

In the middle of General Lee's historical march into the north, which started at the Battle of Brandy Station, General Pleasanton reorganized his corps, and General Gregg now commanded the 2nd Division. Gregg led his cavalry division in engagements at Aldie, Middleburg, and Upperville, Virginia. While his fellow, newly promoted 1st Division commander Major General John Buford was initiating the Battle of Gettysburg on July 1, 1863, Gregg was still moving north.

Buford's quick actions to hold off the Confederate army with only his cavalry division was critical in securing the high ground for the Union Army that was racing up from the south of Gettysburg. Greggs's division arrived midday on July 2 and took up positions to protect the right flank and rear of the Union Army, but on the morning of July 3 he was ordered to move west and away from this critical area.

Gregg refused his orders and requested to stay at his location. He also asked Brigadier General George A. Custer, commander of a brigade in the 3rd Division, to stay and help guard this key junction. Custer agreed, despite having to refuse orders from his division commander.

Midday on July 3, General Stuart's 6,000-man cavalry force started a large raid to flank the Union right and hit their wagon trains and lines of communications, hoping to exploit the large Confederate infantry charge on the Union center, which had just started.

Three miles east of Gettysburg, in a large field, Stuart's force assaulted and collided with Gregg's division and Custer's brigade. A lengthy battle ensued, including hand-to-hand combat and mounted troops.

These two cavalry engagements lead by Buford and Gregg at the start and the end of the largest battle of the American Civil War would prove to be critical.

The telegraphs were clicking away, spreading the news fast: *The war once again is flowing north.*

Before midday on July 1, Ellie received the news. She rode up to Kate's house, dust flying everywhere. She jumped off and ran in.

"Kate, you here?"

"What is the big hurry?" asked Kate.

"Did you hear? It's all over the wire."

"What is?"

Ellie leaned against the doorframe to catch her breath. "The first big battle in the North started this morning, just over the Pennsylvania border near where you grew up."

"Oh, no." Kate slumped into a chair.

"What happened?"

"I had another dream last night," said Kate.

"About who?"

"All I remember is it was cavalry, and our boys were in the middle of it."

"Do they get killed?" asked Ellie.

"One gets hurt bad."

"Which one?"

"I couldn't tell ... all the troopers were wearing black."

Ellie's face was serious. "Whenever you have these types of dreams, something bad happens."

"I know, and I have a bad feeling about this one. We need to get to the battlefield as soon as possible," said Kate.

Ellie looked at her. "You pack the food and water. I'll go home and get two fresh horses—if not horses, then mules. I'll get something for us to ride."

Kate nodded. "Yes, and bring extra clothes. See you in an hour or less. I'll plan the route. Go!"

Let's see: We will need to travel by horse and rail, and as we get closer we can find out where the fighting is. The best and fastest way would be to cross at Kelly's Ford, then ride the thirty miles to Manassas Junction to board a train to Washington, then on to Baltimore. By then we should know exactly where to go—we probably need to continue on to Westminster. That's about one hundred and sixty miles to southern Pennsylvania. If we are lucky, we can be on a train at Manassas Junction by dark, then in Baltimore late tonight.

In Baltimore they encountered trouble boarding a train.

"Look at all these people!" said Ellie. "I haven't seen so many in a long time."

Two days earlier, Stuart's cavalry had clashed briefly with and overwhelmed two companies of the 1st Delaware Cavalry, chasing them down the Baltimore Road and causing a panic in the city.

"Ellie, did you hear? So far the fighting is at Gettysburg."

"I think we have three choices. We can go back home, wait the panic out here, or leave before sunup and ride the rest of the way."

"Let's ride—it's twenty miles to Winchester, then just over fifteen miles to Gettysburg. Without killing our mules we can be there in ten hours. We should leave at five in the morning."

* * *

Stepping onto Hanover Road, right in front of me was Spangler's house. I immediately recognized where I was. Our division was commanded by Brigadier General David M. Gregg. His cousin Colonel J. Irvin Gregg commanded one brigade, and the newly formed "Michigan Brigade" was commanded by Brigadier General George Custer, who was on loan to our division and was positioned on the Hanover Road, where I now stand. To my right was Pennington and Randol's cannons, and behind them on the Low Dutch Road about a half mile away was our brigade, commanded by Colonel John McIntosh, consisting of the 1st New Jersey, the 3rd Pennsylvania, and the 1st Maryland regiments.

Walking slowly on the Low Dutch Road, I reached where my regiment was positioned. I had to pause for a moment. The emotional rush of the midday battle started to take hold of my body as I began to relive the clash. The first thing I remember was the firing of four Rebel cannons:

BOOM. BOOM. BOOM. BOOM.

It was before noon, and I could see some of the smoke from the cannons. My heart started beating faster, and my hands and legs began to shake. Then our cannons returned fire ... where I now stand I am reliving it, I can feel it. I can still smell the familiar scent of burning black powder, watching the artillery duel begin to fill the air with thick, gray smoke. Our horse artillerymen got the better of their guns.

Then the Rebels came from the area near Rummel's farmhouse to attack our skirmish line, which was a small, dismounted force that included two of our squadrons—two from the 3rd Pennsylvania, and a company from another regiment. They were on the far side of the large field in front of me, puffs of smoke revealing where men were engaging each other.

"Rascal, let's keep moving."

Arriving where my regiment had been positioned on the Low Dutch Road, I needed to dismount, and in so doing I fell to my knees.

Mounted at this same spot earlier in the day, and using my field glasses, I could see the battle as if I were a witness and not a participant; that would change. We were here to protect the Union rear and protect the Baltimore Pike, the main avenue of supply and communications for the Army.

Our boys fought hard to stop the enemy and push them back. I could see the 5th Michigan Cavalry colors as they rode in to reinforce the line; they were armed with the Spencer repeating rifles, which seemed to increase their numbers. They were able to hold, but not for long, as more of the enemy reinforcements arrived. A large charge of Rebels rode at them, and they could not hold any longer. The skirmish line and 5th Michigan began to scatter.

Then another Michigan regiment came charging in to support them. Later I learned it was the 7th Michigan, personally led by Brigadier General Custer. Waves of horsemen, maybe 700 men, collided in a furious fight along the fence line at point-blank range—sabers wheeling above their heads, carbines and pistols firing and filling the air with more smoke, making it difficult to see which force held the ground.

We did ... we could see the Rebels retreating, but again General Stuart sent more regiments, causing the 7th Michigan to fall back in a disorderly retreat. We held back and watched as more Rebels poured in.

Again our horse artillery batteries fired on them, but still they came. Then another Michigan regiment charged up to meet the Rebels. This was the first time in this war I was able to watch and not participate, as two large cavalry columns approached each other at such speed until suddenly and violently they crashed into each other. The sound was horrific, so many of the horses flipped end-over-end, and many of their riders were crushed or trampled from the impact.

Watching both sides fighting desperately in the field, I felt helpless. Then finally it was our turn. General McIntosh personally led our brigade into the battle. The 3rd Pennsylvania and the 1st New Jersey charged across the open field, making a fearless, fast, and hard dash into the left flank of the Southern cavalry.

As we closed in on the Rebel force, they were now engaged in their front and both flanks, thus nearly surrounded. The killing and being killed went on, as more were trampled and crushed to death by friend or foe, with or without their mounts.

By this time the weight of our division's three brigades minus our reserves were attacking the Rebels from three sides, and they were forced to withdraw. We were in no condition to pursue much further beyond our original skirmish line.

Sometimes to the victors is the burden of walking the battlefield, finding foe and friends, both two-and four-legged, tangled, mauled, and bloody. The slaughter of men and beast could have been far worse. The intense battle lasted nearly four hours, and the field may have been covered with over four hundred dead or wounded men, and nearly half as many horses.

This time the tables were turned; this time JEB Stuart was the attacker, and we were ready and waiting. Barely three weeks ago we attacked him, and we had to leave our dead and many of our wounded behind.

After the battle several officers estimated there were about 3,000 Rebel cavalry in the battle and a handful of cannons ... we had nearly as many men, but more cannons.

Sometime after 4:30 P.M., as massive thunderclouds were forming, our division was making ready to move away from Gettysburg.

"'There was no blue or gray, just red.' Where have I heard that before?" Gabe mumbled. "Captain Hart, I want to stay and make sure our wounded were moved quickly to a hospital and to escort the remaining prisoners to the holding area."

"Why?"

"The truth, sir?"

"Yes, lieutenant. What are you up to?"

"I have seen deserters robbing the dead. I want to make sure they don't go through our battlefield and rob these men."

"Lieutenant, you have my permission. Do you want a few men?"

"No. I will do this on my own."

"No, take a squad. Pick 'em, or I will."

"Yes, sir. Corporal O'Keeffe, take privates Mott, Gregory, and Smalls, and wait over there."

"Lieutenant, you have until eight o'clock." He pulled out his map and pointed to a spot. "Tonight we will be here."

"Yes, sir. I will only be a few hours behind you, sir. Do you know where the wounded are being sent?"

"Both the wounded and the prisoners are going to a location west of the Baltimore Pike along Rock Creek. Ironically, this was the same area Stuart's cavalry had hoped to move through to reach the Union rear."

"Thank you, sir."

"Anybody but you, I would never—" he told Gabe.

"Don't worry, someone who deserves it may die."

"That does not surprise me."

* * *

"This is agonizing."

"Look, the creek is flowing blood red," Private Smith called out.

"Men, this is only some of the intense slaughter the two armies waged on each other over these three days of conflict," Gabe told them.

"Some? This is appalling," said Corporal O'Keeffe. "There must be many other hospitals spread out all over the battlefield."

"Let's go and move the remaining prisoners to the holding area," ordered Gabe.

He saluted a major as he approached. "Lieutenant O'Shea from the First New Jersey Cavalry, transferring these four cavalry prisoners taken east of here."

"So you're a lieutenant now, and not a sergeant?"

"What, sir?"

"Two ladies where looking for a Sergeant O'Shea, from the First New Jersey. I guess they didn't know you were promoted."

"When were they here?" asked Gabe.

"About an hour ago. I hear they were also looking for a Rebel major."

"Which way did they go, sir?"

"I sent them to where the cavalry battle was."

"Thank you, sir." He turned to the others. "Men, I'm going back to the field."

"Sir, we are going with you."

"No. Head back to the regiment," Gabe ordered.

"Sir, we will wait for you," said Corporal O'Keeffe.

Gabe pulled out his map. "Corporal, have the men meet up with me where Rock Creek passes the Baltimore Pike, here." He placed his finger on the map. "If I'm not there by six o'clock, you are to ride ahead and meet the regiment here. You need to get there by eight o'clock. Got it?"

"Sir, you want us to leave without you?" the corporal questioned.

"Yes. I'll catch up with you."

* * *

On the second day of the battle, their ride up the Baltimore Pike to Westminster, Maryland, was difficult. The Pike was packed with supplies going to battle and wagon trains of the wounded, along with lines of prisoners moving south. When they finally reached Westminster, the Union Army notified them that they must take the Taneytown Road to Gettysburg. After they reached Taneytown, the Union army would not let them proceed until the next day.

"Kate, are you praying? In all the years I have know you, I don't think I ever heard you pray."

"Cause I don't, but I have to admit that on this trip I have talked to God a few times. Do you think He is listening?"

"Our Lord always listens, especially to you."

"Is it because I surprise Him?"

"You surprise everyone, except Him. He hears you, our Lord is always listening."

"Nothing surprises him, not even me—but you know I still try to."

The news they had gotten on the way up had been extremely grim. The look on Ellie's face as they got closer did not reveal what she was feeling and seeing. The condition of some of the prisoners and wounded from both sides was worse than they had thought it would be — and what they saw only told a small part of the story. Every chance they had, they would ask about the cavalry.

"Right now I will do anything to find at least one of them alive," Kate said.

Riding their mules, they finally arrived from the southeast in the late afternoon of July 3 as rain clouds began to blow in. They were directed to turn off the Taneytown Road, near Rock Creek, where several field hospitals were overwhelmed by the wounded from both sides.

It was a huge layout of tents and hospital wagons moving in and out west of White Church Road, all along Rock Creek.

"My God, this is unbearable," Ellie softly mumbled.

"This is horrendous," Kate agreed.

My Lord, why? were the words that flooded both their minds over and over upon arriving. For more than two hours, they walked through as many hospitals in the area as they could—and there were many. Different areas were set up to support each corps. Finally Ellie let go of her mule and fell to the ground onto her knees, partly from exhaustion but mostly from anguish.

"I need to rest for a bit. I'm going to stop looking and help these field surgeons. They are exhausted."

"No, you can't. We must look for our men. They could be hurt and dying."

"No," Ellie replied firmly, looking up at Kate. "Right now, all I know for sure is all these men are hurt and dying, and they need help now."

"I can't look for them alone."

"Then stay here and help."

"No, not until I find at least one of them."

Tears ran down Ellie's face. "Look around you, Kate. Nothing is absolute here. They may already be gone or dead and buried, and we will not have been of any help to anybody. My Lord, the smell of decaying limbs, bodies, feces, and death is so thick I can't breathe. Every time I try to take a breath, my body wants to return my last meal to the mass of flesh upon this earth."

"Then do it. You won't be the first."

"No, I do not want to desecrate the decomposing, soulless bodies any more than they are."

"You said it: Their souls are no longer here."

Ellie was anguished as she glared around her. "I can't stop crying. So many of my Southern boys lay dead on this land."

No sooner had she finished wiping her tears when a young Union lieutenant approached them. "Excuse me, ladies. I hear you're looking for the cavalry."

Kate turned to respond. "Yes, we are."

"See that major over there?"

"Yes. Who is he, and what is he doing?" Kate asked.

"He is organizing that mass of prisoners, and I hear some are from a cavalry battle. Go see him."

"Thank you. Thank you so much," Ellie responded with a smile as she regained her strength and stood.

Kate stared for a moment at her. "Finally! I guess your God wants you to keep looking."

Ellie stopped, turned toward Kate, and stepped in close to her face with a stern voice and resolve that she rarely showed. "No matter how this turns out, we are coming back here to help those field surgeons with all these wounded boys, North or South, for as long as it takes, or you go home alone."

"No matter how long," Kate echoed.

"Major, sir, where can we find some cavalry prisoners?" Kate blurted.

"Over there, in that group."

"Thank you. Would you know where they were picked up?"

"Probably about three miles east of here in a large field. You can go ask them, but don't give them anything."

"Not even water?" asked Ellie.

"Only water," said the major.

"What about the Union cavalry wounded? Do you know where they are?" Ellie asked.

"The few that came in are in that tent behind you."

Ellie looked at Kate. "Kate, he's not there. We looked in that tent already."

"Who are you looking for?" the major asked.

"Sergeant O'Shea, First New Jersey."

"Sorry, don't recognize that name or that unit." He turned to a young man standing near the tent flap. "Private, escort these ladies, and stay with them until they leave the area."

"Yes, sir."

"Thank you, Major." Kate smiled at him before turning away.

Kate and Ellie passed by several wounded soldiers on makeshift beds on the ground. "Hi, boys. You want some water?" Ellie asked.

"Yes, ma'am."

"Me, too."

"Any of you know Captain William Randle McMurphy?" Kate asked.

"You mean Major Mac?" asked one private. "He is a major now, Miss. I mean, he was—"

"Don't say that. You don't know for sure," a wounded Rebel sergeant said.

"Why? What happened to him, Sergeant?" Kate asked.

"I saw him get struck by a saber," said another wounded man. "Then he fell from his horse."

"Yeah, and he's not with us here," said the first private, "and we keep askin' if a wounded major came in, and they keep telling us no, not yet."

"If he's dead, he is still on the field," the sergeant told the ladies.

"Where?"

"About three miles east of here in a large field, just past where the Low Dutch Road meets up with the Hanover Road," a corporal told them.

"Thanks, boys. Take care of yourselves," Kate told them.

"Anybody else want any more water?"

"Me."

"Me, too."

"Here. Pass it around and finish it. We'll get more."

They rode in silence for nearly an hour before Ellie spoke.

"I think we are lost. We must have passed it by now."

"It's getting late. We need to find him soon if he has any chance of surviving."

"I know. Let's try over there. And Kate, you must stop checking all the gray-clothed bodies, or we will never reach the field before dark."

"OK."

"Look over there. Let's ask those Yankees."

* * *

I need to focus on my task. I need to take slow, deep breaths and focus. Get up now and walk. Come on, Rascal, let's go into the field again. Good. I feel better walking into the field where only hours ago we had ridden hard and fast and killed. I now walk among the dead who still lie where they had fallen. This time I avoid looking at the faces of the dead, especially the young ones. There were a few that I remember, looking into their eyes and shooting or striking them with my saber, knowing some went down. I don't want to remember their lifeless eyes and their faces as their bodies start to bloat and attract flies in the day's sun.

Off to my left there's a woman yelling at the dead, weeping as she mourns her loss. I'm relieved that I'm too far to see if he is wearing gray or blue. I remember only seeing Mac for a second ... he had blood on his blouse as he swung his saber. I don't think he saw me. He was not among the prisoners or the wounded we removed after the battle.

As the smell of the dead lying in the sun begins to rise, I thought I had gotten used to it, but that's one memory I will keep with me for as long as I live. I remember there are two shallow depressions on each side of the field, each one concealing small creeks. I am walking over to the far side of the field, toward Rummel's house, to the small creek. This should provide us with some shade and water.

Arriving, I see there is no water fit to drink. A few badly wounded horses and men made their way here to escape the killing; this depression became their final resting place.

I continue on, walking along the creek, toward where our picket line had fought, until I can hear the faint sound of people yelling at each other. As I get closer I can see one woman holding a rifle and using the bayonet end to hold off two Union soldiers, and another woman yelling and waving her arms in the air.

"Rascal, stay here. I'm going to get a better look. I'll call you if I need help."

Moving slowly toward the ruckus I watch my steps to avoid stepping or tripping over the dead. Looking out over the depression to the edge of the field, I can clearly hear the women arguing with the two Union soldiers.

"You're not a soldier. You both are just deserters," one woman shouted.
"No, we are here to remove the dead."
"No, you weren't. We caught you robbing them."
"You're a killer. It was you who killed our friend."
"No, ma'am. I didn't kill her, I didn't kill nobody."
"Not you, him. You shot her."
"Lady, I don't know what you are talking about."
"Yes, you do." With both pistols drawn, Gabe stepped onto the field. One woman was to his right, the other to his left, and the two men were directly in front of him.
Each pistol pointed toward a man.
"Good day, ladies. Do you need my assistance?"
"Gabe, thank God you're here!" shouted Ellie.
Gabe took a few more steps to his right to get completely out of the creek bed and onto the field, toward Kate. He addressed the two men. "You two were at Brandy Station last month. I'm not asking; I know it was you."
The man with the large scar on his face was holding a rifle. The young, slow one was holding a small bag.
"Don't lie to me, private, or I'll shoot you were you stand. You don't remember me, do you?"
"No, sir, we don't."
"I was a sergeant last year when I rode through the Antietam battlefield and first caught you robbing the dead. I should have turned you in then as deserters."
"Yup, I remember."
"Shut up, you stupid kid," the man with the scar yelled.
"Article 20 says that if you're accused of being a deserter, you'll be tried. If convicted, you shall suffer death, or such other punishment as sentenced through a court-martial."
"Dead? You gonna shoot me, sir?"
"Maybe not you, kid. But him I'll shoot for killing a child."
"Lieutenant, you gonna shoot me in front of the ladies?"
"If he doesn't, Scarface, I will," Kate told him.
"There was a third man, a big man. Where is he?"
Click. Click.

Gabe heard the sound of two rifle-hammers locking into firing position behind him.

"Behind you, lieutenant. Did you miss me? They call me Big Joe."

Slowly he tried to glance over his left shoulder.

"Don't think about turning to look at me," Big Joe told him.

Ellie closed her right hand and then showed Gabe two fingers.

"It sounds like you added another deserter."

"Yup, and now it is the four of us, and only one of you."

"I didn't know the army would take men who can't count. What I know is, it's the three of you with one shot each, against me and my pistols with twelve shots."

"He's right. I ain't got no rifle."

"Shut up, boy! If you ain't armed, you ain't no good to us."

"I like these odds. What about you, Big Joe?" Gabe looked over at the boy. "Boy, you want to die today?"

"No, sir."

"Shut up, boy!" said the man with the scar. "He is messing with your dumb head. If the lieutenant lives, we all hang."

"Boy, if you don't want to die today, move away from him." Gabe motioned with his left hand to show the boy where to move to avoid getting shot. Ellie noticed he was waving his hand up and down more than left and right, and he was glancing at her, not the boy. She looked down to see a pistol three feet from her in Gabe's direction.

"Like I said, I like my odds." Just then, two more men came up out of the creek bed behind Ellie.

"How do you like your odds now, lieutenant?"

"If they are with you, your odds are getting a bit better."

"Gabe, don't shoot them!" Ellie yelled. "They did not hurt us."

"They didn't hurt you yet. They killed Brandy, and now they will try to kill us," Kate yelled to her.

"Let's all walk away and forget about this," Ellie pleaded as she fell to her knees.

"No. He killed Brandy. I'm going to make him pay." Kate pointed the rifle she was holding at the man with the scar.

"Woman, you judging me? You ever kill someone?"

"Maybe. But I'm not here to judge you. I'm here to send you to her God," she said, glancing at Ellie. "It's his job to judge you."

"Lieutenant, sir, I don't kill nobody."

"Kate, you got him?" Gabe asked,
"I sure do."

Gabe's eye bounced from the four men in front to the ladies and back again. As Ellie went to her knees, she used her dress to cover the pistol. But now she appeared to be having trouble reaching for it under the fabric.

"No, wait. I need to pray for all of our souls," she told everyone as she rocked back and forth on her knees.

"What? Not now!" Kate yelled to her.

"Yes, Kate. Now," said Ellie steadily.

"Lord, if someone should die today, please let it only be the one who killed Brandy."

"The Boss did it. He did it." The boy pointed to the scar-faced man.

"Shut up, boy, or I will kill you too."

"No, you're not. Because I'm going to kill you first," Kate told him.

"No, Kate. Not yet," Gabe shouted.

"When?" Kate yelled out.

"Not yet."

"Gabe, he goes first no matter what," Kate told him.

"Mr. Scarface, it looks like you're going to be the first one to die. Because she is our Boss. Right, Kate?"

"Yup. And I'm getting tired of waiting."

"Lieutenant, you will be the second. Big Joe, Sam, move apart so it will be harder for him to get the both of you before one of you gets a shot off," Scarface yelled out to them.

Click.

Silence.

Click.

Big Joe and his new friend Sam heard that familiar sound from behind them.

"Don't move, or the both of you will be the first to die." The soft voice was coming from directly behind them and very low to the ground from a wounded soldier, lying in the grass.

"Big Joe, Sam move apart!" the Boss yelled again.

"Shut up! Don't respond. The first one to move gets the both of you killed," the voice told Big Joe and Sam.

"Looks like you're not their boss anymore," Kate snickered. "Who's their boss now? Me."

"Do the both of you want to be executed as deserters?" he yelled to them again.

"I don't think they hear you," Kate told him.

"Please, all of you—drop your weapons and leave," Ellie said.

"No! Gabe, Scarface, and Big Joe stay. They need to pay for killing Brandy. The rest can leave!" Kate yelled out.

"Big Joe, do you hear them? They want to kill us for hurting that girl," the Boss yelled again.

"Is that true, Big Joe? You killed Miss Brandy?" Ellie asked.

Another soft voice on the ground spoke out. "Captain? Sorry, but I can't last much longer."

BOOM.

Right next to Mac's face a pistol went off, practically deafening him and spitting that putrid black-powder smell in his face. The gray smoke gave their location away.

As Big Joe went down to his knees, looking down he saw a hole in his chest.

BOOM.

Mac fired at Big Joe and he fell over onto his face. Sam immediately dropped his weapon.

The Boss swung his rifle at Gabe.

BOOM. BOOM. BOOM.

In an instant, three rounds fired from three different weapons struck Scarface. His body fell back, dead. Ellie pointed her pistol at the kid as the two men behind her raised their weapons. Gabe immediately fired at them.

BOOM. BOOM.

They turned and ran off into the creek bed. Gabe went after them. Just as he passed Ellie, she lunged at him. They both fell to the ground and rolled down the slope. Angrily, he started to shake free. She could see the rage in his eyes. She let go and moved away from him. Seeing the fear in her face, he dropped his pistols and looked at his hands. Ellie quickly reached over and gently placed her soft, white hands over his.

"It is OK. I know you would never hurt me."

"I'm sorry Miss Ellie, but ... but I ..."

"*Shhhh.* It's over."

"Thank you, Ellie, for stopping me from killing those men."

"Gabe, if it had been anybody but you, I would not have. You have done enough killing."

"Ellie, you …" He paused to find the right words. "You killed him."

"No, I didn't. I shot him in the leg. You and Kate killed him."

"Do you think she knows that you—"

"Nope, and don't tell her. Besides, you know she would like the idea that I helped to kill him."

"Is that her first?"

"I hope so. I hope it will be her last."

"Me, too."

"Let's go, Lieutenant. I like the sound of your new rank."

"You do?"

They picked up their weapons and walked over to Kate.

"Yup, she aims to restore your conscience to your soul," Kate told him.

"Is Ellie rubbing off on you, Kate?"

"Don't know. It was a long trip up here, and she did lay into me a few times about my conscience. That's if I still have a conscience and a soul by the end of this war, especially now that I have killed someone."

"Ladies, stay here with the boy."

Both ladies ignored him, and with the boy they walked slowly behind Gabe.

"I didn't know you had a pistol," Kate told Ellie.

"I didn't know your rifle was loaded," Ellie responded.

"Neither did I."

"Good bluff," Ellie told her.

Gabe immediately turned his attention to the smoke and gunfire that came from behind them as he walked closer. He saw one man standing; his hands empty at his side and gray smoke floating in the air around him.

Did that man shoot Big Joe? he wondered.

Gabe looked over to the man still standing, about sixty feet back.

"Who fired those shots?" Gabe yelled. "Who's there? Let me see you."

"I did, Gabe."

Gabe looked down. Fifteen feet away, lying among bodies of troopers and horses, was Mac.

"Captain Mac, your wounded arm—how did you …"

A sergeant who was lying next to Mac mumbled, "I fired first, sir."

"You're wounded too, sergeant —anyplace else besides your leg?" He knelt down next to both of them.

"I don't think so, sir."

"I don't care which one of you did the shooting, you saved me and the ladies."

"Yankee, that's twice now I saved you. It's time for payback, and I'll call it even."

Kate stared at the boy.

"Stop walking, boy. Ellie, this one has to die too." Kate pointed the spent rifle at him.

"No ma'am, I don't hurt nobody. I promise I'll go back to my regiment."

"No, Kate, there has been enough killing. Look around you," Ellie told her.

"He needs to pay for being involved." Kate pulled the pistol from Ellie's hand. "Good—it still has unspent rounds."

"Gabe will make sure he gets what he deserves. He is only a scared boy."

Gabe shouted to them. "Ladies, hurry, bring him over here. I need your help."

"Mac! Oh, my," Kate called out, seeing who Gabe was helping.

"Gabe, deal with these two Yankees. We'll check the wounds," Ellie told him.

"We need to get them to a field hospital now," Kate told Ellie.

"One horse won't be enough. We need a wagon."

"How did you get here?" Gabe asked them.

"We came by mule and train," Kate responded.

"Where are the mules?"

"We got lost, and a Union captain on the other side of Wolf's Hill had us escorted here. Then they took the mules and gave me five dollars," Ellie said.

"Ladies, I'll ride and get some help."

"No. If Union troops find them, who knows what will happen. It's better if you're here."

"I'll go," Kate told them.

"No, now it's my turn, I'll go. Kate, you're better at this doctor's stuff than me. Besides, now I get to ride Rascal."

Gabe looked into her eyes with concern.

"It will be ok, don't worry." She told him.

"Ok, get my men. Go back down the Low Dutch Road to the Baltimore Pike. Go right for one and half miles. That should put you at Rock Creek. That's where I ordered them to wait for me. Tell Corporal O'Keefe what we need, he'll help you."

"See you soon." Kate smiled at her. "Hurry, I don't know how much longer they will last."

"Wait. Let me reload that pistol you picked up. You may need it," Gabe said to Ellie as he took the weapon from Kate.

"No thanks, lieutenant! I won't need it again." Off she went.

"Gabe, where are you going? I need you to help me stop the bleeding."

"Some of these dead may have medical supplies on them, and I need something to tie these men up."

"Sir, like I told the lady, I don't hurt nobody. I promise I'll go back to my regiment."

"Sorry, boy, I want to let you go back, but if I do, she will shoot me." He looked over at Kate.

"Here, take this bag. It's got lots of stuff in it."

"Look inside for something that will work as a field tourniquet."

"Like what, sir?"

"Look for a thick compress and a stick of wood, about six inches long, wrapped up in a handkerchief."

"Gentlemen your belts did good on your wounds, but I need to replace them with better tourniquets," Kate told them.

* * *

"Look, here comes your lady friend," the boy told them.

"Gabe! Ellie did it, she found your men, and they have a wagon."

Ellie rode up with Corporal O'Keeffe and his men. Gabe looked to acknowledge them, as O'Keeffe and his men glanced at the scene.

"Kate, let my men know as soon as you are ready to load the wounded."

"Now, Gabe, now. Men, load up."

"Yes, ma'am."

Gabe approached Ellie. "Are you OK?"

"Yes, I'm fine. How are they doing?"

"OK. You got back fast."

"Your men were already on the way here when they heard the shooting. We ran into each other on the Low Dutch Road. It took longer to find a wagon we could use."

"Lieutenant, you are always full of surprises—but this? When Ellie told us you found two wounded and had two prisoners, this is not what I pictured."

"It's not? I'm glad I can still surprise you, Corporal."

"No, I think you need your eyes checked. You can't tell blue from gray."

"Captain McMurphy saved my life twice." He then turned and pointed to the Yankee prisoners. "These men are deserters who were robbing the dead. I'm not using my eyes to see blue or gray, I'm using my heart to feel good and evil."

"Hurry, men. As soon as you load the two wounded men into the wagon, tie these two men to it. They can walk or run if they have to," Corporal O'Keeffe ordered. "Then help the ladies up."

"Gabe, thanks for letting me ride Rascal. Your men recognized him immediately."

"We're ready, lieutenant."

"Then let's move out, men. Straight to the hospital."

Captain William Randle McMurphy and Sergeant Wilson were with the famous 7th Virginia Cavalry, also known as Ashby's Cavalry. Now their war was over. Mac would live, but his rebellion would cost him his left arm at the elbow. Sergeant Wilson would also survive, with one less leg. After months of recovering, and time spent in limited rehabilitation, they would be sent home.

Riding to the hospital area, Gabe asked, "Will you ladies be staying?"

"Yes, for a while. We want to make sure they have the best chance of making it through."

The group arrived back at the field hospital around six o'clock, as the expected evening storm started. Gabe spotted the major, who was still processing POWs. "Corporal, take the wounded to the hospital. Private Smith, untie these men from the wagon and follow me." The wounded soldiers were unloaded and immediately taken care of.

"Major." Gabe handed him a letter he had written on the way. The major unfolded and read it.

"This states that these men are to be tried for desertion." The major glanced at the prisoners.

"Yes, sir. I can't stay—my cavalry unit is moving out—and I don't know what regiment they are from. It's all in that letter."

Gabe turned and stepped in front of the two boys. "In my letter, I was lenient. But if I ever find out you deserted again, I will hunt you down, and next time the war won't ever hurt you like I will. Do you understand?"

In unison and with fear in their voices they replied, "Yes, sir."

Gabe looked over to the hospital area and saw that his men couldn't stop staring and talking to the ladies. He walked over to the group.

"I need to know, why are you ladies here?" Gabe asked.

"The night of June 30th, Kate had another dream about you and Mac." Ellie explains.

"It was a bad one, so we headed north early the next day." Kate added, and asked him, "Why did you come back to the battlefield?"

"I heard you were looking for me."

"Corporal O'Keeffe, when I first saw your lieutenant, he was wearing Union rags and had gotten the snot kicked out of him by some Southern boys."

"Corporal, are we ready to ride?"

"Ready when you are, sir. We should leave before the heavy rain starts."

"Ladies, we must be going."

"Goodbye, boys. Please stay alive," Kate told them.

"Yes, thank you all, and be safe," Ellie added.

"Men, mount up! Move out! I'm right behind you."

Private Gregory whispered, "Sure you are, Lieutenant." The ladies smiled at his comment.

Kate gently kissed Gabe on his cheek then hugged him as she whispered in his ear, "Thank you. Be safe, and goodbye. I will never forget you, my wounded warrior."

Ellie added, "Thank you for keeping your promise to get the men responsible for Brandy's death—without getting yourself or too many others killed."

"Well, I did have help." He smiled at Kate.

"Yes, you did," Kate blurted out.

"Ellie, your God sent me two beautiful angels to watch over me."

"That he did. What else will he be sending you?" Kate asked.

"I don't know, but I can't wait to find out."

After watching Gabe ride off, Kate turned to Ellie. "Well, Miss Ellie, did you learn anything new about Gabe?"

"Yes. What did you learn?"

"We knew he tries his best to be a charming gentleman. But once again, we saw a fearless man who fights with determination. I get the feeling he likes to pretend he's not as smart as he really is."

"Kate he is also full of rage. I saw it in his eyes. But the instant he saw my fear, he regained his control."

"I saw that, too. You know what you need to do?"

"What?"

"Soothe the savage beast within."

"That's what you do best, Kate. Not me."

"Not this time," she whispered to herself.

Gabe and his men left the hospital to rejoin their division just as the heavy rain began to fall.

First thing the next morning, in the pouring rain on the 4th of July, they were ordered to Emmitsburg, Maryland.

Riding out on the Emmitsburg Road alongside 1st Lieutenant John Hobensack, Gabe said, "You saw it yesterday. What a difference repeating rifles make!"

"Yes we all saw what Custer's Michigan Fifth and Sixth regiments were able to do with them."

"I'm going to do whatever it takes to get some for our regiment, even if I have to start buying them myself. Maybe some of the other companies will get the idea and do the same."

"Let's hope so."

"What was our total regiment count?"

"We brought two hundred sixty-nine men to the field, suffered nine wounded."

"No one was killed or captured?"

"Not in our regiment … not this time."

"What about the other regiments?"

"Our division had about two-hundred-fifty casualties. Over two hundred of them were from Custer's brigade alone. At last count, the dead, wounded, and Confederate taken prisoners were over one-hundred-seventy."

"The Michigan men paid this time for holding the field."

"Yes, they did. But usually we pay a higher price and don't hold the field, so it was a victory for us."

"At Brandy Station we made a big step forward, fighting toe-to-toe with Stuart. Today, we finally whipped him."

"General Gregg was right—that intersection was critical," John pointed out.

"If he hadn't convinced General Custer to stay, we would have been whipped. Adding the regiments from his brigade was the difference."

"Let's hope that someone recognizes what he did today. General Gregg has a brilliant military mind, and he is a great leader."

"What are you saying? He has replaced your wonderful General Lee?" John asked.

"No, Lee is an army general; we still need someone who can go toe-to-toe with him. At least we now have the two best cavalry leaders in the field, Gregg and Buford"

"Yes—we can hope, pray, and write a lot of letters home on their behalf."

"Did you find what you were looking for?" John asked.

"Yes. All is good."

They rode silently in the rain for a while. Then 1st Lieutenant John Hobensack commented on the irony of the weather. "It's not fitting that our Lord has it rain today."

"I think it is fitting."

"Why do you say that?"

"It's a day to wash away the blood of rebellion, not a day to celebrate our independence."

"It might have been better for it to rain during the battle, Gabe. Maybe fewer men would have suffered."

"Maybe, but maybe we would have lost. I think things are starting to look better for our cavalry and this war," Gabe tells him.

Cavalry actions east of Gettysburg, July 3, 1863:

Early that morning Gregg had been informed that a large

cavalry force was moving east. About 11 A.M. Confederate General Stuart reached Cress Ridge, just north of a large field three miles east of Gettysburg. There he signaled Lee that he was in position by ordering the firing of four guns, one in each direction of the compass. This was an error, because by doing so he alerted General Gregg to his presence. General Gregg had positioned the brigades of McIntosh and Custer to block Stuart. As the Confederates approached, Gregg engaged them with an artillery duel, and the superior skills of the Union horse artillerymen got the better of Stuart's guns.

Stuart's plan had been to pin down McIntosh's and Custer's skirmishers around the Rummel farm and swing over Cress Ridge, around the left flank of the defenders, but the Federal skirmish line pushed back tenaciously; and the troopers from Greggs Division fought gallantly even though they had been outnumbered.

Stuart decided on a direct cavalry charge to break their resistance. He ordered an assault by the 1st Virginia Cavalry, his own old regiment, now in Fitz Lee's brigade. The battle started in earnest at approximately 1 P.M., at the same time that Col. Edward Porter Alexander's Confederate artillery barrage opened up on Cemetery Ridge, just south of Gettysburg—the start of what has become known as Pickett's Charge.

The Confederate troopers came pouring through the farm of John Rummel, scattering the Union skirmish line. Gregg ordered Custer to counterattack. Custer personally led the regiment, shouting, "Come on, you Wolverines!"

Waves of horsemen collided in furious fighting along the fence-line on Rummel's farm. Seven hundred men fought at point-blank range across the fence with carbines, pistols, and sabers. Custer's horse was shot out from under him, and he commandeered a bugler's horse. Eventually enough of Custer's men were amassed to break down the fence, and they caused the Confederates to retreat.

Stuart sent in reinforcements from all three of his brigades: the 9th and 13th Virginia (Chambliss's Brigade), the 1st North Carolina and Jeff Davis Legion (Hampton's), and squadrons from the 2nd Virginia (Lee's). Custer's pursuit was broken, and the 7th Michigan fell back in a disorderly retreat.

Stuart tried again for a breakthrough by sending in the bulk of Wade Hampton's brigade, accelerating in formation from a walk to a gallop, sabers flashing, calling forth "murmurs of admiration" from their Union targets. Union horse artillery batteries attempted to block the advance with shell and canister, but the Confederates moved too quickly and were able to fill in for lost men, maintaining their momentum.

Once again the cry "Come on, you Wolverines!" was heard as Custer and Colonel Charles H. Town led the 1st Michigan Cavalry into the fight.

A trooper from one of Gregg's Pennsylvania regiments observed:

"As the two columns approached each other the pace of each increased, when suddenly a crash like the falling of timber betokened the crisis. So sudden and violent was the collision that many of the horses were turned end over end and crushed their riders beneath them."

As the horsemen fought desperately in the center, McIntosh personally led his brigade against Hampton's right flank, and the 3rd Pennsylvania and 1st New Jersey hit Hampton's left from north of the Lott house. Hampton received a serious saber wound to the head; Custer lost his second horse of the day. Assaulted from three sides, the Confederates withdrew. The Union troopers were in no condition to pursue beyond the Rummel farmhouse.

The losses from the intense cavalry battle on East Cavalry Field were relatively minor: 254 Union casualties, 219 of them from Custer's brigade; and 181 Confederate.

Although tactically inconclusive, the battle was a strategic loss for Stuart and Robert E. Lee, whose plans to drive into the Union rear was foiled.

Stuart was blocked from achieving his objectives in the Federal rear, and Pickett's charge up Cemetery Ridge was a disaster for the South.

On the night of July 3rd General Lee had reformed his lines into a defensive position on Seminary Ridge west of Gettysburg. Both armies began to collect their remaining wounded and bury some of the dead. Lee started his Army of Northern Virginia in motion late on the evening of July 4th. General Meade's Army of the Potomac followed, although the pursuit was half-spirited. Combat operations were primarily cavalry battles, raids, and skirmishes.

Dealing with the casualties at Gettysburg for the three-day

battle has often been called "The Harvest of Death." The two armies suffered between 46,000 and 51,000 casualties. Union casualties were 23,055 (3,155 killed, 14,531 wounded, and 5,369 captured or missing), while Confederate casualties are more difficult to estimate but are from 23,000 to as high as 28,000 (4,708 killed, 12,693 wounded, 5,830 captured or missing).

Nearly a third of Lee's general officers were killed, wounded, or captured. Over 3,000 horse carcasses were burned in a series of piles south of town; townsfolk became violently ill from the stench.

The Army of the Confederate States of America would never again invade the North. Lee was now finally on the defense.

* * *

"Ellie, we are almost home. I can't wait!"

"It's going to be nice to bathe like a human being and sleep in my bed again."

"That was the longest month of my life," said Kate.

"And the most depressing of my life," added Ellie.

Love Is a Battlefield

It was a bit chilly for mid-November. She could see the smoke of Kate's fire rising up into the air.

"Here, Kate. I was in town, and I picked up your mail for you. Will you be coming to our house for Thanksgiving?"

Kate quickly looked to see who had written her. "My mother and the Yankee. That's it?" She handed Gabe's letter back to Ellie.

"Yes. What were you expecting?"

"One from Mac."

"Are you coming over or not?"

"What day is that, Ellie?"

"Mac is writing you?"

"Not yet, but one day he will."

"It's on the last Thursday in November, the 26th."

"How long has Gabe been writing you?"

"Yes, tell your folks I will be there. The night after we found Mac at Gettysburg, I made the mistake of writing him a quick letter."

"Why was it a mistake?"

"I wanted to thank him for the things he did for me and you over the past few months. But then he wrote me back, and the letters keep coming."

"What is happening to you, Kate?"

"What do you mean?"

"When was the last time you wrote a letter?"

"Before the one to Gabe? Maybe five years ago."

"You wrote one letter in five years to thank someone. That's a miracle!" Ellie laughed.

Kate grinned. "You know I'm lucky. I don't need miracles."

"Since you met Gabe, you act different. You have worried dreams. You seem to be more caring about people—as if strange, tiny miracles are following you around."

"Stop that! You're having way too much fun with unrelated coincidences."

"How have you been staying in touch with your family?" asked Ellie.

"I don't. But if I needed to, I'd send a telegraph. They are easier and faster."

"That's so impersonal."

"Whoever said I was a personal person?" asked Kate.

"Not me. You should write more often."

"I will when Mac writes me."

"Why didn't you tell me that Gabe wrote you?"

"I don't know. I guess I forgot. It's not important." Kate shrugged.

"Not important?" Ellie's eyes were wide.

"Here, throw it in the fire for me."

"You didn't even open it." Ellie frowned.

"Why should I? If you don't burn it, I will." Kate walked over to the fire and threw in the letter. It immediately caught fire but burned slowly.

Inside, Ellie was also slowly burning. "Why did you do that?"

"Why do you think? I don't want to read it, because he expects me to keep writing him back, and you know that ain't me."

"If Mac writes you, you will."

"Yes, but that's different. Besides, I wrote Gabe once already, and that's enough."

Ellie felt sadness and hurt inside for Gabe as she watched his unread letter slowly burn.

Kate gestured to her. "Open the drawer next to you. Throw all of those into the fire for me, too. Maybe one day he will stop writing. I'm going to fill my water bucket."

Ellie grabbed the letters, turned, and reached out over the fire. Maybe it was the door opening and closing, which created a breeze that blew the cinders from the burning letter into the air. Maybe it was her curiosity. Whatever it was, she could not burn his letters. She quickly tucked them inside her dress.

As Kate walked back in, Ellie was stirring the ashes to hide the fact that she could not burned any more of them.

"All during the war, I have heard stories from mothers, wives, fiancées, and children of how important writing to the soldiers is, and then reading the letters the men sent home."

"Good. So when Mac writes me, I'll write him back."

"It is important to write to Gabe. Just as important for him to write someone. Someone who wants him to come home, who cares about him. Some soldiers pour out their feelings so if they die, they can feel like they were able to leave a part of themselves behind."

Kate looked at her. "Sweetie, did you forget that Gabe wants to die?"

"I know. That's why it is more important for him that someone who cares about him writes him."

"Then maybe you should not have burned them. You could have read them and then written to him."

Ellie said softly, "Maybe I will."

"What? Thanks. Now I know how important it is to write to Mac."

"How many times did you write Gabe?"

"I only needed to write the one."

* * *

On her way home, Ellie stopped by the same spot she and Gabe had sat on a log so many months ago and talked about having fun. It was one of her favorite places on Kate's side of the river. After removing her blanket roll, she sat on part of it and wrapped herself in the rest. Then she pulled out both of his letters.

She started with the older one. She opened it very slowly, as if it were a delicate historical document.

> *Dear Kate,*
>
> *I was pleasantly surprised to get a letter from you. It finally arrived on this first day of fall. I did not think you were the writing type.*
>
> *I'm glad to hear that your friend Mac was doing well, considering he lost his arm. At least he is alive and the war is over for him. How long were you at Gettysburg? I heard there were so many wounded that the Hospital Corps was going to be there for a few more months.*
>
> *We were on the move late on the 4th in the rain heading to cut off Lee's retreat, but as you know by now he got back into Virginia without much trouble. How is my friend Ellie doing? I expect she is keeping the hospital staff busy trying to save*

everyone. She must be exhausted saving all those lives and souls. Rascal is holding on but he will need a break. I'm thinking of sending him home this winter like I did last year. That would be best for him.

I hope my letter finds you safe and in your home. Until we meet again.

Yours,
Gabe

She folded the letter slowly and gently put it back into the envelope. *I wonder where he is now.*

She then opened the second letter—again, very slowly.

Oct 20, 1863.

Dear Kate,
I haven't heard back from you, but I was thinking about you a lot, for we passed by White Sulphur Springs mid-month. Sorry to tell you the place is a mess, except the areas where the officers of both sides use each time the area changes possession.

I have had time to think as we ride many miles these past few months. You remind me of my wife, both of you tough, independent women with a love for life and fun. She was my best friend. While riding for hours a few days ago a light rain began to fall and the sky was so beautiful. Through sunshine or rain, through loss or gain, forever more I will feel no pain.

Gabe

Ellie was deep in thought for several moments after reading the second letter. *He seems to like writing her and is looking forward to her writing him again. He doesn't know she won't be.*

* * *

April 1, 1864.
 Gabe slipped away from his troop as they moved east toward Fredericksburg. The Army of the Potomac's winter headquarters was still camped at Brandy Station.

 He quietly rode up to Kate's home, checking to see if she had any visitors who might want to kill him. He saw no one. He dismounted and looked around, checking the house. Still, nobody.
 "Come on, boy, I can't leave you out here again. Let's get you some of her good hay that you like."
 He led Rascal to the barn and into a back stall, threw some hay down, and removed his saddle. As he walked out, he heard the faint sound of a woman singing. He slowly walked over to the side of the house. Back about fifty feet, there she was, sitting in her garden.
 Not the best singer I ever heard, but she sure puts her heart into it.
 He enjoyed watching her for a while as she took in each deep breath, trying to carry a tune. It was nice to hear sweet words come from that mouth for a change even if she couldn't carry a tune. Each time she wiped at her face, she got more dirt on it. She had dirt to her elbows, and looked more like she was playing in the dirt than gardening. Dirt was flying everywhere.
 With a smile on his face he approached her, she lifted her head, and her smile was so big that her beautiful teeth shined and lit up her face, in sharp contrast to the dirt all over it.
 "Good afternoon, Kate."
 "Good afternoon, lieutenant."
 "Having fun?" he asked her.
 "I'm willing to bet not as much as you. How long have you been there watching me?"
 "Not long. Just enough to watch you dirty your face."
 She got up and walked to the pump on the side of the house.
 "You look stunning in your new officer's uniform. So clean and blue, and you smell great."
 "Thank you. I wish I could say the same for you. I guess two people can make a second first impression."

"How do I look?" she asked him.

"I think you look like I did when we first met. But you smell better."

"Are you saying I'm a mess that doesn't smell?"

"No ... yes. You look like you need a bath."

"If I remember, I did give you a bath once. I guess it is now your turn to repay me."

"What?"

"Just pump the well for now. I think that's all you can handle."

He pumped the well, and as the water came gushing out it shot over the rim of the bucket, splashing them both. He took the blue and gold bandanna from around his neck, rinsed it, and began to wipe her face.

They said nothing.

After several attempts, she took the bandanna from him, and he held the bucket. She slowly began to wash her face and arms. He watch each splash wet her—first her hair around her face, then her upper arms to her shoulders, where her dress sleeves were. Her dress at the neck had been unbuttoned, he watched intensely as she washed her neckline, tilting her head back, watching the water ran down her throat down to where the first button was ...

Splash.

His face was hit with two handfuls of water.

"I had to. You were enjoying that too much."

"Oh, yeah." He turned the bucket toward her, she ran to the house.

He entered right behind her and grabbed her dress. She turned and smiled at him. They stared at each other, their eyes darting from eyes to lips and back to eyes, each one waiting for the other to make the first move.

Slowly moving closer, he pressed his chest against her. She pressed her legs even closer. He couldn't wait any longer, and his mouth went for her lips. She pulled herself in hard against his chest; she also could not wait. They kissed as if they only had moments more to be this close. They knew the world around them would take this from them if it could. He moved her back slowly, back to the table, and gently lifted her onto it. His mouth and lips went for her neck as she struggled to unbutton her dress. She got it open, and he went to the edge of her corset, his lips kissing as he moved across the tops of her breasts. She lifted her dress so he could press closer to her, and down went his holster, his pistols banging on the wooden floor. She pulled off his jacket, and before his trousers hit the floor, her legs wrapped around him. Nothing short of wild horses was going to drag them apart ... except the war ... and the cavalry, they have many horses.

"Shhh," said Kate suddenly. "Do you hear that?"

"No, what? You're hearing things."

"Horses. I hear horses." She pushed him back. He stumbled and nearly fell, his pants wrapped around his feet.

"Put your pants on, you look helpless," she told him. She checked the windows. "I see two—no, four—and two more. That makes six Rebel cavalry soldiers riding up. You are in big trouble, mister."

"You mean *we* are."

"Nope. I'm going to say you tried to rape me."

"What?"

"Just kidding." She buttoned her dress. "It would help your case if you finished getting dressed." She kissed him again. "Stay here. Don't go outside no matter what, OK?"

"I don't know. I'm a soldier; this is what I do."

"Well, you will be a dead one if you challenge them, and I don't want that. Do you trust me?"

"Yes."

"Do you really trust me with your life, again?"

"Yes, again!"

"Good. Then let me do what I do. Let me do my thing. Damn, where is Rascal?"

"In a stall in the barn. I learned my lesson the last time."

"Good thing you're a fast learner." She kissed him again and gave him a big smile, and out she went.

She gave the arriving soldiers a big smile. "Howdy, boys! How can I help you, sergeant?"

The rider in front tipped his hat. "We are looking for Yankees."

She threw her head back a bit and ran her hand through her wet hair. "Haven't seen any of them around here recently. Any of you need medical help or food?" Brushing her hand on the sides of a few horses, then on the trooper's boots, as she walked around them. That's when she noticed Gabe's boot-tracks in the loose sand.

From deep inside the house Gabe watched from the bedroom doorway. He could see more troopers riding around the house. He watched her work her magic as she used her charm to distract the men. He realized he has never seen her show any fear.

"What makes you think they are around here? Anything I need to worry about?" She dragged her feet over the tracks as she moved.

"No. But a few scouts reported that a large Union scouting party crossed the river about an hour ago."

"A large Union did what? What did you say?" She tried to keep them distracted, but one corporal kept looking down at the ground. She could see he was not interested in her. "Hey, corporal, you married?"

"Yes."

"Never you mind," she told him.

Then two more troopers rode up from behind the house. "Sergeant, all looks clear."

"OK, let's go."

They rode off in the direction that they came. She followed them out to the road as they went left away from the river. She watched closely, noticing that as the corporal moved closer to the sergeant they exchanged words as they rode.

She ran into the house. "Go! They know you are here." They ran into the barn and quickly got Rascal ready, he swung into the saddle.

Kate looked up at him. "Why do you keep coming here and risking your life?" she quietly asked.

"To see you again. It's been a year since you saved my life and your letters of course. I'm glad you're getting mine. I will keep writing you, until we see each other again."

Then he rode out of the barn as fast as he could.

Approaching the road, he slowed and looked to the left for the Rebels. He spotted them not more than a hundred and fifty feet down the road, slowly making their way back. An easy shot if not on horseback in full gallop.

Gabe turned right and bolted down the road. The Rebels gave chase and fired their pistols.

I may have just gotten him killed, thought Kate. *He may need me.* She quickly tried to hitch the mule to her wagon when she heard horses approaching at a fast gallop again. Looking up, she saw the Rebels retreat back to where they came from.

Nope. I guess he scared them away. He must have threatened to write them letters. No wonder this war is lasting so long.

As she sat on the wagon, her mind wandered to his last words. *Letter? What letters? I'm not writing him. My only letter to him was just after Gettysburg, nearly a year ago. I burned his letters. I remember because I just came from town and Ellie came in with the mail, and I went through it. My mother sent me another voucher for Alex's benefits. Then there was a letter from Gabe, but none from Mac. I told Ellie to burn Gabe's letter, and I told her I wish he would stop writing me. She asked why, and I threw it in the fire. I watched it burn. I was going to burn them all ... when ... what happened? I got distracted, and Ellie left ... No! I asked her to burn them, then she left. He said, "your letters, I will keep writing you"—but I have not received any more letters from him. What was he talking about?*

A Night to Remember

Eight weeks later, Kate was driving her wagon into town. Looking down the main street, she saw very few people out on this late spring afternoon. Then she spotted Ann and Teresa, Ellie's sisters, leaving the general store. Riding up to the general store, Kate watched them walk past the hotel near the center of the town. She dismounted and walked into the store.

"Hi, John, any mail for me?"

"Yup. Here is one from that Yankee who writes you a lot. Who is he?"

"What are you talking about?"

"You know, they come for your letters."

"Who does? What are you talking about?"

"The girls. Today it was Ellie's sisters. I don't understand why sometimes they pick up some letters and leave others. Like this one."

Ignoring him, she walked over to the door and watched them, climb into their wagon, and ride off toward home. *I wonder what they are up to.*

She sat outside on the steps to open the letter. She paused and turned it around several times, looking it over, then began to think back to Gabe's visit in April.

What did he say? "Your letters, I will keep writing." I'm not writing him, so who is?

This time she looked closely at the outside of the envelope. *It's poorly sealed. This letter has been opened and resealed. I guess I'm not the only one who knows this trick.*

She opened it and began to read.

May 22, 1864

My Dear Kate,

    This letter must be short. I requested my first leave since joining the war and not only was it granted, but I have been selected to attend a ball in Washington. I would like it very much if I could be your escort, so I have included an invitation for you. I will reserve *a room for you at the Taylor Hotel for your convenience. I will wait for you all night at the entrance of the ball if need be.*

Cordially,
Lieutenant Gabriel O'Shea

Also in the envelope was an invitation.

Military and Civic Ball
to be given by the Organization of Eastern States
at The Jefferson Hotel
at six o'clock on Monday evening,
on the 4th of July, 1864

Sir: the pleasure of your company, with ladies,
is most respectfully solicited.
Committee of arrangements: Capt. Richard Smith

She put both the invitation and letter back into the envelope and stared down the main street.

What should I tell Ellie? Nothing. I have no interest in going all the way to Washington for Gabe. If I were a betting girl, I would bet Ellie had this letter for a few days trying to decide what to do with it before she finally decided to let me see it. She is the one writing him.

In a heartbeat, a mischievous grin appeared on her face. *If she is, this could be a lot of fun.*

Standing, she stretched, looked up to the clouds, then turned and walked back in.

"John, from now on, don't give anyone else my letters. I will pick up all of them myself. If someone does come, please tell them that there are no letters for me."

"OK, Miss Kate."

"There are none, got it?"

"Yes, Miss Kate. There are none."

"How often have these letters been coming?"

"One every two months or so. Is everything OK?"

"Yes, everything is perfect now. I'll be stopping in to see you every time I'm in town."

"OK, Miss Kate. You have a nice day."

"Thanks, John. I will ... now."

* * *

Midday two days later, Ellie rode to Kate's house and found her cleaning up after a quick meal.

"Good day! You need anything?" Ellie greeted her.

"No, I'm fine. How are you?"

"Good." She walked around looking for the mail. "Any letters from Mac?"

"No, I haven't gotten any from him in some time."

"Any letters for me to get rid of?"

"Yes, one from Gabe."

"Oh, is he still writing you?"

"Yes, but not in a long while."

"Have you read it?"

Kate paused just enough to raise a bit of concern in Ellie. "Yes."

"Anything interesting?"

"It depends."

"It depends on what?"

I wonder how long I can keep this up. I do enjoy this.

Ellie's mind started going in two directions. *Does she know?*

Kate considered the situation. *I need to know what she is going to do. How much should I push her? Too hard won't be good.*

"It depends on how you feel about what he wrote."

Ellie felt a dry lump in her throat, as if Kate had reached in to pull her tongue out and attached to it was her conscience.

"Gabe asked me to attend a July Fourth ball in Washington."

Relief. I still need to act like I don't know anything. This is hard! How do liars do this?

"Have you started getting your things together?"

"No."

"Why not?"

"I'm not going."

"Why not?

"I have no interest in seeing Gabe. Besides, I don't have the money for the trip."

"He ... he wants to see you. I don't understand you, Kate."

"I don't want to go."

"You had to go to Gettysburg to find both Gabe and Mac in a battle—but you won't go to Washington for a ball?"

If she knew that at Gettysburg I only cared about finding Mac and used Gabe as an excuse for her to be interested in going, she would be furious. Oh, well. I won't be telling her.

"Why don't you go?" Kate asked her. *He wants the woman who is writing him to go, not me.*

Ellie shook her head. "Too many Yankees for me."

"Ellie, even if I wanted to see Gabe, I don't have a gown."

"I can lend you one of mine," Ellie offered.

"Nice try, but no."

"You always wanted to go to a ball as a lady and not as a child. This is your chance."

"OK, but only if you go with me."

"Me, go with you? I can't do that."

"Why not? You know I will need your help. If you don't go, then neither will I."

"OK, but I will need to work it out with my folks."

"How interesting, I will finally get to go to a ball. Not how I envisioned it."

"You always thought your first was going to be at The Springs."

"Ellie, you plan the trip. You like that kind of stuff."

"OK, we have a month. The first thing you need to do is meet me at my home to pick out a gown."

"I know which one I want to wear," said Kate.

"You do? So you have thought about going," said Ellie.

"Only a little bit." Kate smiled. "I like the blue and white one, but you need to fix the bodice for me. I'm not as full as you are."

"OK, stop by tomorrow at noon. I should be done with my work," Ellie said. "Can I see the invitation? How many days will we be in Washington?"

"It's in the same drawer I put his last letters in," said Kate. *Nice touch to ask to see the invitation. She is better at this than I thought she would be.*

Ellie opened the invitation and quickly scanned it. She already had her plan ready. "I think we need to plan for at least a four-day trip. We should leave at sunup on the third, and return on the sixth."

"Sounds good to me. This could be a fun trip." Kate paused. "By the way, what happened to Gabe's letters I asked you to burn?"

Oh, no, thought Ellie. *I was praying she forgot about them.* "Gabe's letters?"

"Yes, the ones I took out of that same drawer and asked you to throw in the fire, last fall."

Ellie swallowed. "Oh, yes. I took care of them."

Smart, thought Kate. *I bet you did.* "Bye. See you tomorrow at noon."

* * *

"All loaded up, Jimmy?" Kate asked.

"Yes, that was the last bag. Two each—do you think you packed enough?"

"If we forgot anything, we can always buy what we need," said Kate. "I forgot to thank your parents for taking care of my place while we are gone."

"I already did," Ellie told her. "Let's go, before someone changes their mind."

"I'm not going to change my mind. Why, are you?"

"Not you, Kate, I mean my folks."

"Yup, our Pa did not want her to go. Just like he didn't want her to go to Gettysburg. You should have heard the quarrel my Ma and Ellie had with him last night."

Ellie's voice was tense. "Jimmy, I don't want to talk about it now. Let's go."

"OK. We have a long trip, we can talk about it later," said Kate. "So, Mama Laura put your Pa in his place again?"

"Shh!" hissed Ellie. "We'll talk later."

* * *

"It's six o'clock. Now arriving Washington Station!" the conductor yelled out.

"Ellie, I don't feel well," said Kate as they stepped down onto the platform.

"What is it, your stomach? Maybe you're hungry."

"No, it is not my stomach. I feel warm."

"Move over here so no one will see us." Ellie motioned her

over to a side bench. "Let me feel your head, hon."

"What? What is it?"

"Nothing. You're not warm. Let's get to the Taylor Hotel and unpack our things."

"OK, maybe you're right. Maybe I'm just hungry for some great city food."

"That always makes me feel better."

July 4. The next day.

"Ellie, I'm not feeling well again," Kate said.

"Do you have a fever?"

"Maybe a slight one."

"Let me feel you." Ellie pressed her fingers against Kate's forehead. "No, I don't think so."

"I feel warm."

"So do I. It is very hot outside."

"No, I don't feel right," insisted Kate. "My head hurts."

"You are fine. What is that you like to say—'If I wanted a pig, I would get one'? So stop whining."

"Do you want me to get all those poor soldiers sick?" Kate looked over to Ellie, who had a grin on her face. "No, never mind. I'm not going down in history as the woman who got all these officers sick and helped the South win the war."

"OK, get me sick. I'll do it," Ellie replied with a grin.

"That's not funny. You should go in my place."

I have been writing him ... I should be the one to go, Ellie thought. "I can't. I won't."

"If you don't, then we don't," Kate said. "Gabe will be waiting all night for one of us, worrying that something happened. When we are only a few blocks from him, acting like little girls instead of women. Now get dressed."

"I shouldn't go," Ellie told her again.

"Why not?"

"I only came to accompany you."

"You want me to go, but you won't. Not even to see Gabe."

"I'm in the North, in Washington, with so many Yankee officers! Just thinking about it makes me sick. See? I'm sweating already," said Ellie.

"You went to Gettysburg," said Kate.

"That was different."

"Don't worry, Gabe will protect you."

"Yes, he would—and he would like doing it."

"Remember I also say, 'Never let the fear of falling off the horse keep you from enjoying the ride.'"

"You do say that," said Ellie, smiling. "Did you make that one up?"

"I don't know. But you can tell everyone that I did."

Ellie paused for a moment. "OK, I'll go for you."

"Good. Now let's get you dressed."

* * *

"Kate, I'm ready. Help me get this corset over your chemises."

Kate fidgeted with the garment. "Hold still! I need to make your corset tighter."

"I don't think it can get any tighter."

"You need to stop eating. You're putting on weight. ... Oh! Unless ..."

"Unless what?"

"You're pregnant."

"That would be funny, but you can't get—"

"Forget it," said Kate. "I was joking. That's not possible with you, and you aren't Mary. Your makeup looks good. Get your dress."

Ellie held it up. "Kate, I can't wear this dress."

"Why not?"

"We had the bodice tightened up to fit you. It's too tight for me now."

"No, it's not. It's perfect now. Before it was too high and baggy. Put it on; I'll show you it fits."

Ellie struggled into the dress.

"Now it is too low and too ... tight. I feel like I'm going to pop out."

"Don't worry. See? I pulled it up a bit." As Kate turned away, she mumbled, "Just don't breathe too heavily."

"What? You did? Where? Will it stay up?"

"I said, don't worry. Turn around. Let's get your sash on—and here, take this shawl with you. You may need it tonight while watching the fireworks."

Ellie wrapped it over her shoulders and back. "The shawl

helps. Good idea."

Kate stood back and looked at Ellie. "Ellie, you're not a child anymore. This dress fits you real nice for a lady. You look lovely."

"Let me see."

"Come here. Take a look at yourself while I put this ribbon in your hair. How does that look?" Kate gestured for Ellie to come stand in front of the mirror.

Ellie looked at her reflection and smiled slightly. "I like it."

"Hold your sapphire pendant around your neck so I can clip it."

"Kate, hand me my earrings. I'll put them on now."

"Not bad. Better than I thought."

"Not bad? You look beautiful! Do you have your gloves and fan?"

"Yes, right here."

"Spray more perfume on; I don't smell it."

Ellie squeezed a few puffs of perfume over her. "OK, is that enough?"

"Yup. You're ready."

Ellie fidgeted with the skirt of her dress. "I'm so nervous."

"Remember, he will be waiting for you out front, so stay there and wait."

"Where is my invitation?"

"Here in your handbag, see?"

Knock, knock.

"Who is it?"

"Miss Kate?"

"Yes?"

"Your coach is here."

"OK," Kate called out, "she is ready."

"I hope so."

She said to Ellie in a low voice, "Do you know how beautiful you look?"

"I do?"

"Remember, you are Miss Katherine Hancock. In your words, you look heavenly. The first thing you should do when you walk into the room is to have them announce you. Then let all the men in the room dance with you, in exchange for the Union Army surrendering. They would gladly do it."

* * *

A civilian quickly climbed up the top steps of the main entrance of The Jefferson Hotel.

"Captain O'Shea?"

"Yes."

"I have been looking for you."

"I'm on my way out. Who are you?"

"Please come with me now." He grabbed Gabe's arm. "Hurry, they are waiting for you."

"Stop! Let me go, or you will end up on the floor." Gabe pulled away. "I'm not moving until you tell me why."

"Sorry, sir. I am Mr. Jones. I work for Congressmen John Starr. He wants you to join him. Now, please hurry a bit, so I won't be late starting the introductions."

"OK, show me the way." Gabe walked along with Mr. Jones.

Approaching a group of officers, he noticed that one junior officer was wearing a uniform he was not familiar with.

"I'm glad you could join us, Captain."

"Yes, sir. Me too, Congressman Starr."

"Mr. Jones, please begin."

"Gentleman, for those of you who do not know each other, I will begin with introductions:

"House Republican John F. Starr, of New Jersey—one of your hosts. Colonel William Sewell, former commander 5th New Jersey Infantry. Lieutenant Colonel Marcus Kitchen, 2nd New Jersey Cavalry. Charles Weeks, Captain of the Foretop, U.S. Navy—currently on board the *U.S.S. Montauk*. Robert Strahan, Captain of the Top, U.S. Navy, currently serving on board the *U.S.S. Kearsarge*. Thomas Kane Captain of the Hold, U.S. Navy, currently on board the *U.S.S. Nereus*. Captain Robert O'Shea, 1st New Jersey Cavalry. Captain Adoniram Judson Wright, 2nd Battery "B," New Jersey Volunteer Light Artillery. And 1st Lieutenant John Toffey, formally with the 33rd New Jersey Volunteer Infantry, wounded at the Battle of Missionary Ridge. His wounds have rendered him unfit for active field service, and he will shortly be appointed into the Veteran Reserve Corps."

"Thank you, Mr. Jones. Honorable officers, I'm glad you could all join us today to celebrate the birth of this nation. You have been selected to attend this ball as representatives of our great state of New Jersey, but above all, for your brave, noble and distinguished service to our country, in this war.

"I would like to start by reading two citations that have been submitted. Colonel William J. Sewell, and 1st Lieutenant John J. Toffey. Also, tonight we will discuss the talk of the day — restoration of the South after the war is won, and the part our state will play."

The group of officers exchanged greetings.

"Lieutenant Toffey, I hear you have been on President Lincoln's staff."

"I am not formally on his staff, Captain Weeks, but occasionally I have the pleasure of escorting the President, members of his family or staff and close friends around the city."

"Is that the uniform of the Veteran Reserve Corps, Lieutenant?"

"Yes, Sir Captain Wright."

"Good choice to wear a jacket cut like the U.S. Cavalry," Lieutenant Colonel Kitchen added.

"Colonel Kitchen, is it true you resigned on June 30th?"

"Yes it is, Colonel Sewell."

"Colonel Kitchen, the First New Jersey, or the second?"

"Captain O'Shea, you should know the first will always be my first."

"Colonel Sewell, I heard a rumor you will be resigning very soon also," said Lieutenant Colonel Kitchen, returning the questioning to the colonel.

"Due to my wounds, gentlemen, I will be resigning effective July 6th."

"The colonel and I have been discussing that—and his future in state government," Congressmen Starr informed them. "Gentleman, today we salute 'Kearny the Magnificent,' so nicknamed by his French comrades before this war. September will mark two years since Major General Philip Kearny, the former commander of our own First New Jersey Brigade, was killed at Chantilly, Virginia—a major loss for our state. With one arm, he was more of a solider than any man with both."

"Congressman, were you responsible for the rumor in Washington that President Lincoln was contemplating replacing General George McClellan with General Kearny?"

"As I said, a major loss for our state. Mr. Jones, please continue and read the nominations."

"Colonel William J. Sewell, citation submitted to Congress as follows: While serving as colonel of Fifth New Jersey Infantry at Chancellorsville, Virginia, third May, eighteen sixty-three. Assuming command of a brigade, he rallied around his colors a mass of men from other regiments and led these troops with great brilliancy through several hours of desperate conflict, remaining in command though wounded and inspiring them by his presence and the gallantry of his personal example." He paused. "Congressman, back to you."

"Men, Colonel Sewell was severely wounded again at the Battle of Gettysburg, Pennsylvania, while commanding his unit along Emmitsburg Road on the second day of the battle, July second, eighteen sixty-three. Captain Wright, you were also there commanding the Second Battery B New Jersey Volunteer Light Artillery."

"Yes, sir."

"The colonel's wounds at Gettysburg have forced him from the field and, after tonight, hopefully, into state government. "

"Sir, have the colonel's actions at Gettysburg also been submitted for awards and decoration? If not, they should."

"Not yet, Captain O'Shea."

"Sir, if I may. I believe we all agree they should be."

"We do, sir."

"Mr. Jones, you heard Lieutenant Colonel Kitchen. Please document and submit to my office."

Gabe leaned over and whispered, "Captain Wright, would this be the first time you agreed with me?"

"Come on, Gabe, call me A.J."

"This conversation would bore Kate to death. Good thing she is not here yet."

"Kate… is she the lady who saved you in the rain during the raid in sixty-three?"

"Yes." Gabe's eyes started wandering around the room.

"Who are you looking for?"

"Kate."

"So I will get to meet her."

"Not if I can help it. Where is Ellen?"

"With Congressman Starr's wife, and Colonel Sewell's, and the other wives. Over there."

"Next is 1st Lieutenant John J. Toffey's citation, submitted as follows:

"While serving as 1st Lieutenant, Company G, Thirty-third New Jersey Infantry, at the Battle of Missionary Ridge, Chattanooga, Tennessee, twenty-three November, eighteen sixty-three, although excused from duty on account of sickness, went to the front in command of a storming party, and with conspicuous gallantry participated in the assault of Missionary Ridge. Was here wounded and permanently disabled."

"Excuse me for a moment, gentlemen."

Gabe walked over to a lieutenant who had just descended the stairs of the grand entrance.

"Lieutenant, I need you to do something for me."

"What is it, Captain?"

"When you came in, did you see a lady outside? She may or may not have been escorted."

"No, I did not notice any."

"Go back outside and look around. There should be a lady, Miss Katherine Hancock, waiting for me out front. She knows me as Lieutenant Gabriel O'Shea. Please apologizes for me and escort her in."

"Yes, sir, Captain. If you like, I can entertain her until you're done."

"Sorry, but as soon as she arrives, I will have a good reason to excuse myself from this discussion."

The lieutenant ascended the stairway, walked outside, and looked around, but did not see any ladies. He turned right and walked into the hotel garden. There, on a stone bench under a tree, sat a lone woman.

"Miss Katherine Hancock?"

He got no response. He moved closer.

"Excuse me. I'm looking for Miss Katherine Hancock. Is that you?"

"Me?" asked Ellie. "You are looking for me?"

"If you are Miss Katherine Hancock, yes."

She was confused for a moment. "Why are you looking for Miss Kate?"

"Miss, you look like you have been weeping. Are you OK? Are

you hurt?"

"I'm fine."

"If you are Miss Katherine Hancock, Lieutenant Gabe sends his apologies that he can't—"

She looked dismayed. "He can't make it!"

"No," said the lieutenant. "I mean yes! He is inside, but unable to come outside at this time. So he sent me to escort you in. Will that be acceptable to you?"

Ellie regained her composure. "Yes, Lieutenant. Thank you. Please call me Miss Kate."

She stood. He offered his arm, she took it, and together they walked to the entrance.

"Good evening," said a man at the door. "May I see your invitations?"

"Miss Kate, would you like to be announced?" the lieutenant asked her.

Ellie paused at the top of the stairs and gazed out into the room. She handed her invitation to the lieutenant, who stepped over to the announcer.

I have seen many halls before, but this room is magnificent. Marble floors, large marble pillars that reach up to the twenty five-foot ceilings, floor-to-ceiling windows with exquisite drapes, very large mirrors, eight crystal chandeliers, and a balcony that goes all the way around the room. This room is quite elegant.

"Miss Katherine Hancock, would you like to be announced?"

He got no response.

"Her escort is Captain Robert O'Shea," the lieutenant told the announcer. Then he approached her. "Miss Kate … Miss Kate?"

"I'm sorry, Lieutenant. This beautiful room distracted me."

"Miss Katherine Hancock, would you like to be announced?"

* * *

From the moment the lieutenant had left the hall, Gabe could not stop glancing at the entrance. The instant she stopped at the edge of the stairs, his eyes gazed upon beauty he did not expect. He needed to move quickly before she was announced and someone else escorted her down.

"Congressman Starr, Colonel, I must excuse myself once more. My lady is waiting for me." Without waiting for their approval, he quickly moved to her.

"If he hadn't moved that fast, I would have been concerned for that young man," said the colonel.

"Colonel, that's one thing everyone in this room can agree with," said the congressman.

"Said like a true politician."

Gabe moved up the stairs briskly and with dignity, trying to avoid attracting attention, but few noticed him.

The announcer spoke. "Miss Katherine Hancock from Virginia, and her escort, Captain Robert O'Shea."

For a few moments she stood alone at the top, with many eyes focused on the breathtaking lady from the state that housed the capital of their enemy. Gabe quickly ascended to the top and reached out to her. For a heartbeat, both of them were not sure who they were looking at. Seeing the joy in her big, bright smile, he lit up and felt warm all over.

"I feel as though you are seeing me for the first time, Ellie," Gabe whispered.

"I am. 'Captain'?" she said questioningly.

He took her arm, and they proceeded down the grand staircase.

"Yes, as of this morning."

She smiled. "And 'Robert.' You are full of surprises tonight."

"My full name is Robert Gabriel O'Shea."

"Are you disappointed that Kate is not here?" she asked.

"No, absolutely not. Ellie, you are also a surprise tonight."

He glanced at her, and she could see his smile.

"Why are you grinning?"

"You, a Virginia girl in Union blue, at a ball with all these officers. Miss Ellie, I'm pleasantly surprised. This evening may end up being pleasantly perfect."

Focus, so you don't fall. With her free hand, she grabbed her dress and lifted it. "Just get me down these stairs safely."

"You are always safe with me."

Now she grinned. "Yes, I am. And my gown is sapphire and white, not blue and gold like your formal uniform."

"What's wrong with my uniform?"

"Nothing. I like your gold sash. And you smell good for a change."

As they walked toward the group, Gabe noticed that in his

absence the wives had joined their husbands.

Glancing at the group ahead of them, Ellie could feel her nerves again. She began to take deep, rapid breaths, and her walk slowed enough to get Gabe's attention. He glanced over and notices her distress.

"Are you anxious, or cold?"

She stopped and looked at him.

"Anxious." She reset her shawl, covering her shoulders and pulling it closed in front.

"Relax. Nobody in this room is tougher than Kate. Breathe slower and shallower. You're making an amazing entrance."

She smiled at the thought of having to deal with Kate. "Thank you for that. I'm ready."

"Kate, this is Congressman John F. Starr and his wife …"

"Elaine," cut in, reaching out to him with her hand. He reached out and gently kissed it.

"Mrs. Starr."

"Colonel William Sewell, Lieutenant Colonel Marcus Kitchen, Navy Captain Charles Weeks, Navy Captain Robert Strahan, Navy Captain Thomas Kane, Captain A. J. Wright and his wife, Ellen, and 1st Lieutenant John Toffey."

"Please call me Kate."

Mr. Jones interrupted them. "The grand opening is about to start."

"Will you be joining us in the Grand March, Kate?"

"Yes, Elaine, if Captain O'Shea will escort me to the floor." She held out her hand. Looking toward one of the large, floor-to-ceiling mirrors, she caught a full view of herself. *If Kate could see me now!*

As the orchestra began and the attendees promenaded around the room, Elaine Starr made it a point to speak to Kate each time she could.

"You are beautiful, Kate. Where in Virginia are you from?"

"Brandy Station."

"How did you two meet?"

"He was wounded when my family found him. I helped nursing him back to health."

"Gabe, I don't think Elaine's intentions at this dance are the same as everyone else's."

"Ell—I mean, Miss Kate—what are the intentions of everyone else?"

"To see and be seen, or to look at potential partners for dances later on, what else?" She turned to look at him. "Haven't you ever been to a ball?"

"Yes, of course. But I always had my focus on the lady I brought and no one else. What are your intentions?"

"To be Miss Kate, of course."

"Miss Ellie, you have true flair."

The pattern of dancers rotated again. "Bye, Gabe."

Then the cotillion dance followed. It picked up the tempo a bit, as the dancers stepped and swirled around the room making intricate figures and continually changing partners.

Elaine whispered to Gabe during their turn around the room. "Captain, does this mean Kate is your savior?"

"Maybe. If I survive this war, Elaine."

Moments later, Gabe saw Ellie across the room, dancing with a general he recognized instantly. He had first spotted that long, golden hair in the cavalry battle at Gettysburg. Quickly, Gabe moved around the floor and positioned himself to intercept Ellie's next partner. But before he could complete his maneuver, she was dancing with Colonel Sewell. Gabe could feel a sense of relief; the young general would never challenge Colonel Sewell. Sewell glanced over at Gabe with an eye that indicated he should relax.

After the dance there was a short break while the musicians played a soft, soothing melody.

"Oh, my, that general was quite forward," said Ellie.

"Was he? That's his wife over there."

"Well, some of you Yankees are foul. He said I was stunning for a Southern woman, and that he could just kiss me."

"He did?" Gabe frowned.

"Yes, he did. Guess what I told him."

"What?"

"I said 'If you try, you will be leaving this room with only one lip.'"

He chuckled. "That's my girl."

"Your girl"—that has a nice ring to it.

"That removed his smug attitude," she said.

"Was it Kate or Ellie who said those words?" Gabe asked playfully.

"Both," said Ellie.

"I think she is rubbing off on you."

"Really?"

Then the quadrille dance followed. This square dance of patterns of four couples offered the New Jersey officers and their wives a chance to dance as a group.

Gabe stayed out of the reel, the Scottish dance that involves at least two couples and the execution of a figure eight. He sat with his friends, relaxed, and focused on one thought: He enjoyed watching Ellie having fun. She smiled the entire time she was dancing, and she looked very comfortable doing so.

The waltz was about to begin when out of nowhere the blond general appeared and reached out to Ellie.

"No, thank you, sir," she said, then turned to Gabe. "This dance belongs to the captain."

Gabe immediately reached his hand out to her, and she took it gracefully. He held her hand gently, as if each part of her was a delicate link to a life he once had. *I know one day I will lose her. Don't hold on too tight. I don't want to feel that pain and loss again.*

Without missing a note of the dance, she floated out onto the floor. He followed.

They moved together as one—lightly, quickly, whirling, swirling, and flowing effortlessly about the floor. Many of the women watching commented that if the North and the South could move as one like they do, the war would never have happened. The young lady from Virginia made a memorable impression on many that night. For both Ellie and Gabe, it would be a night to remember, and it was just getting started.

They walked off the floor and approached the Jersey men's wives.

"Captain, she is your savior. I hope you plan on marrying her."

Ellie blushed for a moment.

"If she is my savior Elaine, we will need to eat, or we may not live much longer." Placing his right hand on her lower back, he gently moved Ellie toward the dining room.

"Are you hungry?" he asked her.

"Yes, very."

The congressman leaned over to Gabe as they passed. "If I may be so bold: She is special. Take care of her, Captain."

Gabe nodded. "I will, Congressman. And I will start with her stomach. Please excuse us as we proceed to the dining room."

"Captain O'Shea, my wife and I will be joining you."

"Captains, may I also join you?"

"Of course, Lieutenant Toffey. It is our pleasure to have you join us" replied Captain Wright.

Ellie noticed that Lieutenant Toffey walked with a severe limp. That image immediately caused the color to leave her face as the memory of the war came streaming back.

* * *

This dining room is incredible! There must be at least twenty tables, each seating four couples.

They walked over to the spread of food.

"It's been a while since I have seen some of these dishes."

"Ellie, do you see anything you like?"

"Yes, many. I could spend the rest of the evening here. Look, they have squab pie. What do you like, Gabe?"

"I'm going to start with the turtle soup. I enjoy it when it's made with green turtle, though I like it better when it's a stew instead of a soup. Do you want to try the cinnamon sticks?"

"Yes, place one here in my dish."

"A.J., what are you interested in?"

"My dear wife, I'm going for the pigeon pie. I'm also looking forward to a variety of vegetables. John, are you interested in the cold ox tongue?"

"No, I'm going for the stewed fricassee. It is the way I like it, with its own gravy. I haven't had this since before the war."

"Eat up, gentleman, for today we eat like kings; tomorrow we eat like dogs," said Gabe.

"Like a dog isn't bad. It's when we don't eat at all that gets to me. I would like to take some with me."

"Look around, A.J. Do you really think there will be any left?"

"This table is empty," John called out.

"What a beautiful flower bowl," said Ellie.

"Ladies and gentleman, what can I pour for your drinking pleasure?"

"I'll have a glass of claret, thank you. You, Gabe, what do you prefer?"

"I'll take the claret, but my preference is bourbon with a splash of vanilla."

"Sir, I can get you that drink if you like."

"No, I will have the wine with my meal."

"That sounds good."

"And sweet."

"Gabe, when did you come up with that drink?

"It's a family thing."

"My wife and I will have the port."

"Me, too."

"Good evening, ladies and gentlemen. I am Second Lieutenant Thomas O'Brian. May I join you?"

Gabe stood up, approached the lieutenant, and gave him a bear hug.

"Yes, Lieutenant O'Brian, please do. And congratulations on your promotion."

"Thank you, sir. Your letter made the difference with my commission as an officer."

Gabe looked to the group at the table. "As a first sergeant, he was influential on the third day at Gettysburg and our actions at the Rummel farm, battling to protect Hanover Road. Thomas and the rest of the Third Pennsylvania Cavalry regiment fought side by side with the First New Jersey."

"Sir, my promotion is not official until July twenty-seventh. That's also when I get transferred to battalion."

"Thomas, this is Miss Ellie Johnson, A.J. Wright and his wife Ellen, and John Toffey."

"This is my wife, Mary."

"Thank you so much, Captain, for helping my husband get his well-deserved promotion."

"Mary, please call me Gabe. And you don't have to thank me. He deserved it."

A.J. turned to Ellie. "Weren't you introduced as Kate earlier?"

"Yes, I was. Kate was not feeling well, so she asked me to take her place. She did not want to disappoint Gabe. It was her name that was announced."

"You do know each other, right?"

"Yes, of course, I met Gabe the day after Kate found him, and we both worked together to heal his wounds."

"So you are also from Virginia?"

"I was born and raised there; Kate came to live there in 'sixty. But I met her when we were children, long before the war."

"Ladies and gentleman, my wife and I would like all of you to come to a private party tonight after the ball," Lieutenant O'Brian announced.

"Who is giving this party, Thomas?" asked Ellen.

"I am, along with a few other low-ranking Pennsylvania artillery and cavalry officers. For gratitude to many of our fellow soldiers during the war."

"OK, I'm in," A.J. immediately replied.

"It will be fun and different, Gabe," Thomas told him.

"Gabe, what do you think?" Ellie asked.

He glanced at her and saw her smile. "Ellie and I are in, Thomas."

"That leaves you, John."

"I'm definitely in."

"OK. Good. It is at the Tavern."

"Everyone, we have another visitor," John announced, "Mr. Jones, I see you are back. How can we help you?"

"Captain O'Shea, Congressman Starr would like to speak with you alone."

"A.J., would you please care for Miss Ellie in my few minutes of absence?"

"Yes, sir."

* * *

Just after Gabe returned to the group, the announcements started.

"Our first speaker tonight will be General Campbell."

The general's introduction was met with thunderous applause. General Campbell immediately started his speech.

"'They insulted the nation's honor; therefore they desired to die by the sword.' Do you remember when Galusha Grow was elected Speaker of the House of Representatives? It was July fourth, eighteen sixty-one, and he gave the Independence Day address."

Many responded with cheers and shouts of approval.

"He continued his speech:

"'In view of this grandest demonstration for self-preservation in the history of nationalities, desponding patriotism may be assured that the foundations of our national greatness still stand strong, and that the sentiment which today beats responsive in every loyal heart will for the future be realized. No flag alien to the sources of the Mississippi River will ever float permanently over its mouths 'til its waters are crimsoned in human gore, and not one foot of American soil can ever be wrenched from the jurisdiction of the Constitution of the United States until it is baptized in fire and blood.'"

The officers, as did Congress before them, offered hearty applause upon the floor and in the galleries.

"Indicative of his humility, Grow then finished with:

"'Invoking for our guidance wisdom from that divine power which led our fathers through the red sea of revolution, I enter upon the discharge of the duties to which you have assigned me, relying upon your forbearance and cooperation, and trusting that your labors will contribute not a little to the greatness and glory of the republic.'"

"Gentlemen, many of us here today bear witness to this nation as it is again being baptized in fire and blood in this red sea of revolution.

"Thank you, and enjoy your evening."

"*Not one foot of American soil can ever be wrenched from the jurisdiction of the Constitution of the United States until it is baptized in fire and blood.* Most impressive."

"John, our Constitution is the heart of this nation."

"It is the soul, heart, and binding force of this nation, and should never, never be compromised by any man," said Gabe.

"Yes, sir. That's why our forefathers wrote it this way."

"Change one word, and the document means nothing, A.J. It becomes a worthless piece of paper."

"Then we have to keep lawyers from attempting to alter it in any way."

"You mean beyond the Bill of Rights and the 11th and 12th Amendments," Gabe corrected him.

"I'm glad President Lincoln did not institute martial law during the riots in New York and Boston last year. History will show he did the right thing," A.J. told them.

"Those days in July must have been tough on him." John added.

"I do believe we all agree with that, John. You get to spend time with that great and God-loving man."

"If President Lincoln did not institute martial law in these times, then no president in any time ever should do it," Thomas told them as he raised his glass.

"Hear, hear! To President Lincoln."

Gabe whispered to Ellie. "That reminds me of the seven days in May we had last year."

"If a president now, or any time in the future, ever tries to do so, it could be the end of this great nation," John added.

"Then God be with us, that no tyrant or false king ever tries to seize power by force or political cunning," Gabe said.

Ellie turned to Gabe. "Can we go out to the lovely garden? I need some air."

"Yes, let's take a walk."

"Gabe," A.J. called out.

"A.J., look for us by the river."

A.J. acknowledged him with a subtle nod.

* * *

"I find this garden relaxing. Gardens are very important in large cities. Do you agree?"

"Yes, they are important, Ellie."

"Come sit with me, Robert." She pulled over her dress to make room for him.

He sat very close and stared into her eyes. *How strange that she called me Robert. I wonder why.* His face showed a bit of sorrow.

"Gabe, what's wrong? Did I do something wrong?"

"No, I'm OK. I haven't been called that name in a long time."

"I didn't mean anything by it. I won't do it again," Ellie commented, her expression concerned.

"Why did you call me Robert?" he asked.

"Part of me thought when you were a young, sweet boy running around, your mother called you Robert. I was also looking for a conversation-starter about your life before the war."

"Well, you picked a subject that hit both." He stood and walked around the tree next to the bench.

"I'm sorry. Where are you going?"

"Nowhere, and don't ever apologize for being yourself with me." He looked up. "The sky is clear and beautiful tonight. The fireworks will have another celestial body to compete with."

She looked up and scanned the sky. "Which celestial body are you talking about? I see many."

"I see only one that is interesting and shines bright."

Confused, she looked over to Gabe saw he had been looking at her.

"Gabe, that was sweet."

"Tonight, after the fireworks, it may be hard to see the stars, Ellie."

"It's harder to see the stars in the city on any night."

"That reminds me of the first time I saw you. The stars are so bright where you live."

He turned toward her and was fixated. From one of the large windows the light from the ballroom was reflecting off of her gown, causing it to glow in a bright, greenish hue, as if she were an angel who came to rescue him.

"What is it?"

"You ... you are glowing."

"What do you mean, I'm glowing?"

"You look like a glowing ... tribute to ... life."

"That is sweet, too. Thank you, but I think you had too much to drink tonight."

I need to move closer to her, I want to be closer. He sat beside her, so close that he could smell not only her lavender perfume, but also the fragrance of her hair.

Ellie felt shy for a moment. *Why is he so close? Does he want to kiss me? No, he is wishing Kate were here so he could kiss her. Stop these crazy thoughts! Just enjoy his company. That is what you really want.*

"You smell wonderful."

"Thank you, Gabe. And for a change, so do you." She smiled.

"Thank you for the compliment. I think it is the first one you have ever given me."

"No, it is not. I have given you many."

"Why are you here, and not Kate?"

"She got sick on the trip here. She is sleeping back in our room."

"This ball—is this anything like what The Fauquier Springs balls were like?"

"Yes and no."

"Do you like it?" he asked.

"It would be better if there weren't so many Yankees," she whispered.

"I am hoping that you can relive a bit of that childhood feeling you got from the Springs."

"I know," she said. "Thank you."

"It is getting late. If you want to see the fireworks, we should start walking over to a good spot on the Mall."

"OK, Gabe, I'm ready. Do you want your friends to come with us?"

"No, I only want your company."

"OK. Let's start walking."

"Let's watch from over there." He pointed away from the large lawn in the center of the Mall.

"Why? This is OK here."

"You'll see. Walk with me a bit more."

As they moved closer, she saw it.

"Oh, it's a river. A gorgeous one! Is this the Potomac?"

"Yes, it is."

"I love the way the city lights flash across the ripples. The water is so calm. Is that normal?"

"Sometimes. Look across the water to the far shore, over there." He moved up close behind her and pointed.

Oh! He is so close, I can feel his warm body against me, and his breath on the back of my neck.

"What am I looking for?"

He looked thoughtfully at the other shore. "This war has been an irony tangled in fate, wrapped in destiny."

She looked across the river too and was silent for a moment.

"See those dim lights?" he asked.

"Yes."

"That is your Robert E. Lee's home."

"What? I knew Arlington was close to Washington City, but not that close."

I won't tell her that the War Department decided to use Arlington as a Union cemetery to let General Lee know how many Union solders he is responsible for killing.

BOOM. BOOM.

They both turned to see the fireworks start.

"Ellie?" asked Gabe.

"Yes?"

BOOM. BOOM.

"Are you cold?"

"A little bit."

"Would it be OK for me to put my arms around you?"

"Yes, please. It is cooler here by the water."

BOOM. BOOM.

"Ooohh! It's so beautiful."

"Yes, beautiful," Gabe whispered to her.

Nothing is as beautiful as you. She has no idea how radiant and gorgeous she is tonight.

BOOM. BOOM.

Ooohh! The crowd expressed its approval.

* * *

As they walked back to the ball, Ellie's voice glowed with excitement. "That was spectacular! I haven't seen fireworks like that since before the war. Gabe, may I ask—what did Congressman Starr want to talk to you about?"

"He asked me how my grandmother was." He paused. "He hadn't heard from her in a while, and he was expecting to, that's all."

"He knows your family?"

"Yes. Look, here come A.J., Ellen, John, Thomas, and Mary."

Ellie had no opportunity to ask further about the congressman. Together the group walked back to the ball.

The political talk of the ball was the Wade–Davis Bill of 1864, a bill proposed for the reconstruction of the South written by two Radical Republicans, Senator Benjamin Wade of Ohio and

Representative Henry Winter Davis of Maryland. In contrast to President Lincoln's more lenient Ten Percent Plan, the bill made re-admittance to the Union for former Confederate states contingent on a majority in each Southern state to take the ironclad oath to the effect they had never in the past supported the Confederacy.

The bill passed both houses of Congress on July 2, 1864, but was pocket-vetoed by Lincoln and never took effect. The Radical Republicans were outraged that Lincoln did not sign the bill. Lincoln wanted to mend the Union by carrying out his plan. He believed it would be too difficult to repair all of the ties within the Union if the Wade–Davis bill passed.

Lieutenant Thomas O'Brian noticed a concerned look on Ellie's face. He sensed that she was uncomfortable with all the talk of rebuilding the South, all the celebrating and the wealth and opulence they were flaunting while the South suffered.

He turned to the group. "Today's celebrations do not truly reflect the spirit of a traditional celebration."

A New York Infantry officer jumped in. "I read in the *New York Times* that, though the South has torn down the flag and rejected the Constitution, the celebration of the Fourth of July remained as the last link of the Union shared between every state, both North and South."

"As I said earlier, our Constitution is the heart of this nation."

"When freedom becomes a memory, and the constitution is outlawed, blood must be shed." A.J. replied.

"This country was born in revolution. Today we fight a civil war to stay as one nation. What is to come in the next century, or the next? Are we to be destroyed from within, like the Roman Empire?" added Lieutenant O'Brian.

"We must remember and learn from the past, or we dissolve in greed and ignorance," the New York officer remarked.

Gabe ended it with, "This nation by the people for the people dies when lions are bought and they become lambs."

The men murmured in agreement.

"Since these may be my last hours of life, I do not want to be here when I can be at a party celebrating. I'm ready to go. What about you, my dear?"

"I'm ready, A.J."

"I just hope I can keep up," John added.

"A.J., I like your suggestion. It's time to go to the next party," Ellie said.

"John, if we need to carry you, we will," said Gabe. "Right, A.J.?"

"Yes, sir."

A.J.'s wife whispered to Ellie, "I wish he would not talk of dying."

"We are ready to follow the Third Pennsylvania! Please take the point, Thomas."

"Yes, sir."

* * *

Gabe and Ellie stopped when a man asked them for directions. Hearing a familiar voice across the street, Ellie looked up to a second-floor balcony and saw a young woman in a dress just like one she herself had brought to Washington. Laughing loudly, the woman turned around and walked back into the room.

A sick woman does not go to a party. That can't be her, but it sounds like her laugh. It had better not be. I don't know if I should be mad at her for lying, or glad she is not sick.

Ellie turned to Gabe and took his arm. "Ready to cross, Gabe?"

Approaching the large front window of the building, Ellie looked in. In a corner were several musicians. One was playing quite vigorously on a piano, another on a drum, one playing a horn and tambourine, one a guitar, and another a violin. It was all in sharp contrast to the orchestra at the ball.

"Gabe, what kind of party is this?"

"Junior officers and enlisted men, and their wives. And some guests, I believe."

"This looks very informal, especially the dancing. That's the best word I can think of: informal."

"Gabe, what time is it?"

"Ten-fifty, Thomas. Why, do you have another appointment?"

"No, but if you want a drink, get it now. From eleven to twelve, it will be difficult to get one."

"Why?"

"Ellie, at eleven o'clock, some real good dancers show up," Thomas replied.

"Gabe, what did Thomas mean by 'real good dancers'?" asked Ellie.

"I don't know, but we are going to find out. What do you want to drink, ladies?"

"I'll have a glass of port."

"Me, too"

"I'll have the same."

"Thomas, that makes it easy three ports for the ladies."

"Look at the way that woman is dressed!" Ellen blurted out.

"Oh, my!" added Ellie. "She moves as if she were in her private quarters."

"So is that how you move in private, Ellie?" asked Gabe with a smile.

"That's not what I meant, Gabe."

"A.J., some of those women going into that room aren't acting like, and aren't dressed like, ladies."

"We won't be going over to that room, my dear."

"Let's move over to the table near the window so the ladies can sit."

"Look over there to that young lady. She is flinging her dress up and throwing herself at those men."

"Oh, my. Oh, no! Gabe look. It's Kate."

"What? Where?" He looked around.

"Back there in the back of the room."

"She looks drunk."

"Gabe, please go get her."

"A.J., just in case, look for Thomas."

Gabe walked to the back of the room. "Men, she needs to come with me."

"No, she is staying with us."

"Sorry, Sergeant, but I will need to pull rank on this one."

"Captain, rank means nothing in this place tonight. She is staying with us."

Kate looked up. "Gabe! What brings you to this neck of the woods?"

"Kate, are you drunk?"

"I hope so. But I think I'm more than just drunk. Are you here to take me to bed?"

"Not exactly."

"You know her?" asked one of the men.

"Yes, she is my sister. So if you don't mind, she is coming with me. Anybody have an issue with that?"

"No, sir. She is all yours."

"Sister? I ain't got no sister."

"Kate, hold on." He bent down and picked her up.

"OK, Captain. Are we on a boat?"

"No. Why?"

"I think I'm getting seasick."

"Maybe you shouldn't open your mouth."

"Why?"

"Someone may think you have no class."

"Yes, sir, Your Majesty."

He carried her to where the ladies were sitting.

"She thinks she is going to be sick. Please help her."

"What did they give her?" Mary asked.

"I don't know."

The ladies returned. "I want to dance some more, Miss Ellie."

"Earlier tonight you told me you were sick. How did you end up here?"

In a loud voice she yelled, "I started to feel better, and I went out for fresh air. When I found this place, I realized this is what I need to get better."

"Kate, why are you talking so loudly?"

"So you can hear me."

"We can hear you. It's not that loud in here."

She hugged Gabe and kissed him on the check. "We are having a lot of fun here, aren't we?"

"Yes. And tomorrow when she says she feels sick, she won't be lying," said Mary.

Kate leaned into Gabe to keep herself from falling. "Gabe, can you get me a drink?"

Gabe held her upright. "Are you OK?"

"I don't know, I think so. But the room keeps moving, and I feel numb."

"Am I your little charmer?"

"Yes, you are my charmer, now sit down."

"Gabe, she has had enough to drink," Ellen told him.

"Kate, sit down, before you fall." Ellen offered her a chair.

"Thanks, whoever you are." Kate looked over to Ellie. "Ellie, I only had two glasses of port, that's it." She held up two fingers, one from each hand.

"That's it?"

"I also had one glass of bourbon. I think."

"You think?"

"What did they give her?" Mary asked.

A.J. whispered to Gabe. "Laudanum. I think she had laudanum."

"That's what I'm thinking."

"Gabe, you think they gave her laudanum?"

"Yes, Ellie. She is showing signs of having some. Do you know what it is?"

"Yes, we give it to the wounded. That's if and when we have it. It's a drug to kill pain—a mix of opium and alcohol. Do you think she was given too much? It can be dangerous."

"No, she will be fine."

Thomas announced to the group. "It's time. It's eleven o'clock, and you should each have a dance partner by now. First, we will see a quick-paced, close-contact waltz by three couples, followed by a few international dancers. After that, we can all join in."

As the music started, the dancers walked in from the back room.

"They are wearing beautiful dresses."

"Oh my!" said Mary. "Look how fast they move. And how close they are dancing!"

"Ellen, look how their bodies touch."

"We see, Ellie."

"I can't see, you're all standing in front of me." Kate moved her chair.

"Gabe, I was told you speak Spanish, and you are familiar with the culture," Thomas said.

"Who told you that?" asked Gabe.

"You're going to like the next dancers. They are part of a diplomatic mission from Europe."

When the waltz was finished, the crowd applauded. From the back room a couple came out, made their way to the dance floor, and walked around as if to judge the space and the size of the crowd.

I have never met anyone from Spain before, Ellie thought, as she closely studied the couple.

The man was tall and thin, with dark skin and eyes. His hair was long and brushed back. He wore black military trousers and a short, black military dress jacket that was open, revealing a tight white shirt that was partially unbuttoned. She wore a long, deep-red dress that covered her shoulders but was tight from the bustline down to mid-thigh. It revealed her slender figure. From there the dress was black and blood-red, with many layers of ruffles flowing loosely down to the floor that showed she wore shoes with heels. Her hair was tied in a bun with red ribbons. She too was tall; her bright red lips were a contrast to her dark skin, hair, and piercing dark eyes. Her beauty was exotic.

The couple walked to the center of the dance floor, turned, and stood pressed tightly back to back, with their heads turned to see one another.

There was no music playing, no sound at all. I could only hear my breathing, as my heart began to beat faster with anticipation.

As the music started they each took a long, slow stride away from each other and paused. Then again another stride, and another, quickening the pace with each step until they reached the edges of the dance floor. Each turned to the left, moving faster circling the dance floor, staying on the opposite sides. The audience was clapping with each step. The dancers turned to face each other, paused, then raised their arms and took several quick strides back to the center into each other's arms. At that moment the female dancer turned and looked straight into Gabe's eyes.

"The man's name is Don Virgil Guerrero de Rivera," Thomas said. "That's his wife, Ernestina, from Cordoba, Spain."

"What kind of dance are they doing, Gabe?" asked Mary.

"I believe they are dancing a type of flamenco, but I'm not sure," Gabe replied.

"Whatever it is, they are very passionate about it."

"Flamenco dancing is very popular throughout Spain. It reflects the Spanish culture."

"What is in her hands?"

"They are called castanets."

"Now that is dancing! What technique and style!" added John.

She flings her dress around as if it's in her way, Ellie thought, *each time revealing her legs. Oh, my!*

"Look at how they touch and move around the dance floor with each other."

"Like making love in a dance," added A.J.

"A.J!" Ellie blushed.

"Tell me you weren't thinking the same thing, Ellie."

"I was thinking it was like watching birds dance!"

"Same thing."

"Look how high she can kick her legs," added Thomas.

"They seem to be inspired by the rhythm — the beat of the music and the handclapping from the crowd," said Ellen.

"Ellen, I agree with you. They do look inspired."

"Thomas, how did you arrange this?" Gabe asked.

"A captain I know saw Virgil and Ernestina dance here in Washington last year, and he told me about them. When I heard they were back, I asked if they would come tonight. Ernestina told me that they like teaching Yankees how to dance."

When the couple finished their dance, the room broke out into thunderous applause. As they caught their breath, the dancers walked around the dance floor, looking into the crowd. Ernestina walked over to Thomas, while eyeing Gabe.

"Is this him?" she asked with a slight Spanish, Mediterranean accent, looking Gabe over.

"Yes, he is the one I told you about," Thomas replied.

Realizing he was the topic of conversation, Gabe asked, "What is going on, Thomas? What did you tell her?"

Feeling a proper introduction necessary, Thomas gestured. "Ernestina Guerrero de Rivera, meet Captain Robert Gabriel O'Shea."

She reached out her hand to Gabe. He took it and gently kissed it.

"Roberto, you speak Spanish?"

"Some, Ernestina, *pero entiendo bastante.*" [But I understand more.]

"And I understand you have been to Spain. *¿A dónde?*" [Where?]

"Mostly Barcelona, Madrid, Sevilla. *Y Bilbao, también.*" [And Bilbao, also.]

"*¿Bilbao? ¿Familia?*" [Bilbao? Family?]

"*Sí.*" [Yes.]

"And your favorite?"

"Barcelona … and Bilbao."

"*¿Por qué?*" [Why?]

"*El océano, por supuesto.*" *[The ocean, I suppose.]*

"*¿Conoce el baile Flamenco?*" *[Do you know the flamenco dance?]*

"*Sí.* Yes, I have seen it performed many times in many ways, and tried a few."

"*¡Jugamos!*" *[Let's play.]*

Gabe took a deep breath. "Yes, let's play." He walked Ernestina to the center of the dance floor, where Virgil was already waiting with a lady who had volunteered to dance with him.

"Roberto, *no se preocupe.* Don't worry. I won't hurt you. But I will lead."

"*Sí, por favor,*" *[Yes, please,]* Gabe mumbled.

"Oh, Mary! I hope the next time Virgil dances, he doesn't pick me."

"Ellie, I'm praying he picks me."

"Me too," added Ellen.

"I want to dance, too," Kate blurted out as she tried to stand. Mary and Ellen each placed an arm on a shoulder and gently eased her back into her seat.

"I don't think you are ready, honey," Ellen told her.

"When you can stand on your own, we will think about it, my dear." Mary paused, and then continued. "Ellen, I really like the way the music and the dance start slow, but then the tempo picks up."

"I do too, Mary. The basic rhythmic pattern of the music, chord progression, and the use of the castanets are impressive."

"Virgil told me that flamenco dancing allows for improvisation by the dancer. The *bailaor* — that's the man — erupts into spontaneous movement to match the mood of the music. It lends a unique quality to the performances of each dancer."

"Thomas, can the dancers also change the pace?"

"I don't see why not. But then the musicians would need to adjust. I guess they work it out as they go."

"Ellie, Gabe looks like he knows what he is doing. I think he has done this before," said A.J.

"I see that," said Ellie. *Oh, my, look how close she is getting to him.*

"He seems to be enjoying it," said Thomas.

"Yes, I see that too, Thomas," Ellie replied.

"If it were me, I would be," added John.

"I think she shows too much of her legs," Ellie said.

"Nope, I don't agree," A.J. added with a grin.

"Neither do I," said John.

"Not just shows—look! She is wrapping them around Gabe and rubbing them on his ... hip and thigh, oh my."

"She does brush her hands on him quite a bit."

"Yes, she does," all three men agreed, in harmony.

"Gentleman, be careful. One of you may be going out next."

The dance ended.

"*Mucho grasia*, Ernestina. That brought back many memories."

"*Mucho grasia*, Roberto. The next time you go to Spain, come see us."

"I will." He turned to Ellie. "Now it's your turn."

"Oh no, I can't! I don't know how."

Ernestina moved in close and whispered to Ellie. "Give your dress and legs life, my dear. Let go. Show him you are worth it." Then she walked off.

"What did she say?" asked Gabe.

"Nothing. Nothing you need to know."

"Follow my lead, and let me be your hero, Miss Kate," he told her.

"That's not fair."

"Oh, so it is OK when you want to use her title, but not me?"

That was all Ellie needed to hear. She placed his right hand on her lower back and pulled in close, at the same time raising her left hand and offering it to him. He grasped it firmly. When the music started, he did not move. They stared into each other's eyes. He started by moving his left thigh into hers, and they began to move together, twirling slowly—once, twice, then a third time. Each time the circle got bigger and bigger, but their bodies stayed very close together. He spun her, and she landed in his arm, face to face, so close she could feel his breath. He never looked away from her eyes.

Taking her hand he slowly moved it across his chest and down his side. Around and around they went, his hands moving over her body, and occasionally she moved her hands over his. He felt her breathing get deeper and deeper, and knew her emotions were building. He wondered if she knew, he could tell she wanted to let go.

Stop holding back, he wanted to tell her.

Some of her hair came loose and began flowing with her. She fought the urge to give in and let loose as she had seen Ernestina do. She needed to feel in control of her emotions, but she knew not why. *It's just a dance, go with the flow—like when you're in the river. Let him take you away for this moment.* She sensed the dance was coming to the end. Before he could reach for her leg, she lifted it and wrapped it around him as she threw her head back. *Now that was a surprise!* thought Gabe. He looked down at her as he held her weight in his arms. Her breath was deep, some of her hair was free and loose around her face and chest, and in that perfect moment she finally let go.

He held her for as long as she wanted. Then she leaned forward and looked at him with a smile that could light up the sun. *If only she could see how much emotion and playfulness she just shared with me,* thought Gabe.

Ellie stood there for a moment, catching her breath. *If he only knew how I just felt. But I could never share that with anyone, not even him.*

They looked over to their friends, who all were applauding and had big smiles on their faces, even Kate.

"OK, gentlemen, now it's your turn. I need a drink. Ellie, will you join me?"

"Yes, Gabe."

A.J. danced with Ellen, Thomas with Mary, and John with a young woman he had met. When they had finished their drinks, Gabe walked over to A.J.

"A.J., we are going to leave now. Thomas thank you. We will be leaving, as it is getting late and Kate doesn't feel well."

"OK, Gabe. Miss Ellie, Miss Kate, we hope to see you all again soon."

"Good night, and thank you all. I hope to see you soon, too."

"Hopefully soon, when the war is over," Gabe said.

Gabe picked Kate up, put her over his shoulder, and headed out the door.

"Gabe, where did you learn to speak Spanish?"

"My grandmother taught me some, Ellie, when I was a child. Those lessons helped me when I spent some time in Europe. She lived in many places in Europe, but Spain was her favorite, in a village called Vista Tierras Altas."

"What does that mean?"

"'The View from the Heights.'"

"Did you like Europe?"

"Yes, very much. You should go some time."

"Are you inviting me?"

He turned to look at her. *What is she thinking?*

"Sorry," she said before he could respond. "I have also been there. One summer, my mother and I went to Ireland, England and all over France all the way to the Mediterranean Sea. I loved it. I dream of going back one day."

"I used to, Miss Ellie. I used to."

* * *

Back in their room, he placed Kate on her bed.

"I will be staying for the night, then I must return to the war and my regiment."

"I hope you don't plan on staying here in our room!" Ellie whispered.

"Gabe! Please stay with us," Kate mumbled.

"No, please don't," Ellie responded, with a bit more concern.

"Sorry to disappoint the two of you, but I have my own room."

"In this hotel?" Kate asked.

"Yes, I'm upstairs. Oh, before I go — have either of you seen one of those balloons that fly?"

"I'm flying now, and I don't have a balloon." Kate giggled.

"Have you, Gabe?" Ellie asked.

"Yes, I have."

Ellie turned to Kate. "See? They do exist, Kate! I tried telling you, but you wouldn't listen."

"I thought you and the boys back home were teasing me," Kate replied.

"Last November, as we approached Fredericksburg, we were ordered to reconnoiter to the Potomac River by way of the Potomac Creek," said Gabe. "Before we reached the creek, in a small clearing we could see a large balloon and several men trying to keep it from going into the trees. It was a balloon outfit, including all the balloons, gas-generators, balloon-inflating boat, gunboat, and tug proceeding up the Potomac.

"We rode over to help get it stable, then we moved it away

from the trees. Finally enough men swam to shore from the boats to help. The balloon-inflating boat was using the cover of the cove to stay out of the wind and current of the river, but as they were inflating the balloon, it started to climb above the tree line as a gust of wind blew it on to the shore on our side of the creek. My troop helped them control it long enough to get it up in the air, and the barge moved away to open water."

"So you got close to the balloon?" asked Ellie.

"I got to sit in the basket while they inflated it. And I spoke to Thaddeus Lowe, the man who was in charge of the balloon outfit. He thanked us for saving his balloon."

"I saw one when I took a walk this morning," Ellie said.

"When?" Kate asked.

"When you were still sleeping. I think they are giving rides."

"I want to see that." Kate said.

"Tomorrow morning I have a surprise"—he hesitated for a second—"for the both of you. That is, if you are up to it, Kate."

"What is it?"

"You'll see. Be ready at eight o'clock. We must be there by half-past eight, or we will miss it."

"Eight A.M.?"

"Yes, Kate."

"I hope I feel better and can get up at eight," Kate mumbled. "Goodnight, Gabe, I'm going back to sleep, huh."

"Goodnight, Gabe, and thank you," Ellie said. "I had a wonderful time."

"So did I, Ellie. So did I. May I kiss you good night?"

"Yes, here." She pointed to a spot on her cheek.

He leaned in, moved from her cheek to her lips, and gently kissed her. She did not move away.

It was a sweet, short kiss —where he wanted it. I like that. Always the gentleman, with a twist.

As she closed the door, she whispered, "Gabe, this is a night I will remember for as long as I live." To herself, she added, *When I'm close to you, I can feel my soul surging like a flooding river.* She dared not say that aloud.

Social Season to Soar

The next morning Gabe met the ladies in the lobby, and together they walked through the city streets. After a few blocks of window-shopping, Gabe found a carriage to take them to their destination.

"To the Smithsonian Institution, in the Mall, please."

"Where? That's a museum," Ellie told him.

"I don't want to go to a museum," said Kate.

"You don't?" asked Gabe.

"Where are we really going?" asked Ellie.

"You'll see."

They rode for a few minutes then the carriage stopped.

"We are here, sir."

"Thank you driver. Ladies, please follow me," Gabe told them.

They walked around the buildings that make up the museum.

"You like dancing with the devil?" Gabe asked Kate.

"I like dancing," she said with a shrug.

"Is it because he's the only one you can't intimidate?" asked Gabe.

"Who said I can't intimidate the devil?" she said with a smile.

"I heard he's hard to intimidate, even for you."

"Did you hear that from Ellie?" Kate shot a look at Ellie.

"No, but I'm sure you hear a lot about him from her."

"Not anymore she doesn't, Gabe, I gave up some time ago," added Ellie.

"Kate, did you intimidate Ellie?"

"No, too much work. She may be harder to intimidate than the devil. I just ignore her."

"Kate, is there anything that intimidates you?"

"I haven't found it yet."

As they passed the last building they walked onto the Mall grounds. Lying on the grass were three large balloons in the process of being inflated.

"How about going for a ride in one of those?" asked Gabe.

"Are you both trying to get me killed?" Ellie blurted out.

"Ellie, we will be going with you," said Gabe.

"What? I'm not going up in that," she replied.

"Yes, both of you are going."

Gabe walked over to the man who was giving orders to the ground crew.

"Mr. Lowe, I want you to meet the ladies I was telling you about—Miss Kate and Miss Ellie."

Mr. Lowe reached out for their hands and placed a gentle kiss on each. "It is a pleasure to meet you both. How beautiful you are this fine summer morning."

"Nice to meet you too, sir, and what wonderful balloons."

"Please call me Thaddeus, Ellie."

"It must be amazing up there, so high up."

"In fifteen minutes we will all find out," Gabe told them.

"No, I can't!" said Ellie.

"It is paid for … and I don't give refunds," said Thaddeus. "It is very safe—all my balloons are."

"Ladies, look." Gabe showed them the tie-lines attached to the ground. "We can't drift away, and the men down there will pull us down when we are done."

"Not even the Confederate army was able to shoot one down."

"That's right, Gabe," said Thaddeus. "The closest they came was from artillery fired at our ground forces situated near the balloons. In February of '63, David Hogan, an enlisted man with the 13th New Hampshire Infantry, was performing sentry duty when a shell that was aimed at me when I was aloft instead hit a cesspool near Hogan, covering him with the unpleasant contents. Hogan was not injured, but a fellow soldier noted that 'his clothes and appetite are utterly ruined.'"

The ladies giggled softly.

"I heard you have given rides to many senior federal officers, including McClellan, Sedgwick, Reynolds, and Hooker," Gabe said.

"Yes, I have—and don't forget George Custer."

"Oh, yes!" said Ellie. "From what I was told, I danced with him last night."

"I fought with him at Gettysburg," Gabe added. "He is one fearless man."

"Let's go, ladies. This is a once in a lifetime chance," said Gabe. "This will be an experience you will remember and share for a long time. Right, Thaddeus?"

"Yes. Each time I go up I pray it won't be my last."
"That sounded encouraging," said Ellie, with a dubious tone.
"Miss Ellie, you know that's not what I meant."
They all climbed into the basket.
"Ready? You can hold on here if you feel you need to."
"Ellie, you can even pray if you like," said Kate.
"I'll be praying the whole time we are up, so don't talk to me."
"My feet are not on the ground. I like this floating feeling," said Kate as they ascended.
"We only have fifteen minutes, so please relax and enjoy the view," Gabe told them.
"How high will we be going?"
"The city has put a height limit on all the balloons," said Thaddeus. "Sorry, but she cannot go above three hundred feet."
"That's OK, that will be high enough," Ellie told him.
"How far can we see?" Kate asked.
"Without glasses, on a clear day, about seven to fifteen miles," said Thaddeus. "With glasses and going higher, as much as fifty miles away. From within the city, about five to ten."
"Thaddeus, can I try with the glasses?"
"Sure, Miss Ellie."
Gabe looked over at her. *That was a surprise*, he thought.
"A little bit like God's view of the world?" Gabe whispered to her.
"Just a little bit."
In awe of the amazing experience of seeing the city from the air, they all were silent for a few moments as they looked around. Gabe broke the silence.
"My grandmother remembered seeing a balloon fly over her house in France when she was very young. She would love to be here," said Gabe softly.
"Did she tell you when that was?" asked Thaddeus.
"I think it was the early 1790s ... she said the French military was learning how to use them to watch the movements of the enemy."
"Thaddeus, how were the balloons used in the war?" asked Ellie.
"Well, we would spot for the artillery," said Thaddeus. "I worked as a FAO by directing artillery fire with flag signals. This allowed gunners on the ground to fire accurately at targets they

could not see. We also tracked troop and cavalry movements."

"What is an FAO?" Ellie asked.

"I'm sorry—it means forward artillery observer."

"Were all the balloons this size?" Kate asked.

"No. We had five-man balloons, all the way down to one-man balloons. Different-sized balloons are used for different purposes. The smaller, one-man balloons can be inflated and sent skyward in a shorter amount of time. Larger balloons carry more observers and can include telegraphers and their gear."

"How and what are they inflated with?" Ellie asked.

"We could inflate balloons with city gas when available, as in Washington and Richmond. For the field, I had to design and have the Navy Yard construct special inflation wagons. Charged with dilute sulfuric acid and iron filings, they generated hydrogen. These gas-generation wagons gave us the ability to deploy the balloons more freely in the field. That was the system on the barge we were using when I first met Gabe."

"Do balloons have names, like ships do?" asked Kate.

"Why do you ask, Miss Kate?"

"You called it 'she,' like it was a ship."

"I guess I did, so that makes her an airship. But I haven't given her a name yet."

"Why not call her Kate?"

"Please don't," said Ellie.

"I can't decide if I should give her a new name, or name her after my first balloon. When I was called up to observe for the army at the First Battle of Bull Run, in July '61, I had to use my personal balloon, the Enterprise."

Kate, Gabe and Ellie looked out over the city in amazement as they listened to his every word.

"Before that, I met with President Lincoln on June 11, '61, and proposed a demonstration with the Enterprise. So on June 17, '61, from the grounds of the Columbia Armory directly across the street from the White House—not far from here, over there ..." He pointed across the Mall, then continued. "... tethered from a height of 500 feet, I dictated a message to a telegraph operator who sent my message. I memorized that message. Do you want to hear it?"

"Yes, please," Ellie blurted out, before anybody else could respond.

Thaddeus recited the message:

"This point of observation commands an extent of country nearly 50 miles in diameter. The city with its girdle of encampments presents a superb scene. I have pleasure in sending you this first dispatch ever telegraphed from an aerial station, and in acknowledging indebtedness for your encouragement for the opportunity of demonstrating the availability of the science of aeronautics in the military service of the country."

"The telegraph cables ran along one of the rigging wires to the ground and were connected to the War Department and the White House below," explained Thaddeus. "The man next to the telegraph operator that was on the receiving end of my message was President Abraham Lincoln."

"Oh my, now that is historical and impressive," said Ellie.

"But what happened to the Enterprise?" Kate asked.

"She was destroyed as she landed in '62. She was getting old and worn out. I should have stopped using her, but the army was slow in getting me more balloons." Thaddeus sighed.

"Look, Gabe, across the Potomac—I can see Arlington, that's Virginia over there," Ellie told him.

"Yes, it is."

At that moment they began to feel their return to the earth.

"Thaddeus, are you married?" asked Kate.

"Yes, my wife is Leontine. In '55, we were introduced at one of my lectures, and she was a pretty Parisian actress and nineteen years old. We have three children, and we hope to have more. Leontine's father, by the last name of Gaschon, was a palace guard of King Louis Phillipe who fled to the U.S. as a political refugee. Gabe, that's why I asked about when your grandmother was in France."

"I don't know," said Gabe. "She has been there several times, Thaddeus."

"Thank you very much, Thaddeus," said Kate as they were helped out of the balloon.

"Yes, thank you," said Ellie. "That was a once in a lifetime experience."

"Goodbye, ladies. I hope we meet again. Remember to always look up, I may float by one day." He smiled and tipped his hat.

Gabe walked with Kate and Ellie to catch a ride back to their room.

"I must go," he said. "My leave is up, and I must report back. So this is goodbye until we meet again, my ladies. I had a wonderful time."

"Goodbye, Gabe," said Kate. "I also had a wonderful morning. Please stay safe, and with good luck the war may be over soon."

"Thank you Kate, I told you, I don't believe in luck."

"Did I tell you I use the power of mind to get people to do what I want? Why don't you believe in luck?"

"Luck is when preparation meets opportunity. Have you ever heard that before?"

"Yes, I have."

"Then you know you're the preparation, and I'm the opportunity."

"I like that," Kate said with a smile.

"Our Lord adds the when, and why," Ellie said.

"Ellie, aren't you ever going to give up on that stuff?" asked Kate. "You know I never have believed in a God."

"I will always believe," said Ellie. "What about you, Gabe? Will you ever believe again?"

"I grew up believing. Now I'm so angry, I don't know. Maybe if I live through this war." His face looked somber.

Ellie grabbed Gabe and gave him a hug like she had never given him before, firm and longer than ever. He held her tight in return.

"Was this trip what you expected?" he asked.

"What a weekend surprise." she replied in a whisper. "You know it did."

"Thank you so much, Gabe," she added. "These two days have truly been an amazing experience. Remember; always keep your eyes focused on what's in front of you, and your heart in the heavens."

He looked into her eyes and gave a slight smile, then off he went back to the living dead.

They both were silent for several moments after he left, then Ellie spoke.

"Kate I'm not ready to go back to our room. Let's go shopping."

"OK," Kate said with a grin. "Do you remember when you didn't trust him? Look how much my little girl has grown."

PART FOUR
Letters, Lies, and Love

August 20, 1864

My dear Kate,

I have been reluctant to write you, but I have bad news I need to share. During the battle at Cold Harbor back in June, the Yankee army moved on the north side of the Pamunkey River and crossed at Hanover Town. En route they destroyed my family's plantation. As you know, we were located three miles north of town. The plantation was looted, all the buildings were burned to the ground, the crops were destroyed, and they took all our animals. They are devastating the farms and towns as they move through Virginia.

Even though our loss is great, I am more proud that we won the battle even though we lost our home. Together you and I can rebuild it.

Love,
Mac

Kate was in such a state of shock and disbelief reading the letter, she could barely finish it and dropped it where she stood.

This did not happen. He must be mistaken. He was right not to share this with me. This is not what I want to hear. Gabe's letters are not full of bad news.

The toll of war was seizing a stronger grip on her resilience. Her essence was becoming as devastated as the South.

My man has one arm and no wealth, and he wants me to start over with him? Like hell I am.

* * *

Ellie's mother came upon her sitting on her bed, her face in her hands.

"My dear child, your brothers are looking for you—what are you doing?"

Startled, Ellie looked up at her.

"Oh, dear—why are you weeping?" asked her mother.

"Um, I'm not … weeping," she replied, sniffing. "I'm reading some letters."

"I'm your mother. I know better. What is upsetting you?"

"Nothing."

"Whose letters are you reading? Are they from our boys? Did you finally get one from Lieutenant Anderson?" Ellie's mother stood over her and glanced at the letters spread out around her.

"No, Mother, these are from—"

"From whom?"

"Not from one of our boys," Ellie said in a soft voice.

"From a Yankee?"

Ellie looked at her mother. "Yes, mother—from the Yankee who helped us bring T.J. and Brandy home last year."

"Oh, yes, I remember him. I think he was a sergeant. Why is he writing you? I thought you said he liked Kate?" Her mother looked puzzled.

"He does," said Ellie. "But she won't write him, so I have been."

"Oh, my. What have you gotten yourself into?" Ellie's mother shook her head slowly and sat down beside her daughter.

"I don't know. Lately I have been so confused." Ellie looked despondent.

"Why?"

"After our trip to Washington, he has written Kate less, making it harder to write him."

"Maybe he is busy," said her mother. "You know, he is in a war fighting for his life."

"I know, but it's not that …"

"Then what is it? What is really bothering you?"

"We had a wonderful time the night of the ball. I …"

"You feel guilty?"

"No … um … maybe. Oh, I'm not sure how I feel."

"Sweetheart, if I remember, you told me Kate did not want to go to Washington and she did her own thing when she was there."

"Yes, that's true," said Ellie.

"Is it something about him?"

"That too, he has so much pain inside."

"You want to help him but don't know how. All you have are his letters, written to another woman," said her mother.

"Yes, yes. I really like writing him. I feel they are helping some."

"Helping him—or you?"

"Me? Why me?"

"Why do you want to help him? Why do you feel you need to?"

"I ... I don't know. Because it is the right thing to do?"

"Was that a question, dear?" Her mother looked into her eyes.

"Maybe," looking away. "I guess it could be. I'm going to have to think about that."

"You do that," said her mother, laying her hand on Ellie's hand.

"How will I know?"

"How will you know what, dear?"

"How will I know when to tell him I wrote these letters?"

"Don't worry, you'll know. Can you read some of his letters to me?"

"Yes, I would like to do that, thank you. I want you to listen to part of this letter he wrote in early '64."

Ellie unfolded one of the letters on the bed and began reading.

Feb 9, 1864.

My Dear Kate,

I have not felt such pain and sorrow since the death of my wife. Our general was forced to leave the field in November due to an increasingly severe case of typhoid. This morning the word spread quickly through the regiments that while staying in Washington his condition worsened, and President Lincoln gave him a deathbed promotion to major general. On December 16, 1863, our beloved Major General John Buford died at the age of 37 in the arms of his aide, Captain Myles Keogh. His wife did not reach him in time.

"Let me also read this part of my last letter to him, because he wrote his letter in response to mine. I wrote it in October of that year. I told him he should move on and let his wife go."

She picked up her letter from the bed and found the passage she wanted to share:

> *The day Brandy died you spoke about your wife, "she died fighting for another's life." Whose life, yours?*
>
> *Why did you feel you both died that day? Why are you so angry? You remind me of a young boy who lost his only toy, and his anger and boredom have him looking for trouble instead of refocusing on the problem and looking for a new toy. Remember, I always say forget the past, don't waste time living in it—it's gone, you can't change it, so look ahead.*

"You know, that sounds like Kate," said her mother. "You are writing like her. No wonder the poor guy is confused. You should write as yourself."

"Mother, may I read you another one?" she asked.
"Of course."

Ellie sifted through the letters on the bed and picked up another.

> *Feb 10, 1865.*
>
> *My Dear Kate,*
> *During the war the Union army and cavalry has been organizing races, and on St. Patrick's Day I was able to attend a few hurdle races. Then this past October I heard there was a cease-fire for races. Gen. George Custer saluted Confederate Maj. Gen. Ramseur at the races in Woodstock, Virginia, on October 9.*

Then on Oct. 20, at the Battle of Cedar Hill in the Shenandoah Valley, Ramseur had two horses shot out from under him and was killed by Custer's men. One day we gather to sing, share coffee, or race, then the next we slaughter each other. I don't know if I can go on killing my countrymen. I can't share this with anyone. All the men around me are from my home state, and they count on me to help them to survive. As the war is nearing its end, I struggle with the thought of killing Southern Americans while I save Northern ones—then wonder how their wives, mothers, and children will deal with it.

In your last few letters you asked about my home and about my family. My folks think that Grandmother has a family secret or two; at least we think she does.

In life you appear to be one person, but in your letters you are another. In life I'm attracted to you because you remind me of myself. Both of us enjoy having fun, and we create fun situations when there were none, and both of us have engaging personalities. Your letters talk of the Lord, but your life says different. In your letters you are extremely passionate and caring.

You asked me about my wife and what happened the day she died. This is hard for me, but I need to do this. She grew up wanting to be in the theater. After our daughter was born she began to realize that her dream might not happen. One day she read in the paper that there was a famous performer appearing, some star on Broadway whom she wanted to go see, I can't even remember her name. So I took her to Niblo's Garden. We were late, and she insisted we take a shortcut though a dark alley. Before I could stop her from going that way, we were attacked by four men. I was caught off guard. Her life was in my hands and I could not save her.

Her last words as she lay dying in my arms

still haunt me. She told me that knowing me and spending the few married years we had together were the best years of her life. She said, "Don't let my dying destroy you. I know why God created you. You have so much to offer to so many people. He wants you to know he will be watching over you. Hold me and feel me as I pass over back to our Father."

As her last breath slowly left her body, I felt the energy of her soul pass through me, and at that moment I felt her love, and so much more love. That moment both excited me and killed me. In that instant were the reality of my full loss and the realization that she was gone.

I thought I would never feel that way again for as long as I lived. Then two things happened in this war that I never expected. The first was the ghost horse and you writing me.

I want a reason to live, to go back to when life and living were fun and challenging, not deadly. I need help releasing myself of my pain and guilt, before and during this war. I like it that you write about wanting to help me with my torrent of feelings in my soul. I think you understand me better than anyone. I hope you feel that I need you to be that person, the one who helps me free myself of my guilt.

I have this strong feeling that I need to protect you. Why do I need to protect you? I often wonder if it is only to prove to myself that I can protect those I love ... or is it because I see you getting into trouble one day, and you won't be able to get out of it, just like my wife did?

I sent Rascal back home again for the winter, he really needed the rest. His back was sore, and his feet were a mess. I do miss him when he goes home during winters.

Yours,
Gabe

Ellie and her mother were both silent for a moment.

"Can I read you one more?" asked Ellie.

"Of course, dear."

Ellie's face looked troubled. "In his next letter he wrote of very disturbing things. He needs help, Mother."

"I'm sure he does, and you are the best person to help him. So please find a way to tell him."

> *I was ready for this war. Many troopers don't want to freeze with fear before battle, then run during it, then can't stop thinking for hours and days of how they let their fellow troopers down. After battle, others focus on the minutes and hours of horror during the battle, when they realized they enjoyed the killing. It works like a strange way to release the many emotions one feels while waiting to die.*
>
> *My first taste of battle and first kill were within minutes of each other. Before a battle I think about how I let my wife down that day she died. In battle I feel I can change what happened. No matter how many I kill, nothing changes, nothing. The war goes on, the men who killed her still live, and so do I. After a battle I craved the way I felt, that rush of energy, strength, and skill, the desire to win and be high and proud on my horse. That first battle was the day I became consumed by the killing. I felt like I was another person.*
>
> *That was before I met you. Now I fear I can't live with myself. I know I cannot kill myself. But now I have killed so many, I know when I die I will not be going to Heaven. I once believed that if I died in battle it would release my soul. I'm not so sure of that now. I no longer feel I can talk to God. But I can write you.*
>
> *Gabe*

"I think I'm going to write him again," Ellie said.

"As Kate, or yourself?" her mother asked.

"I don't know. I don't think I'm ready to do that. Besides, I also need to tell Kate what I have done."

"Which will be harder for you—telling Kate, or Gabe?"

"Gabe."

"Why? How do you feel about him?"

Ellie looked down. "I'm not sure … I think I …"

"Sweetheart, I think you should think about writing him as yourself."

"I don't know if I can."

"Why not?"

"He loves Kate, not me."

"Don't you see what is happening here? He is in love with the writer of these letters. Who is writing them?"

"Me."

"That's right. Not Kate."

"But when we are together, he holds back. What is it that he won't or can't share with me? Is it what happened the day his wife was killed?"

"He holds back because you are making the poor man mad, more than this war. He thinks he is in love with two different women. One he loves on paper, and the other in life. He has no idea who is who."

"What do I do?" asked Ellie.

"That's easy," said her mother.

"It is?"

"Yes." Her mother nodded. "You tell them the truth."

"How?"

"Trust and love. Just show that poor man your love. Show him your heart, all of it."

The Fragrance of Flowers and Fire

March 31, 1865.

After two long days engaging the enemy at Dinwiddie Court House, the First New Jersey Regiment pulled back and bivouacked for the night. Some of the men in the company started a few small fires, and Captain O'Shea unrolled and spread out one of his two blankets on the ground, close to one of the fires. He finally got to enjoy the smell and taste of a fresh cup of coffee.

As he finished reading one of Katie's letters for the third time, Captain John Hobensack walked up to visit with him. As John picked up the unused blanket, unknown to him there were letters caught in a fold, causing them to blow toward the fire.

"Hurry, grab them!" Gabe yelled.

The captain was able to grab two from going into the fire, but a third was blown in and started to burn. He quickly tried to pull it out.

"Sorry, Gabe, I did not see them! Only one corner is slightly burnt." John patted the letter on his trousers to put it out. "I'm sorry it no longer smells like lavender like the others do." He held them near his face.

Gabe held one letter to his nose and took a slow, deep breath. "They do smell wonderful, don't they?"

Before the captain handed Gabe the bundle of letters he took in the pleasant fragrance one last time.

"What are you doing?" Gabe asked.

"I have not gotten a letter in some time, and these smell so good. Again, I'm sorry about this one." He handed them over.

Gabe smelled each one again as he went to put them back into his saddlebag. Before finishing, he paused.

"John, please smell these two."

"This one smells like lavender, and this one smells like … um … soap?" He handed them back to Gabe.

Gabe handed John two more. "Smell these—is this letter the only one that smells of soap?"

"Yes, it's the only one."

Gabe turned it over to look at the front. "This one was sent to me back in '63. But why soap?"

"Maybe she washed her hands before she wrote it."

Gabe put all the letters away. "Why have you come to visit, John?" he asked

"I wanted to talk to you about Major Hart."

"I have been trying not to think about it. But now that you are here, did you find out how it happened?"

"The major rode his first battalion in to support Major Walter Robbins' brigade, but meeting the brigade of the enemy, which had moved on Robbins' right, he was unable to get to him. Major Hart fought with his command, as he always did, with courage and great skill against the enemy. He was shot dead in his saddle. The bullet entered his right cheek and passed through the spinal column."

He never knew what hit him, Gabe thought.

At that moment the bugler began to call taps.

John looked up. "I need to head back to my company. See you tomorrow."

"Good night, John, and thanks for the information and visiting." *I wonder if I'll miss taps after the war,* he thought.

The next morning the call of reveille woke the regiment.

I know I won't miss the sound of reveille.

"Can you smell it, Captain?" asked one of the men.

"Smell what?"

"Spring at last."

Early that morning the word came that the enemy was pushed back, his forces routed, and many prisoners taken. On the 1st and 2nd of April the brigade remained in camp near Dinwiddie Court House, guarding the trains of the corps. For the next seven days they were ordered to locate, capture, or destroy supplies and supply trains, as they shadowed and engaged General Lee's army as it struggled to move west.

The End Is Near

General Lee's troops were soon surrounded, and on April 7, 1865, General Grant called upon Lee to surrender. On April 9, the two commanders met at Appomattox Courthouse and agreed on the terms of surrender. Lee's men were sent home on parole, soldiers with their horses, and officers with their sidearms. All other equipment was surrendered.

The news of General Lee's surrender at Appomattox Courthouse spread fast by telegraph, newspapers, and church bells.

April 12, 1865.

My Dear,

This letter is both sorrowful and joyous, as was this war. I'm full of sorrow for the death and killing, but grateful for finding you. I must include a somber thought for my sake and in memorial to both Major James Hart and our regiment commander, Colonel Janeway. They died a few days apart and our colonel on April 5, only four days before the surrender—a loss that is heartbreaking for this nation and the great state of New Jersey. They were two of the most honorable soldiers and men I have ever met and a loss to humanity.

That same day our troop also lost Corporal Richard Smalls.

The First New Jersey was there to see the surrender yesterday morning. It was both sweet and somber. Lee looked honorable, yet I could feel that inside he was worn and weary, older than his years. The toll he carried these four longs years left scars he will carry through the rest of eternity.

Now it's time to heal all wounds. The war and the rebellion are over, and we are one country again.

Thank you for saving my life. I'm not sure when we will be heading north, but I hope it will be soon. I can't wait to see you. It has been far too long.

Yours Truly,
Gabe

* * *

May 3, 1865.
My Dear,
    For two weeks after the surrender we did not do much; the time dragged by. We were camped near Petersburg until the morning of the 24th of April, when, in connection with the Cavalry Corps we took up our line of march to Danville, Virginia, to operate against the rebel General Johnston's army. After a march of five days we learned that Johnston had surrendered his army to General Sherman. We encamped there for the night, and on the following morning commenced our return march for Petersburg, arriving there on the 3rd of May.
    I'm writing you this because it is over. We are heading north and home. Orders are that on the morning of the 10th of May we will break camp and commence our march for Alexandria, via Richmond and the Orange and Alexandria Railroad.
    Upon arriving in Richmond I requested a separation from the regiment in Fredericksburg, to see you. I will ride to Brandy Station and expect to arrive by the 15th of May. I will telegraph you while in Fredericksburg.

Yours,
Gabe

"Captain, how long are we going to sit around here and waste time? I don't even know what day it is. Each day we do the same, boring routine," Sergeant Mott moaned.

"Captain, it's not that we are complaining, but we are not used to this," added Sergeant O'Keeffe.

"The regiment just got new orders. Tomorrow we move out. Men, your wait is over."

"Sir, where are you going?"

"Sergeant, I'm going with the regiment."

"Yes, but only to Fredericksburg—"

"I'm taking a short leave; I'll meet up with you men in Alexandria in a few days."

Captain Hobensack walked up behind the men. "I heard the same thing. What are you up too?"

"Nothing. Men, get ready to move out tomorrow." Then he walked off.

As soon as the train arrived in Fredericksburg, Gabe led Rascal from the railroad car he had been riding in, gave him some water, and rode off.

After Captain Hobensack saw Gabe walk off, he also requested a short leave and made arrangement for three troopers to receive special permission to leave with him: Sergeants George O'Keeffe and Mott, and Corporal Gregory. Together the four men followed O'Shea.

Even though he had a two-hour head start, they knew where he was headed, and it wasn't home. On the evening of the first day's ride they caught up with him.

"Are you sure you know where you are going?" John asked Gabe as they galloped up to him.

"Yes, I do. Do you?"

"I don't think you ever marched so slow. It's like you are unsure if you really want to see her."

"What? Yes, I do. I'm thinking."

"About what, sir?" Sergeant Mott asked.

"Nothing. Leave me alone, or I'll shoot all of you for desertion."

"Sorry, sir, but we aren't deserters. We have orders," said Corporal Gregory.

"Leave me alone anyway."

They continued to ride for miles in silence.

Then Gabe spoke. "It is hard to imagine the purest gift conceivable when death is all we know."

"What gift is that, sir?"

"Love."

Sergeant Mott smiled, and the men thought about that for the next few miles.

Arriving the next day at Kate's little farm, they were shocked to find that her home had been burned to the ground.

Gabe dismounted and rushed to the black, skeletal remains of the structure. Some boards still stood high, reaching to the sky in defiance, while others were a pile of ash. He stepped over to the deck and reached down to pick up what was left of a leg from one of the rockers he once sat in as he recovered from his wound. He slowly moved the burned wood to his nose and took in its death stench.

Nothing. It's been too long.

He stared for a few moments, then turned and mounted.

He did not wish to go to Ellie's home to inquire what had happened, so they rode into town to see what they could find out.

That evening, Ann and Teresa secretly watched Gabe and the Yankees asking around town for Kate.

The troopers stopped to visit the blacksmith at the livery stable to have their horses taken care of, and one of them asked the old man in the barn, "Do you know where Kate is?"

"No," he replied.

"Do you know what happened?

"No."

"If you did know, you wouldn't tell me, would you?"

"Nope."

The men gathered on the main street to decide what to do next.

"Let's ask at the hotel, and we can also get some hot food and some rooms while we are there," suggested Captain Hobensack.

"I agree. We can ask around tomorrow. It's getting late," said Gabe.

"I want a hot bath," said Mott.

"I can't wait to sleep in a bed," added Gregory.

After checking in at the hotel, Gabe inquired about Kate, but nobody seemed to know where she was.

"Let's get some food," said Hobensack with a grin. "I'm hungry."

"Order me whatever you are getting," Gabe told him. "I'm going to ask about her at the general store. I'll be right back."

No sooner had Gabe walked into the general store, Ann and Teresa rode home to tell Ellie.

At the counter, John, the clerk, looked up to see a Yankee cavalry captain staring at him.

"Can I help you, young man?" asked John.

"Sir, I'm Captain O'Shea. I'm looking for—"

"Kate," the clerk interrupted.

"Yes," said Gabe, looking surprised. "How did you know that?"

"Your letters," he explained. "They came though this post office."

"Please help me find her." He paused. "I get conflicting replies … one man tells me she went to Richmond, and a woman said she went back to Pennsylvania. Some say she just left and didn't tell anyone. Do you know where she is?

He shook his head. "Nope. I haven't seen her since the Yankees burned her home down, the day before the war ended."

"She must have been angry."

"Angry? More like enraged."

"Is that why nobody will talk to me, because of what the Yankees did?"

"Probably," said the clerk. "But they don't like you fellas anyway."

"So why are you talking to me? You're the only one in town who will talk to me about her."

"Like I said, I know about your letters."

"What do you know?"

"Hang around, someone will show up soon. Once the word gets out that you are here, you know … news travels fast around here."

"Yes, it does. I learned that during the war."

"Have a nice meal at the hotel. Get a room and a good night's rest, and see what the new day brings to your door."

"Good idea," said Gabe. "I have a hot meal waiting for me at the hotel now."

"Goodbye, young man," said the clerk. "Go eat. I have work to do."

"Thank you, sir," said Gabe.

"Don't call me sir, I'm not an officer. My name is John."

* * *

Before sunup, three Confederate cavalry soldiers finally made their way back to their home county. Since the start of the war four years ago, fifty-three went to fight. No one was sure how many would return.

"Do you ever think about the consequence of some of your acts, sir?"

"There are no consequences," said the Rebel captain. "Just outcomes."

"If you believe that, then you're willing to do anything."

"That's right. If I'm willing to accept the consequences, then I'm willing to do anything, Sergeant Moore."

"There! I can see a few lights. We are almost home," Corporal Hill informed them with joy in his voice.

After entering the town they headed to the livery stable to rest their tired and worn-out mounts. After removing their gear and saddles, Sergeant Moore noticed that in a stall in the back of the barn rested a memorable bay horse.

"Look at that horse! Does he look familiar?" Moore asked Corporal Hill.

Hill nodded. "Yes—he looks like that horse that ran into me at Slaughter Mountain, back in '62. He stopped me from shooting his rider as he mounted a big gray that had his face shot up."

"Yup, and he is the same horse that knocked me and my mount to the ground at Brandy Station in '63."

"Lieutenant Jones, come look at him."

Captain George Jones was the youngest of six. He had been raised as a spoiled child, had a bad temper, and came from a rich family; a bad combination. He was finally allowed to enlist late in the war, when men were badly needed, and his father, who had already lost two of his four sons, made sure he was made a second lieutenant. Abusive to both his men and his enemies, Jones became daring if only to keep his rank.

Captain Jones had been listening to the troopers talking about the horse.

"Why are you men making a big deal over a stupid animal?"

"Come look, Captain."

He slowly walked over to see.

"I also know this horse. Just before the battle at Brandy Station, my sister Peggy told me that Kate won the race at The Spring on a horse she thought was from the Union cavalry. My sister knew our cavalry got her horse, because she gave it to them. Kate kept her new mount a secret. But just before the race, Peggy got one of the kids Kate came with to slip up. She described him just like this one—a white star between his eyes, and a white blaze shaped like a cross on his nose. That's one of the horses that beat her. Miss Ellie also came in first. My sister did not do well."

Sergeant Moore walked over to the other horses. "These other horses are branded as Union, but he is not."

"It is possible he is or was owned by his rider," Jones told them.

"The same owner for the whole war—that would be rare, wouldn't it?" Moore asked.

"Do you think it can be the same rider?" asked Corporal Hill.

"I don't care. That horse is a fighter. I want to make him a wedding gift for Ellie."

"Captain Jones are you thinking of … taking him?" asked Moore.

"No, I—I will make an offer. Let's go before these soldiers come out here. The sun will be up soon."

"Corporal Hill, stay here. Hide somewhere, and let me know when they come for their horses. We will be in the Tavern."

"Yes, sir." His fellow trooper could hear his reluctance to following orders that he need not follow. But out of respect to the rank he did, and they both understood that.

* * *

The next morning, just before sunup, Hobensack and Gabe sat down to fresh eggs, bread, and hot coffee.

"I hope you find her, sir," Hobensack said to Gabe. "Too bad she isn't around. I wanted to meet her. You men got to meet both ladies at Gettysburg in '63."

Gabe sipped his coffee. "I'm sure she is around here somewhere. I'm going to finish my breakfast, then I'll start looking for her by checking where the mail comes in."

The Captain Hobensack stood up. "Let's go, men. Be safe, and God be with you, Gabe, you know how to find us."

Gabe stood as well. "Men, it was my pleasure to serve with you. Live long, happy lives, and have many children and love your wives."

In the livery stable Sergeant O'Keeffe noticed that more horses had arrived and were tied to a side wall. He walked over to check them out..

"Look over here, Captain," said O'Keeffe. "These horse are Rebel cavalry. They were not here when we rode in."

The other man looked at them and nodded. "They must have come in late last night or early this morning."

"Do you think we should stay around for the captain?" O'Keeffe asked.

"No, he will be fine. The war has been over for more than a month. I want to go home ... I say let's ride."

The four men continued on their ride north.

* * *

Arriving at the general store an hour before sunrise, Kate wrapped a blanket around her and sat in a corner to wait for Ellie. She looked tired and worn. For nearly a month after the fire she had lived out of her barn. Friends and neighbors found out she had moved from house to house never staying long. She really wanted to stay with Ellie, but knowing she could not confront her in her own home kept her away.

Kate gazed toward the east as the first light of day began to show itself and wondered how their confrontation would end. *I must take her down this road, before she sees the letter. I can do this. I must do this, it's what I'm good at. Remember how you felt before the letter came, when you wished you had never questioned Gabe's past.*

The door slowly opened, and she waited for Ellie to walk to the counter of the general store.

While on lookout for the Yankees, Corporal Hill noticed Ellie ride into town, and he followed her. He sat down close to a window at the general store and listened to the ladies talk inside.

"Hi, you're here early. Coming to pick up the mail?" Kate asked her.

Ellie turned her head to see Kate sitting in a corner next to the door. "Kate! Yes, I'm here for the mail. Did you get anything?"

"Just this one." Kate held up a letter and waved it.

"From Mac?"

Kate shook her head. "No, but you know who it's from."

Ellie frowned. "Washington?"

"No."

"Your family?"

Kate put the letter on her lap. "That was your last try. Why did you write to Gabe?"

Ellie turned away, headed slowly for the door. "What are you talking about?"

"You know damn well, you can't act like you're innocent." Kate stood up and blocked the way.

Ellie turned away, sighing. "I told you that you should write to him, and you didn't."

"So you decided to write to him as me, why?"

"How do you know?" asked Ellie.

Kate looked at her. "I know everything. I have known for a while. I read his letters then resealed some of them so you could reply."

"I felt he needed someone to care about him."

"So why not write him as yourself?"

"Because he wanted you."

Kate threw up her hands in exasperation. "You don't even have the strength to say the truth."

"That is the truth."

"No, it isn't," said Kate.

"Then what is?"

"He didn't want you."

"I know. I only wanted to help him survive the war."

"I find that ironic."

"Why?" asked Ellie.

"That you wanted a Yankee to survive this war."

"Not just any Yankee, just this one."

"Well, I need to thank you. Because of what you did, I now see how wonderful he is."

"But you don't care about him."

Kate shook her head. "I do care—maybe not like you do, but at least I don't lie to him. If you play along I'll give you Rascal."

"You can't," said Ellie. "You don't own him."

"I will when we are married."

Ellie looked shocked. "You wouldn't!"

Kate looked at her with a level gaze. "You know I would."

"You have always been about what you want and what you could get, instead of what is the right thing to do."

"Don't bullshit me, you and I always had the same goals. We just had different approaches."

Ellie's voice was steady. "You choose control and at times manipulation to get what you desire."

"And you think because you choose love and God that you're better than me?"

"I care."

"About what? Not the truth."

Ellie hesitated and was silent for a moment.

Kate prodded her. "What's the matter—your guilt holding you back? Do you think you are above reproach?"

Ellie narrowed her eyes. "Why didn't you tell me what happened to Mac's family's plantation?"

"I knew you would find out anyway."

"What else have you been hiding from me?"

She is getting better at this, thought Kate. *Gabe and I are creating a feisty, smart verbal opponent. I'll need to raise the tension.*

Kate held up the letter. "His letters. I saved most of them; I only passed a few onto you. I'll use his letters to keep him loving me."

Ellie looked her in the eye. "This war changed you. It has taken everything from you, your husband, your home, your animals, even your childhood love—in your mind Mac is not a complete man, he lost everything you feels is important."

Kate's jaw clenched. "That's right, and you get to keep everything—your home is safe, and you are lying to Gabe to keep him from me."

"Kate, your outer strength has always been stronger than your inner, and they were always at odds with each other."

"What difference does that make?"

Kate paused and holds her head in her hands thinking of her next step.

She is right. My outer strength was always stronger, but now for the first time they are both fighting for the same thing. "How dare you, trying to bring morality into this? You lied to both of us."

Ellie looked away. "I … I just wanted to do the right thing."

"By deceiving us and you think you love us, how do you justify that with your God?"

She sighed. "I can't."

"That's right, you can't. You did the wrong thing."

"Yes, I did the wrong thing, but for the right reason."

"I'm going to get something more out of it. My new love has everything I want, and he got though this war whole. He is stronger and his family is wealthier than when this war started."

"I at least care about Gabe."

I need to push her harder. "I care. I care about all the things he's going to give me."

"He's smart, he'll see that you don't really care about him."

Kate shrugged. "By then it will be too late, and we'll be married."

"I'll have to object," said Ellie.

"If you find us. I can't take this war anymore. I'm going to take what I want, no matter the cost."

"He won't be happy with you," Ellie mumbled as she wept.

"Why do you think he'll be happy with you? He finds you boring."

Ellie looked hurt. "Maybe, but I understand him."

"I can read the letters to get to understand him when I need to. Look, I still have them." Kate waved the bundle of letters at Ellie.

"That's not love," she replied.

"I don't need to love him." Kate paused. "He loves me, and that's all that matters. He will do anything for me."

"You don't love him," Ellie repeated.

"You don't love him either. You're deceiving him." Kate raised her voice.

"I care about him."

"You keep saying that, but you don't love someone you've been lying to. You're trying to steal him from me."

"I do love him," Ellie cried out. "I'm not stealing him."

"You'll say anything to keep him from me." Kate pretended to cry.

"I wrote the letters—those words are mine. They express how I feel about him," Ellie said through tears.

"You are lying to him—how do you think your God feels about that?"

"His words are for me, he is opening up to me," said Ellie, raising her voice.

"I know. And if you don't tell him, I won't either."

"I wrote to him because I love him for who he is, not what he has."

"Finally we are getting somewhere," said Kate.

"What?"

"You just said you love him—more than once."

"I did?" asked Ellie.

"Yes."

Ellie was silent for a moment, then swallowed. "I do Kate, I do love him. Please help me." Her eyes were pleading.

"Help you with what?" asked Kate.

"I need to tell him the truth."

Kate nodded. "Yes, tell him the truth."

"Why are you agreeing with me?"

"He needs to know the truth so he can choose."

"So those things you said to me is your way of getting me to tell him the truth?"

"Maybe."

"He will make one of us very happy," said Ellie.

"Ellie, if he doesn't pick you, he's crazy and he doesn't deserve you."

"What are you doing? Are you trying to trick me?"

"No. You need to tell him the truth about how you feel, today. He is here now … he needs to pick one of us, once and for all."

Ellie looked at Kate. "I'm sorry I lied. The last thing I wanted was to ruin our friendship."

"I know. I'm sorry I had to push you so hard, but you gave me a hell of a time."

"I guess you are rubbing off on me." Ellie smiled.

"It's about time."

"How did you know he was here already? I only found out late last night from my sisters."

"Two days ago he sent me this telegram telling me he expected to arrive yesterday."

"So, you haven't seen him yet?" she asked.

"Nope. I have been waiting for you." Kate smiled at her. "Ellie, let's go watch this amazing sunrise. I have a feeling this is the start of a new beginning."

Captains, Damsels, and Destiny

As Kate and Ellie left the general store, Corporal Hill approached them.

"'Morning. Miss Kate, Miss Ellie, remember me?"

"Yes, of course! Timmy, I'm so glad you made it through the war." Kate gave him a hug.

"Good to see you, Timmy. Any more boys with you?" Ellie asked.

"Yes, Sergeant Sam Moore. Also there is a certain captain waiting to see you."

John came out of the store and called out to the ladies. "Miss Kate, I have a letter for you, from Mac." Kate walked back with him to the counter.

"Thanks, John. How did I do?" she asked him quietly.

He smiled. "You were entertaining, as always. Did you have to push her so hard?"

"What else are friends for? Besides, she needed it. I'm good at pushing people."

"Yes, you are," he said. "And you pushed her in the right direction."

"You heard everything?" asked Kate.

"Yes, I did. Oh—the Union captain is here."

"Thanks again for getting his telegram to me. Thanks for everything."

"No need to thank me. Go have some fun."

Kate went back outside, and she and Ellie started walking down the main street.

"Where is Timmy?" asked Kate.

"He went ahead. So Gabe will be here today?" asked Ellie in a shaky voice.

"Yes I told you that. You sound nervous."

"I am, a little bit, but I'm not sure why. How do I look?" Ellie asked.

"Let's stop in the hotel and clean up a bit for him. We need to make it hard for him to choose."

"We do?" asked Ellie.

"Yes, of course! Men love it when women do these things."
"OK, if you say so. Good idea to freshen up."

* * *

Corporal Timmy Hill ran to the tavern to report to Captain George Jones what he had learned.

"Four of the Yankees rode out about thirty minutes ago, and a captain owns the horse, and he is still in town."

"Where is he?" asked Jones.

"I think he is still in the hotel, eating" said Timmy.

"What do you mean, you 'think'—weren't you watching him?"

"When I was on my way here Miss Ellie rode in, and I followed her to the general store."

"Ellie is here?"

"Yes, sir, with Kate. They are looking for someone named Gabe."

"Gabe?"

"Yes. Miss Kate was mad at Miss Ellie, and they had words."

"About what?" asked the captain.

"Ellie told Kate she was writing someone named Gabe, and she is in love with him. Kate got mad because she was also in love with him."

"With a man named Gabe?"

"Yes. I think he is in love with Ellie, and he has come here for her."

"What else, corporal?"

"That's it. They argued and were loud, then Ellie started to cry. They were talking fast and at the same time. When John the clerk called out to talk to Kate, I came here."

"Let's get back to the livery stable before the captain does."

"Sir, then what?" asked Sergeant Moore.

"When he shows up, I'll buy his horse. Let's go."

The three men then hurried to the barn. Sergeant Moore scanned the quiet street then closed the barn door behind them.

"You two step back toward that empty stall and wait there."

"Sir, I don't think this is a good idea."

"Who is in charge here, corporal?"

"Sir, the war is over."

"What did you say?" Jones stepped up chest-to-chest with

Sergeant Moore.

"Sir, what if he won't sell him?"

"He will."

"If he was my horse I wouldn't sell him, no matter how much money was offered," said Corporal Hill.

"Me, neither. I can still see him slamming into our horses at Brandy—what an animal."

"Everyone has a price, that's what my Pa taught me."

Just then Captain O'Shea walked into the livery stable and moved toward Rascal's stall.

"Move back," Captain Jones quietly told his men. As Gabe approached he stepped out of the shadows.

Not until Gabe reached the stall did he see the Confederate captain standing next to it.

"Nice horse," said Jones.

"Thanks," Gabe replied. "I didn't see you standing there."

"Not much light in here, is there?"

"No, not much."

"I don't need light," said Captain Jones. "I know what I want."

"What?"

"I want to buy him," he said, pointing to Rascal.

"Sorry, captain, but he is not for sale."

The captain straightened. "I'm Captain George Jones, and these are my men."

Gabe looked around to see two enlisted men with holstered sidearms walk out from behind him.

After looking them over, he said, "I'm Captain O'Shea, and according to the surrender terms you two men are not supposed to be armed."

"How much for the horse?" asked Captain Jones.

"I told you, he is not for sale."

Jones stepped closer to Gabe and put his hand on his pistol.

"Back off, captain," warned Gabe.

"I want him," repeated the captain. "How much?"

Gabe sized Jones up and moved in close so that they were toe to toe. The two captains glared into each other's eyes, neither backing. They were so close they could feel each other's breath and pulsating heartbeats, their blood pounding in strong rhythm.

"Sir, please, he is a Union officer," Corporal Hill whispered to his captain.

"Captain, stand down. That's an order," said Gabe, raising his voice.

George Jones stepped back and started to mumble to himself. Gabe said, "This horse is not for sale because I will be giving him away."

"To who?"

"To my soon-to-be wife, as a wedding gift." He reached for a cloth in a bucket next to the stall and began to rub Rascal. *He will be the first of several wedding gifts, but I know he will be her favorite. What a perfect retirement for my companion. Horses should be recognized as war heroes and given a good home.*

"I also want to give him as a wedding gift," Jones tells the three men.

"My girl is Ellie Jefferson," Gabe said to Jones.

"Elizabeth Lynn Jefferson?"

"Yes. She lives at Brook—"

Captain Jones was red in the face with irritation. "I know where she lives. Is your name Gabe?" He began to pace and mumble in front of the stall.

"Yes. Why do you ask?" Gabe turned to look at Jones, who was struggling to control his anger—his hands began to tremble, and his eyes began to burn with fury.

Suddenly, like an old, rotten tree in a wicked storm, Jones snapped. He reached for his pistol and wildly struck Gabe on the back of the head.

CRACK.

The impact splattered blood on Sergeant Moore's face, and the blow spun Gabe around. The next blow caught Gabe on his jaw. His head flung around and his body followed, toppling to the ground.

BOOM.

The building shook and dust filled the air.

BOOM.

Rascal violently kicked his stall wall again. The barn rattled and groaned as if in pain from the powerful impacts. After the second blow to Gabe, Rascal's head went down, his back raised up in an arch, and he let out deep grunts, his nostrils expanding with each forceful exhale, like a pent-up dragon ready to blow fire from his angry heart. Then the bucking started, and each blow threatened to dismantle his stall and the walls around it. Each buck was more violent than the one before as boards snapped and objects began to fall from the walls.

Minutes ago there would have been five other horses around Rascal joining in the rage. Gabe tried to lift himself up.

"I'm OK, boy ... easy, easy, before you hurt yourself. Easy."

His calm voice barely soothed Rascal's pain and anger. It was enough to stop the bucking, but he continued to grunt, paw and blow, just waiting for the signal to let loose and explode into battle.

Sergeant Moore stood with a smug smile on his face.

"Now that's the horse we saw at Brandy Station and Slaughter Mountain." *I wonder who is crazier,* he thought. *That horse or my captain.*

* * *

"I feel better, don't you?" Kate asked Ellie.

"Refreshed, yes," said Ellie. "But still nervous."

Leaving the hotel, the sounds of several loud impacts suddenly reverberated down the street.

BAM. BAM. BAM.

"What is going on over there?" Kate asked.

"It came from the livery stable—hurry, someone may need our help."

A few early risers out on the street froze in their steps as they looked over toward the stable. Soon several people hurried over to see what was happening.

"Miss Kate, what was that?"

"I don't know, Edwin. Go wake Doc Wilson, in case someone was hurt."

Inside the livery stable, Jones still confronted Gabe.

"For God's sake, he is a captain in the Union army—you could be hanged, we could all be hanged!" said Sergeant Moore.

"You heard him—we aren't supposed to be armed," said Corporal Hill.

"Over a horse? No one in this town will hang me over a horse. This is about a woman, a woman I love, and she loves me."

"What is he saying?" asked Corporal Hill.

"Holster your weapon, captain," said Moore.

Jones pulled his other pistol out, and then pointed one at each man.

"You both are traitors of the Confederacy."

In a shaky voice Hill said, "Sir, the war is over."

"No, not yet, corporal. Not this war. It's over when I say it is over when she is my woman."

"Captain, please don't hurt anybody. We are home, we are tired of the hurting."

"I'm home now, and I have come for my future and my wife."

Gabe looked over at Rascal and saw his rage continuing to slowly build. The horse slammed his body into the boards that separated him from Gabe, grunting and blowing between each impact.

Gabe whispered to him. "Sorry, old friend, but I'm hesitant to signal you to stop ... my life may depend on your explosive fury."

Ellie and Kate reached the barn before anyone else, and upon entering they saw Captain Jones, with his pistols drawn. Both immediately recognized the other men, and as Ellie closed the door she signaled to the people behind her to get help.

Kate spotted Rascal and went straight to him.

"Stop, Kate," said Jones. "Go back outside."

She ignored him.

Ellie approached Jones and talked to him calmly. "George? George Jones? It's me, Ellie. What are you doing?"

"Easy, boy, easy." Kate spoke to the horse in a soft, soothing voice. She reached into his stall. He felt her hand move across his back, and he quieted a bit more.

George looked toward Ellie, who had her back to the barn door.

"Hi, Ellie ... I'm here for you."

In the dim light she was able to see the confusion in his face, like a lost child in the dark who is afraid of the monsters that might come for him.

"Um ... OK, I'm here," said Ellie reassuringly. "George, what have you done to that horse?"

"I had to stop him."

"From what?"

"From taking you away from me."

Kate grabbed a support pole next to Rascal's stall but her hand slid down, unable to get a grip. She looked at it, wondering what she touched. A few gaps in the wall—some caused by wear, but others by Rascals powerful blows—allowed the early morning sun to shine through, revealing to her the blood on her palm. She quickly looked over Rascal but saw no wound, then turned to Jones.

Confused, Ellie asked Jones, "Why would a horse take you away?"

"Not a horse—his owner." He pointed to Gabe, who was on the ground in the dark.

Kate quickly moved to Gabe and gasped as she saw the blood and the gash in his head.

"Is he alive?" Ellie yelled to Kate, purposely loud enough for the people outside to hear.

"Yes, he is," Jones replied, and Kate and Samuel both shook their heads in agreement.

Kate knelt down next to Gabe to check his head. She turned him over, revealing the wound on his jaw.

"Gabe, it's Kate. Can you hear me?"

Gabe stirred. "Yes, but my head …"

"Stay still, and don't touch it. It seems like I'm always saving your little ass."

Gabe managed a smile. "What did you say—you're playing with my ass?"

"Funny, still the same old Gabe," said Kate. "Good thing Ellie didn't hear that."

Kate ripped a piece of her dress, then tried to close the wound in his scalp before wrapping the two-inch gash. With anger in her voice, she yelled to Jones, "Can you get up? We are leaving now."

"No, you can't do that."

"Why not? He doesn't even know who you are."

"Yes, he does, and we both want the same woman."

"What woman, George? Who do you want?" Kate asked.

"Hill, block the door with something. I don't want anyone else in here," he ordered.

Hill found a pitchfork and stuck it through the handle of the barn door.

With his head down, Jones replied.

"I want you," he said.

"Me?" Kate asked.

"Not you—her." He turned and pointed to Ellie.

"Me?" asked Ellie. "Why?"

"I love you," he said. "I always have."

"George, what have you done?" Ellie asked.

Jones pointed at Gabe. "He wanted to take you from me."

"He is still alive, so we can still work this out."

"Yes, Miss Kate, but he beat him," Timmy Hill told her.

"Why?" Kate asked as she stared at Ellie. Jones struggled to get his thoughts together.

"George wanted to buy his horse, but the Yankee would not sell it. When the Yankee told Captain Jones it was a wedding gift, he hit him," said Moore.

"We tried to get him to put his weapons away, but he won't," said Hill.

"George, what do you want us to do?" Ellie asked.

He looked at Ellie. "I want everyone to leave, and for you to stay with me."

"Sir, we will put our weapons down, but I don't think we should leave you," said Moore.

"Slow, Timmy and Samuel, move away slowly," Kate whispered to them. "Let Ellie handle him."

Jones rambled on. "I want to marry you, Miss Ellie."

"George, I will do anything you want … just please stay in control of yourself, OK?"

"I'll try."

"George, what do you want me to do?"

"Marry me."

Kate yelled out, "Ellie, you know you are going to have to ask your father first."

Good thinking, Kate, thought Ellie. "That's true, George—you know how my father can be."

Jones looked confused. "What? OK, whatever you say."

Jones turned to Gabe. "You must die so then she will love me."

"No! George, he must live," Ellie told him, trying to remain calm.

"He can't … he loves you."

Kate called over to him, "No, George. He loves me, not Ellie."

"Liar! Corporal Hill heard your fight … he wrote her letters. He loves her."

"Look for yourself—look at the letters. They are to me, not Ellie." Kate held out the letters and waved them.

Kate moved to put herself between Jones and Gabe.

"Lies!" He slapped her hand and shook his head as he mumbled to himself.

Kate tried again, picking up the few letters she dropped. "George, please look—it's me he is in love with."

"No." This time Jones slapped her across her face. She fell across the top of a barrel, and Jones stepped up close behind her, pressing his thighs up against her bottom. He reached down for her hair and pulled her head back toward him. He licked her cheek, looking for fear in her eyes.

But what he didn't know was that she was incapable of fear. She smiled at him.

"You ready to do this now, in front of all these people?"

Jones didn't let go, enraged. "I'm tired of you ... all my life you controlled me and you teased me. No more."

Gabe struggled to his feet. "Let her go, or the last thing I do in this life is kill you with my bare hands."

Jones turned around to see his men grab Gabe. He threw Kate forward and over the barrel and walked over to Gabe, who was struggling to get loose.

"Stop—stay still, before he hits you again," said Moore.

Without warning Jones struck Gabe again. Surprised, and to avoid getting him hit again, the two men let Gabe go. He dropped like a doll to the straw that was soaked with his blood.

Kneeling, Gabe yelled out to Gorge, "You coward ... you need your men to hold me." He spat blood from his mouth. "You can't fight me without help. You're a coward."

Kate pushed past Jones and put herself between them again.

Jones tried to step around Kate, who again moved to position herself between the two men.

Ellie had moved away from the door and now stood up against Jones's back. She needed him to feel her; she needed to get his attention.

Softly she whispered to him, "George, if you kill him, they will hunt you down, and you will never be able to marry me. Let's go now."

Moore then added, "Sir, a crowd is beginning to form ... let's go now, while we can."

"No, nobody will hunt me down. I will take you to the mountains. No one will ever find us."

Jones pointed his pistol at Gabe once again, ignoring the cries and screams of a few women outside who could hear what was going on.

What damage this war has done to him, Ellie thought. *Two years ago he left here a weak, violent young man, and he has come back a jealous madman. I will save Gabe's life, no matter what it costs me.*

"Now you must die."

Ellie put her arms around Jones. "No ... I will marry you now, right now, if you let him live."

"Ellie, what are you doing?" Kate asked.

"George, let Timmy tell the people outside to get the preacher."

Timmy looked over to Jones.

"Go, do it." Timmy moved to the barn door and without opening it said to the people outside, "Go get a preacher."

Ellie knelt down next to Kate and whispered, "He is all yours. You win again. Take care of him."

She stood up again and stepped toward Jones. She reached out and put her hand over his, the pistol still in his grip pointed at Gabe.

Gabe grabbed Kate's leg, and she bent down to him.

He said to her in a low voice, "One thing you have trouble accepting is that your mental strength is much stronger than your body. So don't do anything stupid. He wants to kill us both, that's the only way he can have Ellie for himself."

Ellie spoke gently to Jones. "George, if you kill him, I will never marry you, and I won't ever talk to you for as long as I live. Now let's get married and get out of here."

Kate was taken aback, surprised. *What is she doing? She can't marry this crazy man. She can't give up now. She would rather marry someone she despises and lose Gabe than get him killed? Either way, she would lose him. I wonder if he could ever find happiness with me.*

That last thought made her mind go blank. She heard nothing. The world was dead silent. Then a voice came to her—not from within her head, but from somewhere outside of her into her ears. It was firm and deep.

Just deal with it.

Kate's mind reeled for a moment. *Now I understand the love Ellie has for Gabe, a love I have never known and may never have. What Ellie can't bear or allow is for Gabe to die because of her. Is this love? I now know they will have a magical union, and Ellie is the ideal partner for him. They are made for each other.*

Kate stood up and pulled Ellie away from Jones. Jones mumbled to himself, unsure of what to do. They could tell he was beginning to lose his sense of reality.

"George, what are you going to do now?" Kate asked him.

Kate saw it in his eyes; she had seen it once before in the war, the instant the eyes show the need to release oneself from all pain through the desire to kill. Jones slowly squeezed the trigger as Kate leaned away.

BOOM.

She flew back and landed on Gabe, who rolled her off and then realized he was covered in blood. The bullet had passed through her and sprayed him with her blood. The air filled with the all-too-familiar gray smoke.

Rascal crashed out of his stall and lunged, only to be trapped again in the next stall.

"Nooooooo!" Ellie yelled.

"Captain, what did you do?" Sergeant Moore called out in horror.

"I ... I was shooting—"

Before he could finish his words, through the cloud of smoke emerged another flash of gray, as if the smoke gave birth to the angel of death. This apparition gripping a saber in his fully extended arm swung at Jones. Jones gasped on his last word as blood streamed from his throat. He fell to his knees, then onto his side. Death and silence were instant.

"Anyone else?"

Both Hill and Moore froze. Before them stood a Confederate officer, the third captain to enter this confrontation.

"No, sir."

"Remove your holsters slowly; you're not supposed to be armed." He turned to Ellie.

"Hurry—get someone to help her."

Doc Wilson, who had been listening from outside with the crowd that had gathered, called out. A group of people were trying to open the door.

"Let me in!" yelled Doc.

Timmy released the door.

The Doc and Gabe's men stormed in. The three Rebels turned toward them, blood still dripping from the tip of the saber.

"No, stop, it's over." Ellie grabbed at the Yankees and then moved in between the blue and the gray uniformed men.

"Over here," Gabe yelled out to his men.

"Captain, are you all right?"

"Yes … take the Rebels out but don't hurt them. I will be out soon."

Gabe rolled toward Kate. He leaned in close to listen to her soft but firm voice that only he heard.

"What happened?" she asked. "I feel like shit …"

"George shot you. Don't move."

"Give me a gun," she said, "I need to put him out of his misery."

"That was done already," Gabe told her.

"Good. You got him?"

"No. A Rebel captain came out of nowhere."

Kate smiled weakly. "Tell him if he had come sooner I would have liked to meet him, thank him, and marry him."

"I will," he paused. "I love you."

"I love you, too," she said with a smile.

Before he could say another word, she whispered again. "Ellie wrote the letters you got after Gettysburg, not me."

"I know."

"You knew? For how long?" she asked.

"I figured it out this April."

"You are slow. I figured it out in May of '64. She really loves you. Do you love her?"

"Yes, I do. Very much," he told her.

"Good. She doesn't know you figured out she wrote the letters. It is important that she admits it to you, so push her. Bring her closer to me."

He turned to Ellie. "She wants to talk to you."

Ellie reached over toward Kate, sorrow in her eyes.

Kate spoke to her quietly but firmly.

"I'm sorry," she said. "You deserve him. I'm sorry I said those things to you. You know I love you. "

Tears ran down Ellie's cheeks. "Forget those words, I never

stopped loving you." Her tears dripped onto Kate's dress.

"You were meant for each other," said Kate. "He brings out the passion in you, and you understand the torrent of feelings in his soul better than anyone. Take care of him and he will take care of you."

"Ellie, I need to see her. Please move over," said the doctor.

Gabe asked, "Any chance, Doc?"

The doctor looked at her wound but soon looked away, shaking his head slowly.

"I'll do what I can to slow the bleeding, but she doesn't have long. Don't move her."

Before Gabe could move away Kate grabbed his leg, looking up at him. He knelt and moved in close to her.

"Gabe, you are everything she needs to open up her heart."

Kate grabbed Ellie's arm also, then turned her head as she coughed up blood. Struggling to speak, she asked, "It's bad?"

Ellie takes a breath but her voice still trembled. "No, we have seen worse."

"You're the worst liar I have ever met, Ellie. I can't feel my legs, and I'm getting cold."

Ellie swallowed hard and kept a brave face. "We are here for you. Please hold on."

"I don't think one of your prayers is going to help, so don't waste your breath on one. With your sympathizing way, your gentleness and generosity of the heart, together you and Gabe will succeed in discovering a fascinating universe under your God. Remember, he is a man who not only understands you but is willing to help you go your way, just to be with you."

She looked at Gabe. "Gabe, move closer. Both of you support and take care of each other. Gabe, Ellie's patience and understanding will help you take hold of your complicated soul."

Gabe looked at her and gently stroked her face. "Kate, I know you are capable of anything, but not of such deep and caring thoughts. Where is this side of you coming from?"

"I'm still full of surprises. I guess your God wants you to hear his words, and not mine." She gritted her teeth to hold back her pain, then smiled for them one last time. She pulled him close. "I now know who you are." Reaching close to her heart, she lifted a small letter out from above her corset. "You must read this."

Gabe shook his head. "Kate, not now!"

"Ellie, make sure to read this. I know you will do that for me." She handed it to Ellie. Looking over to Gabe she ran her right hand in his hair and moved it away from his face, her hand weak and shaking. "Even after the beating you just took, you still look great. I will always love you both." She took a gasping breath. "You are and will always be my family."

Ellie reached over to hold her.

Hurrrrrrr.

They both heard the sound of Kate's last breath leaving her body.

Ellie was close enough to also feel it. It was deep, slow, and flowing like a warm breeze across the mouth of the river. Then Kate's vibrant energy passed into and through her, leaving her with a warm, peaceful feeling that told her Kate would be OK.

She looked over to Gabe who gave her a smile and asked, "Did you feel her leave?"

"Yes," she said, her face full of emotion. "I did."

Gabe held Kate's lifeless body one last time, then turned to look at Ellie. Both had tears in their eyes.

Still clutched in Kate's left hand were the letters written in war. Ellie watched carefully as he slowly removed them and placed them in his pocket.

Ellie staggered over to a barrel next to Rascal's stall and tipped it upright. She collapsed onto it and sobbed. She watched Gabe hand Doc Wilson his blanket roll, and together they opened it and laid it over her.

"Doc, will you take care of her?"

"Yes, don't worry. I will be back shortly."

"OK, Doc," Gabe replied.

After several minutes Ellie asked, "Where do you think she is now?"

"I don't know." He paused, searching for the right words, "But wherever she is, she is telling everyone she is now in charge."

Ellie smiled.

"Why did she risk her life? She rarely showed her compassionate side. Or did she feel she was invincible?"

"We will never know," said Gabe. "But I do know there was much more to that young woman than we will ever know." He was silent for a moment. "Why?"

"Why what, Gabe?"

"Why couldn't I protect her? Why couldn't I save her?"

"What makes you think you were supposed to? Maybe she was supposed to save you."

"What? I never thought of it that way—but why?"

"She lost her husband, her childhood love, and her home—everything that was important to her. Maybe she needed to save something. She wanted to save you."

"Me? She did. I was not in any position to save myself, but again I was caught off guard."

"Gabe, you made it through this great conflict, but you were caught off guard after it was over. Think about how many times you were not caught off guard."

"I guess so."

"She wanted you to go on living. I think she expected she would also."

"Ellie, read the letter she gave you."

Ellie stood and walked over to him. "Here—she wanted you to read it."

His eyes were still swollen with tears. He began to use his sleeve to wipe his face, and Ellie removed a silk handkerchief from her sleeve.

"Here," she said. "Use this."

He looked at it, then grinned with a boyish expression.

"It's only us in here, and I promise not to tell anyone," She smiled at him.

He wiped his face. "It's not that. This is the first time during this war I have shed tears for anyone."

"Gabe, the war has been over for more than a month. You can't blame the war for this."

"I know, it's just been so long since—" He stopped himself.

"It's been so long since what?"

"Since I cried for someone."

"I know."

"How would you know that?"

Ellie ignored him and took both the small letter and her handkerchief from him. She wiped her own tears away, sat down again on the barrel, opened the letter, and began to read. As she read she repeatedly looked up at him.

April 22, 1865.

Katherine,

It was nice to get your letter. Sorry it took me so long to get back to you. When the Confederates came north in June '63, we fled our home in York to go east to Philadelphia. We returned in November, and that's when I finally got your letter. The next spring I wrote to the War Department in Trenton, New Jersey. I was able to get his correct full name but little else. In the fall of '64 I was able to track down his birth information. You were correct to be concerned about Gabe.

The summer after your mother died, your dad took you back to NYC for the summer. I think you were five. You must have had a memorable time. Your letter described a lot of details. Those details helped me track down the information confirming some of your suspicions.

Seven years later, it was the year your father died. You turned twelve. That's when you came to live with me and we spent all of our summers at The Springs and many weeks with Uncle Arthur. From that time on you began to lose touch with your father's family.

You need to be careful how close you get to that young man you wrote so fondly of, but not for the reason you thought.

Andrew Hancock left his home in New York City to go west, but he never got far. In 1832 in Philadelphia he met my sister Caroline who was there as a student, and a year later they married. Your father Andrew had two siblings, Robert and Adeline.

Adeline is Gabe's mother. Your new friend is your first cousin.

I pray this information is helpful and finds you well. Hope to see you soon.

Miss and love you,
Your aunt, Jaclyn

As she read the last sentence, tears dripped onto the letter. Gabe walked over to her. She looked up at him and he appeared as shocked as she was.

She saw the surprise in his face grow as it depleted what little strength he had left. He fell down to his knees, grabbed her legs, and pulled her in close. He pressed his face to her thighs and squeezed her tight. She gently ran her hand over his head. He looked up at her with his face showing the full impact of his loss.

The morning sunlight shone through the small openings in the barn wall, revealing his blood, sweat, and tears, all showing the external trauma of his loss. *But what about his internal stress? What about his heart and soul? How much more loss can he take?*

"God, you didn't let this war take me, but why must you take those I love? Why now? Again, why so many young ones?"

Ellie tried to comfort him. "You're not alone this time. I am here for you, and as long as there is a heaven I will always be with you."

"Did you know?" he asked.

"No."

"Do you know what she was concerned about?"

Ellie wrinkled her brow. "I don't understand."

"In the letter, she wrote that Kate was concerned about me."

"Oh. When we first met you, you had a lot of money in your saddlebags; we thought you might be robbing Southern families. You also told us you were a lieutenant, but you weren't. After you left we didn't think about it. You kept coming back, and we started to like you, but we couldn't help but still wonder, so she wrote her aunt to look into your background. We were being cautious. The war made us so."

He shook his head in disbelief. "My God, we were family and we shared childhood memories but didn't realize it."

"Based on the date of this letter she knew for almost a month."

They stared at each other for a moment.

"That's why she said, 'you are and will always be my family.'"

"I wonder if that's why you felt close to her? After all, you were related, and you both had a lot more in common than you knew.

Why is it that you didn't remember her as a child?"

"I was just thinking about that. She was only five, and I was several years older. I do remember her family coming to stay for a summer. She was too young. I spent a lot of time riding with my friends or going into the city. I only remember her as a little girl, and I don't remember spending any time with her."

"I wonder if your being related to her was why you enjoyed spending time with her."

"What do you mean?"

"In some ways you were very similar."

Gabe let out a long breath. "Let's get out of here. I need fresh air." They stepped out of the barn.

"Captain, over here," Mott called out to Gabe.

"John, please return the captain's saber."

"Good day. I am Captain Gabriel O'Shea. Please call me Gabe. You are?"

"I'm Captain William Smith, 1st North Carolina Cavalry. Call me Bill."

"Why were you in the barn?"

"I rode up as the crowd gathered, and they filled me in as best they could. I knew I could not sneak in from the barn door."

"True, the big door was blocked," said Ellie.

"I headed to the side door. It took some time, but I finally got in quietly. I really wasn't sure what was going on, and I did not have a clear shot. I'm sorry I did not react sooner."

"It must have been hard to kill another Confederate office after the war was over."

"That did cross my mind, but the instant he fired his weapon there was no doubt."

"Where are you headed?"

"I'm on my way home to North Carolina."

"Where were you coming from?" John asked.

"If you don't mind, I prefer not to answer that."

"That's OK."

"Gabe, I'm sure we have crossed paths before," Bill told him.

"I'm sure we did. You must have been at Brandy Station in '63, and again at Gettysburg and so many other times."

"Fate made sure you survived."

"Yes, it did."

"Captain, I'm glad you were here and chose the cavalry."

"When the war started I was working in Charlotte, so in May '61, they came for volunteers. and I joined the cavalry."

"Captain Smith, please use his two men and work with Doc Wilson to make sure Captain Jones's body gets to his family."

"Yes, sir. I will."

"Ellie, who was Jones?" Gabe asked.

"The older brother of Peggy—one of the ladies we beat at The Spring in '63. He was a troubled man who Kate beat up as a boy and who I once courted for a few weeks."

"I guess the war put a lot of things in his mind."

"Do you remember in '63 when your fever came back, and I was telling you about Kate at The Springs?"

"Yes, I think so—something about her dancing with Mac."

"Yes, there were several boys trying to dance with her, and while she and Mac were dancing one of the boys tried to cut in, and they both rejected him. That boy was George Jones."

"Kate sure knew how to make enemies."

"Bill, you're free to go, and thank you. Have a safe trip home, Captain. Go back to your family and enjoy the rest of your life in peace."

"I think I'm going to stay for the funeral—that's if it is OK with you."

"Yes, please stay."

* * *

Many of the Confederate cavalry units of the Army of Northern Virginia were listed among the troops that surrendered at Appomattox. Before the Confederate lines were enveloped, many tried to cut their way through federal lines and succeeded in breaking through and escaped, thus avoiding surrender. Days later they returned home to disband, rather than taking parole with the rest of the Army of Northern Virginia. They were never forced to surrender.

* * *

Before the funeral Gabe and his men talked about what went

on in the barn that sad morning.

"Mott, please release the other two Rebels."

"Yes, sir."

"Please don't."

"Don't what, sir?"

"You don't have to salute or say 'sir.' Call me Gabe."

"OK, Gabe."

"John, why did you and the men come back."

"All the way out, all we could think and talk about were those Rebel horses in the livery stable. So we thought you might need a hand—you know, being a captain, you may attract some unwanted attention."

"Did I."

"Then, as you always do, you may have to fight someone—and without us to order into battle, you may have had to do it all by yourself."

"Yeah, and I though the war was over."

"The war may be over, but there will always be evil to fight," said John.

"Gabe doesn't look for evil, it looks for him," added O'Keeffe.

"Evil and women."

"That was a good one, Mott!"

"No wonder you kept disappearing for days, and the army thought you were being a good trooper, scouting the enemy. You were scouting the enemy's women, and you had two of them taking care of you."

"When we rode into town we spotted the crowd at the livery stable, as we got closer we heard the shot that killed Kate."

"Thanks for backing me up."

"No, sir, thank you for backing us all up and keeping us alive for more than three years. Many of the troopers realized we survived this war because of your help."

Ellie walked up.

"It's time, Gabe. We need to walk over to St. James Church."

"It's eleven o'clock already?"

"Yes."

Even completely dressed in black, she looks amazing. I wonder if she will ever bring up the letters. Why should she?

As they stood next to each other Gabe reached for her hand.

Holding his hand not only warmed it, it made her whole body warm.

Gabe, Mark, Robert, T.J., Samuel, and Timmy lowered Kate into the ground. When they were done, Gabe looked over at Ellie. He watched her walk along the hole, dropping flowers into it, and saw a tear fall from her face. She looked up and straight at him, then approached as she wiped her tears away. Gabe offered his arm.
Walking back to town, he wondered why she was unusually quiet as she held him close and firm.

Conscience and Consequences

"Gabe, we will be heading out within the hour. Will you be riding out with us?" John asked.

"In an hour, I will let you know," he responded.

He turned to see a surprised look on Ellie's face. He reached into her sleeve and pulled out her handkerchief.

"Here, it looks like you need this," he said, handing it to her.

"Do I?"

"Ellie, I should be going with my men."

"Why? Where to?"

"There is no reason for me to stay, is there?"

"Is there?"

"It's been so long since ..." He stopped himself.

"It's been so long since, what?"

"Since I cried for someone?

"I know."

"You said that before ... but how would you know that?"

"Um ... Kate told me."

"Kate also said you aren't a very good liar, either."

Oh, no—does he know I deceived him?

Walking back, he reached into his pocket and pulled out the letters he had taken from Kate's hand.

He read a few parts to her, as if he didn't know who wrote them.

He has my letters. How do I tell him ... what do I tell him?

"This is what I miss, a woman who knows her feelings and knows how to express them. Kate's letters told me a lot about her feelings, and her words helped me get through this war. Even if she had not died, our love was never meant to be. Do you agree?"

"What I don't understand, Ellie, is why George thought you wrote these letters. So now Miss Ellie, it is goodbye. I ride home alone."

Staring at him, her body began to shake, but the words would not leave her tongue. She leaned her head on his chest. He held her closer feeling her body trembling.

"Ellie, will you be able to go on without …" He paused. "I …"

"Wait," she said. "Kate did not share her feelings because she thought that it would be a show of weakness."

"How do you feel about that?"

"I feel sharing one's feelings is a sign of strength."

"Last night I did a lot of thinking about Kate's last words. What do you think she meant by 'You understand the torrent of feelings in his soul better than anyone'?"

"I don't know."

"What about when she said, 'Ellie's patience and understanding will help you grasp your complicated soul'? What 'understanding' was she talking about?"

"I don't know what she meant."

"You aren't a good liar, but since you can't tell me what I need to know, then I must go."

"It's not that."

"Then what is it?"

"I … I wrote the letters. Those words are mine."

"They are?"

"Yes. They expressed how I feel about you."

"I know."

"What? You knew I was writing them?"

"I started to suspect something was going on in April, when the flowers came into bloom. All your letters smelled of lavender, like you. The first letter smelled different, and it was written in a different tone and handwriting. Last winter I tried to write about things that only Kate would know. But then I realized you both shared almost everything. So based on how you replied, I started to think that one or both of you were writing. I was not completely sure until Kate told me before she died. She knew I fell in love with the writer of these letters, with you. She also knew that for a long time I thought I was in love with the both of you."

"Are you disappointed that it was not Kate?"

"No. That was the same question you asked me at the ball."

"Even if she had not been my cousin, I could not be in love with her."

"Why not?"

"Because not until her dying moments could she express such passion for someone. I could not live waiting for that. You are strong, smart, and not afraid to show how you feel." He took a breath. "I love you, Miss Ellie."

Her eyes filled with tears. "I love you too."

After looking at each other for a moment, they kissed.

"I have been waiting a long time for you to do that," she said.

"Since when?"

"At the river, when we sat on the log."

He smiled. "Me too."

"Gabe …"

"Yes?"

"When did you learn that Kate knew you were writing me?"

"This morning."

"What was it that you liked best?"

"Your letters and your words saw through me; they drenched my soul. I was a man in the desert dying of thirst and needing a drink. Each letter exposed a little more of me and made me feel that you cared. I knew that Kate would not write like that."

"She doesn't like to write."

"After my loss I was empty, nothing before you. I am here, now because of you."

"No, don't say that."

"You are my hero," he said. "If you hadn't written those letters, I know I would be dead. They gave me a reason to focus on living each and every day. If you wish, I will spend the rest of my life living to repay you for your life-giving words and feelings. Your divine influence put into words, inspired my mind and soul to enjoy my life again you gave me hope. You have returned me to a living and loving new world."

"Everybody has the potential to be somebody's hero. I'm so happy I am yours and you are mine," she said. "I feel safe with you."

They continued their walk the rest of the way in silence. Reaching town, they stopped and sat on a bench.

"Ellie, now I need to tell you something. Please sit here next to me," he said, still tightly holding her hand for fear of losing her.

"What is it?" she asked. "You still look troubled."

"I feel like … like I'm in distress."

"Distressed, you? Never. Why?"

"I'm being pulled apart."

"Why?"

"I feel like I am going to lose your trust, love, and heart. A few minutes ago you were being pulled apart, right?"

"Yes. But how could I do that to you?"

"Part of you wanted me to know the truth—but another part was scared that I wouldn't understand or forgive you, right?"

"Yes. I won't leave you. I thought you let go of your guilt, your wife's death ... there was nothing you could have done."

"I did, but this is different."

"I know your heart and values. There is nothing you could do that will change how I feel about you."

"Are you sure about that?"

"Yes, Gabe." She moved to stand in front of him, wrapping her arms around his head. Pulling him close against her midsection, he wrapped his arms tight around her lower back. She could feel his strong, tense grip squeezing her and sensed his apprehension.

"Gabe, tell me, what is bothering you so?"

"Ellie, how far would you go to protect your family and the people you love?"

"It depends, but I would never sell my soul."

"What if you did sell it and you didn't realize it until it was too late?"

Her face was serious. "Gabe what do you think you did that makes you feel like that?"

"I killed," he said.

"I know."

"I killed many."

"I—"

He cut her off. "My second month in the war, June '62, near Harrisonburg, my regiment attacked Ashby's position at Good's Farm."

"I remember ... our beloved General Ashby was killed there."

Looking down, he continued. "Yes. In our attack I lost a close friend killed by cavalry cannon fire. When I saw him fall dead, all I could think about was my wife's death. Then something took over me. I was angry and rode hard through Ashby's line. In a rage I felt as if someone was controlling my body, a crazy madman bent on revenge. It was my first time in the war that I killed, I killed two..... and I....I enjoyed it. Then I spotted the horse artillery that fired on us. I rode hard to and through the cannons—" He raised his eyes to hers. She could see tears beginning to swell in his eyes.

"In front of me was a lone, gray-uniformed cannonier. He

picked up a rife. I fired as he turned toward me, and his hat flew back, exposing his face." Tears begin to run down his face. "I ... he ... was a boy ... a child, maybe thirteen. I jumped from my horse and went to his side. He was crying, gasping, and coughing blood as he struggled to speak."

Gabe swallowed hard. "He said, 'I'm James Jefferson from Brandy Station ... tell my mum I love her.'" He died in my arms There was no rifle—he was holding a cannonball rammer. He was unarmed."

Ellie stepped back, her head down looking at her hands shaking, then tears began to run down her checks.

"Can you ever forgive me?"

Nothing in his life was worse than those next quiet seconds ... he was finally in hell.

Then the noon church bells started all over town.

DONG, DONG, DONG, DONG, DONG,
DONG, DONG, DONG, DONG,
DONG, DONG,
DONG.

Then again silence.

"Robert Gabriel ... you know ... I ... you need to forgive yourself. Can you do that?"

"I haven't been able to."

"Yes, you can."

"If you can forgive me? Your forgiveness means more to me than my life."

"No, you must forgive yourself first."

They stared at each other for several long seconds, and then Gabe softly whispered, "I want to. I'll try."

She said quietly, "You know I forgive you, but it is not my forgiveness you need. You need to first forgive yourself and my parents to forgive you."

He shook his head. "They will hate me and keep us apart. We could never be together."

"Don't worry, we will get through it. My folks need to know what happened to J.J. He was always a spontaneous boy who wanted to join the cavalry. Remember, it is never too late to be redeemed."

"How?"

"Three words: trust, forgiveness, and above all, love."

30th of May, 1865.

Captain O'Shea,
Following is the information you request as to the regiment. The regiment arrived at Alexandria on the morning of the 16th of May. On the 21st we marched to Bladensburg, Md. On the 22nd we had the pleasure of receiving our State colors. On the 23rd we took part in the grand review. The regiment was complimented by many for the neat uniform dress and soldierly appearance of its officers and men and for its precision in marching. We are now encamped near Bladensburg, Md.

The health of the regiment is good, and the men are expecting your return.

Walter R. Robbins, Major,
Commanding First New Jersey Cavalry.

Captain Robert Gabriel O'Shea never returned to his regiment.

The End

Epilogue

"Before moving here I was never able to ride on the beach. I love riding here, especially in the morning and evenings. The waves and summer breezes are amazing, Gabe."

"Ellie, I knew you would like it here."

"Do you know if Kate ever had a chance to ride here?"

"Several months ago, while I was in the city, I met up with a few of my cousins, and we talked about the summer Kate was here. Several of the girls told me she did get to ride a few times on the beach. One day Kate would not stop until they took her all the way to the end of The Hook, past the fort."

"That sounds like her."

"They were gone so long that my grandmother had to send someone out to look for them. When they got back they were scolded and not allowed to ride on the beach for a month. After that, no one wanted to ride with her. They did not want Grandma O'Shea to get mad at them."

"You know she would have loved to be here with us," she said, showing off the beautiful smile he remembered seeing on that day they first met.

"I know. I sometimes try to remember what we did together when she was here. In her aunt's letter she wrote that she remembered being here."

"We need to head back, it's starting to get dark. You don't want Grandma O'Shea to send the boys out to look for us."

"OK. Race you to the crossing."

"You'll need that head start you just gave yourself," she yelled out to him. "Come on, Rascal—let's show them who the best team is around here."

Off they rode along the beach toward the crossing. After reaching to the other side they rode up into the heights and through the woods to their home and family.

As the sun set on the Middletown Heights overlooking the lower New York City bay that 4th of July evening, they listened to the bugler from the Fort at Sandy Hook begin to call taps. The music was beautiful on that still summer night and was heard far beyond the limits of the heights.

Watching the fireworks with her descendants, she beams with confidence for her family and their bright future that she had worked hard to nurture, a family that any grand old matriarch would be proud of. Around her are her children, grandchildren, and great-grandchildren. Her keen eyes watch her eldest great granddaughter Jackie playing on the ground in front of her. Standing next to her in glowing tribute is her protégé, Ellie. In her arm is her newborn daughter Katherine, her other arm around her loving husband, Robert Gabriel, who is holding Katherine's twin sister Brandy, both born June 9, 1869.

* * *

This story is in honor all of the people of the United States of America who lived and died during that war 150 years ago. They paid the price to make this country greater than it was, in spite of the toll. Do you deserve that sacrifice?

* * *

In U.S. military bases at home and around the world, at the end of every day or to honor the end of a military life taps is called. Of all the military bugle calls, to this day none is so easily recognized or more apt to render emotion than taps. Up until the Civil War, the traditional call at day's end was a tune borrowed from the French called "Lights Out."

In July of 1862, in the aftermath of the bloody Seven Days battles, with the loss of 600 men and wounded himself, Union General Daniel Adams Butterfield called the brigade bugler to his tent. He thought "Lights Out" was too formal, and he wished to honor his men.

Oliver Wilcox Norton, the bugler, tells the story:

"*Showing me some notes on a staff written in pencil on the back of an envelope, [he] asked me to sound them on my bugle. I did this several times, playing the music as written. He changed it somewhat, lengthening some notes and shortening others, but retaining the melody as he first gave it to me. After getting it to his satisfaction, he directed me to sound that call for 'taps' thereafter in place of the* regulation call. The music was beautiful on that still summer night and was heard far beyond the limits of our Brigade.

"The next day I was visited by several buglers from neighboring Brigades, asking for copies of the music which I gladly furnished. The call was gradually taken up through the Army of the Potomac. [It was also adopted by the army of the Confederates States of America.]

"At the end of one's day there is something singularly beautiful and appropriate in the music and melody of this wonderful and touching call. Its strains are melancholy, yet full of rest and peace. Its echoes linger in the heart long after its tones have ceased to vibrate in the air."

— *from an article by Master Sergeant Jari A Villanueva, USAF, and U.S. Army Military District of Columbia Fact Sheet*

By the final note of "Taps" all lights were to be extinguished, all men bedded down, and all loud talking was to cease. This is the last call of the day.

The Inspiration and Real Story

Several times in March 2012 I called Lauren Schock, owner of Evolution Training Center in West Chester, Pennsylvania, to get updates on one of my two 3-year-old fillies she was breaking. Each time Lauren inquired about my horse Rascal and his racing. She had trained Rascal to race two years before. We knew he was struggling with speed, but we also knew he had plenty of determination.

In April, our phone calls turned to updates on Rascal. Lauren explained to me that she thought he would make a very good jumper, specifically a timber horse. I decided that Atlantic City in late April was going to be his last chance. If he ran poorly, I was set on retiring him from racing and bring him home to rest and transition into my riding horse.

Lauren had other ideas for him, however. She was determined to live her dream of riding in a race. She became the catalyst for getting me out of that rabbit-hole and into the land of amazement. Rascal and I were about to venture into a new world of possibility and a remarkable ride.

My decision would be simple: Rascal had to run decisively well or poorly. So, the opportunist that I am, I asked for a clear and unambiguous outcome that would let me know where we stood. Lauren wanted to live her dream of riding in races and confirm her training instincts. Would Rascal like jumping?

In Atlantic City he ran his usual poor race, so he was hers to train and race. On April 30 he went back to Pennsylvania. Two days later Lauren texted me: "He remembers me." In those three words I could feel her joy and the possibilities.

She had planned to race the following weekend, but getting her trainer and jockey licenses and me getting my owner's license was not going to happen until the following week. She entered him in an amateur apprentice training flat race—two miles, no jumping. Neither Lauren nor Rascal had any experience in this type of racing. It was scheduled as the last race of the day at Willowdale, Pennsylvania.

The week before the race, her husband Todd had not been feeling well, and Lauren had a dream that he would die of a heart attack.

May 13, race day.
Early in the day, Mookie Monster, trained and owned by Lauren, started the day off with a bang. Mookie was in the large pony event for riders 16 years old or under. She and her rider ran well for the win. Winning was and would continue to be Mookie's way.

Then the day slowed to a crawl, and the temperature grew warmer. On all of my race days, my nervousness builds, starting a few hours before the race until shortly after it. I worry about my babies. I set their lives in motion. I pick the stallions to mate with my mares. I try to be at their births, and I help raise them, pick the farm where they will become racehorses, and pick their trainers—all the time praying they have potential and that they try, stay happy, and above all stay safe.

To calm myself I needed to keep moving from person to person and place to place, keeping my mind busy. An hour before the race, I was spent, from walking from our tailgate area to the barn to check in on him and back and also from the stress. The group we were with included child riders from Lauren's lesson classes, her family, friends, racehorse owners, and her other clients.

As the time approached, I needed to sit. I sat down next to Todd in the back of an open hatchback facing the table area, watching the people that came to see Lauren ride.

No sooner had I sat down when one of Lauren's child students came over and asked me, "What does the big, gold 'G' on Lauren's chest stand for?" She was referring to the letter on my silks.

I told her mostly it is for my last name, but sometimes I like to think it is for God. She told me not to tell Lauren that, because "she doesn't believe in God." I told her I knew that, and then she ran off. I looked over to Todd and asked if he believed in God, and he said yes. I told him, "If you lived my life, you wouldn't believe in God ... you would know there is a God." I asked him if he was interested in hearing a story that I rarely shared with anybody. He said yes.

In April 2005, a friend of mine was having a spring get-together. Her home was on a large farm, and during the summer she would host several gatherings. Mostly we drank, sat around the fire, talked, and laughed until late. This time, to mix things up I brought my Yamaha Kodiak 450 quad.

While I was enjoying a drink, several of her friends told her to take me to the nearby sand pits. So she jumped on and off we went. A quarry sand pit is like a theme park for dirt bikes, quads, Jeeps, and any vehicle that lives for sand.

My first pass took us to the water hole, and my first reaction was to drive through it. I like water. But something inside told me don't it could be very deep. After a quick circle around, my friend asked me to drop her off on a small mound. She wanted to enjoy the clear, dark sky and all the visible stars. She said go enjoy myself. So off I went, but "enjoy" is not the word I now use to express what I would feel for the rest of this life.

The first big pile of sand I drove up to up must have been 35 to 40 feet up, about the size of an average telephone pole. So, as I was taught, I drove about a third of the way up, then rolled back down backwards. Then up again, this time a bit faster and further, about two thirds up, then rolled back.

Too high and too steep is what I told myself. *Let's go at this from the other side.*

So off I went, where I found a gradual incline. Straight to the top I went, right to the edge of my little peak. From my new vantage point I was able to look around and see most of the quarry and a few dim lights in the distance. I could not see my friend because there was a small mound between us, and it blocked my view of the smaller mound she was on. I looked down over the edge when I noticed that the dirt bikes had left a trial where they left the earth and flew into the air.

I can do this, I thought, but I would tackle it from the other side. So I turned around and headed back to the other side, back to the steep side where I first tried to challenge my little mountain.

At the base I looked up and told myself, *Go fast, and you should clear the top and pop up on the other side.* So I turned the throttle and accelerated up straight to the top. *Too easy,* I thought as I approached the peak. That's when I saw the lip jutting out that the dirt bikes had created.

THUD, the front wheels hit it, and up flew the front of my quad.

    In that instant I could feel the quad completely airborne and begin to slowly roll over backwards. I could see that my right hand holding the handlebars was slightly higher than the left. It was silhouetted against a gray background of dim light, like a cloud had appeared out of nowhere. I was moving very slowly if at all. There was no sound, not even the engine. Everything around me was still or did not exist. All my focus was on my predicament.

    Hanging in the air, the thoughts of what I had done immediately ran through my mind. Then in that instant I realized I was not going to survive this. *I'm going to die.* I did not think it; I knew and felt it. *This is the last moment of my life.*

    In that instant I felt a force of energy enter into my stomach and quickly move up inside my chest to my head. It went straight to my brain, like a light bulb my brain told me *This is your life.* No photos, too slow; no hair or clothes blowing, no wind, no sound, just the pure energy of my life. *I feel good. I had a good life, I'm ok with dying. I'm ready.* Total serenity and security.

    The next thing I remember I was trying to sit up, but it was difficult. I was buried—more like my face and chest had been pressed—into the sand past my ears by over 550 pounds of metal. My legs were pointing uphill. As I strained to sit up I had to hold myself upright as sand poured from my ears. For a few seconds I stared up the hill. All was quiet, so I turned back slowly to see my quad on its side, not running, and perpendicular to me, almost near the bottom of the incline. I was about halfway up the mound.

    I called out, and within a few seconds my friend came running over. Her first words were "I knew something was wrong when the quad shut off." All I could think of as I looked up at her was that my face hurt real badly. "Is my nose broken?" I kept asking her. She just stared with a confused look in her eyes and softly said no. Later I asked her why she looked at me like that, she said it was because there was so much blood she could not see my nose. She helped me up, and we rode back to her place.

    Her friends who saw us off asked her what she did to me. Another friend of ours drove us to the hospital.

    When the intake person took my blood pressure, I threw up—a sure sign of a concussion. The CAT scan showed little other than a possible minor concussion. The handlebars had hit my face, opening up lacerations from above and below my right eye across my face to the left corner of my mouth. The doctor was shocked to learn that I had not broken my eye-socket or my nose, nor lost any teeth. He said the kid who came in yesterday had the handlebars cut open this throat and almost suffocated to death. He told me I was lucky and that I should see my doctor first thing the next day.

The next morning my doctor checked my chest, because it and my upper arms were sore. When I took off my shirt, we saw that the cross I had on around my neck had been driven in to my skin over my left chest muscle, close to my breastbone. It had left a mark of the head and arms. The cross itself was curved from the partial impact. The gas can had hit me over my heart. I then told him that I couldn't see too well, so he sent me to an eye specialist. Both eyes hemorrhaged, and fluid built up in my retinas. I was diagnosed as legally blind for at least five days. My face still hurt and remained swollen for days.

At my doctor's we pondered what happened. What he speculated was that because the angle of the hill was so steep, the quad's impact was reduced by the momentum as it rolled over me and down the hill. Also, because the sand had been very soft, it was able to absorb and reduce the weight that made contact with my body. He indicated that could be why I survived, because the weight of the quad should have crushed my chest.

For a few seconds after I finished my story Todd said very little. Then we were interrupted, and we walked off to get ready for the race.

Just before a race in the paddock area the riders, trainers, and owners gather and talk as the horses are paraded around for those interested in seeing them. As I walked over to where Lauren was standing, someone yelled out to her, "Lauren do you know what that big 'G' on your silks stands for?" She smiled and said, "Yes, I heard." Those around us laughed.

Together they had an interesting first race. She was not expecting many of the other riders to be yelling and aggressively maneuvering for a good starting position. She had Rascal stay close to the pack, but near the end of the race they had to avoid a rider who had fallen in from of them. She said Rascal stayed on track and did not move to avoid the rider on the ground until she asked him to. That adjustment cost them in the outcome, however, and they would end up sixth. She said he was great and did everything she asked. Now that they had that experience under their saddle, she could not wait for their next race in two weeks to show the other riders she was for real and out to win.

That evening as Lauren was getting ready to load Rascal into the trailer to leave Willowdale, she threw me her cell phone and asked me to take a photo of Todd, Rascal, and her. It would be the last photo taken of the three of them.

The ride back to their home was wonderful. We laughed and talked about the day the whole way home. The day had been exciting. I enjoyed being a new owner in this new-to-me atmosphere of jump racing. This was only the beginning.

Back at the house, Lauren told a friend and me that on Friday night she and Todd had a wonderful romantic dinner. I then followed Todd to the barn to help him with a few minor evening chores. He could tell something was bothering me. I told him that I was not ready to end this day and make the one-and-a-half-hour drive home. He suggested that we order dinner in and I should stay for pizza.

The talk at dinner was about their plans for the following weekend in Ocean City, Maryland. Todd made a comment to me, and again in joking, as I had done several times before since meeting him, I told him, "Respect your elders." "How old are you?" I asked, and he said 34. "OK, then," I said, "I'm 36—don't forget, you may be bigger and stronger than me, but I'm still your older brother." His friend's wife stared at me but said nothing, and as usual Lauren ignored us. I never had a brother myself, but I became brothers with a few close friends I made in my childhood and in the Marine Corps.

Tuesday, May 15, 2012. The day started with Lauren and Todd spending the day together. That evening, while driving home from work on the New Jersey Turnpike, I began to get a familiar and dreadful feeling. It would grow until it filled my chest and left me feeling sad that something bad was about to happen.

When this feeling first started to happen to me years before, I would think one of my loved ones was the target. But later in life I wanted to think I could protect them, so I let myself feel I was the target; I was the one going to die.

I immediately called Lauren and asked her if something were to happen to me, would she want Rascal? She tried several times to convince me that nothing was going to happen. I knew better, so I changed my approach. I told her that my family worries because I have no one who knows my horses—what would happen to them if something happened to me?

"You have Todd," I explained.

"Do you want Rascal, or not?" I asked.

She said yes, and for the next few minutes we talked about his next race.

Early the next day, shortly after I arrived at work, I got the call from a close friend of Lauren's who works with her at Evolution as an instructor. She told me that Todd had died the night before, and I could come over to a friend's home to be with family and friends. I immediately left work and headed west to Pennsylvania.

When I arrived at the home where everyone was gathering, Lauren was seated on a stool in the large kitchen. I waited for her to be alone and walked up to her. We hugged, and she cried in my arms as we spoke for several minutes. Then I told her that I needed to know something: "Was he alone, or were you with him when he died?" She said they were together and proceeded to tell me what happened. She was not sure exactly when he died, but it was sometime between 8:10 and 8:30 P.M. on Tuesday night.

I then walked away and stood in a corner. That's when Todd's mom approached me. She reached out for my hands and held them out in front of us. She was glad I had come and told me how proud Todd was of Lauren and how he couldn't stop talking about the race. He said he had a fabulous day.

My first thought as she spoke was, *Days like that are why we put in all the farm work.* She also told me that Todd really liked me, especially my sense of humor. I told her how I would joke with him about him being my younger brother, and as I did she began squeezing my hands.

"Are you OK?" I asked.

"You don't know?" she asked me.

"I don't know what?" I replied.

"When Todd was 10, his 12-year-old brother was killed in a skiing accident."

I was shocked. "Sorry—no, I did not know. I would not have joked about that."

She said it was OK.

After the funeral I asked both Lauren and his friend's wife

why they did not tell me about Todd's brother the night we had dinner after the race. Both had assumed that Todd had told me about it. He never said anything to me about a brother. I told them if he had, I would not have joked about it.

After talking with Lauren, I then thought about my call to Lauren the evening he died. I had to check my cell phone call log. The time of that call was 6:45 P.M.; we had spoken for 4 minutes and 27 seconds.

Lauren asked me to take Rascal home for a while, until she felt she would be able to ride. So a few days later he finally came home.

One month later, Lauren needed to get back in the saddle and asked me if I could bring Rascal back to her. So on June 16, I gave him back. That day in her barn we discussed and replayed the sequence of events before and after Todd's death as they occurred.

She said that they spent his last day together, and it was wonderful. I asked if Todd told her about the story I had told him at the race. She said he had tried to on the night he died. I asked her what she thought of it. She said she cut him off and she did not want to hear about it. I told her, "You made comments about him not opening up to you like he used to—then when he finally opens up to you with something he wants to share, you shut him down." She said, "I know." I asked her if she wanted to hear it now, and she said yes. So I told her all about our talk. We discussed my call on the way home that Tuesday night, we spoke for over three hours in her barn.

When I got home, I started to write down the events. I did not want to forget or misremember what had happened.

As I wrote I realized that because I did not know what had happened to me on my quad ride years before I rarely shared that experience. Because I was not sure why I shared it with Todd, I decided to research what had happened to me.

Below is an abbreviated extract about near-death experiences (NDE), found on the website of the International Association for Near-Death Studies (*http://iands.org/research/archives.html*):

"A near-death experience, or NDE, is a profound psychological event that may occur to a person close to death or who is not near death but in a situation of physical or emotional crisis. Being in a life-threatening situation does not by itself constitute a near-death experience. It is the pattern of perceptions, creating a recognizable overall event that has been called 'near-death experience.'

"Across the years and around the world, people have described powerful experiences that follow this general pattern that may include few or several of the common features. At its broadest, the experiences involve perceptions of movement through space, of light and darkness, a landscape, presences, intense emotion, and a conviction of having a new understanding of the nature of the universe.

"Many accounts of experiences include only one or two of the common features, but those were so powerful they created permanent changes in people's lives.

"The emotions of an NDE are intense and most commonly include peace, love and bliss, although a substantial minority are marked by terror, anxiety, or despair. Most people come away from the experience with an unshakable belief that they have learned something of immeasurable importance about the purpose of life.

"Overall, the entire experience is ineffable—that is, it is beyond describing. The effects of an NDE are often life-changing, and its details will typically be remembered clearly for decades.

"Some common features include:

- Intense emotions: commonly of profound peace, well-being, love; others marked by fear, horror, or loss
- Incredibly rapid, sharp thinking and observations
- A life review, reliving actions and feeling their emotional impact on others
- In some cases, a flood of knowledge about life and the nature of the universe
- A reliving of the life rather than a dispassionate viewing. The person's life can be reviewed in its entirety or in segments.
- Warped sense of time and space; discovering time and space do not exist

"Whether the NDE was beautiful or terrifying, near-death experiencers commonly say it was unlike a dream, 'more real than real,' the most powerful event in their lives. They struggle to find words to describe it, but insist they now know something new about reality, that "there's more than what is here" (in the physical world). Most feel deeply changed in their attitudes toward life, work, and relationships.

"After a wonderful NDE, people almost always report losing their fear of death and believing that the essential purpose of human life is to develop our capacity to love. However, experiencers often have difficulty finding someone they trust to tell about the event.

"These phenomena are usually reported after an individual has been pronounced clinically dead or otherwise very close to death, hence the term 'near-death experience.' Many NDE reports, however, originate from events that are not life threatening."
—http://iands.org/research/archives.html

Test the fabric of time! Our short gift of life is what we all have in common. It is a gift that allows us to create, but only a few of us learn that what we perceive to be real is what we create to be real.

Write it today, read it yesterday, live it tomorrow.

Do you understand the commandment of time? When you have faith you may begin to feel time, and then learn how to better communicate with creation. Death is a life without faith.

—K.R., August 2013

Where They Are Today

As of this printing:

Lauren Schock is owner of Evolution Training Center in West Chester, Pennsylvania. She is still making racehorses, training them and children, riding, and moving on. To follow her, look up Evolution Training Center on Facebook.

Lauren riding her hunt horse Madam Belvedere

Rascal is timber racing, and yes, he enjoys it very much. His official name is Classy Rascal. To follow him go to Facebook, Equibase, or the NSA (National Steeplechase Association) website.

Rascal ridden by Sarah

About the Author

Ken Roberts was born in Manhattan and raised in Staten Island and Monmouth County, New Jersey. He inherited a passion for horses and rode as a child. After serving in the United States Marine Corps for four years in a helicopter squadron, the modern-day cavalry, he fell in love, got married, and had a child. Then slowly the desire and excitement to ride began to take over.

HMM-265, Kaneohe Bay, Hawaii

Above all he loves his family and meeting new people. He also enjoys many outdoor activities from playing with his dogs, riding his horses, scuba diving, sailing, flying, football, baseball, swimming, hiking, fishing, and hunting to traveling the world. He has visited six of this wonderful planet's seven continents.

After realizing he would not become a jockey, and living one of his dreams, he adjusted his course and became a racehorse owner. It is the best of both worlds: His horses race and he rides some of them.

Then in 2010, as part of his recovery from being conned, he was drawn into a new perspective of the world of horse racing. The next big step, or should we say "jump," would reveal another dimension to what he is capable of feeling.

The pieces of a lifetime of

Author riding *L. Fontanne*, "Ellie"

learning to feel what this world, people, and life have to offer started to come together.

K.R. doesn't just live his life, he feels life. Until recently only his family, close friends, and few others have gotten a glimpse of how deep he can go. This new experience also showed him that this was just part of a lifelong journey.

Where Rebels Roam is his first book, and he feels the need to share his experience because so many people can't feel beyond sight, touch, taste, smell, sound, or what they want. Realize that you can feel beyond the physical, really feel another person, feel across time, learn why you were created and then maybe truly feel creation. I wrote this for those of you who want to share the journey and enjoy as much as life has to offer for as long as you believe you want to experience it.

Enjoy and share the ride …

—K.R.

SAILAWAY BOOKS
Quality fiction and nonfiction for adults, children,
and young adults in print and e-book formats

www.sailawaybooks.com

Made in the USA
Charleston, SC
26 November 2013